THE LAMB'S WAR

BOOKS BY

Jan de Hartog

THE LAMB'S WAR   *1980*

THE PEACEABLE KINGDOM   *1971*

THE CHILDREN   *1969*

THE CAPTAIN   *1966*

THE CALL OF THE SEA   *1966*
(*Including* THE LOST SEA, THE DISTANT SHORE,
A SAILOR'S LIFE)

THE HOSPITAL   *1964*

THE ARTIST   *1963*

WATERS OF THE NEW WORLD   *1961*

THE INSPECTOR   *1960*

THE SPIRAL ROAD   *1957*

A SAILOR'S LIFE   *1956*

THE LITTLE ARK   *1954*

THE DISTANT SHORE   *1952*

THE LOST SEA   *1951*

PLAYS

WILLIAM AND MARY   *1963*

THE FOURPOSTER   *1951*

SKIPPER NEXT TO GOD   *1947*

THIS TIME TOMORROW   *1946*

JAN DE HARTOG

THE LAMB'S WAR

Harper & Row/Atheneum

Grateful acknowledgment is made for permission to reprint lines from "Tennessee Waltz" by Pee Wee King & Redd Stewart. © Copyright 1948 Renewed 1975 by Acuff-Rose Publications, Inc. Used by permission of the publisher. All rights reserved.

FIRST EDITION

Designed by Eve Kirch

Library of Congress Cataloging in Publication Data

de Hartog, Jan
  The lamb's war.
  I. Title.
PZ3.H258Lam 1979   [PR6015.A674]   823'.9'14   78–20201
ISBN 0–06–010995–5

80 81 82 83 84 10 9 8 7 6 5 4 3 2 1

"Quaker Ambulance Service" and "Meeting for Sufferings" in Philadelphia are fictitious organizations. There are Quaker services that resemble them, such as the Friends Ambulance Unit during the Second World War and the American Friends Service Committee. But in order to protect the privacy of Friends who have participated in these services during the period covered by this novel, it is stressed that organizations and characters in *The Lamb's War* bear no relationship to groups or people, alive or dead.

CONTENTS

Ten Kings, which have received no
Kingdom as yet, shall receive power
as Kings in one hour with the beast.
These have one mind, and shall give
their power and strength to the beast.
They shall make war on the Lamb,
and the Lamb shall overcome them.

—Revelation XVII

BOOK ONE

HOLLAND,
GERMANY
1942

CHAPTER ONE

AGENT Willemse of the Dutch Customs Brigade and *Feld-webel* Krautschneider, "Kraut" for short, his German opposite number, had been lying all night in the wet grass underneath the hawthorn bush by the roadside.

It had been like this, night after night, ever since the war began. It was known that cigarettes, butter and other commodities were regularly smuggled across the Dutch-German border, but nobody had ever been caught, at least not in their area. Yet it was their duty to lie there, chilled to the bone, with the icy wetness of the dew slowly descending upon them as the hours advanced. The trouble was that they couldn't even while away the hours with conversation, not even a whispered one. Not only were they not supposed to talk while on duty, but since the German invasion of Holland they were officially enemies, and neither of them knew how to handle that situation. They had known each other for years, always got on very well, sharing rounds of Schnapps in the tavern The Droll Pigeon, which, owing to a quirk of bureaucracy, was exactly cut in half by the Dutch-German border. Now, since two years and two months ago, they were supposed to hate each other. As far as Agent Willemse was concerned, he would have no trouble doing that, considering what the Germans had done to his country, but then old Kraut wasn't a German, really. He was just a fellow customs officer with a wife, two kids, some chickens in the yard, living toward his pension.

They both heard the squeaking of the pedals of a bicycle at

the same time. Willemse nudged Kraut, Kraut nudged Willemse and all of a sudden they changed from two grown men lying wearily in the wet grass into the Boy Scouts they had once been, tingling with excitement. Nobody was supposed to be out bicycling at this time of night; the curfew was on, no human being should be in the open, certainly not along the border. Yet there it came, quite clearly: the squeaking of the pedals of a bike. There was nothing to be seen yet, as it was very dark, but the sound got louder and louder. Kraut whispered, "You jump, I'll cover." Willemse jumped. The beam of his flashlight caught the glinting handlebars of a bicycle. "Halt!" he cried. "Halt! In the name of the law!"

The bike swayed wildly, rolled straight into the hedge on the opposite side of the road, toppled over, and the rider sprawled in the brambles, felled like a shot deer. Willemse ran toward the spot and lit up whoever it was with the beam of his flashlight. He saw to his astonishment that it was a woman, a young woman, a girl, spread-eagled on her back in the brambles, her legs bare. To his bewilderment and confusion, he was overcome by a surge of lust. For one crazy, dreamlike moment he felt like hurling himself upon her and taking her by force, a thought that would not have entered his head in a thousand years, before the occupation. It was the moment the war got hold of him too, the violence, the brutality, the obscenity of it. He was a God-fearing man, and therefore instantly swamped by guilt; he stood paralyzed with shame and confusion when Kraut turned up beside him, pointing the snub muzzle of his automatic rifle at the sprawling girl and saying, *"Um Gotteswillen!"* There she lay, and there they stood, the three of them caught in a totally irrational situation from which it took them several seconds to extricate themselves. Willemse was the first to do so by saying to her, as gruffly as he knew how, "Get up and pull down your skirt, child! What are you doing here? Don't you know there's a curfew on? Where are you going? Where are you from?"

While Kraut covered him with the gun, a grotesque gesture in view of her total helplessness, Willemse pulled her to her feet and saw to his horror that she was pregnant. She could not be older than fifteen, sixteen at the most; her hair was blond, her eyes blue and innocent, her small, rotund belly strained the thin, cheap dress she was wearing. When she finally stood on her feet, her legs bleeding because of the brambles, her hair loose, she

looked so pathetic and lost that when Kraut said, "We had better take her to the post," Willemse asked, "What on earth for?"
He did not know himself why he asked it, it must be guilt. He
had, for one moment of total evil, felt like raping a child; she
now turned out to be a pregnant child as well. All he wanted to
do was to send her packing, go back to their side of the road and
lie down in the cold wetness again, pretending that none of it had
happened, that all was well with the world and that he was still
part of the essential goodness of man. But, of course, it was his
duty to question her; she had no business being here, and Kraut
was sure to report the occurrence, there had to be some record of
it. "Yes, I suppose we had better." Willemse started to pull the
bicycle out of the brambles, which wasn't easy. She wasn't carrying anything on her luggage carrier other than a briefcase; no
parcels, no cigarettes or butter; just a pregnant young girl on a
bicycle trying to cross the border at dead of night. They had better find out what it was all about, for Kraut would have to report
to *Hauptmann* Forster, the head of his section, who was certain
to want to know every single detail.

"Where were you going?" Willemse asked as they walked
down the road in the dark, he pushing her bicycle, she limping
by his side, Kraut covering them with his gun.

"Schwalbenbach."

"What were you planning to do there?"

"Nothing."

"Do you have any relatives there?"

"Yes."

"Who?"

"My father."

"What's he doing there?"

"He works."

"As what?"

"He just works."

Her tone of voice was hostile; and the fact that she was pregnant at so young an age made her such an unknown entity to
both men that they decided to leave the interrogation to a woman. There was only one woman who could do that with firmness
and intelligence, and that was Bertha Willemse, the Dutch
agent's wife. She was schoolteacher in the village, the first dark
houses of which began to loom ahead as they approached the
customs post adjoining The Droll Pigeon. All was still, all was

dark, Bertha did not expect her husband until six o'clock that morning and Kraut's wife did not expect him until seven, as he lived in Schwalbenbach. So it took some persuasion on Willemse's part before he managed to convince Bertha that she was needed at once to interrogate a young female who had been caught riding a bicycle after curfew and, on top of it all, turned out to be pregnant.

That last bit of information was what decided Bertha; she dressed and went to the cell behind the office, where the girl was sitting on a cot, looking sullen and closed. She could not be more than fifteen.

"Well, dearie," Bertha Willemse began, "what on earth are you doing here?"

"Nothing," the girl replied with undisguised hostility.

She obviously was a tough cookie, but the fact that she was pregnant made her vulnerable and in need of help. Bertha was about to go motherly on her, when there was a knock on the door and Krautschneider stuck his head in. "Could I have a word with you?"

Bertha joined him outside in the hall, out of earshot of the girl. He whispered, "I would appreciate it if you would search her. I don't know, but I— There's something about her pregnancy that doesn't look right to me."

"What do you know about that?" Bertha inquired coldly. "Are you a gynecologist?"

Krautschneider obviously didn't know the word. It did not figure in the German handbook for customs officers, which was the only literature he ever read. "I have been told they use girls as gun-runners," he replied. "The underground resistance, I mean. So you had better make sure her pregnancy is real. There is nothing in her briefcase, and that makes her suspect."

"Why should 'nothing' make her suspect?" Bertha could not stand the man, she had always had the feeling that he led her husband into drinking too many rounds of Schnapps after hours in The Droll Pigeon. And God only knew what they talked about when they lay side by side in the darkness every night, it certainly wasn't the news of the day.

"Please do as I ask," Krautschneider pleaded. "I would like to let her go, but I must be sure she isn't carrying any weapons. She says she wants to visit her father in Schwalbenbach, but why is she traveling by night? You know what will happen to her once the *Hauptmann* arrives."

Yes, that was a thought. The *Hauptmann* was a stickler for protocol, a martinet who knew no greater delight or purpose in life than to make things as complicated as possible for as many people as possible. "All right," she said, "I'll have a look. But leave us alone and stop sticking your head around the door. And tell that husband of mine to stay out too."

The girl sat watching her with a look of hostile wariness, a cornered animal. She looked unkempt and shabby with her hair loose and her bare legs smudged with blood, but she was not a working-class girl. More likely a bank teller trying to make off with the petty cash. But she was too young to be a bank teller.

"Sorry, dear, I'll have to search you."

The girl's eyes narrowed; for a moment Bertha thought she would physically attack her. "You keep your paws off me," the girl said. "I've done nothing wrong."

"Yes, you have. Have you never heard of the curfew? What were you doing at dead of night on that bike, without lights, on the border?"

"The men have already asked me that."

"I'd like to hear you answer too."

"Well, you're not going to get it."

"Look, *liefje*," Bertha said kindly, "you had better own up, because things will go badly for you if you don't. At nine o'clock *Hauptmann* Forster is going to turn up; he's not the kind of man to take this lightly. So you tell me what you're up to, and you'd better tell me the truth or you'll be in big trouble. Do you hear what I'm saying?"

"I hear you."

The girl seemed cool and collected, but Bertha, who had been dealing with teenagers for twenty years, detected a crack in the fragile armor of defiance. There was something about the child that moved her. She wondered what it was. Kraut was right— her pregnancy didn't look convincing. For one thing, she was carrying the child far too high. "Show me what you are wearing under your dress," she said calmly.

The girl gave her a level look and said, "You are crazy."

"What is it? Cigarettes, butter or guns?"

The girl gave her another look, then she said, in a tone of indifference, "A pillow."

"Would you mind showing it to me?"

"Why?"

"Because I must be able to declare under oath that you are

not carrying any contraband. Do you understand?"

The girl shrugged her shoulders, rose to her feet, lifted her dress and showed what she was wearing underneath her slip. It was indeed a pillow; a small, round pillow embroidered with the legend *"God is Love,"* strapped to her abdomen with surgical tape. "Satisfied?"

Bertha squeezed the pillow, but it wasn't necessary. The idea of guns being hidden in a pillow with that legend seemed too ludicrous for a woman of her elemental decency. Also, her intuition told her that the child was telling the truth. "All right. Pull your dress down. But you better tell me why."

"Why what?"

"Why you were pretending to be pregnant."

The girl hesitated, then she said, "To protect myself."

"Protect yourself? From what?"

"Well, if you must know: from any man who might get ideas about a girl alone at night on a bicycle."

"Have you been bicycling only in the dark?"

"Yes."

"Why?"

For a moment it looked as though the girl would refuse to answer, then she said defiantly, "Because I have no ID card."

It was typical of their elemental innocence: neither Krautschneider, her husband nor she had thought of asking the obvious question: May we see your ID card? They were all innocents, caught in the calamity of war. Even now, more than two years after the German invasion, they still could not believe that they were enemies and that the world they shared had changed into a darker place. "Where were you going?"

"Schwalbenbach. I want to visit my father."

"What's he doing there?"

The girl shrugged her shoulders.

"Is he Dutch?"

"Yes."

"Does he work there?"

"Yes."

"Where?"

The girl hesitated again, then she said, "In the camp."

Bertha Willemse stared at her, alarmed. Although it was so close geographically that they could see its watchtowers right across the border from their windows, nobody in the village, or

in the town of Schwalbenbach, for that matter, knew for certain
what went on behind the barbed wire. The camp was run by the
SS and the rumors about it were gruesome—so gruesome that
nobody wanted to inquire any deeper. It was better not to know.

"Does he work there as a guard?"

"He's an inmate."

"A prisoner? And you want to *visit* him?"

"Prisons have visiting hours, don't they? Anyway, it isn't a
prison, it's a labor camp."

"Don't you have a mother?" It was an irrational question; but
the girl began to respond and open up.

"She's been dead for three years. I'm the only child. I've always looked after him. He can't look after himself, not properly.
I want to go and visit him and take him things and make sure
he's all right. Do you think I'll be able to get a job in Schwalbenbach, once I get there?"

Bertha Willemse looked at the young, determined face, the
clear blue eyes, the childish mouth, and was filled with horror.
Strange that none of the three of them had realized before what
had made the girl seem so odd, so unreal. It was her total, unbelievable innocence. She was a lamb on its way to slaughter.

"Look, *liefje,*" she said, trying to make it sound authoritative
and convincing. "Camp Schwalbenbach is not the kind of place
where visitors are allowed. I don't know what your father has
done—why he's a prisoner there . . . "

"He helped place Jewish babies in Aryan families."

"I beg your pardon?"

"He was part of a group who tried to find homes for small
children of Jewish families that were being deported. He was
caught by the *Grüne Polizei* and condemned to ten years hard
labor."

"For—for trying to place babies?" Bertha asked incredulously.

"Yes," the girl said.

The war had suddenly come close. Bertha had never been
challenged by it, not really. She had been able to go on being a
devout Protestant, a good teacher who continued to teach history, math and Dutch the way she had before the Germans occupied Holland. She had never been confronted with anything like
the monstrousness this girl represented. Her instant reaction was
that she wanted no part of this. "All right," she said. "I'll talk to

the men." She rose and went to the door. "I'm not going to lock this. While I'm talking to the men, you leave by the side door, the first on your right in the hall. You'll find your bike outside. You don't have much time left before daylight. Follow the road across the border; a few kilometers before you get to the town, turn left and you'll find the camp." She rose without waiting for an answer, opened the door and found the two men, looking sheepish and uncertain, standing in the hall, Kraut still holding his ridiculous gun.

"You'd better come with me into the office," she said. "I want to talk to you."

"But what about the child?" her husband asked nervously.

"Come along, get in there." She opened the door to the *Hauptmann*'s office and pushed them inside. They sat down, uncomfortably, in the armchairs with a feeling of daring, as neither of them had ever sat down in the *Hauptmann*'s presence. She told the men that the girl just wanted to visit her father, who had a job in Schwalbenbach, and that her pregnancy was faked to protect her from assault. She kept on talking until she was certain that the child must be on her way. Finally she suggested that she make some coffee. As she set about it in the little kitchen, she saw through the window in the early light that the bicycle was gone.

A sudden sense of shame overwhelmed her. The girl was on her way to the camp, that evil place no one dared talk about; like Pontius Pilate, she had washed her hands of the child. It was all very disturbing; but as she stood there, staring at the empty road to Schwalbenbach, she knew in a confused way that if she were to allow herself to feel guilty for letting a child bicycle to that camp in total innocence, she would thereby admit to herself that she knew what went on in there. If it was true that evil could triumph only as long as enough good people decided to remain silent, then her husband and all her neighbors on both sides of the border were guilty of a horrible crime.

But what else could they have done? How could they possibly have combated the unspeakable evil in their midst? They were harmless people, powerless people, kind people, people who in times of peace had been rightly proud of their village and their own good-neighborliness toward the Germans on the other side of the border. They did not know what went on inside those barbed-wire fences with the squat watchtowers in the midst of their fields; neither did good Germans like Kraut and the pastor of the Evangelical church in Schwalbenbach, who came to visit the sick whenever his Dutch colleague was away. Nobody knew. It was all based on rumor; there was no proof. For all she knew, the girl might indeed be permitted to see her father. Of course she would. It was ridiculous.

She turned her back on the window, took the coffee into the office and said, "Well, she's gone."

The men looked relieved. Sipping their coffee, they agreed not to mention the girl to *Hauptmann* Forster. She had never been here; she did not exist. They felt good about that. They were protecting the innocent at a substantial risk to themselves; if the *Hauptmann* ever found out, they would be given a severe reprimand, it might even cost them a reduction in their pensions.

Bertha Willemse tried not to remember the face, the eyes, the childish mouth. It became easier as the hours went by.

CHAPTER TWO

I N the officers' mess hall of Camp Schwalbenbach, *Haupt-sturmführer* Heinrich Schmidt, the camp doctor, and *Ober-sturmführer* Kroll, the commandant, decided to have supper at the small table by the window, rather than join the other officers at the large one in the center of the room. They were a noisy crowd, producing the din of male camaraderie which tended to become a trifle tiresome after the third round of Pilsener beer.

Although Heinrich Schmidt had arrived at the camp only a month before and was still in his twenties, barely a year out of medical school, Commandant Kroll had shown an instant prefer-ence for him as a table companion. It was not uncommon for a camp commandant to sup with the doctor at a separate table, as they were the two highest-ranking staff officers; the previous camp doctor, however, had been such a crashing bore that Kroll had taken his rightful seat at the head of the large table, prefer-ring the moronic joshing and banter to the doctor's gory descrip-tions of past operations, alternating with equally gory reminis-cences of past conquests. Dr. Hangwurgen had at times made the *Obersturmführer* physically sick, forcing him to leave the ta-ble before the *Torte*—at least so Heinrich Schmidt had been told, in the strictest confidence, by his batman, who knew every-thing that went on in the camp.

The small table, laid for two, was by the window overlooking the *Paradeplatz,* where the daily roll-calls were held and the oc-casional execution performed. It had been a warm day; the win-dow was open, the sun had set, the first swallows were swooping around the top of the flagpole in the center of the square, and the fragrance of night-blooming jasmine was wafted in by the evening breeze.

The commandant ignored the messroom *Scharführer,* who spread a napkin across his lap. "Anything unusual or amusing happen to you today?"

It took Heinrich a moment to realize that it was he who was being addressed. "Nothing earth-shaking or side-splitting," he replied, trying to ignore the spreading of the napkin on his own lap. "How about you?"

"Oh, nothing, as usual," the commandant replied, "other than a letter I received from Berlin this morning, in reply to our request for films of more recent vintage."

"Ah? What did it say?"

The messroom *Scharführer* stood respectfully to attention, menus at the ready, waiting for his cue. It was all rather heady stuff for a young GP from the provinces.

"It said that our request had been duly filed, but advised us to exert patience as there were many similar requests preceding ours. In other words, 'Down, Schwalbenbach! You are at the bottom of the list and don't speak out of turn again!'" The commandant smiled. "We might as well face it, *Herr Doktor:* as concentration camps go, we are not La Scala in Milan, but the Opéra Comique in Puppenheim. So, no Zarah Leander or *White Hell of Pitz Palü* for us, but twenty-year-old musicals and gloomy Swedish epics about incest above the Arctic Circle, with subtitles. All right, let's see what there is to eat tonight."

The *Scharführer* respectfully handed them the handwritten menus.

"No!" Kroll cried. "Not dumplings again!"

"We also have roast pork and applesauce, *Herr Obersturm-führer.*"

"Too heavy. That's the kind of fodder Caesar's fighting legions must have marched on, we are a chairborne legion." He tossed the menu aside. "A couple of fried eggs, four rashers of bacon, potato pancakes. And more rolls."

"Jawohl, Herr Obersturmführer! Sofort!" The man was about to make off. Kroll stopped him in his tracks by snapping, "First take the doctor's order!"

"Jawohl, Herr Obersturmführer! Zu Befehl, Herr Hauptsturmführer."

"I'll have the roast pork," Heinrich said, "and fried potatoes, and the strawberry pie to follow."

"Jawohl, Herr Hauptsturmführer!"

"Beer?" Heinrich asked Kroll.

The commandant shook his head. "Let's have a bottle of that champagne from the *Hauptmarketenderei* in Lille. I couldn't stand the reek of beer mixed with the scent of jasmine."

The champagne was served from a bucket of ice by the *Scharführer,* the bottle wrapped in a napkin. He poured a little into Kroll's glass, and as the commandant tasted it, a short, impressed silence fell at the main table. "H'm. Yes, excellent. How did Charles Laughton put it, in his role of Nero? 'Delicious debauchery.' You may pour."

The attendant poured, reverently; in the silence, the thin, high squealing of the swallows swooping round the flagpole became audible. Then the din at the central table resumed. Kroll raised his glass. "Here's to the bliss of the forgotten," he said. "May Berlin forever keep us at the bottom of all their lists."

Heinrich raised his glass in response, although he did not quite grasp the implication of the toast. What it probably meant was: the less interference from Headquarters, the better. He certainly had ended up in a backwater, for better or for worse.

"Come, *Herr Doktor,*" Kroll said after the eggs and the roast pork were served and the *Scharführer* had withdrawn into the background, "your turn now. Let's hear some juicy medical gossip. How's Kuhlenbach's clap coming along?"

"I don't think you'd find my report appetizing," Heinrich said with a smile.

"All right, let's talk about something innocuous. Religion. The arts."

"Were you involved in the arts in any way, before the war?" Heinrich ventured.

"What makes you ask that?"

"Well, you seem so—so knowledgeable. Intellectually stimulating, I mean."

The commandant looked at him while slowly turning his glass. Then he said, "I will now present you with proof of a total inner security. I could answer, 'I was director of the Vienna Burgtheater,' or '*Intendant* of the resident repertory company in Kassel.' In actual fact, I was the art, stage, film and book reviewer of a pretentious literary weekly called *New Pathways*. It folded

after nineteen issues. In other words, an intellectual dilettante."
He sipped his champagne. "You see? I no longer feel the need to
gild the dandelion. I have reached the degree of detachment and
security where I can be ruthless without rancor, even toward myself. In other words, the right man for the job." He pierced the
yolk of one of his fried eggs with his fork. "And you, *Herr Doktor?* Of which illustrious medical college were you the youthful
Chief Internist?"

Heinrich hesitated; then the champagne, the swallows, the
fragrance of the jasmine seduced him. "I served as *locum tenens*
for a rural alcoholic GP just before I was called up."

"Must have been fascinating."

"Disgusting. I spent most of my time being ashamed of myself."

"It is the privilege of youth to spend most of its time being
ashamed of itself. You have progressed since then, I trust?"

"Somewhat."

Kroll gave him a searching look. "Don't tell me you still indulge in *crises de conscience?* That's a luxury you can ill afford
in a place like this, young friend." He poured more champagne
for both of them, impatiently gesturing away the *Scharführer.*
"Detachment is the key. *'Auf der Höhe ist es einsam'*—the pinnacle is a lonely place. Well, here's to us: two nonentities on the
pinnacle of power in a forgotten prison camp. Cheers."

They drank.

"One thing you must exterminate with total, brutal ruthlessness, and that is any threat to your inner security," Kroll continued. "Not only *Pax Germanica* must be sacrosanct, but *Pax
Krollania.*" He belched into his napkin. "Excuse me."

Heinrich looked at him uneasily. This line of conversation
held a hidden menace, something he could not define but sensed
quite clearly. "By the way," he said, grasping at a straw, "it
seems they have sent us a religious fanatic with that last convoy
from Holland."

"How so?" Kroll sounded bored. Individual prisoners never
interested him.

However, it seemed the better of two evils to persevere.
"When I made rounds today, I found one of the prisoners messing around with the sick, obviously an amateur. I asked him
what he thought he was doing, and do you know what his answer
was? 'I am making myself available as the body of Christ.'"

Kroll lowered his glass and said, "Good God! What exactly was the body of Christ doing?"

"Putting a dying patient on a bedpan."

"Charming." He pushed his plate aside. "Not a Jew, obviously."

"No, a political prisoner."

"Had Wassermann asked your permission to put that man to work?"

"He did when I called him to task about it. He said his two orderlies had been put on transport yesterday, so he desperately needed help. He said he hoped this man might last longer than the two previous ones because he was not a Jew."

"Nonsense," Kroll said irritably. "When a man is spent he is spent, and it no longer matters a damn whether he is a spent Jew or a spent Hottentot. We are not in the business of supporting freeloaders. What shape is the man in? Can he do any real work, or is he only good for messing around with the sick?"

Heinrich shrugged his shoulders. "Even as an orderly, I don't think he'll last long. He's not young, and they must have given him a hard time during interrogation."

"Ah, don't make any mistake there, *Herr Doktor!*" Kroll wagged a finger at him, an incongruous gesture that appeared to indicate he was getting inebriated, rather quickly, it seemed, for so controlled a man. "You are dealing with a Pentecostal Christian. Given the chance, he'll outlive us all. I have seen them run, literally run to the execution wall, ecstatic at the thought that they were about to meet their God."

"What were they? Salvationists?"

"Jehovah's Witnesses, Saturday Adventists, you name them. The Jews are not the only ones to think they are God's chosen." Kroll filled their glasses again and stuck the empty bottle in the ice bucket, upside down. The *Scharführer,* hovering on the periphery, looked apprehensive. "That's what I meant when I said, 'Exterminate any threat to your inner security with total, brutal ruthlessness.' But shooting them or putting them on transport only makes them more sure of their exclusivity. No, there is only one way to break the neck of their arrogance: Show them they are rabid beasts at heart, that will kill when cornered, just like the rest of us." He snapped his fingers. "Another bottle. Quick!"

The *Scharführer* fell over himself in his haste to obey the command. The central table had fallen silent; people were leaving unobtrusively. Kroll could not hold his liquor; Heinrich was beginning to feel that he was in an awkward situation.

Kroll wagged his finger at him again. "To be God's chosen, to love your enemy, those are luxuries, fools' delusions bestowed upon you by a caprice of fortune. Wait till the enemy goes for the jugular! Wait until their smugness is challenged by—by—well, God knows what. There must be a way to unleash the rabid beast in their saintly guts. There must be! Only that too, alas, depends on a caprice of fortune."

The *Scharführer* brought the second bottle. The hall was empty now and so quiet that a new sound could be heard over the squealing of the swallows: the distant whirring of a lawn-mower coming and going; a prisoner had been allowed to work after curfew to mow the grass outside the barracks. The cork popped. Kroll leaned back in his chair and watched the *Scharführer* pour. The man's hands shook.

"Not as good as the first one. But go ahead."

The champagne hissed in the glasses; Kroll stared out of the window at the darkening sky, full of controlled, enigmatic fury. Not one of nature's gentlemen, one of nature's centurions.

"Are you religious, Schmidt?"

The question took Heinrich by surprise. The clatter of the bottle being placed in the bucket made him aware of the danger. "Not particularly," he replied lightly.

"What is that supposed to mean?"

"Well, my father was—is—a churchy kind of person. I just went along with whatever was expected of me. Like most people, I expect."

"Like most people, you are a coward."

Heinrich smiled. "Were. I no longer go along with it. Not even to humor the old man, which at one time I considered to be my filial duty."

"As now you consider it to be your military duty, I observe."

The *Scharführer* sidled away to the safety of the kitchen.

"I wouldn't say so," Heinrich replied calmly. "I did not have the impression that you expected me to butter you up during our private suppers."

Kroll gave him a mirthless smile and lifted a finger. "Arrogance, Schmidt! Beware of arrogance. It comes before the fall." He took a sip from his fresh glass and tasted it, luxuriously, as if he were tasting more than just the pedestrian champagne some crafty French vintner had foisted upon the German Army. The mower whirred; in the short silences as it turned, the swallows around the flagpole could be heard squealing. The blue of the sky had deepened to dusk; Venus trembled, faint and virginal, in the rising heat of the encroaching night.

"Ah," Kroll said, looking at his glass thoughtfully, "what satisfaction it would give, to teach one of those sanctimonious bastards a lesson! More so than goring a bull, or sticking a pig, or kissing the hem of some smelly saint's garment, for that matter. Amusing, don't you think, to unleash the rabid beast in the body of Christ?" He smiled at Heinrich. "Which denomination did you say the man belongs to?"

"I have no idea."

"Well, small matter. They all share the same gambler's luck: to go to their graves unchallenged. Cheer, that's what they did, cheer, as they ran to the wall. I gave the command myself, for all the good it did. You are not drinking, dear friend."

"I think I've had my share, thank you."

"So have I. More than that. Let's go and join our friends." He rose.

Heinrich followed his example, uncertainly.

Kroll grinned, "Yes," he said, "we do have friends left, *Herr Doktor,* friends who will never betray us: Goethe, Schiller, the mad, despairing Büchner. No dagger in the back there. No Brutus lurking in the shadows of a bookshelf. Arrogance, *Herr Doktor!* Beware of arrogance. Beware of the dagger in the back. Good night."

The *Obersturmführer* sauntered off toward his quarters jauntily, without so much as a stumble to betray that he must be quite drunk. And quite, quite dangerous.

* * *

Heinrich thought no more about their conversation so he was taken aback when Kroll said, the next morning, "All right, show me the man."

"Pardon?"

"Our resident saint. I want to see the whites of his eyes. Let's go."

Kroll had never before betrayed the slightest interest in any prisoner; according to what Heinrich had been able to pick up from his fellow officers and his batman, he never even entered the barracks. So it was with discreet curiosity that he accompanied the commandant to Barracks C, where the lazaret was. Barracks C was set aside for the sick and the ailing; only those *in extremis* ended up in the small ward at the far end of the passage between the tiers of bunks, in each of which lay a body in striped coveralls. One of the Kapos, somewhere in the gloom, shouted: "Atten-TION!" and there was a general scramble as shadowy figures tumbled out of their bunks and lined the passage with their dismal, swaying ranks.

If Kroll was in any way impressed by the appalling human misery that engulfed them as they made their way to the lazaret, he did not show it. He strode jauntily along, ignoring the Hitler salutes of the Kapos and the pathetic efforts of the shadows to stand to attention while barely able to stand upright. Only as he reached the door to the lazaret did he seem to falter.

The sight was indeed shocking. The mere name 'lazaret' was ludicrous for the pigsty where the dying were dumped until they expired, after which they were carted off to the crematorium and stacked there, like cordwood, to await the next burning. The dimly lit room was filled with cots jammed close together; in each lay a dark shape, some restless, others quite still. The stench was suffocating; underneath the cots were overflowing bedpans and basins. One of the bodies rose on an elbow, a skeletal arm reached out to them and a quavering voice called, "Ida? Ida? For God's sake—Ida?" The burning eyes, the eerie, reedy voice would have prompted any newcomer to turn and flee, but Kroll appeared unaffected. Quite the reverse; it was as if some unexpected source of compassion inside him were opened up. "What is it?" he asked kindly.

"Water . . . water . . . " The sick man's breath was foul; his strength failed him as he fell back on the cot.

"Is there nobody here to look after the sick?" Kroll shouted suddenly, in his *Paradeplatz* voice.

Everybody froze. Even the dying in their cots seemed to cease breathing in abject terror. The man who had pleaded for water lay quite still now, as if death itself had put its foot on his neck.

"Wassermann!" Kroll bellowed. "Dr. Wassermann! Who the hell is in charge here?"

A calm voice replied, "I am."

Kroll whipped around and faced the prisoner who had dared

to address him without mentioning his rank. It was Martens the Salvationist, or whatever he was, for whose impending fate Heinrich now felt responsible. If he had not mentioned the man . . .

But again Kroll surprised him. He stared at Martens with no emotion other than, perhaps, a faint amusement. "Are you by any chance the current body of Christ?" he asked, smiling.

Martens stood to attention, but not with the rigidity of terror like the others; he looked at Kroll with interest rather than apprehension. He was of middle height, had thin brown hair going gray and brown eyes; his mouth seemed sensitive, there was little indication of a strong will or determination. Instead, there was about him an odd peaceableness, an air of tolerant understanding; he stood facing Kroll the way the principal of a school might face the leader of a street gang about to attack him.

This was an impossible situation from the point of view of a prison-camp commandant. Kroll and his handful of guards could only expect to keep three thousand famished prisoners under control by a rule of irrational terror. But Kroll did not seem fazed by him. "Name?" he asked.

"Martens, Jacob."

"What are your religious beliefs?"

The question was put detachedly, yet Heinrich braced himself for a sudden explosion of violence from Kroll. It seemed impossible that he could countenance the insidious insubordination of the man who looked at him with such understanding awareness.

"I am a Quaker."

"I did not ask for your church affiliation. I asked what your beliefs are. What is this business about your being the body of Christ?"

"In the sixteenth century," Martens replied, "St. Theresa said to her novices, 'Christ has no body on earth now except yours. No hands but yours, no feet but yours. Yours are the eyes through which His love has to look out upon the world. Yours are the feet on which He has to go about doing good. And yours are the hands with which He is to bless us now.' "

It was either immensely impressive or insufferably smug; but above all, it was incredibly stupid on the part of Martens to preach at Kroll and all he represented.

The commandant looked at the prisoner with amused interest and retorted, "She also told God that the reason He had so few friends was because of the way He treated them. You know, of course, that you can afford the luxury of your convictions only because of a caprice of fortune? God, if He exists, has so far allowed you to keep your halo as a whim or an act of grace, whatever terminology you prefer. Do you pray?"

"Yes."

"In that case, let me give you your prayer for the day: 'God, protect me from the caprice of fortune that would enable *Obersturmführer* Kroll to call my holy bluff.'" At that, he turned smartly around and called, in that spine-chilling voice, "Wassermann!"

"Zu Befehl, Herr Obersturmführer!" The prison doctor, a small wiry Jew, leaped in front of Kroll and stood rigidly to attention, little fingers on the seams of his pants.

"Any information?"

"Jawohl, Herr Obersturmführer!" Bowing, he led Kroll to the desk in the corner and handed him a note-pad. The commandant scowled at it, tore off a sheet, folded it, put it in his breast pocket and marched out without a word. After a brief hesitation, Heinrich followed him. What was the meaning of that exchange? What kind of secret arrangement did Kroll and Wassermann have going?

Outside, the moment they were out of earshot, Kroll said, "Next time, young friend, try to look less apprehensive. I am not a brute, you know; neither are you—yet. To end every argument by destroying your opponent is moronic. What you witnessed was a theological dispute. In chess, one does not slam the board over the head of one's opponent the moment he takes one of your men. You accept that as part of the enjoyment of the game. Otherwise, you might as well play chess with a mirror." He walked on, Heinrich following half a step behind. At the flagpole he stopped. "Intellectually, you'll find this camp insufferably boring. One must take one's mental exercise where one can. Shall we have supper together tonight?"

"I would be honored."

Kroll smiled. "For a man on whom an honor has been bestowed, you look pretty green around the gills. Don't worry, *Herr Doktor,* the god of war will prevail. But even Mars must be given the occasional chance to be playful. *Deo ludens.* It took a brilliant mind like St. Theresa's to perceive the whimsicality of God. You should read up on her. She really has the edge on *our* ruling divine, St. Nietzsche. I also want to hear about your father."

He turned and marched away, a dapper, elegant figure in the execution square.

* * *

One of the traditional privileges Heinrich had inherited from his predecessor was the companionship of Siegfried, the camp dog, a large black-and-yellow German Shepherd, trained to track and retrieve fugitives. Nothing in the animal's daily behavior betrayed that aspect of its training; it was just a large, obedient, almost servile creature, somewhat weak in the hindquarters, which gave it a crouching walk, as if it were forever cringing. Heinrich felt no particular affection for the beast; that evening, however, after supper, as he slowly made his way to the bungalow near the gate that served as both his office and his quarters, he was glad of the animal's companionship.

The pansies bordering the path to the bungalow seemed to be yellower in the evening light, almost luminescent. He crossed the veranda, opened the door and went inside, the dog at his heels. It was an impersonal, dreary waiting-room: blacked-out standard lamp, calendar with nude left behind by his predecessor, newspaper rack with *Stürmer* and *Völkischer Beobachter,* both a week old. He went to his laboratory, took from among the boxes of serum in the refrigerator half a bottle of *Liebfraumilch* and gave Siegfried the bone the *Scharführer* had wrapped up for him. Sipping the wine, he sat slumped on the couch in the waiting-room for a while, his feet on a chair, then he lit a cigar, got up and went to his office. Opening the filing cabinet, he took out a folder marked *"General Emetics in Stock,"* in which he kept his private correspondence; from it he took his father's latest letter and went back to lie down on the couch in the waiting-room.

When the letter had arrived a week or so ago, he had glanced at it and filed it without a second thought. It was in answer to a gloomy, self-pitying one he himself had written, a jeremiad about the inhumanity of the conditions under which both prisoners and guards were forced to live; he had regretted sending it the moment he saw the dispatch rider vanish down the cart track that led to the Schwalbenbach road. Now he opened his father's letter again.

"My dear Heinzl, I do not doubt that the camp is a place

where prisoners as well as guards lose their humanity. Please realize that I do not underestimate the repulsiveness of your new surroundings; but there is not much sense in your asking yourself at this point whether you did wrong when you enlisted with the SS. You know as well as I do that you would never have achieved an internship and completed your studies if you had not 'rendered unto Caesar.' Look at what happened to your classmates: Helmuth a mechanic, Franz a scribbler in some office, and why? Because they refused to adjust to the political reality of the hour. You were realistic, and the result has been that for the past six months you have been able to help a great many sick people. Even in your present post you have an important task. If you can be of help anywhere, it's certainly in the place you now find yourself. You must not abandon your post; you must meet reality as a man, and try to atone in terms of compassion for the callousness and brutality of others. We are living through one of those periods in history (by no means the first) in which the brotherhood of Man seems to be reduced to a fata morgana. So: grit your teeth, play the role allotted to you with fortitude, and do not commit the error, common among the young, of assuming that if you cannot save the whole of mankind you have failed. If you were to salvage only one victim of the Great Flood, you would have done as much as any decent human being could be expected to do under the circumstances. You are one man; for you to aspire to save more than one is laudable, but could easily lead to spiritual pride and, incidentally, to your own downfall. To be able to save another human being means to have power; where there is power, hubris is just around the corner.

"There are not many people to whom I would give this advice, but you have been blessed, potentially, with a strong character, a noble spirit, a tender soul. You are a worthy member of our family, who for centuries have tried to incorporate human dignity in our town, in whatever function they served. Think of them and find strength in their example. Last of all, think of your loving Father."

It was a noble letter written by a noble man, but totally out of touch with reality. In order to function in Camp Schwalbenbach you had to accept its purpose, which was to put prisoners to work, weed out those who were exhausted and forward them to the extermination camp. Once a week he was forced to act as an angel of death, by selecting people for transport. They appeared before him, one by one, on the front porch of the bungalow; after only a cursory inspection he directed some to the left and others to the right. The left-hand column meant death, the right-hand column a stay of execution. He might be able to postpone some executions by directing as many as possible to the right, but it was only a postponement. To help people in this camp did not mean that he could save lives. He could prolong their stay a little, and make life a little more bearable for the sick by allowing them to linger briefly in their bunks. Otherwise, his hands were tied. He could do nothing, for instance, about the sadistic brutality of the Kapos, hardened criminals who acted as trusties and were encouraged to brutalize the other prisoners to their hearts' content.

Once you joined the SS, you renounced your individuality. *Kadavergehorsam,* just like the dog at his feet. "From time to time he needs a refresher course," his predecessor had said. "Occasionally one of them goes berserk during roll-call and runs away. Let the dog deal with him. That way the beast stays in training." Under no circumstances would he himself allow the dog to chase and bring down a prisoner; that at least he could hold to in this dehumanized world.

If only he could get away from here! But what was the alternative? Front-line duty. Ever since the Russian campaign had started, the papers were full of death notices: *"For Führer and Fatherland."* He probably wouldn't last a week. Well, it might have to come to that. If Father's unworldly dream of his helping even one person were to prove an impossibility, he might have to apply for front-line duty just to save his soul, and take the consequences. It would mean the end to a promising career. If only he could return to civilian practice! Slip back into being the tireless *locum tenens* adored by his patients! But there was no hope of that, not before the end of the war. He had sealed his fate when he joined the SS to snatch the one available internship before Helmuth grabbed it. Should he have foreseen this? Had Helmuth, had Franz foreseen it? Had they refused because they discerned, vaguely, the road that led from Heidelberg to Schwalbenbach?

Smoking his cigar, his feet on the chair, gazing at the nude on the calendar, he mused about old men running ecstatically to the execution wall, yearning to meet their God, and the insensate hatred with which they seemed to inspire Kroll. Kroll was a tricky fellow, and most certainly a dangerous man to cross; but those *soupers à deux* were most stimulating. Rather admirable, the way Kroll had handled this morning's confrontation with the prisoner Martens. He was too strong and too powerful a man to demean himself by getting drawn into an emotional contest with an obvious fool who had but a short while to live anyway. Heinrich had had a look at Martens' record that afternoon, just out of curiosity: civil disobedience, ten years hard, confession and disclosure, by coercion, of names of associates. Double-talk for the rack and the electric shock to the genitals; someone had to do that, and, compared to that, his present job was a merciful one, allowing him to keep his humanity intact. Kroll was right: detachment was the key. Do not rail at windmills, or try to save those for whom Caesar has ordained death. To remain uninvolved was more crucial than the pursuit of Truth, or the search for the one victim of the Great Flood allotted to him to save. Father in his letter sounded like Voltaire: each man must plant a tree, cultivate a garden and save one victim of the Great Flood.

The *Liebfraumilch* was good, the cigar superb; in the end, he wound up his portable gramophone and put on Mozart's Clarinet Quintet, which seemed just right for this night of warm, scented summer air and the faint warbling of nightingales in the copse across the fields. For a brief while the celestial music held him on that pinnacle of security where all was beauty, serenity and pure, delicate enjoyment. The hell with religion and its murky emotional appeal; Goethe had said it for all time: *"Wer keine Kunst hat, habe religion."* Only those incapable of appreciating true art needed the opium of religion.

* * *

The next evening, as he was preparing to go to supper, Heinrich's attention was drawn to an unusual sound at the gate. It was near the bungalow, and he could hear anyone entering or leaving the camp, especially with the windows open; the unusual sound was a woman's voice. Some female was having an argument with the guards out front.

He listened, his head out of the window of his bathroom, trying to make out what was being said. One soldier cried, from the guardhouse, *"Wass ist denn los?"* The one at the gate replied,

"Weiss nicht! Eine Verrückte!" A madwoman? He decided to go and investigate.

From the veranda he saw a young woman with a bicycle standing by the gate, talking to the two guards. One of them had taken the rifle off his shoulder. "What's going on there?" he cried. "Who is that woman? What does she want?"

Both soldiers made an about-turn and stood to attention. "A visitor, *Herr Hauptsturmführer!"* the one with the gun replied. "She wants to visit a prisoner!"

He went down the steps of the veranda and joined them at the barrier. The woman was no more than a girl; the most striking thing about her was that she was pregnant. The moment she spotted him she put her head on one side, looked at him coyly and said, *"Gnädiger Herr,* my father is an inmate of this camp, I have come all the way from Holland on my bike to visit him. May I not see him, just for a moment? Please? Please?"

"Nobody is ever admitted to this camp except those who belong here. If I were you, I would go home." Siegfried growled by his side. "Quiet," he said. "Heel." He turned away to lock the beast in the bungalow before going down to supper.

"But I *do* belong here, *Herr Offizier!"* the girl cried after him, with a note of despair in her voice. "I—I am Jewish too!"

He turned around and looked at her. *"What* did you say?"

"I—I am Jewish."

She was lying; not only did she look unmistakably Aryan with her blond hair and blue eyes, but the way she said it made obvious that it was a last, foolish attempt on her part to gain access to the camp.

"What's your name?"

"Martens. Laura Martens. My father's name is Jacob."

He stared at her. She could not have any idea of the consequences of her foolish statement if it were to get to Kroll. *"Fräulein,"* he said, keeping his voice low, "get out of here, fast! There are no visiting privileges. Nobody ever sees the prisoners. Go away—get away from here!"

"Please!" she pleaded. "Please!"

There was something moving about her, something vulnerable; maybe it was her youth, her pregnancy, or even her courage—she must be the first person who had ever turned up at the gate of a concentration camp asking to visit a prisoner. Either she was indeed a madwoman or her innocence was heartbreaking.

Suddenly he heard a voice call behind him, *"Herr Doktor! What's going on?"* Kroll was standing in the doorway of the main building.

To send her away now would be foolhardy, but he risked it. "Go! Quick!" He turned around and strolled casually toward Kroll.

"Who is that?" Kroll asked, looking toward the barrier.

"A young lady who wants to visit a prisoner."

"A prisoner? Which prisoner?"

Reluctantly he replied, "The prisoner Martens."

"Ah! Our resident saint!" Kroll was suddenly interested. "What is she? His wife?"

"His daughter. She is pregnant," he added.

"Let her in." The foolish girl had obviously not followed his advice.

"Why?" he asked boldly.

Kroll looked at him through narrowed eyes. *"Herr Hauptsturmführer,"* he said. "It is I who give the orders here. Let her in." He turned on his heel and vanished into the officers' barracks.

Heinrich returned to the gate. The idiot girl was still standing there, expectantly. The guards leaped to attention again as he approached.

"All right, let her in."

"Jawohl, Herr Hauptsturmführer." One of them raised the barrier. The girl entered with an expression of triumph, pushing her bicycle.

Siegfried rose, growling. *"Fuss!"* he said; the dog lay down obediently. "The guard will take care of your bicycle. *Scharführer!"*

"Jawohl, Herr Hauptsturmführer." The guard took her bicycle away; she looked unhappy about it.

"You'll get it back after your visit," Heinrich said, to reassure her.

To his amazement, the commandant received her graciously. Never before had he seen Kroll in his role of ladies' man. He invited her to come in, to sit down in the lobby, inquired about her journey, how she knew that her father was here. Innocent questions, asked with a smile; then he said, still smiling, *"Herr Doktor,* tell the Kapos to bring her father to my office. At once." He opened the door to the mess hall and said to the girl, "Would you mind waiting in here?"

The girl, obviously reassured by his behavior, entered without a second thought. The hall was empty, but in ten minutes the officers would turn up for their supper. What the devil was Kroll up to?

"Komm, Herr Doktor," the commandant said irritably.

"Jawohl, Herr Obersturmführer." Heinrich went outside to find Kapos to escort the prisoner Martens to the commandant's office. Siegfried followed him, slavishly to heel.

He found a couple of the criminals hanging around the entrance to the lazaret and passed on the order; when they got hold of Martens and started to push him around, he warned them sharply, "That's enough! Just take him to the commandant's office, that's all!"

The brutes obeyed at once, but, even so, he had taken sides with a prisoner. As Martens looked at him, bewildered, he committed a second indiscretion by saying impulsively, "Don't worry. Nothing's wrong. You have a visitor."

"Visitor?" The whole lazaret fell silent and even Wassermann, normally as adroit and wary as a weasel, stood open-mouthed. Heinrich instantly regretted his words, but it was too late now. "It's your daughter," he added.

"My—my *daughter?*"

The man looked so thunderstruck that Heinrich suspected for a moment that he did not have a daughter, that the girl was indeed *eine Verrückte* who had got it into her crazy head to worm her way inside a concentration camp. "Yes," he said. "Blonde, blue eyes, about eight or nine months pregnant. Says her name is Laura."

Martens stared at him as if he were a ghost, then he stammered, in anguish, "No . . . no . . . "

The Kapos had had enough, and Heinrich allowed them to put handcuffs on the poor bastard and drag him off in their own inimitable manner. "All right, Wassermann," he said gruffly. "Let's you and I do rounds now. I'll be dining late this evening."

But he barely looked at the patients, and did not listen to a word the man was saying. In the end he got so worked up that he walked away in the middle of one of Wassermann's reports and headed for the mess hall. He met the Kapos on their way back from Kroll's office halfway to the main building; then the three of them froze at the sound of shrill screams coming from that direction—the screams of a girl, followed by a raucous roar, the roar of a madman.

The three of them ran to Kroll's office where they found the bedroom door locked; inside, the screams and cries rose to a demented pitch. Heinrich was about to kick in the door when it was opened by Kroll, in shirt sleeves. Inside, he saw the girl lying half naked on the bed, her torn dress around her waist; manacled to the radiator was Martens, berserk, thrashing about, blood streaming down his wrists where the handcuffs tore at his flesh.

"Um Gotteswillen," Heinrich stammered, aghast.

Kroll reached for his tunic and turned to the Kapos. "Take him out! Put him in the hole!"

The Kapos approached the chained man warily, then jumped him. After a vicious struggle they dragged him out, screaming, fighting. There was foam on his mouth, his eyes were popping out of his head, he was stark, raving mad. As he was dragged out of the room, the girl turned her head and stared at Heinrich, her eyes wide with shock.

Kroll lit a cigarette. "Well, that was quite a circus," he said equably.

"What in the name of God . . . ?"

Kroll snapped his lighter shut. "A theological dispute. *Quod erat demonstrandum."* He picked up a little pillow with surgical tape dangling from it and tossed it at Heinrich. "Here's your answer to the immaculate conception." He went to the door. "Give her a shot, or whatever, and put her up somewhere provisionally. See you at supper." He put on his cap, adjusted it to its usual jaunty angle and left.

Heinrich approached the bed. The girl gazed at him, but her eyes were unfocused. There was blood on her mouth, her hair was disheveled. Her breasts were small and virginal. He looked at the little pillow. *"God is Love."* It was a nightmare. "Can you walk?" he asked. When she did not reply, he put his arm around her to help her up. She did not move, but lay inert on the bed. He lifted her eyelids, the pupils were dilated. He must take her out of here quickly. Wrapping the blanket from the bed around her, he lifted her in his arms and carried her out of the room.

Outside, the two Kapos were holding down the struggling, screaming Martens, waiting for further orders. The moment the demented man saw them appear, he shrieked: "Laura! Laura!", managed to tear himself free and stumbled toward them; before the Kapos were able to catch up with him, a black-and-yellow streak lunged at his throat.

"Siegfried!" Heinrich shouted. *"Fuss!"*

The dog obeyed at once, but it was too late. Martens had fallen to the ground, blood spurting from his throat. Then the Kapos went for him with their clubs. The girl buried her head in Heinrich's shoulder and tightened her arms around his neck. Carefully, he carried her to the bungalow.

CHAPTER THREE

WHEN Heinrich returned to the commandant's office, Kroll was berating the Kapos for killing the prisoner. "I said put him in the hole, not a hole in the ground!" The guards protested that they had not attacked; Kroll delivered a harangue on legality and restraint and sent them packing, saying that whether he would demote them to the status of ordinary prisoners depended on their future behavior. *"Raus!"* The Kapos slunk out, thoroughly rattled.

After they had left, Kroll asked, with that meaningless smile of his, "And how is the Jewess?"

"I don't believe she is," Heinrich replied. "I think—"

"I am not interested in what you think, *Herr Doktor!* She stated at the gate she was a Jewess, that's why I admitted her to the camp. I heard her myself, over that loudspeaker. She's in your bed now, I presume?"

"Yes," Heinrich said. Something decided him to stand up for the girl, maybe the memory of the look of her as he laid her down on his bed: broken, destroyed, while outside the Kapos bludgeoned her father to death. In no way could this be justified by the Final Solution; this was sadistic viciousness. "I think she just said she was Jewish in order to gain access to her father."

"Herr Doktor," Kroll said ominously, "our guideline is that anyone who says he is a Jew *is* a Jew. And she has no papers to prove the contrary. She has no papers at all."

"Even so, I think she should be allowed to leave."

"Are you mad?" Kroll peered at him through the smoke of his

cigarette. Then he stubbed it out and added, "She belongs in the women's barracks, but I'm going to leave her with you until she is fit enough to work. When is the next cremation?'

"Tomorrow."

"See to it that the body of the prisoner Martens is taken to the crematorium. I will write a report stating that he was killed while trying to escape, and I expect you to sign it with me."

"But—"

"You heard me!" Kroll shouted. "You will sign it! That's an order!"

Heinrich clicked his heels, made an about-turn and marched out.

As he walked to the bungalow, his knees were shaking, but he felt calm and lucid. It certainly wasn't remorse for what he had done to poor Martens that had made Kroll relent and allow him to give a prisoner proper care. It wasn't compassion for the girl he had raped either. Kroll must be afraid of something. What? That Berlin would get wind of it? That must be it. If they ever did, the incident might have serious consequences for him. The SS prided itself on the legality of their acts, at least Headquarters did. Their strict orders were that there should be no excessive brutality. The Jews must be exterminated, all of them, but unemotionally, within the law. What if he were to write a report, in his capacity as camp doctor, on what Kroll had done? The possibility gave him a sudden sense of power. He did not want to risk his own neck, but the mere fact of having that report written and ready to be mailed might give him the leverage needed to induce Kroll to set the girl free.

As he entered the waiting-room in his bungalow and stood still to listen, he heard Siegfried come in behind him and lie down next to the couch. There was no sound from the bedroom. He tiptoed to the door, opened it a crack and looked at her still form in the bed for a few moments. Then he went to her and turned down the blanket. "I have to examine you, my dear. You mustn't mind, I'm a doctor. I am here to help you."

She did not respond. Obviously, she was still in shock. A patient in her condition was best left undisturbed, but if he wanted to write that report he should be able to substantiate it with medical proof.

He examined her gently. She stirred, but did not reach consciousness. He discovered, to his surprise, that there had been no defloration. There were no signs of trauma other than a few contusions on the thighs and upper arms, and some slight abrasions where the surgical tape holding the pillow had been torn off. Kroll's sole intention had been to drive her father berserk. The rape had been a pretense.

It might be fortunate for the girl, but it did not help his report. Had he been able to furnish physical proof of rape, the case would have been a straightforward one; now he would have to go into the whole involuted background of the pretense, and that would not be easy. He covered her up, went to his consulting-room and sat down at the desk, the dog on the floor beside him.

He pulled his writing pad toward him and took out his pen. Where should he begin? The arrival of Martens with the convoy from Holland? The arrival of the girl? As he thought it through, he began to see the weakness of his case. Martens had resisted the Kapos with violence. Kroll had driven him to it by feigning the rape of his daughter, but the only witness to that was he himself, and he had not seen the actual assault. Kroll might have friends in Headquarters who would sweep the whole affair under the carpet if they could. Yet, even if it was inconclusive, the report could be a bargaining tool. It depended on what Kroll would consider to be more of a threat: the report, or the girl at liberty outside the camp.

He glanced at his watch: he was late for supper. Kroll must be asking himself what the doctor was up to. He should perhaps stay with the girl, but that would mean standing Kroll up. Could he risk that? He tiptoed to the bedroom. She was still lying as he had left her: as if she had fallen from a great height. Poor child—what could he do to help her? How to blunt the impact when she woke? Keep her where she was and wait for her to surface was all he could do; but how to give her some reassurance at the moment of awakening? Presently he went outside in the dusk to pick a yellow pansy; as he was doing so, the *Scharführer* from the officers' mess turned up with a message from the *Obersturmführer:* was *Herr Doktor* coming to supper or wasn't he? If not, why not?

He scribbled on the back of the note: "Apologies, delayed by patient in urgent need of attention," and handed it back to the man, with the request that he take it to the commandant. The *Scharführer* saluted—*"Zu Befehl, Herr Hauptsturmführer"*— and made an about-turn, after which he marched back to the main building in the dusk.

Back in the bedroom, Heinrich put the flower in a tumbler

with water and placed it on the night table where she would see
it as she opened her eyes. He lit a candle beside it.

He went back to the waiting-room, leaving the bedroom door
open, lay down on the couch and lit a cigar. He heard the click-
ing of Siegfried's claws on the linoleum and a thud as the dog lay
down in the open doorway to keep both him and her in sight: the
ancient instinct of the sheepdog, forever watching over his flock.

The nightingales in the copse across the fields started their
evensong.

* * *

Laura slowly rose through dark water, through fronds of waving seaweed. As she reached the surface she heard a sound: the
panting of a dog. She opened her eyes. A yellow flower. A candle
flame. Then the dog, in a lighted doorway, staring at her. She
screamed, and sank back among the waving weeds.

* * *

Heinrich, who had been dozing on the couch, jumped up and
ran into the bedroom. He found her lying half out of bed, unconscious. Bending over her, he lifted her back onto the bed; as he
was covering her with the blanket, Siegfried started to bark.
There were steps on the veranda, a knock on the door.

"Who is it?"

"Herr Hauptsturmführer . . . " It was one of the guards.

"What do you want?"

"The commandant wants to see you in his office, *Herr Hauptsturmführer.*"

"Now? At this hour?"

"Jawohl, Herr Hauptsturmführer."

He looked at his watch; it was a quarter past midnight; he
must have slept for two hours. "All right. Tell him I'll be with
him in a minute."

The soldier clicked his heels, saluted—*"Heil Hitler!"*—turned
smartly and vanished.

What on earth could be the matter? Had Kroll finally decided
to let him have it for standing him up at supper? Well, he had
better go and find out. He let himself out quietly and walked
over to the main building.

Kroll was sitting behind his desk, immaculate as ever, writing. "Ah, *Herr Doktor*. Sit down. Would you mind closing the door? Thank you."

"What can I do for you, *Herr Kommandant?*"

"Shut that female up. I can't have her screaming the place down at dead of night, or at any other time. I don't care what you do to her, but if this happens again I'll have her moved."

"She is in no fit condition to be moved."

"What is her condition?"

"She is in shock. She will need an extended period of convalescence before she is able to function."

"How long? A day, two days? A week?"

"A week is not enough. At least two, possibly three."

"And during all that time you are prepared to keep her in your bungalow?"

"Do you have another suggestion?"

Kroll smiled. "My dear doctor, I am not a fool. I leave her to you, as long as you keep her quiet. When she gets better, she shall not show herself at the windows. When you receive patients in your office, lock her in your bedroom. Don't ask for meals for her from the kitchen; take to your quarters whatever food you can pick up, as long as it is clearly intended for your own consumption. The moment her presence is known, out she goes. I have enough problems as it is. Thank you, that'll be all." He resumed his writing.

Heinrich rose, clicked his heels and left.

The night was cool and serene. In the copse across the fields the nightingales were singing. Far away the thin beams of searchlights groped in the sky, too far for the gunfire to be heard. The prisoners' barracks stood stark and angular in the moonlight, with black shadows. As he walked to the bungalow, his first thought was that he wanted no part of this. She was his patient. He was touched by her personal tragedy and concerned that she should regain her freedom, but he had no interest in her beyond that. Kroll had clearly intimated that he should keep her as a concubine. What a damnable idea! She was his patient; whatever else they might force him to do, he would not abuse a female patient.

He entered the bedroom on tiptoe. She seemed not to have moved since he left. He ordered Siegfried back into the waiting-room; as he pulled up a chair and sat down at her bedside, he heard the sounds of claws on the linoleum and knew that the dog had lain down in the doorway again.

The unconscious girl looked totally lost. It was a long time since he had last indulged in pity; it came as an unexpected solace, as if his parched soul were drinking in this sudden flood of compassion. While watching her, his elbows on his knees, his chin in his hands, he indulged in juvenile daydreams. Go to Kroll and say, "This is the deal: you write out a pass for me and the girl, I'll take her back to Holland; in exchange, I will not send a report to Berlin." Either that or escape from the camp together, go into hiding, like so many other people in the occupied territories; there must be thousands of them, in attics in the cities, in the haylofts of farms. But that was nothing but a fantasy. He was an SS officer; no German farmer would dare take him in, no Dutch farmer would dream of doing so.

She moaned in her sleep. He stopped daydreaming and just sat watching her, his elbows on his knees, his chin on his hands, in the light of the candle flame.

* * *

A voice called at the bottom of the stairs, "Laura, wake up! Laura, it is late! Laura!" She couldn't understand why; it was Sunday, she should be allowed to sleep in. She wanted to go back to sleep, but the voice went on calling, fainter now; Mother had moved from the bottom of the stairs to the kitchen. But Mother was dead. She was dreaming this. She must wake up.

She peered through her eyelashes, saw a candle flame and realized she was not home, but somewhere else. She must get up! Odd to hear a voice in your sleep urging you to wake up, like a built-in alarm. She wanted to get up, get dressed, but something was wrong. She refused to confront it. She forced herself back to sleep, but was gradually overcome by such terror that she prayed, "God, dear God, save me, save me, in the name of Thy only begotten Son Jesus Christ. . . ." It worked. She was given peace. But it did not last; slowly, relentlessly, she was forced back into an awareness of her surroundings. She peered through her eyelashes at the candle flame. Next to it was the flower in a glass, a yellow pansy. Next to that something large, green or blue. With over it a white disk. A face.

She closed her eyes tight, sick with sudden fear. Whose face? Then she heard the scrabbling of claws, and terror jumped her. She screamed, screamed, pressing herself in the corner; a hand was put on her mouth, she struggled, bit, suffocated, collapsed. When finally she lay panting, limp, powerless, choked with terror, a man's voice said, *"Liebchen,* you must not scream. You are safe here as long as you do not scream. Do you hear me? You must not scream."

There was something wrong with the man, but he had all the power. She nodded, wishing the hand on her mouth would go away and let her breathe. That was all she wished: for that hand to go away.

Finally it did. She took a deep breath.

"That's better," the man said. "Would you like something to drink?" Then she knew what was wrong: he spoke German.

She wanted to scream, but dared not. She tried to crawl away within herself, to hide, to sleep. Sleep, please, God, let me sleep, please, God, please . . .

*   *   *

He sat at her bedside until dawn. She had lapsed back into shock and lay motionless on her side in the fetal position. Would she have the strength to live on, or would she follow the thread back into the womb and beyond, until her life dissolved in the same mystery from which it had emerged, sixteen years ago? She could not be much older; her face was still childlike, as were her hands. She was totally vulnerable; any more violence would crush her. Her only hope was to be coaxed along, patiently, like a bruised seedling. The curtains should remain closed for her sake too; the bungalow should be her greenhouse, with frosted glass.

As daylight grew, he pondered on the irony of his situation. Here he sat, gazing upon a sleeping young girl, dreaming about tender loving care; in a moment he would have to get up, put on his cap, and after morning roll-call he would start the selection of prisoners for transportation to the extermination camp.

Suddenly he wished he knew how to pray; but it passed. The fear subsided; the irony remained.

*   *   *

After she heard his footsteps go away and a door close, she lowered the blanket and looked about her. A chair. A chest of drawers. The bedside table with the tumbler, the flower and the candle stub. A window, which she had not noticed before: blackout curtains with a sliver of sunlight at the bottom. She looked around the room once more. An open door revealed the next room: a sunlit window, the corner of a red couch, a standard lamp with a black shade. The floor was covered with yellow linoleum. She needed to go to the bathroom.

She lay still for a while, listening, but there was no sound. Feeling weak, she sat up and lifted a corner of the curtain to look outside. Barbed wire. Blue sky. A prison? It took a while before she could muster the strength to swing her legs out of bed, then she slid down until her feet touched the floor and stood up. She felt giddy and as weak as a kitten; but she must go to the bathroom. She walked slowly to the open door and stopped there, leaning against the doorpost, exhausted by the effort. She looked around; the other room was small, dingy. Glass curtains covered the solitary window; they were so opaque that she could not see through them. Apart from the standard lamp with the black shade and the shabby red couch, there were a few uncomfortable-looking chairs and a low table with magazines. It looked like a doctor's waiting-room until she noticed a calendar with a naked woman on the wall. No doctor would have that in his waiting-room. To the right was a door, obviously to the outside; to the left, two other doors. Although she felt so weak that she could barely stand up, she opened one of the doors and found it led to a consulting-room. He must be a doctor, after all. She tried the other door and discovered a gloomy little room with a sink, a gas ring and a refrigerator with a second door beside it. On the sink was a rack of glass tubes, on the gas ring a retort; when she peeked behind the door beside the refrigerator, she found a bathroom. It was small and bare. A toilet, a washbasin, over it a mirror and a shelf with male things: a shaving brush, a soap mug, a bottle of lotion. The curtain was open, outside the window was that fence again, and beyond it a radiant summer day. Wheatfields, in the distance a small wood. An image came back to her, out of nowhere: two sparrows fighting, fluttering as they fell. She turned away from the window and opened the lid of the toilet. She wondered if she should put paper on the seat, but she was so exhausted that she decided to forget about it.

She prepared to sit down, and discovered that she was not wearing panties. Yet she was wearing a dress. What had happened to it? The buttons were gone, it was torn down to the waist. Had she been in an accident? She sat down and looked at her thighs. They were covered with bruises that hurt when she touched them. And on her sides were burn marks that hurt too. An accident? When? Where? The moment she asked herself that, fear closed in again. She hastily flushed the toilet, wanted to wash her hands, but the bathroom was full of fear now. She hurried back to the bedroom. She was halfway to the bed when she heard a door open in the other room. She wanted to run to the bed but couldn't move, paralyzed with fear. Footsteps approached.

"Hello," his voice said. "I'm glad you are up. How are you feeling?"

She was so afraid that she could not utter a sound. She saw him out of the corner of her eye, standing in the doorway, the dog at his side.

"Don't be afraid," he said. "You are safe here. Would you like to eat something?"

She was too terrified to answer.

"Very well. But you must rest. Go back to bed." She saw the movement as he turned to leave; then he turned back and said, "By the way, you must not come out until I tell you, and not show yourself at the window. Now I'll leave you in peace." The bedroom door closed.

She stumbled to the bed, covered her head with the blanket and lay in the darkness, trembling.

*   *   *

Should he have handled her differently? Told her who he was? Where she was? She had obviously been scared stiff; she might not have taken in a word he said. Poor girl. Talk about trauma! To suffer a sexual assault while her father went berserk, chained to the wall; then to see him brought down by a dog and clubbed to death . . . She must have seen it, he had felt her arms tighten around his neck and she had pressed her face into his shoulder; that was why he had brought her here in the first place. She must have taken in at least part of the gory scene. The shock might have been sufficient to bring about temporary amnesia, it was common after concussion for patients to remain unable to recall the impact and the circumstances immediately preceding it; this had been an emotional concussion. Suddenly Siegfried started to bark, footsteps crossed the veranda and the door opened. It was *Scharführer* Krause, the first of his morning's appointments. The girl would be still more terrified by these sounds, but he had to carry on business as usual, conform to Kroll's instructions.

"All right, Krause," he said, "you know where it is, go in and get undressed."

"Jawohl, Herr Hauptsturmführer."

He followed the man into the consulting-room. "Take off your pants and bend over. Let me see what it looks like today."

The man obeyed. The *pruritis ani* was improving. He gave him more ointment.

By lunchtime he had seen four patients, including one emergency: one of the cooks had scalded his hand with boiling soup, a second-degree burn. He had made his rounds of the prisoners' lazarets, first the men's, where there were three dead, then the women's, where all the beds were occupied but no one *in extremis.* Amazing how much more resilient women proved to be; he hoped the same would go for the girl. He found himself thinking of her constantly.

During lunch at the table by the window Kroll did not mention the girl and neither did he. They chatted about the weather, the abysmal movie that was to be shown that night called *Kirstin in Lederhosen,* and the fact that the cows were lowing so loudly in the neighboring fields that either the farmer must be drunk or it was going to rain. It did not look like rain, though; this really was a marvelous summer, like the one two years ago. When dessert was served, he asked Kroll's permission to leave, on the pretext that he had to finish an inventory of the drugs in his pharmacy before tomorrow's mail; when he rose, Kroll said, "Here— take this with you. She'll want something to eat, sooner or later. If she doesn't want it today, it should keep in your refrigerator." It was a piece of *Baumkuchen;* he took the plate along.

She was asleep, or pretended to be. Her forehead was cool, her pulse slow and regular, her blood pressure twelve over six.

He tiptoed to his office, sat down at his desk and wrote: *"Yesterday, June 23, 1942, a young Aryan female by the name of Laura Martens presented herself at the gate of this camp. She requested permission to see her father, Jacob Martens, a political prisoner in Barrack A, who had arrived with transport*

H.S. 62 from Holland. The undersigned was witness to her arrival. . . . "

He wrote on, crossing out words and sentences, scribbling over them, until the pages were such a mess that he had to start from scratch.

It took him all afternoon, but finally he came up with a version that satisfied him. The case against Kroll was based largely on circumstantial evidence and therefore weak, but his insult to the honor of the SS was irrefutable.

"The reason for this report is that Obersturmführer Kroll's actions and behavior insult the code of honor of the SS. We are the Führer's representatives at all times, in all places, under all circumstances. In this camp it is our bounden duty to embody his heroic German values. Judged by these sacred standards, Obersturmführer Kroll has sullied and debased our Führer."

As he leaned back and lit a cigar, it struck him that he was actually nauseated by this sanctimonious crap, more than ever before. He had never been happy with the hyperbole in which the SS bullies couched their screaming speeches, but it had never bothered him to the point of actual nausea. Well, never mind, the objective of this whole exercise was to save the girl, so the end had to hallow the means.

He went to look in on her. She still had not stirred. She must have suffered a relapse; what could have brought that about? He hit upon the answer as he rose and heard Siegfried's claws scrabble on the linoleum. Of course, it was the dog! Every time she had screamed, it had been because of the dog. Did she remember how Siegfried had brought down her father? Poor old beast, poor corrupted beast.

He patted the dog's head, walked back to his desk and stood looking down at the report. Now what? If he could send it directly to Himmler, the evangelical language of his summing-up might tip the balance in the girl's favor; but if a lesser official got his hands on it first, her chances were slender. Only Himmler and his immediate entourage actually believed this baloney; anyone else would instantly smell a rat and toss the report into the wastebasket. How about sending it to Horst Dahlen, with the request that it be put on Himmler's desk? If Horst was still in favor, which he was in no position to know as they hadn't corresponded for over six months.

But he was losing sight of the report's real purpose: to blackmail Kroll into releasing the girl. He should say, *"Herr Ober-sturmführer,* I have taken the liberty of writing an extensive report on your actions regarding Martens and his daughter. Unless you release her at once, the report will go directly to Himmler's aide-de-camp, who happens to be a personal friend of mine." But easy now—wasn't that an invitation to have his bungalow ransacked? The report must be safely out of the camp before he told Kroll of its existence. Dr. Schmidt with the report in his bungalow was a sitting duck; once it was in safekeeping somewhere, he was invulnerable.

He put it in an envelope, sealed it and wrote a letter to his father. *"Dear Vati. Please place the enclosed in a safe-deposit box at the Landbank, in your name. I cannot tell you at this time what the envelope contains, but it may save someone's life."* He thought of asking the old man for a confirmation, but Kroll, once he felt threatened, was capable of censoring all incoming mail. *"When you have taken care of this, please write in your next letter: 'Aunt Anna is as besotted with her African violets as ever.' Insert this phrase among other one-line reports on family members. If at any time I were to die under suspicious circumstances ('a fatal accident' or 'deceased in the course of duty'), please forward the envelope to SS Headquarters, Berlin, attention Hauptsturmführer Horst Dahlen. Love, Heinzl."*

There was no problem about mailing it. The daily courier left before supper, it was quite normal to hand the man a last-minute letter at the barrier before he took off on his motorbike. This he did; his next move should be to convey to Kroll that their roles had been reversed: now *Herr Doktor* and not *Herr Kommandant* held the trump card.

He walked over to the officers' mess in high spirits, and took his place opposite the unsuspecting Kroll with a feeling of self-confidence. As the soup was being served, Kroll asked, "Well, did you have a chance to work on your report this afternoon?"

He froze, then he remembered he had used a pharmacy report as an excuse for leaving the table at lunchtime. "Yes, thank you. As a matter of fact, I had the time to make it quite specific."

"Good," Kroll said, uninterested.

He decided it was time to make a move. "What is more, I mailed it to a friend. For safekeeping."

"How thoughtful of you."

The soup tureen appeared between them; Kroll helped himself

liberally. He even thanked the *Scharführer* with a nod, which was unusual. After the man had withdrawn out of earshot, he said casually, "why don't you come with me to my office after the movie, for a Schnapps and a chat?"

"I wasn't planning to go to the movie."

"Let's make it right after dinner, then. By the way, isn't it time we stopped being so official? Your name is Heinzl, isn't it?"

Only his father called him by that name.

Kroll continued, "I know how you feel. My parents used to call me Schlumpsi. Fortunately, my friends call me Sylvester."

Heinrich's high spirits were gone. Maybe he still held the trump card, but the game wasn't going to be as easy as he had assumed.

"Let's go into my bedroom," Kroll said as they entered his office. "It's more comfortable."

He opened the door to the cubicle in which he lived. The moment Heinrich entered, the scene came back to him: the demented Martens chained to the radiator, the ravaged girl on the bed. "By the way," Kroll said, after opening the wardrobe, "she might want this." He held out the little pillow with the legend *"God is Love."* "You also have a blanket of mine, I believe. Would you let me have it back, please?" He took off his tunic and hung it on a hook inside the wardrobe door, sat down on the edge of the bed and stretched out a leg. "Would you mind?"

Heinrich pulled off the boot for him, then the other.

"Thank you." Kroll settled against the wall. "Do sit down. Oh, sorry, I forgot about the Schnapps. It's in the wardrobe. Or would you rather talk first?"

"Let's talk first."

"All right. Talk."

"You asked for this conversation, you start."

"Very well. You're a virgin, aren't you?"

"I beg your pardon?"

"Aren't you?"

"I don't see what—"

"Dear Heinzl, it is the central issue! Picture yourself: the young, self-righteous son of a puritanical father, career-oriented, member of the SS not out of vocation but ambition. Sounds like a picture of Narcissus, doesn't it? My guess is you've had no other sexual experience than an occasional excursion into commercial fornication, as is common among students. You are not engaged to be married, you have no mistress. 'Virgin' seems the right definition. And that not only in regard to sex, but to life in general. Only virgins think they can keep themselves unspotted from the world. New Testament, Epistle of St. James. Smoke?"

"No, thank you."

Kroll snapped his lighter shut and tossed it aside on the bed. "Now about your attempt at blackmail via your so-called report. A typical example of adolescent, muddle-headed thinking. If it weren't, I would deal with you quite differently. You understand that, don't you?"

"But—but how did you—"

"Come, come, dear Heinzl. You have been as conspicuous about it as a Cub Scout. I told the dispatch rider to come to me, of course, if you were to give him a letter. So let's forget about that. What's more, no one would have given it a moment's attention."

"The fact remains that you did rape the girl in front of her father!"

"Spoils of war, my friend. I don't know how you picture the chiefs of staff of the SS, but let me assure you they know what war means. Also, as you must have ascertained by now, I did not in fact rape her. I wanted her father to believe I did, to wipe that holy smirk off his face and unleash the rabid beast within the body of Christ. You must admit I was successful. Now, I don't care what you do with that girl in the privacy of your bungalow. As far as I'm concerned, you may abuse her, torture her, mutilate her, hack her into pieces and toss her into the crematorium in a gunny sack. It is totally unnecessary for you to go in for blackmail in order to keep your little concubine."

"But that is not my intention!" He heard how shrill his voice sounded. "I want you to release her! I demand that you let her go, tomorrow! And I take serious exception to your intercepting my personal correspondence! It will not stop me from making the truth known, one way or another!"

Kroll drew deeply on his cigarette and stubbed it out in the ashtray beside him on the bed. "My dear young friend, the time has come for you to face reality. Forget about your report. It can only cause trouble for you. You are keeping that girl in your private bungalow. She stated that she was a Jewess, so you are committing *Rassenschande*, a crime against our racial laws. All it takes to send you to the front is for me to declare that you kept the girl despite my strict order to put her on transport the moment she could walk. After that, anything you might care to report about me will be explained as a puerile effort at revenge by a junior officer with a grudge. Now, how about that glass of Schnapps?"

"Thank you, no."

"Suit yourself." Kroll got up and opened the wardrobe; there was a clinking of glass. As Heinrich went to the door, Kroll added, "Remember: I will let you keep your succulent little *Fräulein* only so long as her presence is not advertised and she does not affect your attitude to your work. The moment you show signs of going soft on the prisoners, out she comes. Understood?" He took a bottle and a tumbler to the bedside table. "By all means, be an indoor sentimentalist. But make sure that you remain an outdoor SS officer. That'll be all."

'No,' Heinrich thought, 'I won't let myself be intimidated.' He turned to face Kroll. "Am I correct in assuming that it's my turn now?"

"Your turn to what?"

"To present my concept of the situation?"

"No, *Herr Doktor.* You will not. You will appreciate the fact that I chose to treat you as an equal, in private, rather than have you cashiered and transferred to the front. And make no mistake: I would not hesitate to do just that, despite our pleasant little *entre-temps.* Now let's forget about the whole business and meet again for lunch tomorrow. You were going to tell me about your father."

The only way Heinrich could express his helpless rage was by slamming the door as he left.

In the lobby, he heard the metallic voices of the movie behind the closed doors of the officers' lounge. He went out into the dusk fragrant with the scent of freshly cut grass. Somewhere the lawnmower whirred. As he went down the steps, a shadow joined him: Siegfried.

He walked to the bungalow and sat down in one of the deck chairs on the veranda; the dog lay down beside him. The swallows were out again, they wheeled and swooped around the top of the flagpole.

He tried to reflect on what Kroll had said, but all he could do

was sit there and let the rage drain away. He had been given a
lesson in power. He might hold the trump card, Kroll held the
power. Whatever could be said about the man, in the world of
Himmler and Heydrich he was an excellent commanding officer.
In the world of Mozart and Goethe he was a thug.

After he had calmed down somewhat, he went inside to check
on the girl. She lay there exactly the way he had left her, as if
she were in a coma. Her pulse was normal, and her blood pressure had not dropped appreciably; she did not seem to have an
abnormally low body temperature either. She was just recovering, in near-unconsciousness, from the violent emotional trauma
she had suffered. As he stood there, looking down at her innocent face half turned away from him, her blond hair spread out
on the pillow, he realized that his confrontation with Kroll had
not ended in total defeat. He might have been unable to bring
about the girl's release; but, for the time being at least, she was
safe where she was. Kroll must still be taking the threat of a report to Berlin seriously; the counterthreat that by keeping the
child in his quarters he was committing *Rassenschande* did not
hold water; as a physician, he was justified because she was his
patient who needed constant observation and intensive care. He
did not have the slightest intention of turning the child into his
concubine. Not only was she his patient, but she was much too
young, a mere waif. Well, it looked as though he had saved his
father's one human derelict, at least for the time being. Sufficient unto the day . . .

Siegfried barked; someone knocked on the door. *"Heil Hitler!"* It was Kroll's batman. "With the commandant's compli-
ments, *Herr Hauptsturmführer!"* Standing stiffly to attention,
the man held out a little pillow. "And could I have the commandant's blanket, please? The red one."

He went back inside to collect the blanket and gave it to the
man; then he stood in a quandary, the little pillow in his hand.
He should hide it, in a place where the girl could not come across
it by accident. It might unleash memories she could not handle.

In the end, he put it in the cupboard under the sink in the lab.
After that he lit a cigar, put Schubert's Cello Quintet on the gramophone and lay down on the couch.

The tenderly passionate music brought the memory of lost
summer days, of trysts on the banks of the river while the student string quartet of the high school performed this same Quin-

tet, pert little Maria Haverstock playing the second cello: sensuous wails of longing in the moonlit night. The wind in the leaves; the secretive scent of girls in their dark trysting place underneath the weeping willow. It was as if a darkness were dispelled, leaving him lighthearted, caring, the eager, tender young man he had once been.

He turned the record over and started the lovely Adagio; on his way back to the couch he stopped at the bedroom door. It might be the wrong thing to do; but if it had been he lying in there, beset by images of hell, he would have loved to be wakened by these tender sounds.

He opened the door, left it ajar and went back to the couch; after a moment he heard Siegfried lie down beside him. He got up and opened the door to the veranda. The sound of nightingales in the distance mingled with Mariechen Haverstock's cello. "Out, boy. Out!" Siegfried obeyed. "Good boy. Down."

The dog curled up in the darkness. He closed the door and returned to the couch.

*   *   *

Music ebbed and flowed. Slow waves of sound, infinitely soothing, that took away darkness and fear. Where did the music come from? A radio? Then it stopped.

She opened her eyes and saw that the door was ajar; there was light in the other room. Then she heard footsteps and saw a shadow pass; the music started up again. The footsteps came back; the shadow passed. Surely, nobody who played this kind of music would then come in to do her harm. The shadow must be the doctor's.

What had happened to her? She remembered getting up, going to a bathroom. She remembered a torn dress, and no panties. Blue marks on her thighs, burn marks on her waist. What in the world had happened to her? When? Where? Where was she? The soothing music smoothed out the anguished questions and turned them into mere curiosity. Could she ask him? She should, really. Who was he? German. A soldier. Barbed wire. Prison? A record player in prison? And that lovely music? It couldn't be. It must be a hospital, a military hospital. Hush now. Listen, just listen.

Then it was over. There came the footsteps again; this time

they stopped in front of the door. It swung open, she saw the shadow darken the doorway and stiffened.

"More Schubert?" he asked.

She nodded. When he didn't move, she realized he couldn't see her. "Yes," she said. She had a frog in her throat.

"All right, here it comes."

He went away, leaving the door open wider than it had been. The music started up again. But this time it was not able to hush the questions. For one thing, who was she? Odd question: 'Who am I?' The need to know suddenly was stronger than her fear. She called, "Doctor!"

No answer. She cleared her throat. "Doctor!"

Still no answer; the music must be too loud. She had to know. Slowly, carefully, she got out of bed and went to the door, so weak that she almost went back to bed. Holding on to the door-post, she peered into the next room; the first thing she registered was the smell of cigar smoke. She saw the top of his head, on the arm of the shabby red couch. He was lying on his back, smoking, his legs in the black boots crossed. His green military jacket was open. He was wearing a white shirt. There was a big buckle on his belt. He brought a cigar to his mouth; the hand that held it was slender. The cigar glowed; the hand took it out of sight; blue smoke spiraled to the ceiling.

"Doctor?"

Still he did not hear her, but she did not dare go in.

Suddenly he said, "Come in, Laura. Don't worry, the dog is not here. Your name is Laura, isn't it? Or is it Clara?"

No, not Clara.

"Why don't you join me? There, take that chair."

She didn't move.

The music stopped. He rose; she stepped back into the bed-room. He went to the gramophone and wound it. The music started again. Here he came. "Why don't you lie down on the sofa? I'll get you something to eat."

She did not move; she felt terribly weak, and still afraid. A little less, but still afraid.

"All right, take your time."

He went away, she heard him push something heavy around; he came back, pushing an armchair, and sat down in it, facing her.

They remained like that for a while, she clinging to the door-post in the darkness, he sitting in the armchair, legs crossed, smoking his cigar. He was young, in his twenties. He had a kind face, blue eyes. His hair was fair, his eyebrows almost invisible. His uniform was green; on his collar were the letters "SS" in silver. His boots were beautifully polished; he must have a horse. She had wanted a horse, sometime, somewhere.

Suddenly he got up. "I don't know about you," he said, "but I'm going to have some cake. I'm hungry." He went to the door on the left. She peered around the corner, saw him go in and open the refrigerator. She remembered the refrigerator: next to it was the door to the bathroom. He took out a plate with a slice of cake on it. He sat down again, held out the plate to her and asked, "Like a piece?"

She was tempted, the sight of the food made her feel terribly weak. She could not go on standing there, hiding from him, and was not sure she could make it back to the bed.

"Come, lie down on the couch," he said. "I'll cover you up with my greatcoat. Or I'll get my dressing-gown, that is softer. Come on, make yourself comfortable and we'll share the cake. You must be hungry. How long is it since you have eaten?"

"Don't know," she said. She wanted to add, 'I don't know anything.'

He put the plate with the cake on the floor, rose and came toward her.

She backed away; he walked past her, switching on the light. She watched him take the pillow off the bed, open the wardrobe and take out a blue robe.

He came back, went to the couch, plumped the pillow and put it down. Then he held up the robe for her. "Put this on. I'll put the coat over your legs. It'll be very snug." She understood every word, even though he spoke German. She had been good at German in school. Which school? She could not remember.

"Come along," he said, "don't be afraid. Lie down, make yourself comfortable, we'll have a piece of cake together and then I'll tell you all you want to know. You ask the questions, I'll answer. If you don't feel like any questions, let's listen to music. Come."

She hesitated.

"Would you rather go back to bed? In that case, I'll come and sit with you."

She managed to make it, slowly, weakly, to the couch, and sat down.

"Wouldn't you like to lie down?"

She shook her head.

"Shall I put this over your knees?"

She looked down and saw her torn dress. She wanted to close it, but there were no buttons.

"Here." He stood in front of her, holding up the robe.

She didn't dare move. He seemed to understand. "I know what," he said. "You put it on while I get a second plate." He put the robe beside her on the couch and went to the kitchen. She got up and put it on. The sleeves were too long.

"Here we are!" He came back with a plate, a knife and two forks. "Now make yourself comfortable."

She sat down again, feeling a little sick.

"Would you like my coat over your knees?"

She shook her head.

"Would you like me to go on playing the Schubert, or would you rather talk?"

She did not answer.

"All right, let's start with the cake." He cut it in half, put one part on the other plate together with a fork and held it out to her. "Here, try this. It's delicious. We have our own pastry cook here. He's good."

She took the plate and put it on her knees.

"Well," he said, "cheers." He put a piece in his mouth and ate it. "H'm-h'm! It *is* good."

It did look good. She tried a piece. It *was* delicious. It awakened memories, without shape or form. Hunger for sweets. She loved sweets. That was another thing: she had been good at German in school and loved sweets. Who was she? She looked at him. He smiled. He was a kind man.

Slowly, carefully, as to a child, he said, "Don't worry about any questions right now. Your memory has sustained a shock from which it will recover, but it's a slow process. In time, everything will come back to you; for the present, you needn't worry about anything. I'm a doctor. I am looking after you. This is my office. Where we are now is the waiting-room. The consulting-room is over there. You are in an Army camp. I am an Army surgeon. The camp is a base camp, we aren't going anywhere. So just relax, take it easy and don't worry about any questions; that time will come. Relax—nobody is going to hurt you. You are safe. Now, would you like to hear some more music? Something different? The same?"

She did not really want more, but nodded.

He went to the gramophone in the corner, took off the record, selected a new one from a stack and put it on. As he stood there with his back turned, she felt the impulse to flee back to bed. It was very brief, but there still was a lot of fear inside her, waiting to be let out. Gentle, soothing music started up again.

"Come," he said. "Why don't you try to sleep? Your memory needs lots of sleep to recover." He gave her no time to think; he lifted her legs onto the couch. She didn't really want to lie down, but she obeyed. The pillow was soft. She closed her eyes for a moment and opened them again, startled, as he spread something heavy over her. A coat. He went away; she watched him as he sat down and picked up a cigar.

"Do you mind if I smoke?"

She shook her head. She watched him light it and lean back in his chair.

She looked at the coat. It was a uniform coat. The Army. He was an Army surgeon. This was an Army camp. They weren't going anywhere. She was safe. The music came in slow, gentle waves, swelling, curling on a beach. They flattened out, slithered up the beach, and back again. And again.

*   *   *

When he was sure she was asleep, he tiptoed to the consulting-room to look up Amnesia. The handbook did not tell him much more than he already knew. *"Retrograde amnesia; anterograde amnesia; hysterical amnesia after emotional trauma quicker recovery than after injury to the brain.* SYMPTOMS: *disorientation, especially with regard to time, impaired power of perception, confabulations; see Korsakoff Syndrome."* He looked up the Korsakoff Syndrome. *"Denial of personal past, blanks in memory replaced by fantasies so as to escape from an unbearable truth, deterioration of critical functions, negation of illness or catastrophe that caused trauma, high spirits, occasionally leading to euphoria, plans for the future in painful contrast to reality.* THERAPY: *bed rest, emotional rest, bland routine, eventually psychotherapy and/or hypnotherapy. Vitamin B complex, especially B-1.* PROGNOSIS: *Hysterical amnesia: a period of convalescence varying from one month to one year or more, depending on severity of emotional trauma, followed in most cases by complete recovery, although some retrograde and anterograde amnesia surrounding the actual trauma may persist. In cases of injury to the brain . . . "* Well, that was not pertinent in her case. She had suffered severe emotional trauma.

One year or more! For the first time he thought of the future in a practical sense. Bed rest meant a second bed; he could not go on sleeping on the couch fully dressed. Kroll's instructions had been specific: there was to be no hint of her presence. That would be impossible in the long run; for one thing, he had been able to keep Stolz, his batman, out of the bedroom so far on a flimsy pretext, but tomorrow or the day after he would have to take the man into his confidence and swear him to secrecy. But how could he justify the request for a second bed? Where was he going to put it? The bedroom was too small. Here, the table and his desk took up all the space, and the waiting-room was out of the question. It looked like the couch for him, for the foreseeable future. Or for her. No, to put her on the couch was not practicable; he might be called out during the night, and they should not see her. All right, a few weeks. But after that?

Well, the future would take care of itself. There must be thousands of people in hiding right now, living in cramped quarters. He could ask for a second mattress, put it on the bedroom floor at night and on top of the bed during the day. Yes, that was the answer.

Typical to sit here worrying about their sleeping arrangements first. A virgin, Kroll had said. Well, not quite. But the man had been right about 'commercial fornication,' if one-night stands with nurses fell into that category. After Mariechen Haverstock, he had never wanted to tie himself down. Good thing he hadn't! To step from this camp into a family situation, with an innocent wife and cuddly children waiting for you, would amount to schizophrenia.

So, here they were: sixteen-year-old girl and twenty-six-year-old virgin, caught like flies in amber. Well, not to worry. His first task was to help her recover. Bed rest, emotional rest, bland routine. That would be easy: she had nowhere else to go. As soon as she started to move around, he would ask her to make the bed, sweep the floor, dust, make tea, all at pre-set times. He would have to tell Stolz to leave his vacuum cleaner, mop and bucket. Maybe he should have a chat with Wassermann; according to his ID sheet, he had specialized in psychiatry, been head of a

Jewish asylum. But for the time being he himself could handle her. Only Siegfried, poor beast, would remain banished to the veranda for the foreseeable future.

He put the handbook back on the shelf and tiptoed to the waiting-room. There she lay, fast asleep. Poor girl. Poor, damaged girl. Let's hope Brother Amnesia will be kind to her and blot out the horrendous experience forever.

Slumped in his chair, his feet on the low table, he started to light a fresh cigar, but thought better of it. No sense in nodding off and burning the linoleum. He might as well settle down for the night. So to bed? No, that would really shake her if she were to creep back there later. Ah, the luxury of showing concern! To be able to feel compassion again! That fellow Wassermann was to be envied, despite the ghastly circumstances under which he was forced to work, and his constant fear of death. He must be euphoric, wearing himself to a frazzle, fussing over his patients. Maybe that was the error of the New Order, the essential element it ignored: man's perennial yearning to show compassion.

'Christ has no body now on earth but yours, no hands but yours, no feet but yours . . . '

Suddenly, what Kroll had done to Martens seemed utterly vile, an effort to destroy the one gift that might save the world.

Musing about the gift of compassion, he fell asleep in the chair.

CHAPTER FOUR

"ALL right," he said, "let's go over it again. A large house in the country. Racehorses, yours was called Winnetou. A greyhound called Caesar. Your mother died when you were little. What about . . ."

She got up brusquely and went to the lab, now called kitchen. Obviously, she had been afraid he would start questioning her about her father. "Do you want tea?" she called.

"Too late. I must go and see my patients."

"Will you come home soon?" The anxiety with which she came back to ask it was touching. "Please come soon!"

"Of course. I won't be more than an hour. I'll have to go on to lunch, though. Let's have tea when I come back."

"It will be waiting for you!"

"Lovely. Bye, Laura."

"Bye . . ."

He did not look back, but knew she would remain standing there, staring after him with anxious, hungry eyes. Hungry for what? He did not know. She was no longer the dumb, terrified little creature he had brought in two weeks ago, but he knew no more about her now than he had then. She simply did not respond to his therapy at all; the time had come to seek expert advice.

Dr. Wassermann was in the male lazaret, auscultating a skeletal, middle-aged patient who sat on the table, legs dangling. The place was a mess; the moment Wassermann spotted him standing in the doorway he sprang to attention and the patient jumped off the table, dropping his pants in the process. The sight of the poor wretch standing to attention with his breeches around his ankles was unsettling. "All right, Wassermann, tell this man to leave. I want a word with you."

"Yes, *Herr Hauptsturmführer!*" Wassermann gestured to the man, who turned and fled, holding up his trousers as he went.

"In private. Where can we go?"

"I—I wouldn't know." Wassermann looked about him, at a loss. It had been a stupid question, there was no place in the barracks where they could talk privately.

"What about in there?"

"But—*Herr Hauptsturmführer,* that's the latrine!"

"Well, it's private, isn't it? Or is there anyone in there at the moment?"

"No, no, *Herr Hauptsturmführer,* but it—it's not suitable. . . ."

"Don't be ridiculous, man. I have seen latrines before."

"Very well, *Herr Hauptsturmführer . . .*" Wassermann went to open the door, and hesitated.

"All right. Go in."

Wassermann entered the foul little cubicle. The moment Heinrich followed suit he regretted having made the suggestion. The stench was sickening, the place filthy, enough to make one flee. "My God, Wassermann, you should keep this clean! Have you no orderlies?"

"Yes, *Herr Hauptsturmführer!* But—"

"Never mind. Close the door. Now: you are a psychiatrist, aren't you?"

"I was, *Herr Hauptsturmführer . . .*"

"All right. I—" The place was too cramped for both of them to stand up; Heinrich was about to suggest that Wassermann sit down, but all prisoners were expected to stand in the presence of officers. He sat down on the filthy seat himself; his pants would have to be sent to the cleaner before he sat down anywhere at home. "I have this female patient, the one who saw her father killed by the Kapos. You know the one?"

"Yes, *Herr Hauptsturmführer.*"

"Look, forget about formalities. I have come to consult you as a colleague. The girl suffers from hysterical amnesia. She has been under treatment now for nearly two weeks. Vitamin B-1, bed rest combined with a simple work routine, psychotherapeutic sessions—sort of. It's not my specialty. I thought I could handle it, but I am beginning to have my doubts."

"Why, *Herr*—"

"Cut out the *'Herr'!*"

"Yes, *H*— Yes."

"I'll tell you why. She is beginning to remember things. Isolated incidents, disjointed situations connected with her home and her life in Holland. Her parents had a manor house in the country with racehorses, greyhounds, servants. So far, she has not been able to put any of it into sequence."

"That's normal. She needs time. But are you sure she's telling you the truth?"

"Why?"

"I knew her father; he seemed to be fairly well off, but it was not at all the kind of wealth you describe. You know, of course, that these patients have a most prolific imagination? It sounds to me as if she might be making most of it up as she goes along."

"Of course, of course. Confabulations are a symptom. But, even so, she did seem to start remembering things. At least for a while. It would appear that now we've hit a major block."

"Ah?"

"Her father. She absolutely refuses to acknowledge his existence. She maintains she has no father; every time I probe, she says, 'I have no father,' period. It troubles me, as her father's death was what caused the amnesia. She must have really loved the man, to come all the way from Holland on her bicycle looking for him."

"She must indeed."

"So it would seem to me that, unless she arrives at an acknowledgment of his existence, we'll get no further. Am I right?"

Wassermann looked down at him with bright eyes, alert and attentive. No wonder: this consultation must be like a draft of cool water to a parched man. How sad it all was. How wasteful.

"Well? Am I right?"

"I'm trying to think, *Herr*—er—Doctor. I am not sure you should press her. Let her cope with that episode in her own good time. She will function even without acknowledging her father's existence. For that, of course, would mean acknowledging the dog, the beating, the whole scene."

"Not necessarily."

"Oh, yes. Very necessarily. She can only acknowledge having a father at all by working backward from that scene. And for her to be able to do that may take a long time."

"Why? It was a severe trauma, but surely—"

"Ah, we must not overlook the *real* trauma, Doctor!" The man was alive with excitement now.

"What would that be? The rape?"

"No, no, something quite different. Guilt, I would say. Soul-crushing, life-destroying guilt."

"What on earth could she be guilty of?"

"Patricide."

"You're mad!"

"Look at what happened, from her point of view—" Someone banged on the door of the latrine.

"Go away! Leave us alone!" Whoever it was bolted like a scalded cat. "You were saying?"

But Wassermann stood there, sobered by fright, back in reality: the filthy latrine, the SS officer on the toilet, the murderous henchman virtually at his throat.

"Sorry, Wassermann. I did not intend to scare you. Go on. You were looking at her relationship with her father from her point of view. What were you about to say?"

But the shouting had thoroughly rattled the man, who now stood rigidly to attention, his eyes no longer those of a doctor but of a prisoner.

"Come on, Wassermann! Out with it!" .

"It—it was nothing, *Herr Hauptsturmführer!* Just that—that she blames herself for her father's death. Subconsciously . . ."

Heinrich wanted to shake the man, to free him of the terror that had rendered him tongue-tied, but he should go easy on him now. This was obviously all he would get out of the poor brute this time. Astute fellow, though. Must have been good, once.

"All right, Wassermann. Thank you. You may open up."

"Jawohl, Herr Hauptsturmführer!"

Wassermann obeyed; outside the latrine he leaped to attention once more. The whole business was sickening. On his way out, Heinrich turned in the doorway. "By the way: the dog. Can I let the dog back into the house, do you think? The poor brute has been sleeping on the veranda all this time, and it's getting him down. Will she react negatively to having him around?"

Wassermann, standing stiffly to attention, gave him a strange look that he could not interpret. "I do not believe so, *Herr Hauptsturmführer.*"

"Despite what he did to her father?"

Wassermann seemed to smile. Then he said, "She doesn't *have* a father, *Herr Hauptsturmführer.* She'll defend that concept tooth and nail. The dog won't make any difference. Nor will you, *Herr Hauptsturmführer.*"

He frowned. "I don't care for that remark, Wassermann. I think you are forgetting yourself. Do not make me regret treating you as a colleague." Without waiting for an apology, he turned on his heel and left.

On his way to the mess hall he thought over their conversation. The guilt made sense, it explained the mystery of her mental block. He should let the questioning about her father rest awhile. She would function, as Wassermann had indicated. She already did; she was turning into quite the little housewife. The whole situation was a bit like a musical comedy: frilly curtains, dainty teacups, flouncy apron—they had been intended to make her feel at home, but resulted in the set for a musical comedy; at times he expected her to burst into song: "Oh, what a curious ha-ha-ha" from *Der Fledermaus.* Well, why not? Maybe they should start singing while doing the washing-up; it might help release the tension.

Kroll eyed him in a peculiar manner as he sat down to lunch, and said, "I'd like to see you in my office afterward. It would not be wise to discuss it here. The walls have ears."

He was too startled to reply. What was up? Was Kroll planning to have her removed? The mere idea set his heart pounding. He would have to escape with her! Anything but allow Kroll to take her away . . .

When, finally, he sat facing the commandant in his office, he had decided to give her an overdose of phenobarbital rather than let Kroll toss her into the truck to the extermination camp. He was ready to shoot the bastard if it came to that.

His cold fury must have communicated itself to Kroll, who said lightly, "I want to talk to you about the prisoners."

"Which prisoners?"

"In general, in general."

It clearly was an evasion; come on, you bastard, out with it!

"What about the prisoners?"

"Your attitude needs to be clarified."

"To whom?"

"To me." The steel showed again.

"What do you mean?"

"Hiding with Wassermann in a latrine, of all places! What were you up to?"

"I needed his professional opinion."

"On what? The color of your feces?"

He had had enough. *"Herr Kommandant,"* he said, "you do your job, I'll do mine. Stop raking me over the coals; if you think I do my job badly, say so."

"Very well," Kroll said. "Let me put it more clearly. For an SS officer to hide with a prisoner in a latrine is, to put it mildly, unwise. You had better inform me of the exact reason for your need to do so. Why did you need his professional opinion?"

"He was a psychiatrist before—in civilian life. The girl under my care is not responding to standard therapy. I felt the need to consult him."

"Therapy for what?"

"Amnesia."

Kroll gave him a pensive look and lit a cigarette. He snapped his lighter shut. "I think I must remind you of one of my conditions for your keeping that girl as your companion. I warned you that if I were to get the impression that she made you go soft on the prisoners, she would have to go. You remember that, I'm sure."

"In what way could my consulting Dr. Wassermann be taken—"

"As I said, for you to hide with him in a latrine not only provokes ridicule, it establishes a personal relationship between you. This is in flagrant contradiction of the basic rule imposed on you the day of your arrival: *never* become intimate with a prisoner, *never* treat any one of them as an individual, only as a number. The only way to keep them in line, three thousand of them, is by treating them like cattle, by keeping them off balance at all times, by never letting up on our rule of terror. The moment you become personally intimate with one of them, you endanger us all. Today you were playing with fire. Don't let it happen again."

He could stay and argue, but it would be no use. Worse: it might be counterproductive. "Will that be all?" he asked.

Kroll contemplated him. "Yes."

At the door, the sharp voice stopped him. "One of these days I will be forced to put you to the test. And you had better pass it."

"Or else?"

"Or, much to my regret, I will have to put an end to the fairy-tale of Heinzl and Gretel." Kroll smiled. "It would be too bad, for I do enjoy your company at mealtime. If you'll allow me to say so, you are a damned fool. Why don't you grow up?"

With a shrug, Heinrich let himself out. The fear came only as he walked back to the bungalow. What test? What devilish plan was being hatched in that bored, malevolent mind?

* * *

She knew she was not supposed to peek through the glass curtains, but she saw him coming. She hurried to turn the gas high so the water would be boiling when he came in. She was excited, for she had concocted something that she hoped would surprise and please him: two pieces of *Baumkuchen* with jam in between. It was just like a cake. It would be the first treat she had made for him.

There he was. The water boiled at the right moment. She poured it into the teapot, which she then placed on the tray with the two cups and the little pitcher of milk. She turned to him with a smile, the tray in her hands; then she saw his face. Something had happened, something unpleasant.

It made her feel faint. She put the tray down shakily. "What is it?" she asked. "What happened?"

It seemed to startle him. "Why do you ask?"

"You—you look as if something had."

He shrugged his shoulders and took off his cap. "Some problem in the camp," he said. "Is tea ready?"

"Yes." She felt reassured, a little. She poured out a cup and put it down in front of him. It clattered on its saucer.

"Honestly," he said, "there's nothing. I just need a moment to shift from one thing to the other. Delightful. Do we have anything to eat with it? What about the cookies I brought in yesterday?"

"Ah," she said, "wait and see." She hurried to the kitchen and took the plate with the *Baumkuchen* out of the icebox. She put a knife on it, picked up the two plates she had set out on the sink and went back into the room, the plates in one hand, the *Baum-*

kuchen in the other. "Ah! Look at that!" he said. Then, because her hands were still shaking, the knife slid off the plate. She tried to catch it; before she knew what was happening, the *Kuchen* dropped to the floor.

It shattered her. She was on the verge of tears. He said, "Never mind! The floor is clean, we can still eat it. Here—see?" He picked up the two slices, which had separated, leaving a sticky blob of jam on the floor. "That's nothing," he said. "Just get a cloth. Do you want me to do it?"

"No, no!" she hurried back to the kitchen, close to tears, looked for a floor cloth, opened the closet under the sink, groped inside, felt something soft and brought out a little pillow. *"God is Love."*

The past reeled back with flashing speed.

Blows on her face. *'Bitch!'* More blows. *'Bitch! Bitch!'* Blows, again, again—

She hid her face in her hands, felt his arm around her shoulders. "Laura! *Liebchen!* Laura, dear Laura—I'm so sorry, terribly sorry. . . ."

His closeness, once she surrendered to it, gave her a sense of security. His arm around her, his voice trying to comfort her stemmed the terror that threatened to overwhelm her. She raised her head and looked up at him. His eyes were kind and full of understanding. "Don't be frightened. All is well. Don't try to remember, not at this point. Maybe someday you will, but there is no hurry, none at all. When you do, I'll be there to help you. You are young, and healthy, and very courageous, you proved that. Eventually, in the future, you will have the strength to face it, but there's plenty of time. Relax. Don't ask questions, don't look back. Look up. Look at me." His eyes were blue and kind and understanding. "I'm the nightmare-catcher. I catch them and put them in a sack and shake them out, outside. Whoosh! They're gone. Shall we have our tea?"

She wanted to flee to her bed, hide under the blankets, but dared not leave his sheltering presence.

"Come," he said. "Let's eat what is left of that wonderful treat you made. It looked delicious." Gently he urged her back to the couch and sat down beside her. "There. Will you pour, or shall I? Oh, it's poured already. Here." He reached over and handed her a cup and saucer. She wanted to take it, but was sure she would drop it. She hid her face in his shoulder.

"Hush," he said. "Hush, hush."

He stroked her hair, slowly, soothingly. He went on and on, until she slept.

* * *

After lowering her onto the couch, cautiously so as not to wake her, his first thought was: 'Damn Wassermann! Imagine if I had let in Siegfried! What would have happened then, if that damn little pillow was enough to blow her out of the water?'

He sat down in his chair, looking at her as she lay there. Gradually his anger subsided. Maybe Wassermann was right after all, maybe the sight of the pillow had brought back only Kroll's attack on her, not the demented man chained to the radiator. Even so, it would be prudent to let Siegfried sleep outside a while longer. Poor, dumb beast, how bewildered he must be! One moment man's best friend, the next: Out!

Could he light a cigar? She seemed not to mind his smoking; on the contrary, each time he lit up, her face took on an eager expression, expectant almost. Why? Ah, if he knew that, they would be farther down the road. What was it she expected of him in those moments? A magic wand?

He lit the cigar. Excellent. Dutch. Wait a minute! Maybe her father had smoked cigars . . . No, not if Wassermann was right. She blocked out any memory of him because of 'soul-crushing, life-destroying guilt.' He could see that: after bicycling for maybe weeks, risking assault and arrest, and then to bring about your father's death! Enough to shock a grown man out of his senses. There was no hope of her facing *that* truth and then turning around to make the tea.

She stirred, opened her eyes drowsily, an unfocused, roaming look; then she lapsed back into sleep. Unless she was able to cope with her father's death, though, she would be unable to piece herself back together. Any identity she might eventually assume without having faced that central experience would be a makeshift one, turning her into an emotional cripple. Or not? Was that the mute plea in her eyes? 'Give me an identity, any identity; I am shattered, I cannot put the pieces back together, help me *be* somebody, anybody'?

How could he do that? A makeshift identity, built on what little he knew? To start with, she obviously loved music. Maybe he should play more for her. Also, she was very bright. Maybe he should stimulate her mind, read Schopenhauer with her, Hegel, argue out philosophical points. It also would help her command of the language. She spoke German well, but her vocabulary was small, and she needed the tool of language to build up a new identity. Goethe, Schiller, Otto Julius Bierbaum. Old Otto might be a plagiarist, but he made the German language sing as no one else had. Lovely idea: at night, after his work was done, to close the door on the outside world and tell her about old Otto and his famous elegy *"Oft, in der stillen Nacht,"* shamelessly stolen from Moore's *"Oft, in the stilly night, ere slumber's chain has bound me, fond memory brings the light of other days around me . . ."* He hadn't thought of that poem for years. It was the one he had recited for Oral English, at his final exam. It brought Mariechen Haverstock back again, the final school ball, their trysting place under the weeping willow. The soft, yielding kisses. The scent of the crushed rose on her dress. How innocent they had been then. How innocent the world.

Smoking, he looked at the sleeping girl. She needed time, an ocean of time. Well, that they had—a sunlit ocean with nothing to be seen on it but waves. Wave after wave of the same days, the same nights. The daily routine of the camp never varied; nothing would disturb it until, ultimately, the cheers of victory. Or defeat: the desperate bite, the brief bitterness of the capsule of cyanide they had been issued and nicknamed 'The Last Friend.' But that was far away, beyond the horizon. Two years, ten years, a hundred, it made no difference. Like death, Judgment Day was an abstraction.

He put down his cigar and rose cautiously to his feet. She did not wake up. She lay on that couch like the Sleeping Beauty. Waiting to be wakened, unformed, for him to shape. Patiently, unhurriedly. How had Shakespeare put it? *"Time must have a stop."* He should read Shakespeare to her.

Well, he had better go and feed poor, banished Siegfried on the veranda.

*   *   *

She recovered from the shattering episode of the little pillow by thinking about what he had said. *'Don't try to remember, not at this point. When you do, I'll be there to help you.'*

Yes, she was sure he would be. She had to trust somebody, and it was not difficult to trust him. He was kind, and infinitely patient. *'Don't try to remember, not at this point.'* She obeyed him. No memories; whenever forbidden curiosity about herself reared its scary head, she said: 'No! Not at this point!' It was amazing how she could turn her back on questions; the moment something stirred in her mind that was at all frightening, she went and did something: polished the floor, washed the dishes, made her bed, put his mattress on top. There were a hundred things she could do to take her mind off things.

As the days went by, it seemed there was less and less to do. Maybe she had started to do things faster, picking up speed as she went along. The bruises on her thighs had turned from purple to green, then gold; the burns on her sides, which had gone on hurting for a long time, had finally healed. How on earth could she have burned herself in those spots? Where? When? Ah! *'Not at this point!'*

But it became difficult as the days went by. Once she had finished her doll's-house chores, there was nothing to do except wait. Waiting for him meant getting impatient if he stayed away longer than usual, and finally peeking between the opaque glass curtains, although he had forbidden her to do so. Well, forbidden—if he had, she would not have done it. He had never actually said as much, and so she did, and saw things that were upsetting. Rows of people in striped prison suits standing rigidly to attention while a few of them prowled among their ranks and started to beat those who faltered. A row of officers stood watching the spectacle, and he was among them, looking on as those people were being beaten. It needed all her faith in him, her utter belief in his goodness, for her not to start remembering. But she told herself: 'Don't. Don't remember anything, or he'll be angry.'

That was what worried her most. The men who did the beating were very angry; he stood and watched them without doing anything, or saying anything, which meant he was angry too. Whatever happened, she should never never rouse his anger. She would die, just die, if ever— 'Stop! Don't think about it, don't probe, let it be.' It would have been the moment for her to start doing something, but there was nothing left to do. She could polish the floor again, but it would make no difference. She could wash up once more, but everything was clean. Her bed was made, so was his mattress. If only there were something else she could do but wait, wait, wait . . .

At last he came home, and life started. She didn't care any more what he did outside, she reveled in his presence, his kindness, his patience, his unflagging fascination with her. He told her she was "bright" and "quick on the uptake"; to please him, she started to learn things by heart: poems, pages of philosophy, essays, bits of plays. He read to her in his beautiful, manly voice, and she watched carefully which book it was and where he put it; after she had finished her chores, she learned by heart what she had heard the night before. Whole scenes from a play called *Der zerbrochene Krug,* poems by someone called Bierbaum, especially the one that he seemed to like best: *"Oft in the stilly night."* His face when she first recited it to him was worth the hours of interminable waiting.

"Listen—I want you to hear something. *'Oft in the stilly night, ere slumber's chain has bound me, fond memory brings the light of other days around me . . . ' "*

"Liebchen!"

" 'The smiles, the tears of boyhood's years, the words of love then spoken . . . ' "

"Laura! I can't believe it!"

" 'The eyes that shone, now dimmed and gone, the cheerful hearts now broken . . . ' "

He cried out in admiration, his eyes shone with pleasure and surprise as she recited the whole poem without tripping up once. When she was through and he was extolling her cleverness, she hardly took a breath before starting the whole thing all over again in German: *" 'Oft in der stillen Nacht . . . ' "*

It was worth it. It was worth every hour she had spent hammering those lines into her head. She trusted him utterly, with abandon; all she wanted was a chance to show him how she trusted him, how she wanted him to have power over her, all power of decision: what mood to be in, what to do, what not to do. She would do anything for him, anything at all, if only he would never be angry. If ever he were to be angry with her, her world would cave in.

It was a fragile world of small joys and hopes, but full of lurking fears, like creepy-crawlies waiting to come swarming out of the woodwork. The thing that held them back was her utter faith in him. If he said, 'Don't remember,' it was not only best for her but essential to her very existence. He was the center of her world, and his power was such that when, during the hours he was not there and the creepy-crawlies started to show their ugly heads, all she needed to do was say his name, "Heinzl, Heinzl, Heinzl, Heinzl," and they would scurry. Sometimes she would sit in his chair and think his name, 'Heinzl, Heinzl,' and her mind would turn into a blank, a dove-gray emptiness. 'Heinzl, Heinzl. Heinzl.'

Sometimes the hours without him stretched almost beyond endurance. She would go to stand behind the curtains and peek, waiting for him to come toward the house with the dog. She hated the dog, but as he so obviously loved it, she made up her mind to love it too. "Siegfried! Dear Siegfried!" It didn't sound right, and he gave her the shivers, but she forced herself. "Siegfried. Dear Siegfried. Kitty-kitty." No—that was wrong. Well, so what, kitty-kitty was good enough for— No! She must not betray him, not even by thinking nasty things about his dog! For he would know and it might make him angry like those sinister men prowling among the ranks, beating others who vainly tried to protect the backs of their heads with their hands. Those were the moments when the questions became almost uncontainable, but she managed. She was bright. She knew that if she let herself slip into asking questions, the first one would be 'Who am I?' and she would be in trouble. She was his. All she ever wanted to be was his. She was his creature. His creation. She loved to think that: his creation. And that creation was becoming fuller, deeper all the time, with poems in French, in English.

> *"Two households, both alike in dignity,*
> *In fair Verona, where we lay our scene,*
> *From ancient grudge break to new mutiny,*
> *Where civil blood makes civil hands unclean."*

"Laura! Terrific!"

> *"From forth the fatal loins of these two foes*
> *A pair of star-cross'd lovers take their life,*
> *Whose misadventured piteous overthrows*
> *Do with their death bury their parents strife."*

"Laura, darling, magnificent! Do you know the whole of the prologue?"

> *"The fearful passage of their death-mark'd love—"*

Siegfried growled, and she froze.

"God dammit!" he cried. "When did he sneak in?! Out, you bastard, *out!*" He kicked the dog out; when he came back, he found her sick with terror. He comforted her and apologized and was angelic and warm, yet he did not understand it was not the dog that had terrified her, but his anger.

Finally she thawed and brought the tea, the *Baumkuchen* and his cigar, which she lit for him. And he put on the music, heartbreaking music, flowing along like a river, a river of tears.

*   *   *

As the weeks went by, she became the perfect German *Hausfrau.* Nothing was too much for her, her inventiveness was touching, she would do anything to please and surprise him. She kept the place as neat as a pin and as welcoming as a real home; so much so that Heinrich was struck by the thought: 'If only the others don't find out!' He instantly suppressed the idiotic notion—but even so. What if they were to break in here, just to get a rise out of him? Ludicrous! It's of such stuff that nightmares are made.

Eventually her presence became known. It could not be avoided, everyone in the camp knew everything about everyone else: how Halberstadt selected the most delectable girls from each new convoy, discreetly, but not discreetly enough; how Berchenau went for the boys; how—well, such was life in Schwalbenbach, such was revolting life in unspeakable Schwalbenbach. Her presence became known even though no one mentioned her; in the end, he had her meals brought in by Stolz, and ordered dresses for her from the warehouse, where the prisoners' clothes were stored. She did not know where they came from, she tried the dresses on delightedly and made a choice. The waist had to be taken in, or the hemline taken up; Stolz produced needle and thread, then a sewing machine. The whirr of it created a homelike atmosphere; he watched her contentedly, smoking. She began to develop a charming personality, sweet, bright, sensitive to his moods; but she remained very vulnerable. Fear never quite left her; he sensed it flare up whenever there was a sudden noise outside, like Siegfried pushing his empty dish around on the veranda, or Stolz climbing the steps with his tray.

Gradually she gained confidence and turned into a delightful companion, eager to learn, eager to please. Terribly eager to please; her life seemed to be centered on him to the exclusion of all else. If he was moody, she became despondent; if he was pleased, she radiated joy; if he was awash with daydreams while listening to Franck's Symphonic Variations or Sibelius' Second, she sat watching him with adulation. She never asked for any expression of emotion on his part other than his approval; it was touching, but a little oppressive at times.

One night, while listening to Vivaldi's Four Seasons, he found himself reflecting that she was really just another Siegfried. It seemed a callous thought at first; but the way she sat there, watching him, was exactly how Siegfried used to observe him before the poor beast was banished. It was one of those moments when her dependence on him as the center of her universe suddenly became ominous. Would this doting, servile creature, who now asked nothing else from life but to please him, awaken one day to the fact that she was a forgery? The true Laura was still asleep in the haunted forest, covered by leaves and cobwebs, her existence all but forgotten. There could be no doubt: Laura the little German *Hausfrau* with the sewing machine had nothing in common with the Laura who had decided to go and look for her father, faked pregnancy, bicycled from Holland to Germany and turned up at the gate, her head on one side, saying, 'But I *do* belong here, *Herr Offizier,* I'm Jewish too!'

Would that other Laura, when she awakened someday, rise in wrath and assail him with the fury of a woman betrayed? Maybe it was Vivaldi's melodious summer thunderstorm, but he had a brief vision of a new ending to the fairytale of Heinzl and Gretel, in which Heinzl discovered that his doting little playmate was not a *Hausfrau* but Hippolyta, Queen of the Amazons, with a spell thrown over her.

Nonsense! The gratuitous musings of an idle mind on a stomach replete with good food, lulled by the sensuous delight of a first-rate cigar. Without him, she would have remained where she was: spread-eagled in hell, her dress around her waist, her demented father thrashing in his chains. Whatever the future might bring, when the Sleeping Beauty ultimately awakened, the first thing she would feel toward him would be gratitude.

Vivaldi stopped spinning his golden strands of summer and changed to the gossamer of fall. All became peace, beauty, tenderness, tinged with nostalgia. His cigar had gone out. It had only been half-smoked, but he selected a fresh one from the box on the table. She startled him as she struck a match and leaned forward, hands cupped, to light it for him. She must have sat there waiting, the matchbox on her lap, watching him like a lynx.

But he thanked her with a smile, leaned back in his chair and relished the one sensuous indulgence this Spartan life allowed: the first smoke of a virgin cigar.

* * *

A few days later she was in the kitchen, about to put on the water for his tea, when there was a knock on the door to the utility room.

A voice whispered, *"Fräulein, Fräulein, bitte machen sie auf!"*

The door opened to a crack. *"Fräulein, bitte, bitte!"* A gaunt woman in a blue-striped smock with a shaven head appeared in the doorway. Her eyes looked mad; she held out a shawl. *"Bitte, Fräulein, bitte!* They have taken my Lieschen, they have taken her to where the officers live, she is only thirteen, and she has a bad cold, please would you see to it that she gets this? She's so delicate . . ."* Something happened to the woman's eyes as the whispered words gushed out of her, tears spurted from them, little sprays of water. She held out the shawl and pleaded, *"Fräulein, Fräulein,* for the love of God, for the sake of your Christ, see to it that she gets this to put around her shoulders! Her name is Lieschen, Annelieschen Rosenbach . . . "* Suddenly she stopped, listened, dropped the shawl and vanished.

Laura stood stock still. She looked around for a way out, a means of holding the terror at bay. The shawl, the shawl had to go, if the shawl was no longer there, maybe she could convince herself it had never happened. She did not know how to operate the furnace, but she stuffed a newspaper down inside, set fire to it; when it was burning, she put the shawl on top. She opened the vent below and heard the flames roar. She managed to reach the bathroom just before she was sick.

A few moments later Heinzl came in, calling, "Laura! Where are you?" She appeared, but saw his eyes go distant. Fear struck her like the lash of a whip.

"Someone has been here," he said, his voice hard and menacing. "Someone has been here while I was gone! Who was it? Answer me! Who was it?!"

She stammered, "A—a woman . . ."

"Woman? Who?"

"I don't know. She . . . she . . . just came . . . I was in the kitchen. . . ." Her voice choked with fear.

"What did she want?"

"She . . . she wanted . . ."

"Well?" He put his hands on her shoulders, she closed her eyes. "Don't be afraid, I am not blaming you. Just tell me what the woman wanted! She must have wanted something. What was it?"

She opened her eyes, unable to utter a word.

"Don't be afraid," he repeated, more gently. "Just tell me what she wanted. Had you met her before?"

She shook her head.

"What did she want?"

She began to feel his rage again, that terrifying rage. "She gave me something . . . to give to . . . give to . . ."

"To me? A letter? A message?"

"A shawl. To give to her little daughter, who has a cold, and . . ." She covered her face with her hands.

"What did you do with it?"

She answered, without looking up, "I burned it."

She heard him go into the kitchen, open the door to the utility room, open the furnace. There was a sound of metal; she looked up and saw him fish the smoldering shawl out of the furnace with the poker. He stood looking at it; there was an acrid smell of smoke. Then he pushed it back in and closed the furnace. As he came back, she was so terrified that she covered her face with her hands again.

He put his arm around her shoulders. "Laura," he said kindly, "I must talk to you. Come, sit down." He took her to the couch and made her sit down; he sat beside her. "Are you listening?"

She nodded.

"This is a prison camp. The woman you saw was one of the inmates. It has never happened before, and I'll see to it that it never happens again; she must have slipped away from the guards. You must face it: this is a concentration camp. I am the camp doctor. Not by choice. I had no choice, they just sent me here. I am trying to do what I can to help people, but it is not easy. So far, you are the only one I have been able to help."

She did not want to know any of this, all she wanted was for him not to be angry any more, to hold her, kindly.

"I have something to read to you," he said, and got up. She tried to cling to him. "Don't worry," he said, "I'll be right back."

She watched him as he went to the consulting-room, and felt an awful weakness, for without him the ground under her gave way and she was sinking. He returned, sat down by her side again and put his arm around her. "There now, there now! Why are you shivering? I told you I'm not one of them. Listen: It's a letter from my father. *'My dear Heinzl, I do not doubt that the camp is a place where prisoners as well as guards lose their humanity. Please realize that I do not underestimate the repulsiveness of your new surroundings; but there is not much sense in your asking yourself . . .'"*

She no longer listened. She did not want to know anything; as long as he was not angry with her, she did not care where she was, who she was. If he turned on her again in anger, the way he had done just now, she would give up, just give up and die. She listened to his voice, savored being held, safe in his arm. Slowly she became herself again: content, a blank.

"See? This is what I am about, here in the camp. What I hope to achieve. Now about that woman who broke in here. She must have been in great distress. I will not deny that there are things going on in this camp that are unspeakable . . ."

She refused to listen. She refused to think of the woman any more; she refused to remember her. She closed her mind to what he was saying and listened only to the sound of his voice. He could do with her what he wanted, anything at all, as long as he would never be angry with her again.

*   *   *

One evening, as he was standing to attention among the row of officers during roll-call, one of the prisoners ran amok. Shrieking, the man ran toward the gate. The Kapos started after him, but Kroll's voice called out, beside him, *"Halt!"* Then they all looked at him.

He had been miles away, daydreaming. He realized what was asked of him. There was no way out. Kroll had warned him: *'One of these days I will put you to the test, and you had better pass it.'* There was only one way he could save her life.

With an odd detachment he called, *"Siegfried! Fass!"*

The black-and-yellow streak flashed; he did not watch. There was a terrible howl of pain, then Kroll, beside him, said, "Good."

"Siegfried! Fuss!"

The dog returned.

The Kapos finished the prisoner off. Roll-call was resumed. When it was over, he fled to the bungalow.

* * *

Peeking through the glass curtains, she had seen it happen: the running figure in the prison suit, the dog overtaking him and bringing him down, the two men beating him with sticks. Now she stood quivering on the brink of terror. One move, and she would fall. One thought, and she would remember. She must not fall, she must not remember. Whatever she did, she must not move.

She was standing with her back to the door when she heard him come in. The door opened. She heard his footsteps, the claws of the dog on the linoleum. She heard him sit down in his chair. Then she heard the sound of sobs.

The sobs slowly drew her away from herself, and finally made her turn around. He was sitting in his chair with his head in his hands, weeping. She stood looking at him for a long time; then, slowly, she went to his side. He sobbed, sobbed. She put her hand on his shoulder.

He grabbed it, covered it with kisses; his face was wet with tears. He clung to her hand, sobbing; she knelt beside him. His eyes, when he looked at her, were desperate. "I had no choice! I had to do it, for *you!*"

She pulled his head to her shoulder; holding him, she began to stroke his hair. As she did so, something within her reached out to him, a new tenderness.

"Laura! . . . Laura . . ."

She went on stroking his hair until he calmed down. When she tried to get up to get a washcloth, he would not let her go. So she put her arm around him and led him to the bathroom; at the washstand she moistened the cloth with cold water and dabbed his eyes that were swollen with tears. He clung to her as she led him to the bedroom. She made him lie down, but when she wanted to leave, he pulled her to him. She gave in and lay down by his side, her head on his shoulder; suddenly his mouth was on hers.

The kiss overcame the terror. She began to forget what had happened as they kissed, kissed. The terror drew away completely when his kisses became frenzied, demanding. Dimly, she was aware of his hands, his weight, of the invasion, and then the pain. He hurt her, terribly, but a great joy dawned in her. It flared into triumph and ecstasy as he cried, "Laura! Now! Now . . ." Then he slumped on top of her, his frenzy spent.

She lay gazing at the ceiling, with triumph swelling inside her. Now he would never be angry again, never leave her. Now he was hers. All hers.

She began to stroke his hair again, but this time it was different.

*   *   *

He had done the unforgivable. He had made love to his patient. He should feel crushed now with shame and remorse; but he felt only tenderness, love and a new sense of security. As long as this was waiting for him in their sanctuary, nothing in the world outside could harm him.

He wondered what had possessed him; what had lashed him on and on in his mad flight until, with a cry of blissful surrender, he had felt his seed spurt inside her. At that moment he had felt free. Free of fear, shame, guilt, of the ghastly knowledge that he had set a dog onto a man to kill him. No one was responsible for another's fate. Karma. It was written. Every man was drifting down to the sea alone; no one could stop the river that carried him to oblivion.

"Laura," he whispered. "Laura, love . . ."

They kissed. They kissed and kissed. Finally they fell asleep in each other's arms.

After waiting a long time outside the open door, Siegfried came in, stealthily, and lay down beside the bed.

CHAPTER FIVE

"YOU must have been asking yourself why I allow you to keep her," Kroll said, helping himself to salad.

"I presumed you had your reasons. Do you mind if I light up?"

"By all means."

Heinrich lit his after-dinner cigar from one of the candles the *Scharführer* had placed on the small table by the window. Dusk came early now; summer was drawing to a close. The window remained open, but there was a chill in the air and the fragrance of dying roses.

"Well," Kroll continued, "all the world loves a lover, and you and your ghostly Ophelia cloistered in the bungalow fill an emotional need in the beholder." He wiped his mouth with his napkin. "This wine, by the way, is excellent."

"I'm glad you complained to the *Hauptmarketenderei*."

"Others may have."

"Well, whoever it was got results."

Kroll waved aside the cheese platter which the *Scharführer* presented to him and said, "Later." Heinrich in turn shook his head. The man withdrew.

"I gather you're no longer interested in the affairs of the world," Kroll continued, "but you may have noticed that the tide of war is turning against us."

"Yes, Russia has been a disappointment so far," Heinrich said noncommittally. Kroll was too dangerous a man to confide in, however innocuously.

"Somewhat more than that," Kroll said. "Unless you call death a disappointment."

"I call it an abstraction."

"Touché." Kroll pulled a cigarette case from his breastpocket, took out a cigarette and tapped it on the case. The *Scharführer* struck a match for him. "You realize, don't you, that if, by a caprice of fortune, you and I and Ophelia were to cross the Styx together, we would be joined in the nether world for all eternity?"

Heinrich smiled.

"I understand your reticence," Kroll smiled. "I hope you interpret my *valse triste* tonight as a sign of appreciation. You have proved a witty and nimble partner at these verbal chess games of ours. Anything to while away the hours in a tedious place like this; but even in the secular world, I'd have appreciated your company. I suppose I sound somewhat nostalgic."

"It's the *Margaux*," Heinrich said. "Maybe we should order champagne tomorrow."

"H'm, I think not. By the way, I've set the evening roll-call one hour earlier as from today. We want to give ourselves time to count them at our ease; dusk is the hour of dissimulation." He tipped the ashes of his cigarette outside the window. "It'll be winter soon."

"Indeed."

"There is no need to turn yourself into *Le Muet de Portici*, you know. Caution is a laudable trait in Caesar's legions, but there's a critical point beyond which you become a bore."

"Forgive me. That was surely not my intention."

"No matter. By the way, how is Ophelia's therapy coming along?"

"There seems to be little more I can do."

"She still doesn't remember anything?"

"No."

"Not even her father?"

"Especially not her father."

Kroll shot the stub of his half-smoked cigarette out of the window, a tumbling spark. "Well, I do. I found myself thinking of him the other night, and wishing someone had told him in time."

"Told him what?"

"The story of Servetus."

"Servetus? Who was he?"

"You should know! He too was a doctor. The only man to oppose Calvin publicly during the reign of terror in Geneva. A rumpled sort of fellow with steel-rimmed glasses, rather like Schubert. He was burned at the stake in the market square. And to prove the ultimate vanity of all theological disputes: until recently one of the best restaurants on the market place in Geneva was called *La Rotisserie Servetus*. In the end, all his embodiment of the spirit of Christ resulted in was to have a restaurant named after him."

"Fascinating."

"Who knows," Kroll said. "Long after the three of us have crossed the Styx, Martens may have a restaurant named after him too, somewhere." He beckoned the *Scharführer*. "It's unlikely there will ever be a restaurant called 'Schlumpsi Kroll,' but, well, you can't have everything."

"*Zu Befehl, Herr Obersturmführer?*" The *Scharführer* stood to attention.

"I'll have the cheese now," Kroll said, "but only if there's Gorgonzola."

After the man left to get the Gorgonzola, both officers were silent for a while and listened to the whirring of the lawnmower in the distance.

"Probably the last time we'll hear that, this year," Kroll said.

"Yes. They're expecting frost tonight." ·

"And the swallows have left too."

Heinrich listened and indeed there was no sound of squealing high up around the flagpole.

"Autumn is a melancholy season," Kroll said. "One of the great discoveries of adolescence: I am unique, for, to me, autumn is a sad season. Lots of bad poetry."

"And some works of genius. Vivaldi."

"Ah, yes. *Le quatro staggioni.*"

The Scharführer judged this to be the right moment to present the platter with the Gorgonzola. Kroll looked at it balefully. "On second thought, I don't think I'll fight the melancholy of dying roses with the smell of goat cheese."

The *Scharführer* turned to Heinrich who waved it away too. The man withdrew.

Kroll gazed out of the window at the darkening sky already tinged with the green of winter. The first playful gust of night breeze came whirling across the fields and blew out one of the candles. Kroll nipped the wick between finger and thumb. "I detest the smell of snuffed candles. Well, I think I'll retire early tonight." He rose; Heinrich followed his example. "Nothing personal," Kroll added, smiling. "Full moon tonight. We may be called out by some madman running amuck. Good night."

Heinrich clicked his heels. "Good night, *Herr Kommandant.*"

A few minutes later, he too left the mess hall, casually returning the *Scharführer's* salute. Outside, in the chilly dusk, the faithful shadow rose to join him. "Heel, Siegfried."

Together they walked to the bungalow where the other faithful shadow waited behind the glass curtains.

In the deserted mess hall, the *Scharführer,* clearing the tables, was joined by his opposite number from the kitchen. "Well?" the cook asked.

"There wasn't much," the *Scharführer* replied. "Other than that things are going badly in Russia. He's gone to listen to the English radio, so tomorrow there may be more. What's on tomorrow?"

"Fish," the cook said. "It's Friday."

BOOK TWO

GERMANY

1945

CHAPTER ONE

WHEN, in May 1945, after months of delay because of the Arnhem disaster, the Canadian Division of the British Army of the Rhine finally invaded Germany proper, the Quaker Ambulance Service, Northern Unit, followed closely in its wake. The unit, consisting of four ambulances with two medics in each and a jeep with the leader, George Weatherby, motored unhampered through the flat, peaceable countryside.

All around them, fields were being tilled by well-fed and healthy-looking farmers and their families; the only sign of deprivation was that the plows were pulled by cows rather than horses. The people might as well have been Belgian or Dutch; some of them waved, as if this were a liberation rather than an invasion. There were few refugees, nothing like the massive exodus the unit had encountered in liberated territory.

Toward nightfall of the first day they approached a small town on the horizon, the first in Germany. About three kilometers short of the town a dispatch rider on a motorbike emerged from a side road and flagged the jeep down. George Weatherby signaled the convoy to pull up; the cumbersome ambulances came to a squealing halt. "What's up, Corporal?"

"Hi there!" the dispatch rider shouted over the rumble of the idling engines. "RHQ orders you to turn off here and have a dekko at the camp over there. It's pretty fruity, you can smell it from here. RHQ doesn't want the men to go in, there may be typhus. But somebody had better, or those birds will break the fence down."

"What kind of a camp is it?"

"If you ask me, the kind all those wild stories are about. They all look like skeletons. Well—good luck! And hold your noses!" He revved up his engine, swerved around, one foot dragging, and raced back the way he had come, down a cart track through the fields.

George followed him, signaling the convoy to do the same. The camp was visible in the distance: squat watchtowers, a cluster of barracks surrounded by a high fence; it looked like any prisoner-of-war camp. The Nazi flag still fluttered from a tall pole over the tarred roofs.

The four ambulances drew up alongside the jeep on the parking lot outside the gate; George and the eight other members of the unit got out to have a look. They were all in their twenties, of various nationalities; all of them Quakers and therefore conscientious objectors. Their task was to occupy themselves with the civilian victims of the war; POW's were left to the Red Cross. This camp, at first sight, looked like a POW camp; only the inmates, cheering hoarsely, on the other side of the barbed-wire fence, were not wearing uniforms but striped convict suits. The camp looked orderly and well kept; the barrier at the gate was painted red and white like that of a railroad crossing, the short drive leading up to it was bordered by beds of tulips; over the gate, in wrought-iron letters, was the legend *"Arbeit macht Frei"*—"Labor Liberates"—which seemed to indicate that it was a work camp of some sort. Inside the enclosure, bordering a path leading to a bungalow, was the vivid yellow of daffodils.

A Canadian Gun Section, consisting of two heavy trucks and a jeep, had obviously just arrived; soldiers in battle dress were standing about in twos and threes by their vehicles, parked just outside the gate. As the nine Quakers approached, George Weatherby heard the prisoners cheering over the rumble of the Army trucks' engines. The throng behind the barbed-wire fence and the barrier was waving and shouting—the kind of welcome one had come to expect by now.

The sergeant of the section, a heavy-set Canadian with a florid face, came running toward the Quakers from the barrier, crying, "Doc! Quaker Doc!" George had met the man before; on those previous occasions the sergeant had always addressed him as 'Conchie Doc.' Something must have upset him, this time.

"All right, chaps," George said. "Let's go in there and have a dekko."

"No!" the sergeant cried. "Not all of you, just you yourself! I won't allow anybody to go in there until the general arrives. This thing is too big for me."

"But if there are sick, it's our duty to look after them," George said.

"It's *my* duty to see that nobody gets killed while I'm in charge," the sergeant snapped, obviously under stress. "This is no ordinary camp, this is not a *Todt* camp like the others, this is a concentration camp!"

George Weatherby looked over the sergeant's shoulder and his heart sank. A concentration camp . . . This was going to be a trial. He set his jaw and thought: 'It can't be worse than Arnhem, nothing can. Let's get on with it.' Soldiers were guarding the gaily painted barrier. Behind it milled the crowd dressed in white-and-blue-striped prison clothes, waving, cheering. There was something odd about the noise they made; it took George a moment to realize that it was feebler than the raucous yells with which they had been welcomed in other camps.

"Well, let's go," he said to the sergeant, and to the others, "You just hang back, chaps, I shouldn't think we'll be long."

"Maybe we'd better spray ourselves with DDT powder, Doc," the sergeant ventured as they approached the gate. "They're sick, they're all sick, you'll see."

"Would you rather I went in alone?"

"Hell, no! I'll go, I'll go. If you say it's all right, it's all right. But if I get typhus, it's your responsibility."

"Well," George drawled, "in that case, you'd better stay where you are. I'll let you know when I consider it safe for you and your men to come in."

"No, I'll come, I'll come, hell," the sergeant said, "if you go in, hell."

George went toward the gate. He took in the high barbed-wire fence, the empty guard towers. The bungalow directly behind the fence was painted green and white, the daffodils bordering the walk that led to it must have had a lot of nursing. He faced the hoarsely cheering crowd in their striped suits behind the gate.

"All right, Jake," the sergeant said to a corporal who was guarding the barrier with two men. "Open up."

"Sarge, they'll all spill out if I do," the corporal said nervously. He was young, freckled and also very pale.

"Okay," the sergeant said, pulling his pistol. "Back, you people, get back! *Zurück! Zurück!*" He brandished the gun. A few voices behind the gate took up the cry, *"Zurück! Zurück!"* but they had no effect, nobody moved and the cheering did not abate. It was hoarse, like the whispered barking of Army guard dogs whose vocal cords had been cut. Now George Weatherby saw the faces: skeletal, hollow-eyed, inhuman. He had never seen such faces before. A stolid calm settled his stomach, the defense mechanism of detachment took hold. Somebody had to go in there, it might as well be he. The sergeant was right, disease was probably rampant in there; in any case, they were all starved to skeletons. "All right, gentlemen," he cried. "Now let's all be sensible, shall we, and make a little room so we can open these gates. Yes, yes, you are free. Congratters!"

They cheered louder; but the sergeant by his side brandished his gun and bawled, *"Zurück! Zurück,* you, *zurück!* You'll have to pass a medical examination first!"

"Don't worry, we won't run away," a surprisingly educated voice called from behind the fence. "We are just excited, as you would be under the circumstances, would you not?"

The voice spoke English, but it obviously belonged to a cultured German. None of the skeletons, cheering with gaping death's-heads, waving grisly thin arms and hands, staring at them with sunken eyes, could have spoken like that; behind their ghostly ranks some fat, smug German must be hiding. But, whoever it was, he was their spokesman.

"Sir," George called into the crowd, "would you be awfully kind and tell your people that we are delighted to see them, that we are here to set them free, but that they cannot leave the camp until they have had a medical examination? Perhaps they'd be good enough to let us through?"

Out of the mass of skeletons, one worked his way to the gate, turned to the crowd and cried, *"Meine Damen und Herren! Ruhe! Bitte, meine Damen und Herren, hören Sie zu!"*

Damen? There must be women among them! The voice, cultured and persuasive, went on haranguing the crowd behind the gate until they fell silent. Then he turned around and said, "You can open up now." He was a scarecrow, like the rest, his face a death's-head with sunken eyes.

"Thanks so much," George Weatherby said. "That's awfully civil of you." He turned to the sergeant, who was still brandishing his gun. "Well, shall we?"

"All right, Jake, open up," the sergeant growled. "But slowly, slowly now . . ."

The soldiers gingerly lifted the gaily colored barrier. The moment they did so, the cheering resumed and the mass of prisoners pressed forward.

"Damn it, I told you so!" the sergeant cried. "Back, you people! Back, back, I say!"

But he panicked needlessly; the soldiers pushed against the pressing throng with their rifles and found it alarmingly easy to contain the mass of prisoners, who staggered and tumbled, toppling like dominoes. Good God! Those people could barely stand!

"Easy now, easy, take it easy, please!" George cried. One of the skeletons came staggering toward him, arms outstretched, eyes crazed, cried, "God, God!" stumbled and fell. George bent over the man and touched his shoulder. "Get up, friend. All is well. You are free now."

"I'm afraid in his case it's too late," the cultured German voice said beside him; it was the scarecrow with the sunken eyes. With his foot, the man turned the body over, effortlessly. The gesture was so callous that George felt outraged.

"You can go on in now," the scarecrow said. "We won't give you any trouble. Most of us are civilized people, you know." His breath was foul, his body and the filthy rags he was wearing stank to high heaven. "My name is Dr. Alfred Wassermann, I'm the inmates' physician. Or, rather, their medicine man."

"I'm George Weatherby, leader of the ambulance unit you see out there. We'll try and take care of you until the Red Cross arrives."

"I am honored," the prisoner said stiffly, and he made a little bow. "Are you not Army?"

"No, we are—Quakers. The sergeant and his men are soldiers. Canadians. Sergeant, meet Dr. Wassermann."

"Hiya, Doc," the sergeant said uncomfortably. "Pleasure, I'm sure. The name is Dickinson, but call me Sarge."

"I'm honored," the prisoner said, making a little bow again. He turned back to George. "Would you like to go in now?"

"Indeed."

Without thinking, George stepped over the body of the man at his feet; realizing what he had done, he turned and caught the eye of Boniface Baker, one of his medics. "Take care of him, will you?" Boniface nodded and beckoned to Len Whitfield, his teammate.

"After you," the doctor said, with another of those little bows.

George walked through the gate, the sergeant at his side. The moment they entered, the mass of prisoners, cheering eerily, stretched out their skeletal hands and pressed in upon him. They touched him, plucked at his clothes, caressed his face, kissed his hands, sobbing, laughing, saying in broken English, "Thank you, thank you, friend, friend, God bless you, God, God bless you, God . . ." The stench of their emaciated bodies, their foul breath nauseated him, but he went on pressing their thin, feverish hands, saying, "Hello there, hello, how are you, how nice to see you, congratulations, hello . . ." He had no idea how many there were—hundreds. He heard the high, keening cries of women, but could not discern any among them, there seemed to be no difference in the death's-heads that surrounded him, shouting, cheering. Above their haunting cries he heard the voice of Dr. Wassermann: "Let me take you to the hospital. This way, please." A hand gripped his arm and steered him toward the first building, across the yard.

"This way, Sergeant!" George called. "The sick bay is this way!"

"I'm not sure I have any business there," the sergeant muttered, but joined him. Slowly, haltingly, they made their way through the pressing mass of prisoners; when they entered the first barracks, the stench became so stifling that George stopped involuntarily. The inside was dark and cavernous; slowly his eyes became used to the darkness, and as he moved forward once more he heard a soft, multitudinous lapping sound, as of gurgling water; it took a moment before he realized it was applause. The people in the tiers of bunks all around him had half risen, like corpses from their coffins, and were applauding his arrival with the last vestige of their strength. He saw there was more than one person in each bunk. "How—how many have you in here?" he asked the doctor.

"I don't know exactly," the scarecrow replied. "There are two hundred and fifty bunks per barracks, as a rule we sleep two to a bunk."

"And how many barracks?"

"Six."

"So that makes three thousand inmates, roughly?"

"Roughly."

"Is this the hospital?"

"No. The hospital is at the far end. But these are all sick."

"What are they suffering from, mainly?"

"Typhus, dysentery, tuberculosis. Starvation is the major cause of death."

"What did they feed you?"

"A bowl of thin soup, three hundred grams of bread and five grams of margarine per day."

"Well, they'll soon be getting a meal that'll stick to their ribs!"

"Don't make it too hearty," the doctor said dryly. "Increase the bread to seven hundred grams, and put some meat in the soup, but no more for the time being. Normal rations would kill us."

"Sorry. Of course. How stupid of me. Well, shall we go on?" He could no longer just stand there gazing at the dying wretches, most of whom had slumped back after the strenuous effort of their welcome.

"This way," the doctor said, moving to the door again.

"I thought you said the hospital was in the back."

"That's right, but let's go around the other way."

George had not realized his nausea was so obvious.

The moment they appeared outside the barracks, the mass of prisoners began to press around him again. As George passed, many cried out their names, trying to impress their identity upon him. "I am Professor Habermann from Munich— anthropology . . ." *"Bonjour, bonjour, Charles Latour, Maître d'Orchestre de l'Opéra de Lille!"* He shook hands as fragile as birds' wings. "Hello there, delighted to see you, Professor. Yes, sir, yes, sir, *Carmen,* eh? *Madame Butterfly!"*

"Hello there, sir, hello, sir, my name is Hendricks, I'm a dentist from Brussels!"

"Ah, Belgian, eh?" George said, winking idiotically. "And you, sir . . .?" He had nearly collided with a tottering, obviously delirious skeleton barring his way, stretching out its hands, chanting, "Praised be the Lord, praised be the Lord, praised be the Lord . . ."

"Quite, quite," he said. "Yes, it's wonderful . . ." The doctor pushed the creature aside, but it went on wailing its praises.

Suddenly the mass of people around him came to a halt. He saw that they had reached a gate in a fence between the buildings. *"Lassen Sie uns durch, meine Damen und Herren—bitte,*

bitte!" They made way. Behind the gate George saw a crowd of what looked like elderly midgets, in plain coveralls far too large for them, torn and dirty. The doctor said, "These are the children." Their cavernous faces looked ageless; they backed away as the men entered, with the wariness of scavenging dogs.

"Hey, kids," the sergeant cried, "who'd like some chewing gum? Here, catch!" But Dr. Wassermann stopped him. "No candy!" he said urgently. "Don't give them any, please. They must get some proper food first, please!"

"Oh, I see . . . Sorry, kids. I have to do what the doc says."

The children, if that was indeed what they were, displayed no emotion. They simply stood there, watching, their eyes wary and huge.

"This way," the doctor said.

"To the hospital?" George asked.

"Let's look at the crematorium first."

"Look, Doctor, we are trained orderlies, all nine of us. We have a pharmacy, a field-lab, anything you need for a first-aid emergency. So why don't we have a look at the hospital, and send my men in? That's what we are here for. That's our job."

"I see," the doctor said, with an odd reluctance. "I think it might be better if we talked this over first. We are all right for the moment. My patients have had enough of an emotional strain for one day. Let's take this step by step."

George gave him a knowing look: the disaster-syndrome. He had come across it before. What was it, that moved these physicians, who must have done such heroic work, to resist the arrival of medical help? It didn't make sense, but by now it was a familiar stance. The doctor of the labor-camp just across the border had taken twenty-four hours before he finally accepted the nine male nurses. It was obviously not the patients who had to be approached 'step by step,' but their half-crazed doctors. Talk about 'emotional strain' . . .

"All right," he said. "As you wish, Doctor."

They passed through a gate in a high wall; inside were a few concrete buildings with wide, squat chimneys. The doctor pushed open a door in one of them. The sergeant gasped, "Jesus . . ."

They stood still in the doorway. Stacks of naked, emaciated corpses were piled up like cordwood. Near a gaping black oven stood a cart untidily filled with bodies, arms and legs sprawling.

"My God . . ." George whispered.

"The SS left in a hurry, before they could deal with today's batch," the doctor said, without emotion. "As you can see, they were methodical. To stack them in an orderly manner they stretched the arms and locked the thumbs. Very methodical. Everything they did was very methodical."

"Are . . . are these natural deaths?" the sergeant asked, with an audible effort.

"Yes. That is, if you call murder by untreated infectious diseases and systematic starvation a natural death. Which undoubtedly they *will* call it, should they ever be brought to justice."

"But where are they?" George asked.

"They fled early this morning, just before you arrived, in six cars, with a truck full of records. I hope you catch up with them. Is there a chance, do you think?"

"That you'll have to ask the sergeant," George replied. "We are civilians."

"Ah, yes, I forgot." The doctor looked at him with his feverish eyes. "Quakers, you said? In that case, there is someone who will be very glad to see you."

"Oh?"

"We have a young Quaker girl here. A Dutch girl. Shall I go and get her?"

"Let me go with you."

The doctor put a hand on his arm. "Please. It's better if you wait here. I'll go and get her. I'll be right back." He hurried away.

"Well, I don't know about you," the sergeant said, "but I'm not going to hang around here. This place gives me the creeps." He went toward the gate in the wall.

George followed him; outside the wall, in the open space where the small groups of staring children were watching them motionlessly, the sergeant said, "I think I'll go back to the boys. You'd better wait here for that guy. See you when you come out."

"Okay," George said. He watched the sergeant march past the staring children to the gate in the wire fence. The mass of prisoners, packed closely together, were waiting for him. The moment he opened the gate they surrounded him and he vanished; occasionally his red beret could be seen above the crowd that moved slowly toward the exit.

George leaned against the wall of the crematorium, willing himself to hold down the nausea.

Then a skeleton with paralyzed legs dragged itself across the open space in front of him toward a dirty outhouse. When he saw it was a child, he turned his face to the wall and vomited. As he stood there, retching, his head against the wall, he heard a voice behind him. "Mr. Weatherby? Here is Laura Martens."

He turned, shaken, to face the scarecrow and his companion, a fair-haired girl in a flowered dress, clean and attractive, a bizarre presence in those surroundings.

"Mr. Weatherby," repeated the doctor, "I want you to meet a fellow Quaker. She is from Holland, and her name is Laura Martens."

Martens? Weren't those the people Boniface Baker had been asked to track down in Westerdam? George held out his hand. "I'm delighted to meet you, Laura Martens."

She seemed to hesitate, then cautiously shook hands with him, as if it were something she had not done in a long time. Her hand was ice cold.

"I assume that you and Miss Martens have a lot to talk about," the doctor said. "Why don't you take her along for a chat—outside the camp?"

"Oh? Well, of course, I'd be delighted. We have someone with us who'd love to meet you, Laura Martens. Let's go."

He gestured toward the gate, but she did not move. The doctor did, and when he started to walk toward the prisoners behind the fence, she followed. Obviously, the sergeant had left the camp, for the mass of prisoners was back again, waiting. This time, however, they did not wave and cheer. They were oddly silent; when the doctor opened the gate, they made room for him only reluctantly. The girl clearly was afraid of them, for she did not move; George took her arm and urged her along, but as they tried to follow the doctor, the prisoners refused to budge.

"Bitte, bitte, meine Damen und Herren!" the doctor cried. *"Um Gotteswillen, lassen Sie uns durch!"*

But the prisoners stood their ground, staring at the girl with such hostility that the doctor said, "I think maybe it would be better if you were to fetch the gentleman in question while I stay here with Miss Martens. It might be best if you hurried."

"All right," George said, and walked boldly toward the ranks of the prisoners barring his way. "Come on, gentlemen, if you don't mind. Let me through now, please!"

There was a tense moment, then they moved aside for him. He walked through their fetid ranks toward the red-and-white barrier in the distance.

* * *

Boniface Baker, driver of #1 Ambulance, was munching a
sandwich in the cab of his vehicle when he was struck by a sudden silence behind the gate. Until that moment the prisoners had
been waving, shouting; suddenly they fell silent and turned
around as though watching something inside the camp. Had
they captured a German officer, or a guard? To his surprise, it
was George who ducked under the barrier and came straight for
his ambulance. Boniface clamped the rest of his sandwich between his teeth and wound down the window.

"I say, old chap, would you mind coming with me?" George
looked pale. "Laura Martens is here. The Quaker girl you were
asked to inquire about in Westerdam, remember? The one with
the grandmother in Indiana? The doctor here puts up the usual
resistance to our barging into his hospital, so why don't you go
and chat up the girl? It might break the ice as far as he's concerned."

Boniface received the request with mixed emotions. This camp
was so sinister that he had sat there watching those skeletons behind the barrier, wondering whether he would be asked to go inside and what he could do to avoid it. Despite his apparent detachment, the corpse that Len and he had picked up and carried
out had shocked him by the discovery of how little it weighed,
and made him flee to the security of his ambulance. And now
here was George, as white as a sheet, asking him with the bored
drawl of British self-control to go inside and meet a girl. There
didn't seem to be much he could do about it; he had better see it
through. "Okay," he said, put his sandwich on the seat, opened
the door and jumped out.

When the two of them walked toward the barrier, Boniface
was struck by the difference in the attitude of the prisoners who
watched them approach. No more waving, no more cheering, no
more arms stretched out toward them in a delirium of joy. The
scarecrows in their striped rags were watching them now with
evident suspicion.

The corporal lifted the boom; George said to the prisoners,
"Come on, you chaps, let us through, won't you? Please, come
on now. There, that's better. Thank you. Thanks so much!"

They made their way through the tightly packed crowd; Boniface was nauseated by the stench. He had never smelled an odor

like this, the stench of roasting meat from burning tanks had been less repulsive. To combat his revulsion he tried to focus on their individual humanity, but that turned out to be pointless. They all looked alike. Suddenly there was a space around him; the prisoners hung back. Beyond a low fence, ahead, stood one of the prisoners in the company of a blonde girl in a flowered dress. The moment he set eyes on her he recognized her. She was older than her picture, but, given the circumstances, she looked comfortingly normal. To come upon a normal human being in this nightmare was a relief. She looked clean, she looked healthy, she had filled out since that picture was taken. He smiled and said, "Hi. I'm Boniface Baker. How are you?" He held out his hand. When she put out hers, he found it was ice cold. "And is this your father?" he asked.

"I'm sorry," the man beside her said. "My name is Dr. Wassermann. Her father is deceased."

"Oh, I'm sorry to hear that." Well, at least he would not have to tell him he could not go home again. "But your grandmother will be delighted to hear that you're not only alive and well but in such obvious good health." This, for some reason, was off the mark. She looked at him stonily; the prisoner beside her frowned; George looked as if he had committed a social offense. What was wrong?

"Let's go over to the bungalow," the doctor said, "I'm afraid there may be problems if we don't."

The moment they started to move, the crowd moved with them. The menace in the air was unmistakable; it was obvious now that it was directed at the girl.

When they reached the porch of the cottage, the prison doctor said, "Well, Laura, why don't you go inside? We'll see what we can arrange for you. I would lock the door if I were you."

The girl turned around without a word, hurried up the steps and went inside; they heard her bolt the door behind her.

"What does—" George started, but the doctor put a hand on his arm and said in a low voice, "Let's go. I'd like a private moment with the two of you."

This time the prisoners did not accompany them. They stayed behind at the cottage, a silent, malevolent crowd.

"May I go with them for a moment?" the doctor asked as they reached the barrier.

"He is the representative of the prisoners," George added.

But the corporal shook his head. "Sorry, Doc. I can't let any of them out. Sergeant's orders."

"Where is the sergeant?"

"In his tent."

"All right. Doctor, if you'd be kind enough to wait here a moment, I'll go and see him. Bonny, would you mind staying with the doctor, please?"

"What's the matter with her?" Boniface asked when they were alone.

"Not now," the doctor whispered. The corporal kept a wary eye on them, his Sten gun across his chest.

George and the sergeant came back together.

"Sorry," the sergeant said to the doctor. "I've just had contact with Headquarters, and their orders are: Nobody is to enter or leave the camp until tomorrow morning, when we receive reinforcements."

"But this concerns an urgent case that I cannot possibly discuss in public!"

"Okay, Jake, boy, why don't you go and look at the sights?"

The corporal sauntered off.

"Okay, shoot," the sergeant said.

The doctor didn't look happy, but obviously realized that this was all the privacy he was going to get. "It concerns the Martens girl in that bungalow. Her life is in danger. The only way to save her is to send in an armed patrol to bring her out."

"And who is threatening that person's life?" the sergeant asked.

"My fellow inmates."

"Why?"

The doctor hesitated. "She was the camp doctor's concubine."

"Was he one of those SS bastards?"

"Yes, but let me explain . . ."

"Sorry, Doc, I won't be able to help you."

"But this is a matter of life and death! The people here are out of their senses! Now that they are liberated, they want revenge; the only one they have left to vent their anger on is that girl. But she's innocent. They don't know the whole story. I've been here since the beginning, I know how it came about, what happened, why she had no choice. This was forced upon her. Now, unless we take her out of the camp before it gets dark . . ."

"Doc," the sergeant said, unmoved, "that's a matter between

your people and the woman. My orders are under no circumstances to become involved in the internal affairs of liberated countries, as far as their treatment of collaborators is concerned. And what's more, my standing orders are: no one in, no one out."

"But she's not a collaborator! She's a victim!"

The sergeant shook his head. "Whenever we enter a town that's been liberated and we see women dragged off with their heads shaved and we hear them scream and yell, of course our natural instinct is to come to their aid. A bunch of guys tearing the clothes off one helpless female and covering her with tar and doing God knows what else is not something we normally would allow. But those are our orders. So, I'm sorry, there's nothing I can do. If your people want to shave that girl's head and tar and feather her, I'm sorry for her, but I can't interfere."

"She's innocent!" the doctor cried. "And they won't just tar and feather her, they'll kill her! Don't you understand? All the SS officers are gone! The man with whom she was forced to live is gone! All they have left to serve as a scapegoat is that poor creature in there. She is innocent, I swear to you she is innocent! She had no alternative, it was the only way she could survive!"

"If that's so, the other prisoners will be aware of it too," the sergeant said.

"But that's what I've been trying to tell you! People here have been put on transport every week. There is hardly anyone in this camp who was here when the girl arrived. Do you know what happened to her? She came here to find her father. The moment she entered the camp she was grabbed by the commandant, who raped her, in front of her father, and—"

"Sorry, Doc," the sergeant said, unmoved. "There's nothing I can do. I don't want to hear about it, it's none of my business. My orders are that nobody can leave the camp. The woman will have to stay in that bungalow until tomorrow morning, when my superiors arrive. Let *them* sort it out."

"I don't care what your orders are, man!" the doctor cried. "That child will be dead by tomorrow morning!"

"Doc," the sergeant said calmly, "we may all be dead by tomorrow morning. That's the name of the game." He turned and walked away.

The doctor, exhausted, leaned on the barrier. "My God," he said, "they're all the same . . ."

"I'll tell you what, Dr. Wassermann," George said pleasantly, "why don't you tell us a little more about the girl's background, and then I'll labor with the sergeant in private. I'm sure, once he knows the full story, he'll reconsider. But it may be difficult; I was there when he spoke to Headquarters. His orders are indeed that nobody is to leave the camp, and that no soldier shall go in. But tomorrow morning . . ."

"Tomorrow morning will be too late," the doctor said. He sounded tired. "But why should I beat my brains out? While I'm wasting my time here, at least a dozen others are dying. They need me as badly."

"Come on, come on," George urged. "Just tell us, we'll do the rest. What was it you said about her father?"

The doctor sighed. "Three years ago she turned up at the gate, looking for her father. The commandant had a score to settle with the man, so he had him brought to his quarters and chained to the radiator. Then he proceeded to rape the girl in front of her father's eyes."

"Good God . . ."

"The man went berserk, when they took him outside on the way to his barracks he attacked the guards. They finished him off with blackjacks. The SS doctor carried the girl to his bungalow, and she has not been outside since, until a few minutes ago. This morning he fled with the rest, leaving her behind. To people who don't know any better, she's a Nazi whore. She hasn't a ghost of a chance. The moment darkness falls, they'll go in there and take her, and God only knows what they'll do to her. Well— do me a favor and give her a decent burial, will you? If ever there was an innocent victim . . ."

He turned away and tottered off, with dignity, despite his state of degradation.

*   *   *

George Weatherby, his jaw set, watched the man disappear. "I'll go and see the sergeant," he said determinedly. "This is becoming ridiculous."

But when he arrived in front of the sergeant's tent, he had second thoughts. Maybe it would be better if he could show the man the file on the girl, with the report on her background. It might mollify him, for, as George remembered it, it was a sad story.

The files were kept with the drugs, in #3 Ambulance; he

found the one marked *"Martens—Jacob & Laura, Westerdam, Sept. 1944,"* and reread it, seated on the running board.

There was the snapshot of a young girl with long blond hair and braces on her teeth, with on the back of it *"Laura, 12 years old."* The other snapshot, a man in his fifties, balding and rather dour: *"Jacob Martens, 1940."* There was the first Red Cross message, addressed to Stella Best, Rebekah Baker Friends Boarding School, Pendle Hill, Indiana, dated December 1941: *"Laura well. Self being purified in crucible of divine concern. Jacob."* The second Red Cross message, dated June 1942, and addressed to the same Stella Best: *"Regret to inform you that both father and daughter disappeared without trace. Sympathies, van Loon, neighbor."*

He reread the accompanying memorandum. *"This request was made by Stella Best, widow of John Best, a Quaker missionary killed during the uprising of 1904 in West Africa. She is Headmistress of the oldest Friends boarding school in the Midwest. Jacob Martens is her son-in-law. He was married to her only child, Lily Best, who died in 1939 of cancer. He is, or was, manager of one of the branch offices of the Netherlands Farmers Bank in Westerdam. At the time of his disappearance he was Clerk of Westerdam Monthly Meeting. His daughter, Laura, who was fifteen at the time the second Red Cross message was sent, is a birthright member of the same Monthly Meeting. A special effort to locate them seems in order. Stella Best requests that you extend to them the sheltering arms of the Society of Friends."* It was signed *"Ethan Woodhouse, Clerk, Meeting for Sufferings, Philadelphia, Pennsylvania."*

And there was the report Boniface Baker had written after he had made his inquiries in Westerdam, where they had stayed only twenty-four hours. *"Today, Sept. 4, 1944, I visited first the neighbors and then the town hall. The neighbors were most uncooperative, all I could get out of them was that the father and the daughter had both disappeared on the same day, June 3, 1942. They said that they were 'taking care of some of the Martenses' belongings' because the house had been confiscated by the Germans and sold to a family of Quislings. Part of the Martenses' belongings was an old mongrel dog, half blind and decrepit, called Caesar. My visit to the town hall was more productive: I talked to a man called van Haren, ex-member of the underground resistance, now head of the 'Ordedienst': the civil-*

*ian security forces. He told me he had been a member of the
same cell as Jacob Martens, their objective was the placing of
Jewish babies with Aryan families at the request of the parents
who had received information that they were about to be deported. On June 3, 1942, Jacob Martens had been arrested, tak-
en to the town hall and interrogated by the Gestapo. Under torture, he had disclosed the names of the other members of the
cell, who were arrested the same day, with the exception of Mr.
van Haren, who was known to the others only by his first name.
Martens was tried in a German court, condemned to ten years
hard labor and shipped to Schwalbenbach concentration camp;
this was the last information on him received in the Netherlands. His daughter, Laura, aged 15, with whom he lived alone,
was picked up by the underground and placed with a farmer's
family in the boondocks for the sake of her safety. After Jacob
Martens was shipped to Schwalbenbach, she disappeared. No
one knows for certain what happened to her, but van Haren
guessed that she had gone to find her father. He blamed himself, at least in part, for this: in order to spare the girl unnecessary anguish, he had told her her father had been 'put to work
in a labor camp' where he probably would be given some admin-
istrative job in view of his background. She had managed to get
the name of the camp out of him the last time he saw her, and
he still blames himself for the fact that he didn't realize why
she was so insistent that he tell her exactly where her father
was. As to the neighbors, van Haren was most scathing about
them, calling them 'vultures' who had 'picked clean' the modest
Martens house the very next day after his arrest. Before I took
my leave, he warned me, with some embarrassment, that if we
found the father (which he considered most unlikely) we should
warn him not to come home to Westerdam. He, van Haren,
knew how hard it was to resist Gestapo torture, but the fact remained that Martens had given away the names of the other
members of the cell, most of whom died in various camps later.
It would be advisable for Martens to stay away for at least a
few years, given the present mood of the citizens of Westerdam.
As to the daughter, she could come home, of course, but she
would not find much left and a restitution of the stolen property
might take some time, in view of the father's wartime record. As
far as van Haren knew, there were no relatives other than the
grandmother in America. No members of the small Quaker*

*Meeting to which both father and daughter had belonged were
left. In my opinion, this closes our investigation. Signed: Boniface Baker, QAS."*

It was a good report for the purpose, to inform Ethan Woodhouse, General Secretary of Philadelphia Meeting for Sufferings, of the result of the inquiry he had requested. It bore the
hallmark of its writer, Boniface Baker, young Philadelphia
Friend, placid, thorough, unemotional. But the very qualities
that made it proper for MFS rendered it useless in the case of
the sergeant, who would be swayed only, if at all, by something
more emotional, harrowing. Well, it was worth a try anyhow.
The girl's face haunted him, her ice-cold hands, her eyes beyond
hope.

Who knows, the sergeant might turn out to be accessible when
one labored with him in private, as the Quaker saying was.

* * *

When Boniface Baker returned to the cab of his ambulance,
he found the half-eaten sandwich still lying on the seat. He
climbed inside; the moment he closed the door and wound up the
window, he felt the sense of security the cab always gave him, a
feeling of being isolated from the outside world. Dusk was turning into night; the mass of prisoners, indistinct now, still surrounded the bungalow. At the barrier, a cigarette glowed—the
corporal on guard, smoking. Boniface put his head back and
closed his eyes. How was he going to tell that old lady in Indiana
what had happened to her son-in-law and her granddaughter?
He had conducted the investigation, so he would be expected to
write the final report. Maybe it would be better to send the report to Meeting for Sufferings and let Ethan Woodhouse take
care of the rest. But, whichever way he would phrase it, here at
last was the answer to the question that was put to all pacifists,
sooner or later: 'What would you do if your sister or your mother
was raped in front of your eyes?' The standard reply had been, 'I
can't answer hypothetical questions.' Now it no longer was a hypothetical question; here was a Quaker who *had* seen his daughter raped in front of his eyes, and the answer had turned out to
be that you went berserk and attacked your tormentors. Paci-
fism, non-violence, the Peace Testimony—in the face of the horrors of camp Schwalbenbach, they had been proved to be a senti-

mental luxury. Where was 'that of God' in monsters like the commandant who had set up this exercise because he had a score to settle with the father? Where was that of God in the SS doctor who took the child and kept her as a latrine for his sperm? Where was that of God in the henchmen who had turned this camp full of human beings into tottering skeletons? Where was that of God in the skeletons themselves who were about to kill the girl, in God only knew what repulsive manner? Would George be able to convince the sergeant that she should be released at once? But it was fruitless to count on that of God in the sergeant either. The sergeant had reached his moment of truth, as had the vengeful creatures now hovering around that cottage, waiting for the night. As had her father, when he betrayed his friends.

But maybe the whole thing was exaggerated. Only the doctor said that the prisoners were planning to finish her off, and he was obviously overwrought. The girl herself looked pretty hale and healthy for someone who had been a sadist's slave for three years. Whatever that SS doctor might have done to her, at least he had kept her in fighting trim. And weren't they all being a shade sentimental about her? Once she had made the choice to let the man use her body in exchange for her life, she must have made some kind of peace with herself. You couldn't wring your hands and sob your heart out over lost innocence for three years, for heaven's sake. No, for her to come out of this as a well-stacked blonde in a flowered dress with no symptoms of emotional trauma other than cold hands meant that, like everyone else, she must have arrived at some arrangement with the devil. This was where the principles of Quakerism became a luxury that only the secure, well fed and well housed could afford. Those who had chosen not to make that arrangement were all dead. How, by the way, had Dr. Wassermann managed to hang on while, as he said himself, people were shipped out every week? There must have been many doctors among the inmates. How come that, of all the prisoners who had been here three years ago, only Laura Martens and Dr. Wassermann were left?

How easy it was, how frighteningly easy, to rationalize cowardice! Or wasn't it cowardice? Whatever it was, Boniface could not see himself leaving the security of his cab and galloping in there as a knight in shining armor, to save the damsel in distress. Kid stuff. The girl had chosen the life of a heifer over death, so she was about to be slaughtered like one. That was the sober truth. Depressing how one instantly rationalized betrayal and defeat! *'Lord, I cannot do otherwise, for I have discovered the truth: vanity, vanity, all is vanity.'* Maybe Ecclesiastes had found himself faced with a similar choice: either go and save someone's life at the risk of his own, or write an undying poem on the vanity of it all while, behind his back, forgotten brutes gang-raped a forgotten girl.

'To every thing there is a season, and a time to every purpose under the heaven: a time to be born, and a time to die; a time to kill, and a time to heal . . .'

Maybe Ecclesiastes had shouted those lines out loud to himself over the shrieks of the female. It sounded despicable. It *was* despicable. It spat in the face of all that Friends considered made life worth living. Yet, there it was: the sonorous words still sang, stirring the soul with their beauty thousands of years later, and who remembered the girl and the gang who had perpetrated their horror while the poet's back was turned? Vanity, vanity: 'God, give me the gift of poetry and I will turn my betrayal into undying beauty.'

At the barrier, a cigarette glowed briefly in the darkness. Over the roof of the cottage the first stars became visible in the darkening sky. The silent mass of prisoners surrounding it merged with the darkness. Soon, no one on the outside would be able to see what went on inside. Pity the ambulance had no radio. He would have turned on some music, nice, loud music, like the finale of Beethoven's Ninth.

*   *   *

Laura did not know how long she had been sitting there on the couch in the dark, gazing fixedly at the door, when suddenly there was a brief rumble overhead. She heard the sound of the trapdoor to the attic being opened, then Heinzl's hushed voice: "What are they doing?"

"They're still out there. Nothing's changed. Stay where you are." She sounded calm, yet she felt that the slightest touch, one loud noise would unleash panic inside her.

"No," he said. *"Mein Gott!* I must get out of here, I must! I'm going crazy!"

She heard him move; some grit from the ceiling, invisible in the dark, settled on her hands. "Don't be ridiculous," she said. "They don't know you're here. Stay where you are."

But there was a rumble and his bare feet, his legs in long drawers dangled from the ceiling. He hung like that, suspended, for a moment; then he dropped, landed on the floor with a double thud, lost his balance and rolled onto his back. She could not bear to see him like that; she got up to help him to his feet. As she bent over him, he grabbed her arms. "Laura, Laura, for God's sake, Laura! Save me, *Liebchen, Herze-Liebchen,* save me, for God's sake, save me!"

"Don't be a fool," she said, terrified as she felt her self-control slipping. "They think you drove off this morning with the others. Go back to the attic and stay there! Nothing's going to happen, the Americans are here. They are all over the camp . . ."

"No, no," he said, "it's not true! Don't lie to me! I know, I've been listening to them, I can hear every word! They are waiting out there until only a few guards are left at the gate; then they'll break in here and get us. I know! I heard them!" In the corner Siegfried growled.

"Shush!" she warned.

"I told you, they are not human! What do you think they'll do to us? They'll tear us apart, limb from limb!"

"Then what do you want? Why are you coming out? You're crazy!"

"I have to get out of here!" he cried, scrambling to his feet. "I can't stand it any longer! Anything, anything is better than lying up there, waiting, listening to them, waiting for them! I must get out of here! Where are my clothes?" He started to grope around, stumbling over furniture, making a lot of noise.

"Don't be silly, Heinzl! Get back up there! Suppose they come in, suppose they search this place, who will they find? Me!"

He stopped.

"They don't know you're still here! They think you left with the others this morning! Can't you see?"

There was no reply.

"Come, get back up there. They won't come. And even if they do, before they are through with me you'll have plenty of time to get away. Just dash through the gate and surrender." She sensed that she had convinced him.

"Laura . . ." He put his arms around her. "Lauraschen, *Liebchen,* I cannot do that!"

She pushed him away. "Up you go!" She could not stand his tenderness now.

He tried to kiss her.

"Hush!" she said.

"What?" He listened.

Silence.

"They're coming," she whispered.

But he did not move. For a moment she expected him to say, 'No, Laura, I cannot let you do this.' But instead he began to tremble. Then he hissed, "I can't stand this any longer! Siegfried!"

She heard Siegfried's claws on the linoleum. "What are you *doing?* They don't know you are here! Why don't you believe me?"

"They know *you* are," he said in the darkness, "I'm doing it for *you.*" He pulled away from her, she heard him move to the door; then it opened, and he whispered, "Siegfried! *Fass!*"

Growling, the dog leaped out. Someone screamed, a scream of pain and terror. Heinzl closed the door and shot the bolt. Outside, on the veranda, she heard a rumble as if something heavy was being dragged away; then a different, ghastly scream that made her cheeks go cold. "My God, what's that?"

"They got him," he said in the darkness. "I told you, they're not human. Listen."

The screams became shrieks of agony. "They're tearing him apart," he said with eerie calm. "This is the end, *Liebchen.*"

* * *

When he heard the screams, George Weatherby ran to the gate. The guard called, "Sarge! Sarge! Come here! Quick!" He saw soldiers running toward the barrier, and joined them. A searchlight flashed on and lit up a group of prisoners in striped suits who scurried away toward the barracks.

"What the hell is going on?" the sergeant asked.

"They got hold of Siegfried," a voice said, behind the barrier. The searchlight swung around and revealed Dr. Wassermann.

"Who is Siegfried, for God's sake?"

"A dog. The camp dog. He was trained to bring down fugitives. They have torn him apart."

"You mean, with their bare hands?" the sergeant asked incredulously.

"They could hardly do anything else. They don't have any weapons, you know."

"Jake! Get the bullhorn!" The corporal ran off, came back a moment later; the sergeant took the megaphone and his voice, increased ten times in volume, bellowed, "EVERBODY INTO THE BARRACKS! THIS IS A WARNING! ANYONE WHO SHOWS HIMSELF OUTSIDE BEFORE SUN-UP WILL BE SHOT AT SIGHT! I REPEAT: UNTIL SUN-UP NOBODY IS ALLOWED OUTSIDE THE BARRACKS! THIS IS AN ORDER OF THE COMMANDING OFFICER OF THE CANADIAN FORCES!" The searchlight swept the empty space between the barracks, then swung back to the bungalow. There was nobody to be seen. "Okay," the sergeant said, "that ought to do it. You turn in, Doctor. The order goes for you too. I can't make any exceptions."

"As you wish. Good night." The German doctor walked calmly back to the barracks.

"Let's hope I put the fear of God into them," the sergeant said. "But the moment you spot someone leaving those barracks, Jake, even if it's only for a piss, give him one warning shot, and if he doesn't obey, shoot to kill. Let's hope we get those reinforcements tomorrow morning. I sent a signal that should blast a buffalo out of his armchair. But you never know."

"What did you signal, Sarge?"

" '*Trying to contain camp infected with plague full of corpses and insane prisoners. Help. Urgent.*' Let's hope some brahmin will hit the panic button. All right, boys: turn in, everyone except the watch. But keep your boots on, you're under red alert. Jake, call me immediately if you hear or see something move, anything at all." He and the soldiers disappeared in the direction of the tents, leaving the corporal and two guards at the barrier. George remained behind too, staring toward the bungalow in the darkness. After a while he turned and walked slowly back to the tent where the nine of them bivouaced overnight. As he passed #1 Ambulance, he saw a shadowy shape behind the wheel. He walked over and asked, "Aren't you turning in, Bonny?"

"No, I think I'll hang around for a while."

"Why?"

"If that doctor was right, there's no telling what they'll be up to on a night like this. There won't be any moon for hours."

"But there's nothing you can do!"

"I know. But I'm just as comfortable in the cab as in the tent, with all of you snoring your heads off." He seemed about to wind up his window, but George stopped his doing so by leaning against the door and saying, "I tried to persuade the sergeant to let her out, but without success. And he won't let us in, either. The doctor says he doesn't want us in there; so for the moment we're stymied."

"I gathered that."

"Well, let's see what daybreak will bring. It took twenty-four hours last time. So why don't you get some rest? Tomorrow is likely to be a tough day."

"Don't worry about me, George. I'm a big boy now."

It sounded uninviting, but George was suddenly moved to say, "I know, it's always a defeat, to have to give in. As a Quaker, you feel that it's your fault, failing to convince a man to do the right thing, from within himself, I mean."

"Et cetera, et cetera," the boy said. Not exactly an invitation to carry on this conversation.

But George decided to persevere. He remained silent for a while, then he asked, out of the blue, "Why did you join the QAS? I never asked you that."

"Why should you?"

"Well—I don't know. Maybe tonight is the night to reflect on our motivations."

"My motivations were that I no longer felt it was enough to sit on a mountain in central Pennsylvania and plant little trees."

"Was that your alternate service?"

"Yes."

"What made you change your mind?"

There was a silence. Obviously, Boniface Baker was not in the mood to bare his soul. But after a while he said, "Well, one night, a short while after D-day, a couple of Legionnaires turned up at our work camp with a movie of the landing on Omaha Beach. They were two old men in their sixties, with fore-and-aft caps and pot bellies, and mad as hell at us. Old men like them would occasionally give us a ride to town just for the chance to cuss us out on the way. 'Yellow-bellied cowards,' you know the kind of thing."

"Indeed I do," George said. "One rather large lady in Paddington station once gave me a white feather."

"Oh? What was the meaning of that?"

"Just a derisive thing. Badge of cowardice, you might say.

Rather touching, actually. Sort of went out with the First World War. I'm sure very few people on that platform knew what it meant. Must have taken her to be my mother. But go on: your old veterans with their movie of D-day."

"Well, it was pretty gruesome. I knew about the violence and the slaughter, but only as abstractions. That night, in the movie, it was all there; one shot in particular: a guy staggering out of the sea, looking dumb, holding something that kept on slipping from his hands, and each time he'd bend over and pick it up again. When he was out of the water, he fell on his knees, and I saw it was his guts."

The boy said it calmly, almost off-handedly, but it was obvious the incident had made a deep impression on him. George wondered how to react; in the end, he couldn't think of anything except, "I say! Poor sod . . ."

Not something a foreigner would at once recognize for what it was: the British shrinking away from expression of emotions, other than trivial ones; the impulse that had made the Battle of Britain pilots sing, "Death, where is thy sting-a-ling-a-ling?" But the boy was well into his story now, he took it in his stride.

"I couldn't stand the sight of those dangling guts any longer," he continued, "so I got up and walked out. I was standing out there, near the generator shed, looking at the stars, when one of the old men came out to take a leak. He spotted me standing there, and when he was through he came over to me and said, 'Beautiful, ain't it?' I said, 'Yeah,' but he didn't mean the stars. 'Beautiful, you boys, so strong in your faith, refusing to fight because of Jesus. But let me ask you one question: what about the poor sucker who had to take your place?' I asked him what he meant, and he said, 'When the Army needs a certain number of recruits and one drops out, they don't take one less; they draft someone else who otherwise would have slipped through the net because of fallen arches, or a squint, or because he's a bit retarded. How about that guy with his guts dangling out? For all you know, he may have been pulled in after you were allowed to go and plant little trees because of your conscience. Makes you wonder, doesn't it?'"

"Tough argument, that."

"I thought it was. Next day, I went to see the camp director. He threw up his hands and said, '*That* old stuff!' He came up with a lot of counter-arguments, but I couldn't forget that guy going down on his knees, how dumb he looked, amazed. As the old man said: a bit retarded. I know none of it made sense, rationally; but that's when I decided to leave the mountain and enlist as a medic, with the Army. I somehow wanted to join the rest of my generation, not be separate any longer."

"I see. Yes, I do see."

"Of course my mother, who's a widow, and Ethan Woodhouse and the rest of the Establishment raised the roof when they heard what I was planning to do. Stretcher-bearers on the battlefield bear arms, and that was a breach of our Peace Testimony. So, what with all those weighty Friends lined up against me, and ten or fifteen generations of Quaker saints called Baker breathing down my neck, I knuckled under and enrolled with QAS."

"I see . . ." What was most striking in the boy's story was the evocation of those fifteen generations and the phalanx of weighty Friends that had barred his way. It was difficult for an English Quaker, any Quaker other than a Pennsylvania one, to imagine what it was like not to be part of a quaint minority, but of the Establishment. That, probably, was the key to Boniface Baker's calm, almost placid self-assurance, which set him apart from the rest. He was a kind enough boy, but there was a regal streak in him, the kind of poise and unconscious authority that came with fifteen generations of Quaker ancestors and being part of the Establishment.

George was silent for a while. Then he said, somewhat lamely, "None of our emotional impulses make any rational sense, really." He knew he was expected to divulge his own motivation now, but somehow it didn't seem right. It certainly was much less dramatic than what Boniface Baker had told him. It also was, for an obscure reason, as if the young Pennsylvania Quaker would listen to him with just a hint of indulgence, a member of some ancient aristocracy listening to a voluble commoner. Nonsense, it was time he went to bed. One thing was certain: none of this was doing the poor girl in that cottage any good. They should be thinking of ways to help her in her predicament. "Well," he said, "I'd say let each of us see what he can come up with to winkle that sad creature out of her bungalow before it's too late. I think I'll have a look at the others now. May turn in for a spot."

"Do that," the American boy said noncommittally.

Obviously, the upstart from England had not lived up to expectations. George left the dark shape in the ambulance's cab to brood in silence, surrounded by the ghosts of his formidable forebears—for all the good it might do poor Laura Martens, waiting for death.

*   *   *

Well, there went George Weatherby, wandering off into the night, leaving Laura Martens' fate right in his lap. Lucky girl! All she had, from here on in, was Boniface Baker, planter of little trees, ambulance driver with the conchie brigade.

But maybe the situation wasn't as grim as it seemed. There were no prisoners to be seen in the compound; the sergeant had effectively shooed them all back into their barracks. As long as the guards kept their eyes and ears open . . . There sure as hell wasn't anything *he* could do at this point.

Yet he felt somehow compelled to stay awake, slumped morosely in the corner of the seat, gazing into the darkness toward the camp. For what? Nothing, unless it were some sort of wake over the dead body of the Knight in Shining Armor, the birthright Friend. Right now, as he sat there gazing morosely at the darkening sky, it seemed as if everything he had always taken for granted, the power of the Testimonies, the godly lives that went before, the Presence of God, Shekinah of the soul, the whole ball of wax was a self-delusion of privileged Friends, a way of making a materially comfortable group of people feel emotionally comfortable.

What good the queries, the advices, the exhortations of George Fox, the saintly examples of Elizabeth Fry, John Woolman, William Penn, now it came to protecting a helpless girl from the fate that awaited her?

"The Power of the Presence will protect thee." Yeah-yeah. Well, at least he knew the truth now. *'And the truth shall make you free.'*

It was sad, infinitely sad, to at least some people; but all he could think of, after fifteen generations of solid pacifists, was going in there with a gun.

*   *   *

It had become silent outside. Suddenly Heinzl turned on the standard lamp.

"Are you crazy?" Laura whispered.

"They're gone, for the time being . . ." He came toward her, soundlessly on his bare feet, stood still in front of the couch and held out his hand. "Here," he said. "Take one."

In the palm of his hand were two capsules.

"What—what do you—what are they?" she asked, to gain time to think.

"They'll come back. We don't have a hope. Take one."

"But—but why don't you give yourself up to the Canadians? This is your chance! If you open the door now and run fast . . ."

"*Liebes,* I've had plenty of time to think it through up there. We don't have a chance, even if I were to give myself up. Do you think they'd handle me with kid gloves? We listened to the radio, you know what they said. All those who are guilty of crimes against humanity will be tried by an international court of justice. What that means is they won't lynch us the moment they lay a hand on us, they'll lynch us after six months or a year. Our time is up, *Schätzerle.* These have been marvelous years. I've been very, very happy with you. If we had been given a lifetime, I would have married you and been the happiest man in the world. But our time is up. Here—take this. Put it in your mouth, crunch it like a piece of candy. You won't feel a thing. It will be over in a second. Go on."

"Yes . . ." she said, thinking frantically.

"Laura," he said, taking her hand, "believe me: you cannot go home again. The rest of the world will judge you exactly the way that rabble outside judges you. The life we shared was a fairytale, but to them, *Liebchen,* you will never be anything but a Nazi whore. So—let's go together. Don't allow them to turn our dream of love into a nightmare. Death is nothing. It's a door. Let's go through that door together. Come. Take it."

She did not know what else to do. She took a capsule and hid it in her hand.

"Put it in your mouth," he said. "Put it in your mouth and crunch it." She was so terrified, so confused that for one horrible moment she saw no other way than to obey him. Then, rallying, she asked, "Why now? There's nobody out there right now. Nobody is about to break in. Let's wait until they come for us. It may be hours yet. Why don't we use every minute that is left to us?"

She felt his determination waver. "Come." She rose and put her arms around his neck. "Make love to me, just once more."

He searched her eyes, very close, then he said, "It's no good, Laura. I just can't. I—I must listen. They are much slyer than the Canadians. They'll lull them into a sense of security, then they'll come slinking out of the barracks . . ."

"Come," she urged, her heart thumping, "let's have this last hour together. We'll put the capsules on the night table, and then, the moment they come . . ."

Again he searched her eyes. She needed all her strength not to break down under that probing look. "Laura," he said, sadly, "you are very much afraid, aren't you?"

She could not help herself, she nodded.

"Believe me, you won't feel a thing. You just crunch it, and within a second it's all over. Believe me, I know. We've seen it time and again, on prisoners—"

Suddenly her legs gave way. He misunderstood. He caught her and said, concerned, "Come now, come now! One second—is that really so terrifying?"

She slumped on the couch and hid her face in her hands. She felt him sit down beside her. He put an arm around her shoulders and pressed her against him. His lips nuzzled her ear. She could feel the warmth of his breath in her hair. "My darling, my little angel, my love, my heart, my life," he whispered. "Weren't we happy? Hasn't it been wonderful together? Don't many people have less happiness in a lifetime than we had these few years? Why allow it to end in horror, just because we don't have the courage to do this?"

She knew what he was about to do, before she felt him take her fist, pry it open and take out the capsule. Then he whispered, "Come, *liebchen,* open up. Let me do it for you. Come, open up . . ."

She shook her head, and grabbed his hand, trying to take the capsule from him. "I want to do it myself, please, please!"

He looked at her for a moment, then let her take the capsule. "Now . . ." he whispered. "Now . . . !"

She threw the capsule away, into a corner of the room, and burst into tears, hiding her face.

Suddenly she felt his hand on her throat. She screamed, her bladder gave way, she wet herself. She tried to escape, fell half off the couch, but again she felt his hand on her throat. He said, "Laura Laura! I don't want to harm you! I just want to kiss you once more." She stopped struggling. He lifted her chin, and she felt his lips softly on hers for a brief moment. Then he said, "I won't force you, my love. If you can't, I'll go it alone. Listen: the moment you hear them drag me away, go out the back door, run to the gate, calling *'Kamerad, Kamerad!'* Will you do that?"

She looked at him incredulously. The terror had left his eyes. He looked at her as he had looked in the past when it all began: full of tenderness and concern.

"I—I—" She did not know what to say.

"I didn't realize you were so afraid. This is the best way, then. I think I hear them now. Farewell, *Liebes.* Farewell, my darling heart." He kissed her once more, put the capsule in his mouth and walked to the front door.

She wanted to jump up, hold him back, but was unable to move. Petrified, her hands in front of her mouth, she stared at him as he opened the front door.

"Good evening, ladies and gentlemen, here I am. Let's get on with it."

He pulled the door shut behind him. Outside, on the veranda, she heard a shuffling noise. Somebody hissed, "Shhh!" There was the noise of a short struggle. She jumped up, ran to the door, listened at the crack, heard footsteps crunch on the gravel and fade into silence. This was her chance, now she must slip out the back door and run for her life to the barrier. If she didn't do it now, she'd never make it.

Then she heard, somewhere in the camp, a wild cheering. Everything around her seemed to collapse, everything, everything, the whole world. She fell to her knees and started, jabbering with fear, to crawl around, groping for the capsule.

* * *

At the sound of the spine-chilling cheers the searchlight hissed and flashed on, the beam swept the open space, lit up the barracks and caught a few running figures in its white circle.

"NOW THAT'S ENOUGH!" the bullhorn bellowed. "WE SHOOT TO KILL! GET BACK INTO YOUR—"

Suddenly a mannikin jumped into the circle as into a spotlight on the stage, spread its arms and shrieked, "Shoota me! Shoota me, you coward! Shoota me!"

"Okay, Jake, turn it off," the sergeant said. "The hell with them. Let 'em do what they fucking well want in their God-damned stinking camp."

"Who do you think they did it to this time, Sarge?"

"How the hell should I know? Hey, Doc, are you out there somewhere? What were those people yelling about? Have they got hold of the woman?"

A cry came back from the darkness: "No! Not yet!" It was not the doctor's voice, but a voice full of hatred.

"Sweep 'em again, Jake. Let's see what the hell is going on."

The searchlight flashed on again, hissing; the beam slowly moved, lighting up the barracks, one by one, the parade ground, finally the cottage. There was no one to be seen.

"Okay, that seems to be it." The sergeant turned off the searchlight himself. "I forgot my fags. Anybody got one for me?"

Boniface had had enough. He walked back to his ambulance and climbed into the cab. The moment he leaned back in the seat he felt the security of the cubicle relax him, like dope. So they had not got hold of her. Not yet. He closed his eyes and prayed, 'God, protect her, protect her with Thy wings . . .'

He was overcome by a feeling of contempt. To sit there and pray, because he was too yellow to set foot inside the camp! But what could he do? Run to the gate, rip a Sten gun from the hands of one of the guards and run to the cottage? The thought was ludicrous. They would stop him, they might even shoot him down, they were jumpy enough to do so. And had he really come to the point where the only solution he could think of was violence? What about St. Paul's armor of God: *'Stand therefore, having your loins girt about with truth, and having on the breastplate of righteousness, and your feet shod with the preparation of the gospel of peace. . .'* That had not always been a pious platitude. His own ancestors had been among the Quakers of Philadelphia who in 1754 had hidden Indian refugees in their cellars and their attics and stood in the doorways of their houses, hand in hand, to await the lynch mob, unarmed. Or was that a legend? No, Friends had a passion for truth, it must have happened. Those families had somehow found the strength to face the onrushing rednecks without weapons. Where had they found that strength? Had they too started by praying, 'God, protect the Indians with Thy wings'? Had one of them been overcome by contempt for the pious balderdash? What had happened to make those families decide to take in the fleeing Indians, stand in their doorways together and face down death? Had they believed that God would really protect the Indians with His wings? Of course not. How was God supposed to do that? Wings, indeed.

'Present thyself as an instrument.' How often had he heard that bleated during meetings for worship by well-fed, prosperous Friends? Yet the ancestors of those same people had, two centuries before, stood in their doorways in the power of the Lord, at the risk of their lives. 'All He has is thee.' If only he could put that into practice, here, now!

But how? By standing in the doorway of the cottage? *'Meine Damen und Herren,* I represent God, and I command you to leave the girl alone.' After everything he had seen, the war, the camp itself, he was no longer capable of believing the old, saccharine Quaker appeal to that of God in every man; they would trample him underfoot. What if the others joined in, the way his forefathers had, standing in that doorway, hand in hand? All nine of them?

Suddenly he realized that he was no longer idly ruminating. He was facing a real choice. He was faced, unexpectedly, with his moment of truth.

Did he imagine it, or was it getting lighter? Indeed, he could now discern the roof of the cottage. The moon was rising. Soon it would be lighter still. Then, finally, sunrise. Was it really necessary to go in for all this? A few more hours and dawn would break, reinforcements would arrive. But the prisoners, bent on revenge, must come to the same conclusion: if they wanted to get the girl, they would have to do it soon, before the guards at the gate could see them. This was the moment. It was now or never.

He could not believe it yet. He was being emotional. He should not act hastily. The soldiers would not allow them to enter anyhow. Desperately, he folded his hands, closed his eyes and prayed, 'God, if Thee is real, if that story of the Friends in their doorways is true, then manifest Thyself to me *now!* Lead me. Lead me, God. Let me be Thy instrument. God, let me embody

Thee.' He waited. He did not know quite what to expect, a hand on his shoulder, or a voice like the one George Fox had heard from the apple tree. Perhaps he would start to quake.

But nothing happened. He just sat there, hands folded, eyes closed. There came no answer from infinity, no Light filled the empty vessel of his waiting. All he registered was the stench of gasoline and a growing sense of having been betrayed.

He opened the door and smelled, stronger than the gasoline, the sickening stench of the camp. One of the guards coughed; near the gate a cigarette glowed briefly. He could discern the white sections of the barrier. It was getting lighter all the time. If he was going to do it, he should do it now.

"Bonny?" The voice sounded very close.

"George?"

"Yes. Can't you sleep either?"

"No."

"I've been thinking."

"So have I."

George appeared beside him, a dark shape in the night. "I'm afraid all I've come up with is Walter Mitty stuff. Like galloping in there and liberating her like a knight of some sort."

"With a Sten gun that you would yank from the hands of one of the guards?"

"No, that idea had not occurred to me."

"I think there is something else we might do. On condition we believe in the Quaker Testimonies."

"What would that be?"

"You remember the Friends in Philadelphia in 1754? Standing in the doorways of their houses to protect the Indians they had hidden in their cellars? Know the story?"

"I may have heard it in Sunday school."

"How about us going in there, the nine of us, to stand in the doorway, hand in hand?"

He found himself hoping that George would say, 'Are you crazy?'

George said, after a moment, "Why don't you suggest it to the other chaps?"

"All right," he said, "let's go."

* * *

George Weatherby watched the faces of the others in the tent while Boniface Baker told them the story of the Quakers of Philadelphia and the Indians.

Len said, "It just might work. What do you think, boys?"

There was a murmur of approval, but it did not sound whole-hearted.

"I must confess that I don't really believe in that—not quite," said Oscar.

"In what?" Boniface asked.

"In our power to stop them."

"So you don't believe in it," Boniface said, "but the least we can do, as Quakers, is what her grandmother asked us to do: extend to her the sheltering arms of the Society of Friends."

Then François said, with his lilting French accent, "And it would not be *us* who stop them. It would be *la Présence*. God."

"But how?" Len asked.

"We might go into meeting for worship on that porch, instead of standing in the doorway," said Charles. That was surprising, he was the least Quakerly of them all; at least, he had appeared to be. "A lot of people, nine, to stand in one doorway," he added practically.

George Weatherby pictured them as they would be seen from the camp: a half-circle of people sitting there, heads bent in prayer. Everyone must recognize prayer when they saw it. "If we do it at all," he said, "then that would be the way to do it."

A deep silence fell. It was a strange moment; for some reason it sent a shiver down George's spine. Then he realized what was happening: they had gone into meeting for worship. They sat like that for minutes on end, quite still, in silence; then Len said, "All right, let's do it."

One by one they rose and ducked out of the tent. George was the last to go; it had been pretty impressive, but he was the leader, he was responsible. Or was he? The sense of the Meeting had been clear . . . He followed them.

The others reached the barrier first; when Boniface went to raise the boom, the guard called, "Hey, you guys! What's the big idea?"

"We're going to the cottage," Boniface replied.

"Does the sarge know about this?"

"No."

"Then I can't let you in. My orders are nobody in, nobody out. Sorry."

"What the hell is going on?" It was the sergeant, approaching in the darkness.

"We want to protect the girl in the cottage," Boniface replied.

"How?"

"By sitting down on the porch and holding meeting for worship."

"Meeting for *what?*"

"A Quaker service," Len explained. "A prayer group."

"Prayer group?!" the sergeant bellowed, exasperated. "What do you take me for? I've got fifteen men! God knows how many people they've slaughtered in there already! Do you think I'm going to allow you nuts to provoke those people some more?"

George felt the moment had come for him to intervene. "Sergeant," he said, "could you and I talk this over in private?"

"No!" the sergeant replied roughly. "No fancy talk, no religious bullshit. Nobody's going to enter that camp, those are my orders."

"Sergeant," George said carefully, "the people in that camp are sick. We are here to nurse them. They're not only physically sick, but emotionally. These eight boys here are under my command. We obey your orders as long as there is any fighting, but when it comes to doing our job as an ambulance service, then it's *my* orders they obey. My rank is first lieutenant, and I consider it my duty to enter that camp to prevent those people from committing any more murders."

"Okay, Lieutenant," the sergeant said, with heavy irony. "If you want to pull your phony rank on me, then that's where the buck stops. As long as you realize that it's *your* responsibility, yours alone. I'm not about to risk the life of any of my men to get you out of there. If those jokers want to cut your throats, it'll be *your* baby."

"Very well," George said. "Would you order the guard to let us in?"

"Jake!" the sergeant called. "Let 'em in. The hell with 'em."

The boom was raised.

The nine went inside, in single file, Boniface in the lead with a blacked-out flashlight. There was no one to be seen in the diffused moonlight; the black silhouettes of the barracks stood starkly outlined against the starry sky with the unreality of a stage set. It was a peaceful scene, yet to George the menace was unmistakable. Their boots crunched on the gravel as they walked down the path toward the bungalow; the steps of the veranda creaked; they sat down in a semi-circle, facing the camp.

Once they were seated, George became afraid. The sergeant was right: if the prisoners were determined to get hold of the girl, they were not going to be restrained by nine unarmed pacifists. The only hope seemed to be that the inmates might mistake them for soldiers; they were wearing uniforms. Then he saw Boniface Baker put the flashlight down in the center, facing them, its small shutters open, revealing their seated figures like a footlight. George's first impulse was to turn it off. But it was too late now. Here they sat, the nine of them, like the bait in a trap.

They bent their heads and centered down in the silence. From the barracks, silent, ghostly figures slowly moved toward them in the moonlight.

* * *

Laura listened, her eyes wide in the darkness, her heart banging in her chest. They were out there on the porch! Any moment now the door would open! Thank God she had finally found the capsule. The moment had come to swallow it. She closed her eyes and thought: 'Be brave. It will be over in a second. Think of—' Suddenly, totally unexpectedly, a soundless cry tore loose within her: 'Help! God, Christ, help! Let me live! I want to live!' Her muscles went as taut as cords; then the moment of frenzy was spent. 'Come,' she told herself, 'put it in your mouth. You won't feel anything. It will be like—' She heard a sound behind her.

She turned her head and stared into the darkness. She heard panting, getting closer. The panting of a dog. It could not be Siegfried. Siegfried was dead! She listened, heart racing, open-mouthed. *Pant, pant, pant, pant* . . . Then she realized what it was: the beating of her heart in her throat. She sagged with relief. How silly, how— A sound in the kitchen: a crack! Then a squeak. They were trying to open the back door! Or was it her imagination? Why did the ones on the veranda not come in?

A crash, the jangle of glass. The jam jar on the windowsill! The one with the parsley! They were climbing in!

Terror lashed her into frenzied action. It was not her mind, it was her body that suddenly knew what they would do to her if they caught her here in this room. She made a dash for the front door, grabbed the knob, heard the floorboards creak behind her and tore the door open. She saw a flashlight, low on the ground. She turned to run back into the house, but a hand grabbed her from below. The capsule! The capsule! But the hand that held her wrist pulled her down. She discovered she had no strength, no strength at all; she knelt down, in utter terror. Dark shadows were crouching all around her. Behind her, the floorboards creaked again. This would have been the moment to crush the capsule. But the hand held hers in an iron grip. She saw, in the moonlight behind the lantern, a movement. There they were. Rows and rows of them, waiting for her to be thrown at their feet. She closed her eyes, bent her head and waited, swooning, for them to kill her.

*   *   *

From the corner of his eye Boniface saw a movement in the doorway to the cottage. The others, eyes closed in prayer, did not appear to notice. Any moment now hands would reach out from the doorway, grab the girl and drag her inside. What had possessed him to think that the nine of them could keep these people from avenging their dead? There they were! He could discern, vaguely, striped prison suits in the doorway.

In front of him, less than ten paces away, a whole crowd of them faced him menacingly. The girl beside him sat with her head bent; he held her hand in a powerless gesture of protection. Then someone detached himself from the crowd in front of the cottage, stood still at the bottom of the steps, climbed onto the porch. There was a massive shuffle, the ranks closed in. He wanted to jump up and cry, 'People, please, please don't do this!' Suddenly a civilized voice asked, in formal English, "Would you have any objection to my joining you?" It was an old man in prison clothes.

A voice from the crowd called, "Rabbi Hirsch, don't do that! You must not do that!"

The old man lowered himself arthritically to the floor, his back to the crowd. In front of the cottage the murmur grew, in the doorway behind Boniface sounded whispers. The old man put on a convict's cap and started, face tilted upward, to rock in prayer.

The hubbub of voices subsided. The whispering in the doorway ceased. Then a gaunt, shorn woman appeared at the bottom of the steps and climbed onto the porch, staring at the girl. The rabbi grabbed the skirt of the woman and said, *"Komm, Frau Rosenbach, setzen Sie sich hin."*

The woman looked down at him. Then she looked at the girl.

The rabbi said, *"Komm, Frau Rosenbach, danken wir Gott für unsere Erlösung vom Bösen."*

The woman sank slowly to her knees by the rabbi's side. She bent her head and seemed to be weeping; the rabbi put his hand on hers.

The crowd growled. Inside the cottage sounded whispers again. But Boniface knew, with a sense of awe and jubilation, that some unutterable grace had descended upon them.

*   *   *

George saw Boniface break meeting by shaking Len's hand. The others followed his example and shook hands, the rabbi too. The only one who remained motionless was the woman. Boniface helped the girl to her feet and put an arm around her shoulders. The moment they rose, the prisoners closed in on them; as they went down the steps, they were surrounded. But, confident now, they walked on, the rabbi leading them with the woman at his side. The wall of prisoners grudgingly gave way as the rabbi slowly led them to the gate. Some of them spat, some were crying; as she passed them, Laura covered her face with her hands.

When they reached the gate, the guard raised the boom for them. Laura let herself be led toward the first ambulance. George opened the doors; Boniface said, "I think she should be sedated."

"I'll get it," George said.

They helped Laura into the truck. Boniface said, "Come, Laura. Sit down, relax. You are safe now."

She obeyed.

George went to get the sedative, reconstituted some milk and heated it on the portable stove in the tent. When he took the steaming mug into the ambulance, she was still sitting as he had left her: on the edge of the bunk, head bent. Boniface took the mug over to her. "Laura? Here, take this."

After a moment she looked up. Her eyes stared blankly. She reached out, took the mug and said, in a whisper, "Thank you."

Boniface said, "You're welcome."

George went out, closed the doors of the ambulance and walked to the edge of the fields. Day was breaking; a farmer was plowing with a team of two cows. The black earth curled under the plow. The farmer spotted him and waved.

Not knowing what else to do, George waved back.

CHAPTER TWO

LATER that morning the bombing of the town of Schwalbenbach started. Scores of planes came over, flying low. The drone of their engines drowned the cheering of the prisoners, who yelled and shouted and waved as if the pilots could hear them. The town was three miles east of the camp, but the planes released their bombs overhead; like schools of small black fish, the clusters floated down in a slow curve. Minutes later the earth shook. Within half an hour the town was ablaze; a huge, roiling black cloud reached up until it covered almost half of the sky.

Everyone was gazing at the spectacle when a growing roar drowned out the steady sound of the oncoming planes. A column of wagons of war, ten abreast, came churning across the freshly plowed field toward the camp, chasing the farmer and his cows. Tanks, armored troop-carriers, mobile guns, followed by a train of field kitchens, ambulances, trucks with food and supplies, and a tail of runt-like jeeps. The rattle of the half-tracks, the whine and snarl of the engines, the clanking of metal inside the trucks drowned even the distant thunder of exploding bombs and crumbling buildings as the armored column lined up in front of the camp.

The dust was still settling when a jeep came careening through their ranks and stopped at the barrier. Out jumped a white-helmeted, goggled general in battle dress with riding boots and two pearl-handled pistols. The sergeant, standing at the gate with George Weatherby and Dr. Wassermann, sprang to attention; so did the doctor. George did not quite know what to do and ended by smiling engagingly as the swaggering warlord advanced on them. The general, tall and broad-shouldered and theatrically covered with dust, snapped the goggles onto his helmet with a practiced gesture and revealed a pair of bright blue eyes set in pink ovals where the goggles had been. "I'm General Harry Schickelgruber," he said. "Anyone making a crack about it being Hitler's name gets kicked in the balls."

None of those present, standing to attention, moved a muscle; it seemed as if with the general a power of awesome proportions had arrived on the scene, intimidating everyone, even Dr. Wassermann.

"Well," the general said, "where's the plague?"

"The—the plague, sir?" the sergeant stammered, standing to attention with parade-ground rigidity.

"Hell," the general said, "some joker sent a message that he'd come upon a camp with the plague. Is this it?"

"Ye-yes, sir . . ."

"Is there plague or ain't there?"

"Yes, sir . . . well . . ." When the general looked at him with those pink-ringed blue eyes, the sergeant added, "I had to make sure, sir, that someone would come."

There was a silence; everyone expected the sergeant to be demolished by the general's wrath. But he said, "I see. You been in the Army awhile, haven't you, Sergeant?"

"Yessir. Fifteen years."

"I thought so." The general took off his gloves and slapped them together with clouds of dust. He turned on George. "And who have we here?"

"My name is George Weatherby," George replied with a flutter in his stomach. "I am the leader of the Northern unit of the QAS."

"The what?" The general looked at him sideways; it was obvious that he did not consider George a member of the priesthood of war.

"The Quaker Ambulance Service. We have been with you since D-day."

"I see," the general said, with a hard set to his mouth. "The conchies, eh? Well, it takes all kinds." He turned to Dr. Wassermann. "And you? Do you speak English?"

"Yes, sir." It was distressing, but Dr. Wassermann had reverted to the servility he must have shown his jailers.

"Are you the chairman of the committee?"

"Excuse me?"

The general turned to the sergeant. "Haven't you organized a committee of inmates yet?"

"No, sir . . ."

Without turning around, the general called, "Charlie!"

"Yes, General!" A lithe young officer jumped off the jeep and joined them.

"This man speaks English. Get a committee of inmates set up. I'll meet with them in half an hour's time in that cottage over there. Tell Rusty to go check it out."

"Yes, General."

"All right, Sergeant," the general said, tapping the sergeant on the shoulder with his gloves, "show me around." Then to George, "You come along. Let's hear what you have to say."

"It—it's quite a place, General, sir," the sergeant ventured.

"I'm sure it is," the general said casually. "We've come across one or two. Does this one have a crematorium?"

"Yessir."

"Corpses?"

"Yessir. Stacks of them."

"Charlie!"

"General!" The young officer was at his elbow in a flash.

"Don't let the burial detail start before we've had some batches of civilians from the town over there view the place. At least, don't fill up the trench until they've been given the chance to puke in it."

"Yes, General."

"All right," the general said, "let's take a look." He moved ahead, boots creaking, pistols dangling, with a rolling gait. At a signal from the sergeant, the corporal at the boom raised it respectfully.

George followed the general as he walked past the silent ranks of awed inmates, gaping at him with wary curiosity. There was no cheering, no applause. He marched through the barracks with the ghosts rising half out of the coffins of their bunks, through the compound with the little old men that once had been children, into the nightmare of the crematorium. He cast a glance at the ovens, the stacks of corpses, grunted, turned around and marched back to the gate, boots creaking.

When they came out of the camp, the armored column had finished lining up. The green-sheathed, rubber-booted specialists of the burial detail stood to attention at the general's approach. "Lieutenant," he said, in that casual tone, "there's a lot of bodies there, but don't start dumping them before warning my aide-de-camp here so we can have a proper religious service." He turned to George. "Do the people in there have a choir?"

"I—I hardly think so."

"Charlie!"

"Yes, General!"

"Let's bring in the choir from that Russian POW camp we liberated this morning. Have them sing each time you dump a load."

"Yes, General. I think it's a secular choir, though. I doubt whether they know the proper hymns."

"Don't worry your little head over that, son," the general said. "I don't care what they sing, as long as it's slow. It'll be in Russian, so what the hell."

"Very good, General."

"Cottage ready?"

"Yes, General. But Rusty thinks it's still occupied."

"Occupied by whom? Santa Claus?"

"There seem to be women's things in there, sir."

The general turned, for some obscure reason, to George again. "Don't tell me there are any gray mice left in this camp?"

"Pardon?"

"Fritzies, man! Female personnel!"

"I don't believe so," George said.

The general looked at him with his pale eyes in pink oval patches. "Then who are the women?"

"Oh—well, er, there was a girl in there whom we managed to—who—who has nothing to do with—she's Dutch."

"Where is she now?"

"In one of our ambulances."

"Charlie!"

"Yes, General."

"Have Security check a woman in one of the conchie ambulances."

"Yes, General."

The general slapped George on the shoulder with his gloves.

"Let's you and me have a sitdown with the pill brigade and see what needs to be done. After that, I think you'd better leave them to it. They'll take care of it."

"But we have, thus far, always—"

The general was not interested. "You and your vehicles move out," he said. "Tootle over to that town over there, see if the civilians can use you. The Air Force is making a lot of customers for you right now, by the sound of it." Without waiting for a reply, he turned away and strolled toward the bungalow, boots creaking, pistols bobbing.

* * *

During the meeting with the general and the Red Cross brass, the lamp tinkled softly with the tremors of the bombing; at a given moment someone asked, "What are they pulverizing that town for, does anyone know?" The general answered casually, "Pockets of resistance." They continued their deliberations.

After the conference, George had to admit the general's order made sense. There was nothing left for the unit to do that the Red Cross people couldn't do more efficiently, be it on an impersonal basis. And maybe that was all to the good: no man could approach the challenge of the camp on a personal basis.

The general left to shower and change; when he returned, pink and hale and smelling of after-shave, he looked just as intimidating in a bathrobe as he had in uniform.

"What about this woman?" he asked. "The bathroom is full of her junk, and there are things of hers in the closet. Has Security checked her yet?"

As if in answer to a divine summons, there was a knock on the door and Bonny Baker appeared, looking adolescent without his beret, his boyish hair tousled, his eyes blazing with anger. "Are you in command here?" he asked the general.

"Hunh?"

The general's entourage froze with shock.

"Somebody is harassing Laura Martens," Bonny said, "She's under sedation in my ambulance and some bully is giving her the third degree. Call him off, please."

"Who in hell are *you?!*" the general bellowed.

George felt he should intervene, explain the situation, but he was dumbfounded like the rest.

"My name is Boniface Baker," Bonny said coldly. "I'm a Quaker, and it's my task to look after people like Laura Martens. She's being treated as if she was the enemy. She's a poor, tormented girl who was raped by the SS in front of her father and saw him butchered. The camp doctor who lived in this cottage took her and made her his mistress. You know the story of the woman taken in adultery, and what Jesus said to those who wanted to stone her?"

"Hell's bells!"

But Bonny was not to be deterred. It was, in a crazy way, magnificent, like trying to talk a mad bull into meekness. " 'He that is without sin among you, let him throw the first stone.' That's what Jesus said, and they all crept away, and—"

"Now, listen—!"

"And he asked the woman, 'Where are your accusers?' or words to that effect, and she replied, 'Gone.' So he said, 'Neither do I condemn you. Go and sin no more.' So get that bully off her back and let her sleep. Goodbye." He turned around and left.

The general looked stunned. "He one of yours?" he asked George.

"Er—yes," George replied.

"Good for him!" the general cried. "I'd rather hear that boy than Billy Sunday any time! Why do my chaplains never give me that stuff? 'The woman taken in adultery'! Terrific! Charlie!"

"Yes, General!" There he was again, instantly, *premier danseur* of the warlord's ballet.

"Call off Security," the general said. "Tell that girl to come here and clear out her junk. I want a word with her." He turned to George. "What nationality did you say?"

"Dutch."

"Okay, Charlie, arrange for her to be repatriated. Quickly, before I change my mind." The general grinned and patted George on the shoulder. "Christian charity doesn't last long, y'know; wears off faster than a bottle of booze. And, Charlie, give those inmates something to do, the ones that are hopping around. Keep them busy, and out of mischief."

"What would you like them to do, General?"

"How should I know? That's *your* department. Have them tar the roofs of the barracks, or something."

"Yes, General." The lieutenant called Charlie turned to

George and said, in a tone of cheerful intimacy, "Shall we go? You know where she is."

George nodded, and he was about to follow the man when the general shouted, "Hey! Have a look at this! Where did you find that, Rusty?" He was holding a small pillow.

"Under the sink in the kitchen, General," replied a small, wiry Pfc who had been fussing around in the background, bringing in luggage, carrying out bed linen.

"Well, if that doesn't beat them all," the general cried. " *'God is love,'* and that in this charnel house! This is even better than the baby pictures in the other one, isn't it, Charlie?"

"Indeed, General," Charlie said, and he nudged George out the door.

* * *

"Tell me," the Security officer said, "did he have any scars? Birthmarks? Anything else that might identify him?"

Laura felt so groggy that it seemed as if this whole conversation was taking place in a dream. As if presently Heinzl would wake her up and ask, *'Liebes, hast du gut geschlafen?'* "He had a birthmark on his left thigh," she replied.

"On the inside? About three centimeters wide, shaped like a crescent?"

"How—how do you know?"

"So it's him." The officer wrote something in his little book.

"Did you find him?"

"Yes," he replied, without interrupting his writing.

Suddenly it became reality for her. "Was he . . . Did they . . ."

"Yes," the officer said impassively.

The door was opened and the American Quaker climbed into the ambulance. "Okay, friend," he said, "this is it. Out!"

"I *beg* your pardon?!"

"I'm the medic in charge of this patient. She's been sedated, you have no business cross-examining her. Out. You can come back tomorrow."

There was an altercation that she did not follow. She thought about Heinzl and what they had done to him. She prayed to God, with all her might, that he had been given time to crush the capsule. He must have, or she would have heard screams. All she had heard—

The row between the two men suddenly stopped. Another officer had appeared in the doorway. He had a little mustache, and seemed to have more authority than the one who had been questioning her. "The guy is right, Masterson," he said. "I'm afraid you'll have to wrap it up."

"But listen! I'm just—"

"Sorry. Adolf says wrap it up. I have orders to bring her in. He wants her to clear out her belongings."

"Can I carry on with this tomorrow?"

"No way. I'm supposed to repatriate her. Forget about her, Masterson. There's plenty more where she came from. Are you able to walk?"

She only realized he was talking to her when he repeated his question. "I? Oh, yes . . ."

"All right. The general wants to see you. Let's go."

"But what about the people in the camp?" the American Quaker asked. "What will they do to her?"

"Don't worry," the officer said. "The place is swarming with troops." He held out his hand to her. "Come, let's go." She rose.

"Hey! Wait a minute!" The American Quaker barred her way. "This patient is in no fit condition—"

"Listen, old buddy," the officer with the mustache said, "let her forge the iron while it's hot. He's in a good mood now, God knows how he'll feel an hour from now. If you really want to help this—this person, do as I say: let her get this over with, I'll repatriate her and when he wakes up she'll be gone. This way, please."

The Quaker helped her down the steps of the ambulance and took her arm. "Don't worry," he said, concerned. "The general is okay. I know what it'll mean to you to go back in, but don't worry. Do you think you can make it?"

She nodded, dazed, and let herself be guided along. At the barrier a guard with a gun jumped to attention and asked, "Has the lady got a pass, Lieutenant?"

"I have orders to take her to the general. It's okay."

The soldier lifted the boom.

The moment she set foot inside the camp she was overcome with terror. She tried to hold back, but the American beside her urged her on, gently. When the gravel crunched under her feet, she could no longer contain herself and ran toward the veranda, beset by the compulsion to get inside as quickly as she could. A

soldier at the door stopped her. "Hey! Wait a minute! Where
d'you think you're going?"

"It's okay, the general wants to see her." The officer opened
the door a crack. "General, I've got the girl here."

"Send her in," a man's voice called from the living room.

The officer opened the door and said to the Quaker, "You and
I wait outside."

On the couch sat a man with his stockinged feet on the coffee
table. He was wearing a jumpsuit with the legend *Notre Dame,*
and his gray hair was close-cropped. "Hot dog!" he said. "The
woman taken in adultery. Rusty!"

"Yes, General." A small red-haired soldier appeared in the
bedroom door.

"Get those things you stacked on the dresser."

"Yes, General."

"Or do you want to go and get them yourself?" he asked her.
"I think Rusty's emptied all the drawers, but if you want to
check, you're welcome."

She shook her head.

The red-haired soldier came back with a stack of underwear,
toilet things, her robe, her pajamas. It brought home with a sudden, unbearable poignancy the fact that Heinzl was dead. He
handed her the stack without a word, but his eyes were hostile.
"Thank you," she whispered. The feel of the silk pajamas at the
bottom of the stack made her almost burst into tears.

Then she heard the general say, "All right, Rusty, out!" The
red-haired soldier muttered, "Yes, General," and vanished.
"And close the door!" the general yelled. The door was closed.
There was a silence, then he said, "Okay, honey. Sit down." He
pointed at the other end of the couch. She obeyed and sat down,
with the stack of her belongings on her lap. The general looked
at her appraisingly. "Was he the one they killed last night?" he
asked.

She felt tears wriggle down her cheeks and shrugged her
shoulders.

"What happened to the rest of the staff?"

She did not reply.

"Look, honey," the general said, with unexpected kindness. "I
don't want to give you the third degree, but there are a few
things I'd like to know because they're important. So, relax. If
you don't want to answer, don't. But give it a try. So: what happened to the other officers who were in the camp?"

"They left."

"Why didn't he?" When she did not answer, he asked, "Because of you?"

She didn't want to talk about it, but she replied, "He—he thought you might understand."

"I? How did he know I was coming?"

"An American doctor, he thought."

"Oh. What exactly did he do? Kill people for sport?"

She shrugged her shoulders. It was hopeless.

"You lived with him, didn't you?"

She nodded.

"Then don't tell me you didn't know what he was up to in the camp."

"He never talked about it." She wanted to get away now.

"You never saw anything through that window over there?"

She looked at him with the beginning of fear, but his eyes reassured her. "I wasn't allowed to look."

"Was he okay? I mean, did he treat you decently?"

She nodded.

"Did he ever force you to do things that you didn't want to?"

She had no idea what he meant, but it seemed best to humor him. "No."

"He was an educated man, I gather."

She nodded.

"I had a look at his books. Goethe, Schiller, highbrow stuff. And then the gramophone records. Mozart, Schubert, Sibelius."

Sibelius . . . all those nights . . . Her heart sank.

"Well," the general said, "I suppose that if he and I could have talked it over I might have understood what made him tick. Not approved of what he did, mind you. Understood. We too are slaughtering helpless people, right now. You can imagine what that town is like. Better still: don't try."

She had no idea what he meant.

"Listen."

She listened and heard a distant rumbling. Bombs, probably. She had no idea what he wanted of her. She wished he hadn't mentioned Sibelius.

"Well," he said, and he lifted his feet off the coffee table. "Let's hope for the light at the end of the proverbial tunnel, right?"

She had no idea what he was talking about. She could hardly bear it any longer.

"Okay." He rose; he was taller than Heinzl. "You're from Holland originally, aren't you?"

She nodded.

"If you want to go home, I'll have you repatriated. But before you leave I'd like to have another talk with you about this man." He patted her shoulder. "Take it easy now. I'll see to it that they won't bother you any more. Charlie!"

The door sprang open. "Yes, General?"

"Get an escort for this girl, as far as the gate. I'll want to see her again before she is repatriated." He walked away, into the bedroom.

The American Quaker was waiting for her on the veranda. "Come," he said, concerned, "I'll take you back to the ambulance."

"Hold it," the general's officer said. "You'll need an escort." He whistled and gave orders; four soldiers with guns joined them. "All right. Let's go."

She went down the steps to the path; as she felt the gravel under her feet, she could no longer hold back her tears. The soldiers escorted her out of the camp; the Quaker put his arm round her shoulders, as he had this morning, saying, "All right, all right, everything is all right now, you're safe."

*   *   *

"Come on, chaps," George said, "let's get organized. Bonny and I will take the jeep and have a look at the town. Len, you take charge of preparing the ambulances for action. Harry, you check the first-aid kits, we may have to fan out and work in pairs, once we get there. François, arrange with the Red Cross for a truckload of emergency rations; let's divide them among the ambulances. Oscar, see if you can get a load of clothing, shoes, blankets, the works, and remind them that we're likely to meet both sexes, so not just men's clothing as we were given last time. Barry, you're good at flanneling the water boys, see if we can't get a tank truck to join us; the first thing to go is always the water supply. All right, Bonny, we'll go and have a look at that town."

On the road to Schwalbenbach, Boniface and George met a column of civilians trudging toward the camp; behind them, in the distance, stood a huge black cloud of smoke, orange and yel-

low at its base with the glow of fire. As they drew closer, they
saw that the column was herded along by Canadian soldiers, rifles at the ready, who waved as they passed. The civilians
seemed to be in shock; they trudged along with staring eyes and
faces without expression.

"They must be the general's visitors to the crematorium,"
George said. "I heard him give the order."

"Did you see those faces? I wonder what the town's going to
be like."

"Well, we'll soon know."

The smoke, bellowing black and greasy from the buildings at
the end of the road, was shot through with red flashes. Over the
sound of the jeep's engine they could hear the rumble of explosions.

"They aren't still shelling, are they?" Boniface asked.

"No, I think those are just exploding gas mains and collapsing
houses. It was the same in London during the blitz."

They entered the outskirts. It seemed unlikely that anyone
could be left alive in the ruins of Schwalbenbach. The city was
like a colossal funeral pyre. As far as they could see, every house
was burning; the air crackled with huge sounds of fire, the heat
was almost unbearable. All around them, the thundering crashes
of collapsing façades made the ground shudder. The tires
crunched on broken glass; as they turned a corner, they found
the road blocked by a mound of masonry as high as a house.
People were digging at its base, clearing away the rubble with
their bare hands.

"Let's find out what's going on there," George said. "There
must be people buried under that lot."

He stopped the jeep and they joined the people who were digging. Nobody seemed to notice; all of the diggers looked as if
they were in shock, like those they had seen on their way in.

They started to help removing the rubble. Lumps of masonry,
blackened timbers, the smashed statue of a saint—the building
must have been a church. They managed, together, to lift a
heavy beam and uncovered a hand. Small, slender, so white with
dust that they assumed it to be another statue until George spotted a gold ring on one of the fingers. They dug the body from the
rubble. It was a woman; when they uncovered her head, they saw
she was a nun. Her face, eyes closed, white with dust, looked serene, as if in prayer.

A man's voice called in German, "Here, everybody! We have found the entrance!"

At the base of the mound a hole had been dug; at the bottom of it three men were trying to lift a heavy hatch. Boniface and George came to their aid; together, they managed to pull it open. Once they had done so, nobody dared descend into the black hole.

"Hello! Anybody down there?" one of the men called.

Another said, "Hush! Listen . . ."

From below came a sound. The crying of a child. One of the men switched on a flashlight and lit up a flight of steps leading down into the darkness of the crypt. He went in, Boniface and George at his heels. At the bottom of the steps they hesitated. It looked as if there were no one in the dark, echoing vault except the child crying in the distance. Then the flashlight shone into the crypt and revealed rows upon rows of people, sitting or lying on the stone floor, motionless, frozen with shock. They appeared to be alive, yet none seemed to be conscious. Old women, young women, children; dressed in coats, nightgowns, sheets; groups of them huddled closely together; all of them covered with white dust, all of them staring straight ahead, petrified.

The three men slowly walked through them toward the crying child: a little girl, all alone on one of the tombstones. In her arms she held a toy horse.

A woman's voice behind them said in a singsong, "Praised be the Lord! Praised be the Lord! Praised be the Lord!" The beam of the flashlight swept past the staring faces until it found her. She was a nun.

* * *

Laura awoke and tried to sit up, but she felt so drowsy that she slumped back on the bunk. Then she heard a tremendous roar and managed to get to her feet.

She peered through one of the little windows in the back doors of the ambulance and saw, in the nearby field, a huge yellow bulldozer with a sort of scoop digging a long trench, pushing the earth before it. Then she saw a column of civilians, men and women, being driven toward the camp. She thought they were prisoners as she saw them pass through the barrier; but later they came back, still escorted by soldiers; some were weeping. It was a strange business; they all looked stunned.

She went back to the bunk and sat down, her hands in her lap, eyes closed. She was all alone now. There was no one to hold on to, she had lost her entire world—Heinzl, the bungalow. The ambulance in which she was cooped up stifled her, yet she dreaded the moment when the doors would open and she would be forced to go out. What was to become of her? She remembered the general telling her that she would be sent home. But home had been the bungalow, and he had taken it away.

Sooner or later she would be on her own outside, in a world she did not know. Then what would she do? What on earth would she do? She was overcome by longing for Heinzl. It became so bad that she jumped up and went back to the little window. The lumbering yellow bulldozer had almost disappeared in its own trench, pushing huge loads of black soil up the slope at the end of it, like a beetle. The sun had set; the sky was turning green in the twilight of the moors. It would linger for a long time, then night would rise slowly until it had darkened the sky. She was sitting on the bunk, lost in reverie, when she heard a loud, chugging roar. She went back to the little window; the bulldozer came lumbering toward her, its empty scoop lifted high, a soldier in a slick green cape at the wheel. Noisily it clattered past and vanished from sight. The roar of its engine died away.

Where was Heinzl now? It could not be that he had just dissolved into nothing in that empty green sky. Or was that all there was, a dark emptiness into which people's souls vanished without a trace? Again she felt, as she had while she was asleep, that Heinzl was still near her, alive, aware. There was nothing scary or sinister about it; it was not his ghost or something; it was an awareness of his presence, the knowledge that somehow they were still together, wherever he might be now.

How she yearned to join him! To escape, the way he had, from the future that now terrified her! How stupid, how idiotic not to have swallowed that capsule! If only she still had it . . .

She wandered back to her bunk and sat down again, her hands in her lap. They were the youngest part of her. She had never liked them. But Heinzl had. Suddenly, there he was on his knees in front of her, kissing her hands. She jumped up and wandered back to the little window. She was tempted to open the door and face the future now. But what was that sound? Singing? It could not be. Yet there it was: singing by many voices, a choir.

She held her breath and listened, certain she was imagining it; but it drew closer, a choir of male voices approaching from the camp, together with the chugging of the bulldozer. She pressed her cheek against the glass, trying to look sideways, but she could see nothing. The singing grew louder, as did the roar of the bulldozer, and suddenly there they were: a column of men in uniforms she had not seen before, slowly marching four abreast, singing in a strange language. Then she wanted to close her eyes but could not; the ghastly spectacle that followed the marching men was so compelling that it forced her to look. From the scoop of the bulldozer, now lifted high, dangled spindly arms, stick-like legs, death's-heads.

The huge machine lumbered past. The green-sheathed driver was now wearing a white pad over his mouth and nose. The singing was drowned by the roar of the engine. It slowly diminished as the bulldozer with its gruesome load drew away and lumbered toward the trench in the field. The singing men lined up along the edge. Then out of the camp came a column of prisoners, hundreds of them, in their blue-and-white-striped suits. They lined up behind the choir; at a sign from an officer, the driver of the bulldozer pulled a lever, the scoop tipped, the corpses tumbled helter-skelter into the trench, out of sight.

The engine stopped. The sound of the singing came across the field. It was beautiful; Heinzl had had a record that sounded just like it. Suddenly she longed to open the door to listen, but she did not dare. She watched the bulldozer as it turned cumbersomely around in the field and came back, its empty scoop lifted high, followed by the choir, now silent. Who were those men? There they came, in their long greatcoats, followed by the prisoners in their convict suits.

Afraid to be seen, she sat down again on the bunk, hands in her lap. Suddenly, there he was, kneeling in front of her, lamplight glinting on his naked shoulders. 'Laura . . . love . . .' He lifted his head, lips parted. So real was his presence that she fell back on the bunk. The engine roared past and drew away into the silence.

Exhausted, she lifted her legs onto the bunk and was drifting off to sleep when with heart-stopping suddenness the doors were yanked open. She lay stock still, eyes closed, pretending to be asleep. She heard someone climb into the ambulance, sensed he bent over her. She hoped the pounding of her heart would not be visible in her throat. He remained bent over her for a long time; then, making as little noise as possible, whoever it was went out again and closed the doors gingerly. She lay still for a long time; he might be watching her through the little windows. Finally she peered through her eyelashes.

The two small, wedge-shaped windows were empty. It was getting dark. In the distance the roar of the bulldozer started up again. There came the mournful choir again, singing that heart-breaking song. It drew her irresistibly to the little window; it seemed as if the choir was crying for Heinzl, for Siegfried even, who had only been obeying orders too.

The bulldozer, its raised scoop with dangling limbs outlined against the darkening sky, lumbered past on its way to the trench. The silent column of prisoners followed. She waited until the last of them had passed, then, her heart in her mouth, she opened the doors of the ambulance and jumped out. Under cover of the falling night she followed them to the trench. She went as close as she dared, saw the giant arm that raised the scoop slowly being lowered, then there was a snort from the engine, the scoop dipped and bodies cascaded into the open pit. It was a terrible sight, and the choir sang for all of them; suddenly she was seized from behind. A hand covered her mouth, her wrists were grabbed and pulled behind her back. She was pushed into the middle of the crowd of prisoners on their way back to the camp. Nobody looked at her, they all walked with their heads bent, shuffling. The hand that covered her mouth trembled; she realized that if she wished she could break free and scream and bring the Quakers running, the soldiers, the general; but something inside her betrayed her, something to do with Heinzl. As if, in some way, they were taking her to him.

Slowly, shuffling, the mass of prisoners passed through the gate. Then, half-conscious, yet aware of what was happening to her with disembodied clarity, she was taken behind one of the barracks and thrown to the ground. Her clothes were ripped off; she struggled and cried, "No! No!" Then, with a shriek of pain, she felt that her chest was being scratched; a voice hissed in German, "Whore, whore! Filthy Nazi whore! You spread your legs for the SS while they were killing my child! This is for *her,* you slut! This is for *her!*" She shrieked with pain as lashes lacerated her breasts, then something was being done to her hair, a searing pain, a sudden coldness; she was dragged away by her legs amid a murmuring mass of people. She thought she was being dragged to the crematorium, but they hoisted her to her feet, slammed her against a post and tied her to it. It must be the execution post Heinzl had told her about, to which all those people she had heard being shot had been tied. This was it; now she herself would be shot. It would hurt, terribly, but Heinzl was waiting for her, of that she was certain. Even as she cried and wept and begged for mercy, she knew that this was the only way, that she never could have lived on without him, that she was about to join him on the other side, wherever that might be. There was an acrid stench as they slapped something on her head. It was tar. Instinctively, despite her panic, she shut her eyes; then she realized that within moments she would be dead anyhow. "Heinzl!" she whispered. "Heinzl, Heinzl!" She felt the tarbrush rub her stomach, her pubic hair. The voice hissed, "That's what you would like, wouldn't you? For us to kill you! No, you filthy whore! You shall live and remember Annelieshchen!"

"No, no!" she pleaded. "Oh, please, let me go, let me go, please let me go . . ." The tar bit her skin, burned her tongue, its stench choked her, she gasped for breath. "Please, please!" she wailed. There was no answer, only whispers, the sound of shuffling drawing away. 'God,' she prayed, 'God, have mercy, for the sake of Thy only begotten Son, let me die now, let me die, let me go to him, let me go . . .'

But there was no answer, only the roar of the bulldozer, far away.

*   *   *

Boniface Baker ran breathlessly through the gaps between the tanks, the half-tracks, the mobile guns, the trucks, toward the Friends' ambulances. "George! George! They got her! They got Laura!" A prisoner in striped overalls was standing by George's truck; he recognized Dr. Wassermann. "Doctor! They—"

"Yes," the doctor said, "I know. You'd better bring a blanket."

"What happened to her? Is she . . . ?"

"No," the doctor said, "she is not dead. At least not when I last saw her. Get a blanket and a flashlight. Quick!"

Boniface ran to his ambulance, tore open the doors, grabbed a blanket off the bunk and ran to catch up with the doctor and George, who were hailed at the barrier by the guard; George shouted they were on their way to a patient. What could have happened to her? Boniface's stomach was a tight knot as he entered the camp, silent and ominous in its emptiness. 'Calm down,' he told himself, 'calm down, this way you are no good to anybody, calm down.'

"Did you bring the light?" the doctor asked.

George flicked on a flashlight, the feeble beam groped ahead of them.

"This way."

They turned the corner of one of the dark barracks and doubled back; Boniface was bewildered. "Where is she?" Then he stood still, his eyes wide with horror.

The lantern beam had caught in its faint ribbed light a naked body tied to a stake, slumped forward, head down, dripping blood. The body stirred, lifted its blind head at their approach. Then he saw it was she. Her hair was gone, her head and face and chest were covered with blood. "Laura!" He rushed toward her and smelled that it was tar, not blood. Despite his relief, he was overwhelmed with disgust as he saw what they had done to her. They had tarred her head, her face, her breasts, they had even tarred her pubic hair. What hung from that post was a whimpering, sickening obscenity.

Together with others, he undid the rope; she slumped against him. He tried to support her, but she was slick with tar and slipped from his grip. George caught her as she fell; together they supported her. They wrapped her in a blanket and Boniface started to wipe her face with a corner of it, but the doctor cried, "Don't! You'll burn her skin! Take her with you and clean it off properly."

They supported her as she walked, slowly, drunkenly, to the barrier. When finally they reached it, the guard challenged them again.

"What's up, buddies?" To Wassermann he said, gruffly, "No prisoners allowed at the gate. Get back to your barracks, please. Now, who's this—this person?"

"Our patient, old chap," George replied, in his British officer's voice. "We are taking her to the ambulance."

"Oh. All right . . ." The soldier seemed uncertain, but the sight of the tar-covered head made him stay where he was; it must look like blood to him too.

George opened the ambulance doors, they helped her inside, stood for a moment holding her, not knowing what to do with the tar-covered body, then George said, "Wait!" He pulled a rubber sheet from the rack and spread it on the bunk. "Gently, now . . ."

They lowered her; again she slipped from their grasp and fell clumsily, her legs half off the bunk, her horrible black skull rolling back and forth in agony.

"I'm going for help." George left.

Boniface was alone with the moaning body. He lit the lantern, then he sat down beside her, took her hand and said, "You'll be all right, Laura. I know it's terrible, but you'll be all right. Believe me, you'll be all right." Someone opened the doors and shone a flashlight inside; it was George, accompanied by an officer. They climbed into the ambulance; the officer said, "I'm Dr. Howard. Now, what have we got here?" He bent over Laura. "Well, you're a mess, aren't you?"

"Is there anything you can do to get that stuff off her?" George asked.

"Yes. Lard would be best. Go to the Red Cross quartermaster and get plenty of it. Also a couple of rolls of cotton wool. Or have you got that here?"

"Yes, we have."

"All right then, go get the lard and I'll have her cleaned up in a jiffy. At the same time you might call Sergeant O'Henry for me, please. Tell him to bring our bandage kit." He took her pulse and said lightly, "Well, well, they scratched you up pretty badly too, didn't they? Now, whatever you do, my dear, don't open your eyes. They'll be the first thing we'll clean, but you'll have problems if you open them at this stage. And don't open your mouth either. Just stay as you are, we'll see to it. Give us half an hour and you'll be as good as new."

Laura did not react, she just lay there, rolling her head from side to side, moaning.

"Is this all they did to her?" the doctor asked Boniface. "Or has there been sexual assault as well?"

"I—I really don't know."

"Well, we'll check. Usually there is, you know. We've come across these before. I don't know what makes people do this. Some prehistoric thing, I'd say. All right, dear, all right, calm down, you'll be all right. Just give us a little time and we'll have you cleaned up. Then a good night's rest, and tomorrow your only problem will be that your hair is a little shorter. Maybe you won't even mind that."

He kept up the reassuring patter until George returned with a stocky medic carrying an armful of bright yellow cubes. "This is marge, Doc," the medic said. "they wouldn't let us have any lard."

"Never mind. This will do just as well." Howard turned to Boniface and said, "Now, please, the sergeant and I would like some elbow room. And I'm sure the lady would like some privacy too. Just leave her to us and we'll have it done in no time. Thank you."

Outside in the night, George and Boniface were joined by somebody in a hurry. "Good evening. The general wants to see Billy Sunday. Is he around?" It was the general's sidekick.

"Who?" Boniface asked, puzzled.

"Ah, there you are. Would you please come with me? He wants to talk to you about this girl. I gather there have been problems."

Boniface followed him back into the camp, to the cottage, where the general, in jumpsuit with *NOTRE DAME,* lay on the couch, drinking from a bottle. "Charlie, stay around while I talk to this man. What's happened now? I hear they got hold of the girl. Is that so?"

"Yes, General."

"What did they do to her?"

"They cut off her hair, tarred her and tied her to a stake. I don't know what else they did."

"The bastards." The general took a swig from the bottle; Boniface saw it was champagne with the label *"Hauptmarke-tenderei Lille."* "Is Howard seeing to her?"

"Yes, he is, General," Charlie replied.

"Okay," the general said. "What are you folks planning to do with her?"

"I don't know, General," Boniface replied. "I suppose we'll look after her until she's able to function again."

"Where? Do you have a place to look after people like her?"

"We haven't thought it through yet. But we'd better hang on to her and take her along with us, for she can't stay in the camp. And she can't be repatriated either."

"Why not? I gave the order!"

"I know you did, but it won't work. If this is what they did to her in the camp, you can imagine what they would do to her at home. I was told her father should stay away; well, so should she. What's more, she has no home left. I've been there. It's been sold to other people, after the neighbors picked it clean. What she needs right now is a sheltered environment. She hasn't been outside this cottage for three years. She should be taken care of, somewhere safe and protective."

The general took another swig and asked, "Hasn't she got any relatives?"

"She has a grandmother in America."

"Is that all?"

"That's all."

"What about the girl herself? Does she want to tag along with you folks, go to America, or what?"

"I have no idea."

"You mean nobody has asked her what *she* wants? What shape is she in right now, Charlie?"

"Sir, they really messed her up."

"Okay, help me off this damn couch."

Charlie rushed to his aid and hoisted him to his feet.

Good God, Boniface thought, for this ranting lush to crash in on Laura in her present condition . . . "General! Please! She is in no fit condition to have visitors; why don't you—"

"Listen, boob," the general said, his face close, with rancid halitosis, "make up your mind: either you're a reverend or you're a doctor. What shall it be?"

"I'm a medic, General, and—"

"So am I," the general said. At his commanding gesture Charlie opened the door for him. He set out toward it, then he turned around, mumbled, "Scuse me" went back to pick up a half-bottle of champagne off the floor beside the couch and stalked out.

Boniface started to follow, but Charlie held him back. "Don't be a fool," he said. "Let him go."

"But she's not fit to—"

"He's the only chance she's got. Sit down."

"But—"

"Sit down!"

He sat down, miserably. To have the poor girl, in her present condition, importuned by that drunken—

"Take it easy," Charlie said. "He may do her some good."

"What do you mean, good?"

"Who knows? She may hit the jackpot. Relax, man! He won't rape her, the place is full of doctors. Anyhow, she wasn't exactly a fly-button popper, last time I saw her."

Boniface closed his eyes and hid his face in his hands.

"Don't knock it, friend," Charlie said coolly. "Right now, Adolf is God around here. God for one night maybe, but God all the same. He'll be back in the saddle tomorrow. So, why don't you relax and wait to see in what mysterious ways God works His wonders to perform? One thing you can bet your life on, though: when it comes to performing wonders, I'm the one who'll get stuck with the job. Glass of champagne?"

Boniface shook his head.

Charlie uncorked one of the live men by the general's couch. "Ah," he sighed, "what wouldn't I give to spend the night with a girl and a bottle of bubbly, and damn the war! Well, here's to Adolf and the woman taken in adultery. Boy, you really got the better of him there! Amazing that he let you get away with it. But don't count your chickens yet, he may still get even with you. Elephants have long memories. Cheers!"

He drank from the bottle, his head back.

Boniface thought of Laura, mauled and broken. There was nothing he could do but wait with a feeling of powerless rage, and watch her captors drink champagne.

*   *   *

She drifted in and out of consciousness, at times underwater, floating, dream-like, among swaying weeds in green, gold-flecked twilight. Occasionally she surfaced and saw faces bent over her, observing her, while hands massaged her body.

She had no thoughts, no words formed in the twilight. She had no feelings, other than the hands on her body and a vague, weepy sorrow that threatened to overwhelm her if she did not let herself slide back into the water, among the waving weeds. Gold-flecked water.

There was a distant noise. Voices. The hands stopped massaging her, a cover was pulled over her. She opened her eyes; her eyelids hurt, her forehead hurt too. The faces were gone. The voices rose in anger. A slamming noise; then silence. Everyone seemed to have gone, but suddenly a new face appeared above her. It was familiar.

The man gazed down on her with an expression of horror and revulsion. He said, "Jesus Holy Christ..." She smelled champagne, and closed her eyes. She did not want to see that face. Tears welled in her eyes, ran down her face. They hurt. God, let him go away! It was not just that the smell of champagne evoked unbearable memories. The way he stared at her made her realize, for the first time, how she must look now.

The door slammed. There were other voices; she opened her eyes. Through her tears, she saw the faces she knew look down on her again. "He made you weep? Good for him! That's what we needed to wash out your eyes. Okay, Sergeant, let's get on with the abdomen. Easy, now. Let's sedate her, she seems pretty worked up."

The hands started to massage her again.

*   *   *

"Charlie!" The general came marching up the garden path, fighting mad.

"Yes, General!"

"Go and talk to Higgins, find out what it takes to get that girl into the United States."

"How is she?" Boniface asked.

The general ignored him. "Get with it! Quiz Higgins, and don't come back without the answers. I want her shipped to the United States; not next month or next year: tomorrow. Go and stamp on his corns. Make him squeal, the Limey shit. Who's been drinking my champagne?"

"It's the matter of her entrance visa, sir."

"Don't change the subject, you sly little runt! Beat it! And take Billy Sunday with you, for all the good he'll do."

"Yessir. Come on, Baker."

When they stood outside on the porch, Boniface said, "I'll go and have a look at her."

"No!" Charlie grabbed his arm. "You come with me! When

he's in this mood you do what he says—at once. He says go and see Higgins, we go and see Higgins. Now."

"Who is he?"

"Our legal officer. By the way, he's English, so watch your step. He's a sticky one."

Captain Higgins was having a late supper in the empty officers' mess that had once belonged to the SS and was now requisitioned by the Army. He was a red-haired satyr with mustaches that bobbed up and down as he chewed. He welcomed them cheerily by lifting his fork, took a swig of beer and said, "Hello, there. Jolly dee of you to join me. What'll it be? Tonight we have the tormenting choice between hot dogs and hamburgers. I've tried them both, and both pong out of the pan. The beer is good, though. If the Krauts knew one thing, it was how to brew beer. Pity we're smashing up their breweries."

"Higgins," Charlie said, "we've a small problem for you. It concerns an entrance visa to the U.S. for a young woman they might consider a security risk."

Higgins' jollity collapsed. "This is an awfully awkward time to snare me with a legal problem, old fruit. Why don't you come and see me in the morning, during office hours?"

"Sorry. Adolf's orders. He wants to know tonight."

"Oh, he does, does he? Napoleon! Join the Hussars and see the pyramids!"

Charlie, unperturbed, explained Laura's case. Boniface was surprised to hear that he had it all, complete and lucid, in his mind. Obviously, the prima ballerina of the general's ballet was more than just a sycophant.

"All right," Higgins said, chewing. "To start with: Adolf can't do anything about this one because it concerns the U.S. immigration service. As a Canadian, he'll have to get used to the fact that there are areas where even he can't do a damn thing."

"We realize that," Charlie said patiently. "But can you give us an idea of what she would need, to get into the States?"

"Oh, yes, I can give you an idea, all right." Higgins wiped his mouth and called for more beer. "She'd need either a visitor's visa or an immigrant's visa. She will not get a visitor's visa, they're not being issued at this time. It'll have to be an immigrant's visa, which means she'll have to be vetted by U.S. security. So she hasn't got a hope. Beer, Corporal! Don't let me languish, boy!"

"You think they'll turn her down because of her history?" Boniface asked.

"You bet your bippy they will. They'd as soon admit the Great Whore of Babylon. So tell Adolf that he can't pull this one. Sorry." The beer arrived.

"You know I can't go back to him with that," Charlie said wearily. "Come on, Higgins, dream up some fancy way of getting her in there. I don't care what it is. Smuggle her across the Canadian border, anything; because if I go back to him without—"

"Take it easy, old chap," Higgins said, and he uncapped the bottle with a plop. "He isn't God Almighty, you know; he is a damned good soldier with a bad case of megalomania. Take away his pistols and his bullhorn, and what have you got?"

"Higgins," Charlie said, "I know all that. Now let's pool our resources and see if we can't come up with a far-fetched device that I can present to him tonight. God willing, he'll have forgotten all about it tomorrow. So get cracking. What other way would there be to get this girl into the United States now? Not next month or next year: now."

Higgins drank, wiped his mustaches and said, "All right. There is one way, as far as I can see offhand, by which we could get her in there without being stymied by their security. Take her to Canada, stick her in a plane, cross the border and push her out, with or without a parachute."

"Higgins," Charlie said, "can it. I may have to face Adolf tonight, but you'll have to face him tomorrow. Get with it."

"All right," Higgins said cheerfully, "let me see. U.S. security would have to obtain their information from the local intelligence in her home town. What is that?"

"Westerdam, Holland."

"Well, the answer is to bomb that source before they give away the details about her. Do you follow?"

"Higgins," Charlie said, with a patience that was becoming impressive, "stop the game. What way is there of getting this girl into the U.S. now? Do you hear? *Now.* I have to go in there and tell him it's done."

"Well, old man," Higgins said, with a grin of satisfaction, "I'm afraid you'll have to commit hari-kiri on his doorstep. It can't be done. He's off his rocker. And so are you, to cater to his delusions of grandeur."

"Bravo," Charlie said, unruffled. "Who governs the entry of

civilians into the United States other than their immigration service?"

"Nobody does. They are supreme. She either has to become a wetback or— Wait a minute! There's one other possibility: she can marry an American soldier. It has to be a soldier."

"Why?"

"If a soldier or an officer wants to marry a foreign female— anything except a Kraut, for Krauts are out—he has to get his general's permission. For his general to give permission, he has to research the background of the female in question, which would be my job."

"Okay, you've done your job. Now what?"

"I beg your pardon? What have I done?"

"You have researched this girl and you advise your general that there's no objection."

"I've done nothing of the sort! I wouldn't know her from Adam!"

"Higgins, cut it out! Tomorrow it'll be you who's called on the mat, so get off your high horse and talk sense. You've researched the girl and she's okay. You inform the general that she can marry anybody she likes as long as he's an American serviceman. Is that correct?"

"One of these days," Higgins said, holding his beer bottle up to the light, "I'm going to write a book about corruption in the British Army of the Rhine."

"So," Charlie said calmly, "you give clearance, the general approves, some American soldier marries the girl. Then what happens?"

"Well, if my scenario is up to snuff, U.S. immigration is informed that MI5 checked the female's credentials, that she is clean, that she married an American citizen, and that she should be admitted to the United States as the legitimate spouse of that U.S. citizen or the citizen will write to his congressman or to Harry S Truman and raise the devil. That should fix it."

"You're sure of that?"

"Good Lord, no, of course I'm not sure! But it's her only chance, as far as I can see. A totally hypothetical situation, mind you. Where do you propose to find an American soldier prepared to marry that tart?"

"I have to present a plan to Adolf, that's all I'm about now. Who would perform the ceremony?"

"They would have to find the proper civil authority. Normal-

ly, that might present a problem, but if an Allied general tells
the *Bürgermeister* of a pulverized German town that he has to
marry an orang-utan and a hippopotamus, he'll do it, on condition there's a town and a *Bürgermeister* left. Now, what else can
I do for you?"

"That'll do," Charlie said. "I think I can work with that.
Thank you."

"Don't mention it, old fruit," Higgins said. "Kiss Adolf good
night for me. And tell him there's a new line in straitjackets he
should try on. So should you, for that matter. You're bonkers,
know that?"

"Night, Higgins."

"Tata, Squirrel Nutkin. Good hunting."

Outside, on the dark parade ground, Charlie asked, "Do you
want to come back with me and see this through, or are you going to back off at this point?"

"No, no, I'll come."

"Right."

The general was on to another half-bottle, otherwise nothing
had changed. "Well?" he asked.

Charlie told him.

"Where the hell do we find an American?" the general asked.
"At this hour of night? Well, it's your baby. Go and find one,
Charlie."

"I did, General," Charlie said.

"Boy! You're really something! Where is he?"

"Right here, General." Charlie looked at Boniface with a
smile.

The general left Boniface no time to recover. He asked, with a
glint in his eye, "You an American citizen?"

"I—er—yes—"

"Fine! That settles it. Is Higgins taking care of the paperwork,
Charlie?"

"I'll go and tell him, the moment we have the details, General."

"Well, hell, you have them! What are you waiting for? Go and
rassle up a *Bürgermeister* and have the two of them hitched before we move on. I want that girl married and off my back."

"Very good, General."

Charlie turned to leave, but Boniface did not move.

"What's the matter?" the general asked. "Don't tell me

you've got cold feet, now you're asked to practice what you preach?"

"I'd like some time to think this over, General."

"Oh, you would, would you? Well, I'd like to be back home! Charlie would like to snort about Toronto in a sports car. And the people who are being burned to a crisp in yonder town would like to have wings. Get out."

"Sorry, but this is a personal decision that I have to think through."

"Are you crazy? You come in here with your collar back to front, smack me across the kisser with the woman taken in adultery; as a result, I'm made to feel that I should do something about that girl, and now you have the gall to say it's a decision you have to think through? Get the hell out of here! You sky-pilots are all the same! Get the hell out, and get married!"

Outside, on the porch, Charlie said, "I wouldn't make a song and dance about it, you know. All it is is a device to get her in. You marry the girl, she's admitted to the United States, you deliver her to her grandmother; six months later you divorce her. So what's the big deal? She won't get another chance like this one. How much time do you think he's going to spend on her problem? Tomorrow he moves on and forgets all about her; then you might as well toss her in with the rest of the corpses. But, look, it's none of my business. I just obey orders. All I've to do now is find a *Bürgermeister;* you take it from there. Happy dreams." He walked away into the darkness.

Boniface sat down on the steps of the porch, trying to gather his wits about him. This went too far. To come to the aid of Laura Martens as they had done this morning was one thing; but *marry* her? Just to enable her to go to her grandmother? It was an outrageous imposition. He was not about to go that far; it was preposterous. There must be another way of getting her into the United States, there must be.

Well, he had better get some sleep. His mind was always clearer in the morning. Surely he would think of something, anything but marrying Laura Martens just to give her his nationality. They would have to find themselves another fall guy.

That was what rankled, the way they had decided the whole thing over his head. He was willing to help her as much as he could, but he'd be damned if he'd let a drunken general and a couple of cynical jokers run his life for him.

* * *

George Weatherby agreed, the next morning, to take Laura Martens with them to Schwalbenbach and see whether they could find someone to take care of her, maybe those nuns. To leave her in the camp was impossible; she still was heavily sedated, she could stay in the ambulance. It was unlikely they would be transporting any patients before they had been able to set up a temporary lazaret.

When they reached the ruins of the church, they parked their ambulances. In the distance throbbed the quivering hum of fires raging in the center of the city.

"She still asleep?" George asked, as they walked to the entrance of the crypt.

"Yes," Boniface replied. "I'll check on her from time to time."

They entered the crypt. There seemed to be more people today, maybe because now there was plenty of light; rows of lanterns had been suspended from the ceiling and attached to the pillars. The day before they had been received by petrified, shell-shocked people; now everybody was moving about. The wounded and the sick lay on blankets or on the bare tombstones; as they passed them on their way to the nuns in the back, some of the patients reached out to them and cried, *"Bruder! Bruder! Bitte, bitte! Um Gotteswillen, Bruder...!"*

It was a harrowing scene, and Boniface felt a momentary impulse to ignore their pathetic pleadings, but he took one of the hands stretched out to him and asked in his best German, "Hello, there, how are you? What can I do for you?" It was an old man on a makeshift stretcher; his hand was cold, he looked confused.

"Oh, but we speak English," a woman sitting beside the old man said. "I'm a teacher. Father speaks English too because he worked in America as an engineer. Didn't you, *Vati?*"

The old man on the litter gazed up at Boniface, unfocused, the way Laura had the night before when she had been given the sedative. *"Hilfe..."* he moaned, *"um Gotteswillen, Hilfe..."*

Boniface lifted the blanket. The old man's trousers were torn and soaked with blood. He put the blanket back, said, "One moment, please," and walked toward the others at the far end of the crypt. Two nuns were helping to put up the emergency equipment and introduced themselves as Sister Ursula and Sister Theresa, nurses.

"I have an old man with an open fracture of the tibia," he said. "We'll have to do something about him soon, there has been loss of blood."

"We'll get to him when his turn comes," one of the nuns said cheerfully.

"But—"

"No buts! He is in God's hands, we must accept His will."

He smiled bleakly and beckoned Len. Together they went to look after the old man.

They labored in the crypt all day long and well into the night. It was extraordinary how the vault with all those people came together as a world apart, dislodged from the total chaos outside. Boniface went to check on Laura occasionally; each time he found her exactly as he had left her: on her back, her face turned to the wall. Toward evening she seemed to awaken; after discussing it with George and Len, he sedated her again rather than allow her to wake up in these frightening surroundings. The longer she slept, the better.

Dawn was breaking when finally they decided they needed a rest. The tank truck had arrived as well as a chuck wagon Barry had managed to wheedle out of the Red Cross, complete with roly-poly cook. They had their meal, sitting on the running boards of their ambulances: soup with noodles and Spam. The cook was stirring something in an enormous pot, sufficient to feed everyone in the crypt; smoke rose home-like from the wagon's chimney. The nuns came out for a breath of fresh air and stayed for soup; Boniface mentioned Laura to them after he heard them refer to a *Hospiz* for refugees and displaced persons they were supposed to take charge of, if it was still standing. They said they would be happy to take her in, anybody was welcome, let them all come, the Lord would provide. *"Koch, gibt's noch etwas Suppe?"* The cook ladled out massive portions; it seemed to give the nuns as well as everyone else a new lease of energy, maybe he had laced it with something, as cooks were rumored to do during battles. After coffee, everybody sprang to their feet and trooped back inside. It was quite light now, sunrise over the ruins.

Before following the others Boniface went to have one more

look at Laura, even though she was sure to be out like a light. He opened the doors of the ambulance, shone the beam of his flashlight inside and saw that the stretcher was empty.

He stood staring at it, dumbfounded, for a moment before he turned away and asked the cook, the only person in sight, "Hey, listen! Did you see a girl run out of here?"

"A girl?"

"A girl in battle dress, from that ambulance. Did you see her make off?"

"Hell, no," the man said. "What was she? A nun?"

"No . . . Never mind." It dawned on Boniface what this meant: groggy with the sedative, she had gone to find a bathroom or a secluded spot and lost her way. There was not a soul to be seen in the wasteland around him, dimly lit by the dawn. "Laura?" he called. "Laura! Where are you? Laura? Laura!"

She could be anywhere. Should he go inside and alert the others? Should they organize a search? But he wandered into the moonscape alone.

"Laura! Laura, where are you? Laura . . . ! Laura . . ."

*   *   *

Demented, half in reality, half in the hereafter where Heinzl was waiting, Laura roamed through the destroyed town, drunk with the sedative they had given her. She wandered aimlessly among the ruins, clambered up and down dunes of rubble, stumbling, falling, scrambling back to her feet, through ghostly valleys reeking of death, calling Heinzl's name. In the end, she was no longer sure she wasn't a ghost wandering among the ruins, whimpering, *'Heinzl! Heinzl! Liebes! Wo bist du?'*

Suddenly, after turning the corner of a ruined house, she saw an old woman in black, staring at a pond. *"Gnädige Frau?"* she asked the woman, breathlessly. *"Gnädige Frau. . ."* But what could she ask her? 'Where am I? Where is Heinzl?' She turned away and ran on, calling for Heinzl; even as she did so, she knew that she had gone out of her mind. Heinzl was dead; she was left behind, alone, lost among the ruins. Why had she run off? She had wanted to go back to the camp. But why? They would kill her. She had nowhere to go. Nowhere at all.

Ahead of her lay the remnants of a broken bridge. She went to where it ended, halfway across the water. She sat down on the edge, feet dangling, and looked down. Below her was the river, glinting in the daybreak, full of dark objects carried along by the current. Refuse. Broken furniture. Dead horses. Human bodies. It was a ghastly sight, yet: one step, and after a brief struggle she would be with Heinzl.

But what if there were no other world in which they would be reunited? What if this was all there was: the river, the swirling bodies? She would be just another corpse carried off by the current. Why had she not taken the capsule when he held it out to her? What had kept her from going with him? The stupid will to live. It had blinded her to the fact that, without him, there could be no life. He had taken it all with him, including herself. As long as she had been with him she had known who she was; now, who was she? She would never be able to answer that question now.

'Come,' she thought, 'jump!' But now she could see the faces of the corpses below. She could not do it. She would end up looking like them. Crazy, for who would care?

The sun rose, the corpses turned into people and she stayed where she was: on the brink of nothing, not knowing where to go, or what to do, other than just to sit there, at the end of the road.

*   *   *

When Boniface reached a river and the ruins of a bridge, he had given up all hope of finding her. But suddenly there she was, outlined against the sky, sitting at the end of a broken bridge, far out over the water. It was a great relief; but as he approached her he noticed something odd in the way she sat there. She seemed poised on the brink of nothing, an image of total despair.

So strong was the impression of despair in the lonely silhouette on the edge of the bridge that he realized there was nothing left for her. No home, no father, nothing. Only the grandmother in America.

He walked down the bridge and sat down beside her. "Hello, Laura. . ."

She did not reply, but went on staring at the river. He looked down and saw what she was staring at: bodies, countless human bodies, drifting by with the stream. It was a scene of such utter desolation that he knew he had to do it, now, or it might be too late. He took a deep breath and said, "Laura, I know you feel there is no way out, no future. But there is your grandmother. In America."

She did not react, but went on staring at the river below. Was it the sedation? Ah—if it were only that . . . But the way she sat there, staring at those corpses, told him that she was at the end of her tether. "Laura," he said, "you *can* go to America. I'll take you there, if you want me to."

She gave no sign that she had heard him. Finally he blurted out, "Laura, would you marry me?"

He regretted it the moment he had said it; it seemed as if everything suddenly hung in the balance: his life, the future, her life.

She slowly turned her head and looked at him. Her face was red and swollen, her eyes were slits, he could not make out the expression on that face. Then she asked, "Me?"

He wanted to take it back now, postpone it. "Well," he said, "it was just a thought."

Then she asked, "What was that? About a grandmother?"

"Well, grandmother. Er—your grandmother. In America."

She stared at him.

"The one who asked us to look for you. She would love to have you, I know."

She turned away and looked at the river again. Finally she said, "I have no grandmother." He was about to protest when she added, "I don't remember anything. I don't know who I am. I don't know where I came from. I forgot it all after—after I came to the camp."

He looked at her, shocked. An amnesiac? No one had mentioned that! In that case, she not only had no future, but no past either, other than the three years with the SS doctor . . . There really was no other solution than for her to go to her grandmother, the only one who could tell her kindly, lovingly, who she was.

"Look," he said, "in order to get you into the United States, we must obtain a visa for you as an immigrant. Tourist visas are not issued at this moment. The U.S. Immigration and Naturalization people . . ."

It suddenly occurred to him what he was doing. There she sat, in the depths of despair, staring death in the face, and he treated her to a lecture on the policies of U.S. Immigration and Naturalization. She was an amnesiac, she needed time to digest the concept of having a grandmother, of starting a new life in America, detaching herself from the only past she knew. What she needed at this moment was to be taken back to the ambulance, put back in her bunk and given time to let it all sink in.

Well, he had, for better or for worse, taken on the general's incredible assignment: proposed marriage to a total stranger.

"Come," he said, "let me take you to the ambulance. It is not far."

He helped her to her feet and put his arm around her shoulders. Walking slowly, he began to lead her back to the ambulances among the ruins.

*   *   *

As she stumbled along, his arm round her shoulders, Laura slowly recovered. It was difficult to switch from looking death in the face to believing there suddenly was hope. There had been no way out, no place to go; now, all of a sudden: *'Laura, would you marry me?'*

America. The first things that came to mind were cowboys and Indians. A horse called Winnetou. But that was what she had told Heinzl when he had urged her to remember. 'What do you remember? Tell me! Anything!' She had answered: 'A greyhound called Caesar, a horse called Winnetou.' It had been nonsense. But was it? She wished she knew. It didn't matter; what mattered was that suddenly a way had opened, out of nothing.

There were the ambulances, the kitchen wagon, the fat cook, and the English Quaker with his little mustache. "I say, is all well?" the English Quaker asked.

"Fine," the boy answered. *'Laura, would you marry me?'* What was his name? An American, that was all she knew.

The fat cook said, "We were worried about you, young lady. Did you get lost or something?"

"Yes, she got lost," the American answered. "Laura? Would you like something to eat?"

She shook her head.

"Hey, listen!" the fat cook said. "How about some waffles and maple syrup? And a cuppa coffee?"

He was the only one who didn't look at her as if he wanted to find out something. *"Ja,"* she said.

"Ja?" the cook asked, heaping something on a plate. "You German?"

"Dutch," the American answered for her.

"Aha, Dutch!" The cook seemed pleased. "Lots of Dutch folk where I come from: Medicine Hat, Ontario. They raise—"

Suddenly, nausea rose in her throat. She turned away, ran behind an ambulance and vomited. She tried to shake off a hand that held her forehead, an arm that supported her; then she gave up and, weak as a kitten, let herself be taken back to bed. There was talking; the two Quakers were standing in the doorway. Someone covered her with a blanket; the whole place seemed to reel about her. God, she was going to throw up again . . .

"Keine Schlafmittel mehr!" a woman's voice said sternly.

She peered through her eyelashes; one of the nuns had joined the Quakers in the doorway.

"Then what do we give her?"

"No more sedatives. Nothing. Just let her recover." Recover. Recover. Recover.

America. Grandmother. She had no grandmother. She didn't want any grandmother. America, yes; grandmother, no. Could she have one without the other? She was so groggy, so tired. *'Laura, would you marry me?'* An American. Indians. Cowboys. A horse called Winnetou.

She woke with a jolt when the ambulance started to move. The motion, when it became continuous, rocked her back to sleep.

* * *

In the driver's cab, on their way back to the camp ten hours later, George said, "Bonny, you're out of your mind! It's one thing for us to help the girl as much as we can, but this is ridiculous! You have let yourself be bullied by the general and his sidekick into something irresponsible."

"It's only a formality, to give her a chance to live."

"She'll live, even if you don't marry her and take her to America!"

"How? Where?"

George talked about the nuns; they would care for her in their *Hospiz* until she was fit enough to go back to Holland, where she could receive proper treatment to cure her amnesia, or whatever it was. George worked himself into a state about it; the more he did, the less sense he made. Finally he asked, "Why? *Why* do this?"

"Because I feel called to do it, I suppose."

"Don't give me any Quaker talk! What does that mean in plain English: 'called'?"

Boniface had had enough. "George," he said, "it is *my* life, and I am entitled to live it the way I want. I won't take any interference from you or anyone else. I want to give this girl the chance to go to her grandmother, the only person she belongs to—"

"How do you *know* that? Have you researched her background, apart from the file they sent us from America and that one visit to her neighbors? Shouldn't you at least find out whether she has relatives in Holland or somewhere else in Europe?"

"If she has, they don't seem too worried about her. Right now this is the only chance she has to get out and I'm going to give it to her. Now will you lay off?"

"Get out of *what?*" George persisted.

"Cut it out, George!"

George cut it out, grumbling. He waited until they had reached the relatively smooth road leading to the camp; then he asked, "Will you promise me one thing?"

"What's that?"

"Will you talk to the prison doctor?"

"About what?"

"For all we know, she may be emotionally damaged to a degree that to take her for your wife, even as a ploy to get her into the States, would be irresponsible."

"Toward whom?"

"Her. You may do her more harm than good. For God's sake, before you go ahead with this, talk to Dr. Wassermann. He seems to know her."

Well, it couldn't hurt; it might even be helpful. "Okay," he said. "I will."

* * *

It was not easy to find Dr. Wassermann in the darkening beehive of the camp. Blackout was maintained, but the activity was still frenetic. Long lines of prisoners were waiting in front of the mobile UNRRA office and in front of the soup kitchens. Everyone looked the same in their striped convict suits; in the dark Boniface couldn't even tell the men and the women apart.

Finally he managed to locate Dr. Wassermann. The doctor was running down the aisle between two rows of bunks in Barracks C, on his way to the lazaret. The stench in the barracks seemed worse than before, the place was just as overcrowded. "Where do they all come from?!" Boniface asked, shouting to make himself heard over the wails, the retching, the delirium of the fevered.

"Reaction!" Wassermann replied, dodging around a stack of bedpans. "Liberation: death! I have more terminal cases than ever! What do you want?"

Hurrying along beside him, Boniface tried to explain; only when he mentioned America did the figure in the darkness stop. "You mean you will take her to *America?* How?"

"As my wife. I'm an American. I'm planning to marry her."

"Marry her? When?"

"Tomorrow."

There was a silence; Boniface braced himself for the same assault the information had provoked from George.

"But—but that's admirable!" the doctor cried. "That's—*ausserordentlich nett!* How does one say it in English? That's remarkably civil of you!" The British understatement sounded bizarre; you had to be English to get away with that kind of thing.

"I'm glad you don't think I'm crazy, or irresponsible . . ."

"Not at all! You—you are a true Quaker! You might be a Jew!" He laughed. "Forgive joke. I think she is a very lucky girl! Quakers are not like Mormons, are they? I mean, you may take only one wife? I could recommend others whose lives would be saved if only they could get to America! I'm sorry, you must forgive bad humor."

"Herr Doktor!" Someone came running and delivered a message breathlessly.

"Sofort," the doctor said. He took Boniface by the arm. "Come," he said. "Here we cannot talk."

They left by a side door and found themselves in an even smellier place, although it was in the open. "Sorry," the doctor said. "It's the only place where we can be sure of a moment of privacy. Tell me what happened."

Boniface explained about the general and Laura's flight and

how he had found her sitting on the ruined bridge, staring at the corpses below. "It had something to do with the way she sat there. I had to come out with it right away, the bit about America, her grandmother. That's why I asked her to marry me: she looked as if she was about to jump in that river."

"I should say so!" the doctor exclaimed. "Had you arrived on the scene a few minutes later, she might indeed have jumped! Schmidt took me to see her in his bungalow a couple of times, and I instantly spotted a suicidal tendency, but—Forgive me, I'm digressing. Now, tell me. What was her answer?"

"Well, she didn't really give me one. She just said she didn't remember any grandmother; in fact, she doesn't remember anything. I got her back to the camp, still under sedation. Did you know she was an amnesiac?"

"Of course! But don't let that stop you, for God's sake! Once she's over the various shocks she has suffered these past days, she'll function quite well. She may not react for a while. She may act like a—zombo? Is that the word? In a trance, sleepwalking. Don't mind that, just go ahead and marry her. Tomorrow, you say? May be too soon. She's apt to be still in shock."

"It *has* to be tomorrow; the Army moves on tomorrow and the general with it. The general is the one who pushed this through with the German civil authorities."

"Pushed it through!" the doctor snickered. "Bombed it through, you mean! *Mein Gott,* they must all be in shock in that town! It's probably highly irregular. Do you think you can make it stick, vis-à-vis the American authorities?"

"The general's legal officer seems to think so."

"Well, it doesn't matter at this stage. Marry her tomorrow, by all means. My God, the lucky girl! On her behalf, let me thank you, from the bottom of my heart. From all our bottoms of our hearts. You are doing a noble thing! Noble! Now I must go and look after my patients. Death waits for no man."

Boniface held him back. "But is it responsible?"

The doctor stared at him in the dark. The stench was sickening. "What do you mean, responsible?"

"My colleague Weatherby is worried it may be a psychotic condition—her amnesia."

"Her amnesia will dissolve eventually, once her life becomes peaceful, civilized. But there's no cause for you to worry yet. For the next few months, until she is safe and secure, she will be—

what do you call it? Quakeress?—an ideal Quakeress. She will do all she can to personify your ideal." Suddenly he seemed to peer at Boniface with a new awareness. "But you will be careful, won't you, to keep it a formality? I mean, your marrying her? Let it go no further! Do you grasp?"

"Doktor Wassermann!"

"O mein Gottchen," the doctor whispered, "even here! Hush!" They waited. The calling voice drifted away. "Listen," the doctor whispered, "I do not have time to tell you her full story, but she is *Dornröschen.* The young girl asleep in the magic forest, the fairy tale, *komm!"*

"The Sleeping Beauty?"

"Ja! The Sleeping Beauty. Marry her by all means, but *um Gotteswillen* do not become emotionally involved!"

"Why? Is she—married already?"

"No, no, nothing like that," the doctor said impatiently. "Look, I do not have the time. You are a noble young man, I wish you well. But for you to fall in love with her would be a tragedy, for both of you."

"You mean, there is a psychotic—"

"I mean: the Laura you will come to know is not the real Laura. The Laura I know is not the real Laura. She herself does not know the real Laura. Who she has been, so far, is the Laura Dr. Schmidt wanted her to be."

"I don't understand."

"O lieber Herrgott! How can I be expected to give you a full diagnosis in a latrine, with people dying all around us? Look: the very day she arrived in the camp she suffered an emotional trauma of such severity that it brought about a state of amnesia that has stayed with her all these years, despite Schmidt's efforts. Well—imagine the trauma to be turned from the daughter of a devout Quaker into the sexual serf of an SS officer! But there was no trauma, because her amnesia had cut all ties with her previous identity. She adapted instantly and became his creation: the image of a faithful, submissive *nette kleine Hausfrau."*

"You mean, in order to save her own life?"

"In the first instance, maybe; but in reality she adapted in order to acquire an identity, to be somebody, not just a blank. But while she was turning herself into the Laura Schmidt wanted her to be, the true, real Laura was in hibernation. The core of her personality had withdrawn into some inner sanctuary, some sub-liminal cavern of the self."

"Doktor Wassermann!" It was the same voice, more desper-ate this time. *"Doktor Wassermann, sind Sie da?"*

"Ja, ich bin hier!"

"Verzeihung, aber meine Mutter . . ."

"Um Gotteswillen: ein moment, bitte! . . . Sorry," the doctor whispered. "I must go. But do realize this: Schmidt is gone. She is spinning like—like a kite that has lost its string. Now you come and say to her: 'I will marry you. Only to take you into the United States.' But she will see in you not the man who will take her to America, but the man who will give her a new identity, without which she cannot function in the long run. She is a cha-meleon. Schmidt wanted *eine nette kleine Hausfrau,* she became *eine nette kleine Hausfrau.* Your ideal may be Florence Night-ingale, or Greta Garbo; whatever it is, she'll adapt to it instantly. But beware: inside that girl a time bomb is ticking away—"

"Doktor Wassermann! Meine Mutter!"

"ICH KOMME!" He turned to go; then he put a hand on Boniface's arm. "Beware! Once the girl starts to awaken, there will be a change of behavior, violent changes of mood, even physical violence is possible. Take her to her grandmother in America; there, arrange for professional psychiatric treatment, and flee. Flee, Mr. Baker!"

"Herr Doktor! Ich glaube sie ist tot!" The voice broke in a sob.

"I must go! Goodbye." The doctor ran off in the darkness

"And without me?!" Boniface called after the receding shad-ow. "What would become of her without me?"

The silence was so long that he thought the doctor had not heard him; then the answer came from the darkness: "In her pre-sent condition, Mr. Baker, she'd jump off that bridge without you. Any bridge. So: marry her tomorrow! And many thanks, on behalf of all of us!"

Boniface slowly made his way out of the camp. The doctor's parting remark left him no choice—he had to go through with it. Not as an instrument of God; any decent human being in his po-sition would have to do it, if he wanted to adhere to the basic val-ues of a civilized society like America. Europe right now was a jungle, like the camp and the town on a larger scale: disintegration, greed, lawlessness, cruelty. She would simply perish if she were left to survive in that jungle on her own.

As he found his way through the throng of stinking bodies milling in the square, he no longer felt like a pawn of the general and his cronies. She could only be salvaged by an American, and it just so happened that he was the only American around. No big deal, to save this poor girl merely by giving her his nationality. It was no heroic deed, but neither was it irresponsible, that much he had picked up from what the doctor said. As to the man's warning not to fall in love with her, that seemed pretty unlikely. Poor girl—with a face like a boiled beet, those eyes like slits, that hair like a clipped poodle—no, that was one danger he could discount. He was as prone to falling in love as the next man, but not with that sad, soiled creature. For the way she looked might be temporary, but he would never forget that, willingly or unwillingly, she had been an SS officer's concubine for three years. It did not bear thinking about, and he felt deeply sorry for her; but when it came to falling in love, that man would forever be hovering in the background. He hadn't given her SS doctor any thought so far, but he could picture him clearly: a bull-necked, monocled, bald-headed sadist, reading Schiller and Goethe while torturing helpless people to death; a monster who set a police dog on poor wretches. Love was said to be an irrational emotion, an instinct made palatable by romance and tradition; but he could not see himself falling for the ex-mistress of such a monster.

He had better make his position clear to her before they went through that phony ceremony. There were a few other things he should explain; she should know what she was doing when she said "I do" or whatever they were supposed to say in German. He could not have her go through the ceremony like a mindless doll.

He was about to enter the ambulance where she lay sleeping when George Weatherby accosted him in the darkness. "Bonny?"

"Yes?"

"What did the doctor say?"

"He said it's okay."

"You are planning to go through with it?"

"Tomorrow, fourteen hundred hours. I'd like you to be one of the witnesses. The other will be Charlie what's-his-name, the general's man. I spoke to him an hour ago."

He went to open the doors, but George held him back. "Look, Bonny, I know it is not my responsibility as the leader of this unit, but I feel it to be my responsibility as a Quaker. The wedding ceremony contains a vow—"

"It's not going to be a marriage after the manner of Friends, George. A civil ceremony, only to obtain a piece of paper. I'll divorce her as soon as I can."

"Bonny, the ceremony is sure to contain the words 'to love and to cherish, in sickness and in health, until death do us part.' As a Friend, how do you feel about making that vow, knowing you are going to break it? Knowing that one of our Testimonies is never to swear an oath? Answer that. Please."

Bonny was silent for a while, trying to restrain his anger. Then he said calmly, "In that case, you had better not be a witness." He knocked, opened the doors and climbed into the ambulance.

* * *

It was dark; the two little wedge-shaped windows in the back doors were deep blue, with five stars in them: two in the one on the left, three on the right. She was lying on her back, her hands under her head, still half asleep, when there was a knock, the doors opened and the top half of a man with a lantern appeared in the opening. "Laura? May I come in for a moment?" She couldn't see who it was, but the voice was familiar.

He climbed in, sat down on the bunk opposite hers and put the lantern on the floor. "How are you feeling, Laura?" he asked. It was the American.

"I'm fine," she said cautiously. Had it been canceled? He sounded odd.

"That's good. There are some things to discuss that are pretty important and urgent. It's necessary that you understand the situation clearly before you go through with it."

So it was not canceled, but he sounded business-like, distant. She wondered what had changed. Last time he had been very concerned about her, his arm around her shoulders.

"Are you well enough to take in what I'm saying to you?"

"I'm well enough." Best to listen to his voice and watch his eyes. That's how Heinzl had always given himself away: by his voice and his eyes. Never mind what he said.

"All right, then. First, I'm sorry I rushed at you with that proposal of marriage this morning. You must have wondered if I'd gone mad."

No, she hadn't. Or had she? Somehow, though, it was not a very nice thing to say. Something had happened. Perhaps it was canceled after all, and he was trying to break it to her gently.

"Now, this is the situation. As far as we know, at this moment, you have no other relatives than your grandmother in America, who asked us to look for you and your father. She is the logical person for you to go to, because for a variety of reasons it is not possible, right now, for you to return to Holland. Now, are you prepared to go to America?"

"Yes," she said. So, not canceled after all.

"Right. Now, the only way you can enter the United States, as things are now, is by marrying a U.S. citizen. I happen to be one, and I'm prepared to give you my nationality. Okay?"

"Thank you," she said. Was that what he wanted to hear? Anyhow, it couldn't hurt, to thank somebody.

"That's not necessary; any man in my position would do this for you. It's no big deal—all I'll be doing is to give you a preferred immigrant's status by marrying you. But the moment you are in the States with your grandmother, I'll start divorce proceedings. Is that clearly understood? It's going to be a marriage of convenience, a formality, nothing more. You understand that, do you?"

He sounded so stern now that she whispered, "Yes . . ." He was beginning to frighten her. What *had* happened since this morning? Had he heard something? Seen something? Her face! She remembered the man who had looked down at her as she was being cleaned up, his horror and revulsion, the way he had said 'Jesus Holy Christ' . . .

"Do you understand what I'm saying?"

"I—I understand," she whispered. Whatever he said was all right, so long as she did not scare him away. It suddenly became real: America. She would go to America unless she scared him away.

"I do want to make something else clear. I won't take advantage of the situation. Do you understand?"

She did not. She was about to say yes, but maybe it was better to be truthful. "Not really," she said, in a small voice.

"What I mean is: you need not be afraid that I'll bother you. I mean, expect any physical attentions from you. This is strictly a device to get you into the States, and nothing more. I am saying this so there will be no misunderstanding. Know what I mean?"

She knew what he meant: 'Jesus Holy Christ.' She wished she had a mirror. "I understand," she said.

"Okay," he said. "The ceremony is set for tomorrow afternoon, fourteen hundred hours—two in the afternoon. It will be performed in what is left of the town hall in Schwalbenbach. The general's aide-de-camp has been able to find an acting burgomaster prepared to do it. It will be a mere formality, but enough to get you your visa—we hope. We will get the rest of your personal documents later from Westerdam: birth certificate, parents' wedding certificate and so on. For the time being, MI5 will guarantee your identity."

Westerdam. Heinzl had never mentioned that name. So they knew where she came from. She didn't want to know. She didn't want to know anything other than that he would go through with it tomorrow. He was mad. He might come to his senses. She had better say yes to anything. America . . . She probably was going to wake up tomorrow and discover she had imagined it all.

"Any questions at this point?" He rose and picked up the lantern.

"Would you—would you have a mirror?" She asked it unthinkingly, but it was too late now. "A—a small one," she whispered. "Just for one moment . . ."

He was silent. She could not see the expression on his face. Why had she asked that stupid question? Why remind him of the way she looked?

"I'm sorry, I don't carry a pocket mirror," he replied. "But one of the others may. I'll go and find out." He went to the door, hesitated, and from a shelf picked up something which he put on the floor beside her. "Here's a flashlight. There's a rear-view mirror in the cab of this ambulance. Use that." He opened the doors. Standing in the blue square of the night, he said, "I wouldn't worry if I were you. You don't look too bad. And it's only temporary. Good night." He closed the doors after he left.

She felt reassured. His business-like gruffness had been a sham. He was a sweet man. He must be; she remembered how he had found her on that bridge, how kind he had been, kind enough to ask, *'Laura, would you marry me?'* She had not understood that it was to be a formality to get her a visa for America, she still didn't quite understand and she didn't care. As long as she didn't scare him away. As long as it wasn't canceled at the last minute, tomorrow. She shouldn't take any risks between now and fourteen hundred hours tomorrow. She would not go and look at herself in a mirror. She didn't want to see what she looked like; she might lose confidence altogether. Seeing reality was not going to help; she herself had to keep the dream going: tomorrow Laura Martens from Westerdam would become Mrs.— She didn't know his name! She should have asked him that, instead of the stupid request for a mirror. She was going to be Mrs. Somebody at fourteen hundred hours tomorrow, and she had no idea who.

Suddenly, sorrow hit her, so deep that she almost cried out in pain. Heinzl, Heinzl . . . !

She did not grieve about never having been given the chance to become Laura Schmidt. It was the thought of him somewhere, alone, bewildered, lost in space, or hell, or wherever he was. She felt, for a moment, the urge to stay behind, to say, 'I don't want to go to America, I want to stay with him.' But that was nonsense. Heinzl had gone the way all the others had gone: up in smoke, his ashes blown across the fields, the woods. She could not believe he had been buried with the rest, one of the bodies with the dangling legs in the scoop of the bulldozer. She must not think about that. He was gone. There was nothing for her to hang on to that would do *him* any good; only for her own sake: a grave to go to; some flowers now and then; sit at his feet and whisper and giggle, or just remember how they had whispered and giggled, how they had loved each other.

'I will not expect any physical attentions from you.'

Poor boy. Poor, kind boy. As if she could ever bear to have another man touch her!

"Heinzl," she whispered in the darkness, "Heinzl, it is just a formality. I only go because you are gone. We'll be together again, somewhere, sometime. I know we will."

She knew nothing of the sort. She had whispered it to help hold back the tears. It was stupid just to lie there, crying.

Tomorrow, fourteen hundred hours.

What could she wear? She didn't have a thing . . .

*   *   *

The next day at two p.m. German time Boniface Francis Baker of Media, Pennsylvania, U.S.A., and Laura Martens of Westerdam, Holland, were united in wedlock by the acting burgomaster of Schwalbenbach in the basement of the town hall. Witnesses were François Perseil of the Quaker Ambulance Service, Northern Unit, First Lieutenant Charles Harvey, British Army of the Rhine, and Captain Higgins, ibid.

The acting burgomaster was almost in tears with fatigue or shock or some other emotion connected with the collapse of his world: the *Rathaus* gone, the town gone, the Third Reich about to go, the burgomaster missing and God knew who else. Only he and a clerk of the court were left; both of them looked as if they had not been out of the clothes they were wearing since the beginning of the bombardment of Schwalbenbach that had turned their world into rubble. Part of the clerk's clawhammer coat was burnt, but it did not appear to bother him; the funereal expression on his face must be a permanent one. The acting burgomaster was in bad shape, hands shaking, stumbling over the phrases of the marriage ceremony; it took a prodding cough on Higgins' part to help him over the actual declaration that the couple in battle dress facing him were now man and wife. The moment he uttered those final words, Higgins cried, "Wizard prang!" and slapped Boniface on the shoulder. "Hey, aren't you going to kiss the bride?"

Boniface, bewildered, placed an awkward kiss on Laura's swollen, brick-red forehead.

"Splendid," Higgins said. "Now I hope these Krauts are going to provide me with a copy of the wedding certificate as proof that the deed has been done, or I'll need a blood-stained bedsheet. Will you arrange for that, old fruit?"

Lieutenant Harvey took it all in his stride, made sure the documents were signed in triplicate, and one copy of each went to the groom. "Don't lose those, Baker," he said, "or you'll be in trouble with the Americans. For all we know, the Air Force may be back, or some loony Russian squadron, and blow even this basement to kingdom come. There's a lot of careless bombing going on, right now."

"Don't worry, old man," Higgins said impatiently. "He can always apply for the copies from our files."

"They wouldn't seem too safe either," Charlie said dryly.

"Well, let's get going. Adolf must be chomping at the bit. We're due to roll at fifteen hundred sharp."

"Ta-ta, dears," Higgins said, on his way to the door; to the clerk of the court he said, "Toodle-oo, old sport!" A few moments later their jeep could be heard taking off with racing engine, spraying grit as its tires spun in the rubble.

Boniface, Laura and François felt awkward, alone with the two Germans. The acting burgomaster was now weeping openly behind his desk, his head in his hands. The clerk was unaffected; as they prepared to leave, he stopped Boniface and said, in strongly accented English, "Ze price will be fifteen marks." As Boniface had no money on him, François paid.

Outside, about to climb into the cab of the ambulance, François took Boniface's hand and said, "I do not know about you, but I felt *la Présence* in there."

It seemed to Boniface, at that moment, the height of gentle Quaker lunacy.

BOOK THREE

UNITED STATES

1945

CHAPTER ONE

REBEKAH Baker Friends School, Principal's office," the black girl said. "Who? . . . Just a minute, please." She covered the mouthpiece with her hand. "Philadelphia Meeting for Sufferings for thee."

The spry white-haired woman behind the principal's desk picked up the phone. "Stella Best."

"One moment please, ma'am," the operator said at the other end. "Here comes Mr. Woodhouse for you."

Ma'am! That young woman was certainly not a Quaker. They should do something about these denizens of the world they were bringing in, especially on the telephone, which to many people was the first contact with what some gushing journalist had called "the world's most selfless charitable organization."

"Stella?" The voice had the Olympian quality that only a life-long bachelor could retain.

"Yes, Ethan."

"How is thee, Stella?"

"I'm fine. I just received a letter from my granddaughter. About her and Boniface Baker."

"Ah, yes . . ."

"Thee knows about that, I presume."

"Yes . . . yes indeed."

"Well, it came as a bit of a shock, I must say. Or, let's say, surprise. But I'm delighted that she's safe, and well."

"Yes. Sorry about thy son-in-law, though."

"Oh, yes. Yes, that's very sad. But, at least, Laura's all right.

Who is this Boniface Baker? Any relation of the late Francis, the Wall Street broker?"

"His son. Only child."

"Ah? Well! At least they won't be destitute. The boy seems an enterprising young fellow. He certainly swept her off her feet, didn't he?"

"Thee—er—thee hasn't heard from him personally yet?"

"No. Why?"

"Well, er—there is a report he wrote which I think thee should see."

"All right. Mail it to me. I'm fascinated. Anything to get to know him better."

"Well—er—I thought I might take it to thee myself, considering how unreliable the mails are. As it happens, I have to be in St. Louis next Sunday for a conference. I thought I would come by. Would thee feed me?"

"Of course. Will thee stay the night?"

"No, I'm afraid not this time. I'd arrive—let me see . . . I'd arrive at nine thirty in the morning with the Super Chief; and I am supposed to change trains that same night in Chicago. So I won't be able to stay longer than just a few hours."

"When will this be?"

"Day after tomorrow. Would that be all right with thee?"

"Of course. I'll meet thee at the station."

"Oh, don't bother! I'll take a taxi."

"Not in this neck of the woods thee won't. We adhere to the gasoline testimony, here in Pendle Hill. I'll meet thee with the chaise."

"Oh—oh, all right, then. See thee day after tomorrow nine thirty a.m., if the Super Chief is on time."

"Thee cannot tell me in a few words what the report is about?"

"No, I'd better not try that. The whole thing is rather complicated. Let's postpone that until I see thee."

"All right. Just as thee likes."

"Wonderful, Stella. Bye, now. I'm looking forward to this."

"Yes, yes. So am I."

She put down the phone. Something was wrong. Ethan had sounded shifty.

She rose and walked over to the window. White clouds came sailing over the prairie. The summer wind stirred the leaves of the sycamore trees. On one of the upstretched arms of Becky Baker's statue sat a mockingbird, warbling away in the somnolent afternoon. What on earth could be the matter? What kind of report? It had seemed simple and straightforward: Jacob Martens had died in the camp, Laura survived and married a boy called Baker, a Hicksite Friend from Philadelphia, member of the Quaker Ambulance Service. Had she overlooked something? "Kuala," she said, "let me have the file on my granddaughter, if thee will."

The black girl rose, went to the filing cabinet and brought the folder.

"Thank thee."

The girl, with languorous gait, strolled back to her chair.

"Dear Grandma, how are you? I am fine. You will have heard by now from Bonny or his mother that he and I were married last week. We haven't passed Meeting yet, but that we may do once we are in the United States, there are few Friends here and their Meetings are messed up because of the war. The fact that we married in such a hurry does not mean that we acted hastily, or under the pressure of creaturely urges. There was a practical reason which we'll explain to you once we are in America." Pregnant. What else? A little more than she had bargained for when she asked the Quaker Ambulance Service to look for the girl. But then, what about the "creaturely urges"? Odd term, that; she hadn't heard anyone use it since her childhood, and even then it had sounded quaint. Where had the child picked it up? Jacob Martens had been a fervent Friend, but even so . . .

"We do not know yet when we'll be coming home, it depends when Bonny will be demobbed." Now, what the devil did that mean? Sounded like a tomcat's operation. Probably some British Army word. *"There are rumors that we will be allowed to leave as soon as victory has been officially declared. In the meantime, I am working here in the Hospiz, mainly among displaced children. I act as an interpreter and keep track of deliveries as they arrive from UNRRA. Bonny and I have meeting for worship every day, and sometimes one of the Sisters joins us, or a passing Friend from London. We have many covered meetings, sometimes the Spirit moves among us mightily."* That sounded like a direct quote from George Fox's Journal; could it be the child was a larger-than-life Quaker as her insufferable father had been? She should not think of him in those terms, but good heavens! His letters had been like tracts; even his last Red Cross message had been a sermonette: ten words about his soul, two about his

daughter. *"I am so looking forward to seeing you again. Isn't it a long time ago? I remember the toy horse with the Indian you gave me, ages ago. Of course I have no longer got it, but I often think of it, especially now I am about to go to America."* Nonsense. She had never given the child anything like that. When she had last seen her she was still crawling around in a playpen; she couldn't remember what she had given her, but it couldn't possibly have been that; more likely a teething-ring, or something with bells. *"Well, Grandma, I am going to close. I am so happy that way has opened and that we are about to be reunited. Not just my heart, but that of God in me rejoices. Yours in love, Laura."* "That of God rejoices!" Sanctimonious claptrap! Alas, it sounded as if the child was indeed like her father, worse luck. Poor Lily! How she must have suffered, with her delightful humor and her earthy common sense, belabored daily by that pompous bore! Oh, well. Let's have a look at the other letter, the one before.

"Dear Grandma. You must be surprised to hear from me. I am sure you must have thought I did not remember, for I have had a difficult time which makes me forget things from before I came to the camp. I spent three years in Schwalbenbach. I had a difficult time, but I am all right. My father died there, so they told me. I wasn't there, so I wouldn't know. They told me he died peacefully, because the hard labor was too much for him. There are also other stories, which I do not believe. In any case, he died a saint, so the doctor told me. He was martyred for his faith. The doctor died too. I myself had an easy time compared to others. I never went hungry, I was never beaten or bothered by the dog, and I never had to go to roll-call or show up for Auslese, as this doctor protected me who had taken a liking to me. He is dead now. I was liberated by the Canadian Army, and am part of the northern unit of the Quaker Ambulance Service. We work among the civilians of Schwalbenbach. You may not recognize me when we meet, for I am different from the photograph you sent to the QAS. My hair is short now, and I have gained some weight. But I am fine, Grandma. I must stop, because the page is full. Love, Laura."

Something didn't sound right. Neither letter sounded right. Why? She could not put her finger on it. "Kuala," she said, "come here a moment."

The black girl put down the sheet she had been about to insert in her typewriter, rose and joined her.

"Here." Stella handed her both letters. "Read these, and tell me what thee thinks of them."

Puzzled, the girl took the letters. "Who are they from?"

From any other secretary this would have been a fatuous question. They all listened in on private conversations and read private correspondence. But Kuala was different. She obviously had not read these.

"From my granddaughter."

"Oh?"

"Just read them, dear. Then tell me what thee thinks."

The girl read the letters, slowly, with the earnest concentration she gave to everything.

"Well?"

The dark antelope eyes looked at her with contemplative detachment. "I think they are beautiful."

"Sense nothing wrong with them?"

To her surprise, Kuala pressed the letters against her chest and closed her eyes. Like all Kikuyu women, especially of her exalted class, she had second sight, or believed she had. There was a moment of reverent silence in which, despite herself, Stella waited with something akin to awe for the oracle itself to speak. Then the black eyes opened and rested their limpid gaze on her once more. "I sense a great pain," the girl said.

"What makes thee say that? To me they read like the letters of a child of nine."

"I couldn't say why," the girl replied, and handed back the letters.

"All right." Stella put them back in the file, and rose. "I'm off to the museum to see if I can find that Harrison book." There was no reason why she should go and hunt for the idiotic book at this moment, but she wanted to be alone to think.

"I am sure I sent the book back," the girl said. "I'm positive."

"Never mind, dear. Even the Friends Historical Library can make mistakes. Once they have gotten over the shock, they cannot but rejoice in losing the idiotic book in the mail."

"I found it quite interesting," the girl said tartly.

It was time she fled from the company of her betters. "That's because thee has a noble soul and a forgiving disposition." She went to the door. "Or, as Miss Harrison would have put it, a quaking heart. She would have hated to be asked what exactly she meant by that, I'm sure."

"Why don't we ask her?" Kuala suggested, with a hint of the

imperial condescension to which she had been born.

"Because Miss Harrison, like Jacob Martens, has gone to her just reward. At least, let's piously hope so."

Goodness! Why on earth did she have to drag in her poor son-in-law? He had reached his goal at last, and died a saint. Chances were he had indeed. She should be ashamed of herself. "Martyred for his faith." That was an impressive witness, even if it did not speak to her condition. She probably had that in common with ninety percent of the women of her age, when asked their honest opinion about their sons-in-law.

Hastily, she clattered down the stone steps. The tapping of her heels echoed in the vaulted stairwell. Outside, the mockingbird was flushed from Becky Baker's statue by her opening the front door. With angry protest it fluttered into the trees and vanished.

During the walk to the old Meeting House she was, out of the blue, overcome by one of those acute, heart-wringing bouts of yearning for John. My God! Forty years, and still pining for him as if he had died last month! But she could not help herself; she walked the rest of the way with her face screwed up into a grimace, in an effort to fight back the tears. What was the matter with her? Other widows rose from the ashes like Valkyries, not like half a person, condemned to suffer like a dog for the rest of her living days! Oh, John, John . . . She hurried down the sunlit road faster, sneering at the cringing creature hidden behind her mask of dour virago. This was ridiculous!

She decided not to go to the museum, or anywhere else gloomy and heavy with memories of the dead. Instead, she went shopping in the latest department store that had sprouted on Baker Street: a place called Woolworth's where they sold frivolous junk at flea-market prices. She spent half an hour among the counters, and came out with a TODAY ONLY summer dress, three hands too long but irresistible at the price of one dollar, and a box with a dozen teaspoons made of a new material called plastic, costing five cents. And as she stood waiting her turn at the cashier's, she saw something she might give to Kuala to make up for her bitchiness: an earthenware elephant, bright blue, sitting on its haunches, a length of twine dangling from its outstretched trunk, the ball of twine in its back. Only after she had paid fifty cents for it and was on her way back to the school did it occur to her that perhaps some little devil had prompted her to cock a snook at the sacred black elephants of Africa with this tasteless caricature from Muleshoe, Texas.

* * *

"Dear Stella, how is thee, how is thee!" Ethan Woodhouse
loped down the platform toward her, arms outstretched. Beside
the locomotive of the Super Chief hissing clouds of steam stood
Stella, small and slight, up to her knees in the swirling white
cloud. As always when he saw her, she activated a protective instinct in him. He bent over to kiss her cheek, and she said,
"Good heavens! I had forgotten how tall thee is. How do other
women kiss thee, Ethan? On a stool?"

"Alas, few women feel so moved," he replied, smiling, and saw
in her eyes that her prickliness was a pretense. What a pity he
was carrying that message of doom. Poor creature . . .

"Where's thy luggage?"

"This is all I have with me." He picked up the small suitcase
he had put down to greet her. "I'm only staying a few days in St.
Louis."

"What's going on there?" she asked, as they made their way
toward the underpass among the throng of passengers and the
redcaps with their dollies.

"Oh, one of those conferences. Thee doesn't mean the old
chaise, the smelly one with the sleepwalking horse?"

"What else? It's no more than seventy-five years old. Quite
young, for a carriage."

They emerged from the underpass into the sunlit station
square. Among a row of parked cars stood the yellow chaise with
the black leather top that he remembered from his boyhood. It
suddenly seemed yesterday that he had been taken, a frightened
beanstalk of a boy in plain dress, across this same station square
by his Uncle Peleg to the same yellow chaise, where they had
parted with the words, "Well, follow the Light, boy," and, "Yes,
Uncle."

"Well, well," he said, as he lifted his suitcase into the chaise,
"time has stood still."

"Don't rush to conclusions," she said, "thee'll be amazed how
liberal the school has become since thee and I were eldered together. Remember?"

"Indeed I do," he said, mellowed by the innocence of the past.
"The time I made a mouse with my handkerchief during meeting, and thee giggled. What was it old Master Obadiah called
it?"

"Creaturely activity during the holy silence," she replied, and clambered lithely into the chaise before he could give her a helping hand. She was as nimble as a child; he wished he could say the same. He hoisted himself into the seat, sat down beside her on the hard leather cushion and smelled the scent of the past. It was as if a cellar door opened that had remained closed for years. "Smells moldy."

"It always did." She grabbed the reins. "Back, Betsy, back!"

The old mare obediently pushed the chaise backward. Behind them a Klaxon barked angrily. She took no notice of it, clacked her tongue and slapped the old horse's buttocks with the reins. The mare started to plod down Baker Street.

"Surely this is not the horse we had at the time?"

"Don't be silly. I know thee is a city slicker now, but surely thee hasn't forgotten that horses don't get older than forty, at the maximum? How long ago does thee think it is that we were at school together?"

"Must be fifty years."

"Fifty-four."

"Good heavens. Makes one think, doesn't it?"

Baker Street hadn't changed much. There were a few new signs: REXALL'S DRUGSTORE, TYBORN GASOLINE. But the façades with their nineteenth-century windows were exactly as when he first saw them, through a prism of tears, from this same chaise. Baker Street. The name made him return to reality. How was he going to handle that report? Should he give a general introduction first, to soften the blow? He had to support her somehow, stand by her in the trial ahead. Because that's what it was going to be, alas. He had assisted many people in moments when the love of God and the innate goodness of man appeared to be heinous lies, but this time . . . O Lord, o Lord. He suddenly feared he would fail her. This tiny creature with the huge eyes was still as fey and vulnerable as when he had fallen in love with her at the age of fourteen, with the befuddlement of the awakening adolescent. She had had no eyes for him, though, only for that cousin of hers, big, bumbling John Best. 'What a waste,' he had thought, as a nineteen-year-old, when they invited him to their wedding; and 'What a tragedy' when, four years later, he was told that John Best had been killed during an uprising in Africa, where they had gone as missionaries, principals of a Quaker school. Only much later had he heard what had happened to

Stella herself after the murder of her husband, and he still cringed from the image it evoked. This frail, sensitive, fragile little creature . . . And now her grandchild! He suddenly felt powerless in the face of man's inhumanity to man, even in this idyllic little town, safe in the heart of the safest continent in the world.

They had reached the Richmond Pike. In the distance, at the end of the dark tunnel of trees, he saw the patch of sunlight where the school gate was. Only as they were about to turn into the grounds did he see the old Meeting House on the other side of the road, hidden by the foliage of sycamores, with behind it a glimpse of the sunlit lake. "Stella," he said, "could we . . . Is it still in use?"

She reined the horse and stopped the chaise. "What?"

"The Meeting House. Could we go inside?"

She gave him a searching look. "Why? Does thee think that would be more appropriate?"

"Yes," he replied.

She clacked her tongue, slapped the horse with the reins; after a sharp turn they entered the burial ground of the Meeting House. They drove between tombstones; the noise of the wheels was deadened by the grass in the track. It felt like a secret place where nobody had penetrated for years, except the squirrels, the woodchucks and occasionally, at dusk, a wolf from the prairie. "How long has it been a museum?" he asked, when they stopped in front of the steps to the porch.

"Oh, about forty years. After the death of Grandmother Saraetta." She jumped from the carriage and tied the reins to one of the hitching posts.

He followed her up the steps to the double doors. They were chained and padlocked and carried a sign: HISTORICAL MUSEUM OF THE RELIGIOUS SOCIETY OF FRIENDS.

"In our day they used it to store lumber, does thee remember?"

"Yes," she said, rummaging in her purse for a key.

The padlock clacked open, the chain rattled down and dropped on the floor. "Go ahead." The door swung open.

"After thee, Stella."

She went in, ahead of him.

*   *   *

The moment they started down the aisle Ethan took her arm. It was dark inside; it smelled of dust and cobwebs.

"Here?" He had guided her to the first row of benches.

She sat down, her purse on her lap. She felt a vague, formless fear. That report must contain something terrible, or he would not have come personally and gone in for all this.

"All right," she said, when he sat down beside her, "let me see it."

"In a moment." He kept his hat on; she realized he intended to have meeting. "Come on, man," she said bitchily, "don't look at me as if I had made an indecent proposition! Hand me that report, let's have done with it."

He took off his hat and put an arm around her shoulders. "Stella, I'm afraid thy granddaughter has not been quite open with thee in her letters. I understand the girl made it appear her father had died of natural causes, and that she had had three fairly rough years . . ."

"Well?"

"I don't know of any way to tell thee this gently, Stella. Thy son-in-law did not die like that. He was killed because he attacked his guards, after his daughter had managed to enter the camp looking for him."

Something within her went cold. "I don't understand."

"After he was killed, the German camp doctor took her in, and—and forced her to become his concubine. She lived with him for three years."

For a few moments she stared at him, motionless, horror-struck. Then she said, "How dear of that boy to marry her after all that." She said it harshly, to hide her shock.

"I don't think thee should look at it that way. As I understand it, they merely married to enable her to enter the United States, which otherwise would not have been possible because of her— well, history. Thee is the only one she has in the whole world, and she wanted to join thee."

"Well," she said, "how about that?"

"I wish I could have spared thee this, Stella. Let's hope that, as usual, time will heal all wounds."

That put a halt to the sudden impulse to let herself go and sob on his shoulder. "Oh, I'm sure it will," she said. "Is there anything else I should know before I read that report myself?"

"Well . . ."

"Is she with child?"

That startled him, as only a bachelor could be startled. "Is she *what?*"

"Well, what else is there? Thee had better tell me now, as I'm going to read it anyhow. It's dear of thee to want to help me, but, believe me, I can handle it. So, better let me have it." She held out her hand.

He hesitated, pulled a few folded sheets of paper from the inside pocket of his jacket, but instead of giving them to her he put the papers between them on the seat and took her hand. "Stella," he said, "I did not tell thee everything."

"Oh?"

"Her father attacked his guards because the commandant of the camp raped her in front of him."

She pulled her hand out of his.

"He went berserk, tore himself free, they set a dog on him and then beat him to death."

She wished she had something to hold on to; she was about to be sick. For a moment all she could think of was how to stop herself from being sick.

"Stella . . ."

"Please," she said, "please leave me. For God's sake! I saw my own husband murdered by—" No, not that! She turned her back on him.

"Stella . . ."

"Please, Ethan, please! Please go away! I'm all right. Please."

His hand touched her shoulder, briefly; then she heard his steps draw away, the squeak and thud of the doors closing.

Well, the monstrousness had now engulfed her grandchild. It was as if, with Ethan, the actuality of it had drawn away from her, leaving a dark, tormented rage, a despairing rebellion against the God of Love on whose image she had been reared until her entire concept of life and death had been distorted, rendering her incapable of coping with the monstrousness when it came. Poor, poor child! No wonder her letters had sounded so sanctimonious and odd. What else could she have written? 'Granny, I was raped in my father's presence and saw him clubbed to death, and then I became a whore to the enemy'? Oh, my God! Instead of the image this should have evoked, there was, suddenly, with hallucinating clarity, that monstrous moment: John, in shorts, running toward the wall, trying to vault it, then the shot, that awful stillness for one interminable second, before he slowly let go and thudded down, on his back. O God, mercy, mercy! Mortal terror hit her, she twisted around and saw, beside her on the bench, the folded sheets of paper. She grabbed them and read, *"Dear Ethan Woodhouse . . ."*

And there it was. All of it. This time not phrased with circumspection, but recorded bluntly, explicitly, all of it. The child on her bicycle, determined to find her father. The commandant taking her to a bedroom, where she found her father shackled to the radiator. The German raping her.

She hid her face in her hands, and there came the tears. The tears, the tears, the river of tears, the source of which was a dear body slowly letting go and thudding on its back at the bottom of the wall, among the sunflowers she had planted, in the shorts she had ironed only the night before. Oh, stop it, stop it, hysterical old fool! She jumped up to tear herself loose from that moment, the moment she had been frozen in loneliness for the rest of her living days. Distraught, she wandered aimlessly about the empty hall, past the glass cases full of mementoes of people who were gone forever, like John, like the miserable Jacob, poor martyred saint, like Lily, like young Stella, wife of Dr. John Best, happy, fulfilled, full of tenderness . . . Oh, stop it! Stop it! She banged the lid of one of the cases in despairing rage, and was brought to her senses by the thought: 'Careful!' Rubbing her fist, she looked at the contents of the case, to calm herself. *"First schoolbook on the frontier, reputed to have belonged to Cleopatra Baker, first principal of the Rebekah Baker Friends Boarding School"* . . . A faded, worn shawl: *"Belonged to Lydia Best, martyr of the Shawnee removal, 1833"* . . .

All the mementoes in the case were remnants of past pain: Becky Baker, raped and killed by the Indians; Lydia Best, blown to shreds by the explosion of a riverboat full of Indians . . . all those people, who had seemed so impossibly saintly when she was forced to learn about them as a child, had suffered the "great pain" the black girl had sensed from Laura's letter. And here she herself was, suffering like the rest of them, her life frozen at the moment when the body fell among the sunflowers at the foot of the wall. There must be, somewhere among these dusty mementoes, a *Book of Faith and Practice* that had belonged to him, which she had donated years ago: *"Belonged to Dr. John Best, Quaker missionary in West Africa, killed during the uprising of 1904."* And still he was as real and alive as when she had opened the door and cried, "John! Come back! Come back, John!"

She gripped her purse, walked toward the doors, but suddenly it became too much, too much. She had no strength left, no faith, she could not cope with these horrors, not cope at all. She wanted to flee, remembered the report, went back to fetch it, sat down to read it all again, and slumped, her head in her hands.

That was how Kuala found her. Suddenly she heard the gentle singsong voice ask, "Stella Best? Is thee all right?"

She looked up, saw the antelope eyes, and wished she could free herself of the implacable hatred for those black apes to whom he had devoted the best years of his manhood and who had killed him for his pains, as they would have killed a baboon swinging itself onto that wall. "I'm all right, Kuala," she said hoarsely. "It's just—I . . ." She could not go on. The hatred for them choked her and filled her eyes with tears, until all she saw was a blur standing over her, commiserating. "Here," she said. "Read it . . ."

She watched, immured in hatred and despair, as the black girl, serene and tall in the diffused light, stood reading about little Laura and what they had done to her.

Then she asked, "Well? Thee was right, wasn't thee?"

There seemed to be nothing else to say. The monstrousness was there between them, and she was paralyzed by it. Then the girl said, "Would thee like to have meeting, Stella Best?"

"O God," she said, as the knife twisted in her heart. "Yes . . ."

Kuala sat down beside her. They joined hands, bent their heads and centered down in silence.

Almost at once a great stillness pervaded her. It was as if, in the silence, a shadowy crowd of people joined them, whose love and awareness were all about her. She said, in ministry, "There has been great pain all the way, all the way. When will it ever end?" Then she broke down and sobbed on the lap of the child by her side. As she lay there, crying for John, for all those years when life had been light and full of tenderness and love and promise, she felt a hand stroking her hair, gently, and wished she could kill the devil within her who whispered, "The hand of the apes that killed him."

This was the worst: that his wonderful life of joy and generosity and laughter, the whole radiant, glorious man, had left her nothing but hate, an impotent rage against the animals for whose sake he had squandered his life, the grinning morons who had shot him like a baboon, a thing, that moved one moment and then—*bang!*—it was dead. 'O God,' she prayed, without faith or hope, 'Rid me of it, rid me of this hate, it kills me!'

"Hush, Stella," the girl's voice whispered in the silence, "hush, hush . . ."

With inexorable gentleness, the black hand went on stroking her hair, until all was still and dark within her.

CHAPTER TWO

A few months later a New York City police car, siren howling and blue light flashing, pursued a speeding black station wagon up Hudson Street. The station wagon cut recklessly in front of a bus, ran a red light and caused a panel truck to brake so violently that it skidded. Finally, at the intersection of Hudson and Houston, the police car managed to overtake the fugitive vehicle and block its way, at which the driver gave up and squealed to a stop.

The officer put on his cap, took his pad, got out and approached the miscreant with a marble face. He was welcomed by a roaring German Shepherd of intimidating dimensions trying to smash the side windows of the station wagon with its bare teeth, to leap at his throat. The officer put his hand on his gun; then the window on the driver's side was wound down and he saw a woman in her fifties, wearing a cartwheel hat that was now awry, looking startled and confused. He let go of his gun and opened the flap of his pad. "Well, neighbor? Where's the fire?"

The dog went berserk and roared so deafeningly that the woman could not hear him.

"Get out, lady!" he shouted. "This way it's not going to work!"

The woman wrestled with the frenzied animal as she tried to back out of her seat. "Quiet, Sally!" she cried. "Quiet! Down! Sit!" But the dog obviously was not trained; it took a while before she could get out of the car and close the door.

When at last the woman stood before him on the sidewalk,

panting and flustered, she said, with a nervous laugh, "She can't help herself, really. All it is is playfulness. She failed her final exam because she made off with the red-and-white cane of her blind trainer. Then, during the high-vision test, she pulled him right underneath the ladder and he hurt his head. But she—"

The officer interrupted her. "May I smell your breath, please?"

She gazed at him, flabbergasted. "My breath? Why?"

"Because you drove sixty miles an hour in a thirty-mile zone. You passed two vehicles in violation of the law. You ran a red light and didn't obey my summons to pull over and stop."

"But when was I summoned?"

"As from the tunnel, by visual as well as audio signals."

"By whom?"

"By me, lady," the officer said, his patience wearing thin. "I've been following you for six blocks, siren howling, lights flashing. Don't you know the meaning of those signals?"

"But I couldn't hear you," the woman said, "my dog—"

"You should have seen me!"

"But you were driving behind me!"

"Don't you ever look in your rear-view mirror?"

"Never," she said firmly. "It makes me nervous."

The officer sighed.

"Doesn't it you?"

"What?"

"Make you nervous?"

"No," the officer said. "That's why I'm still alive."

She laughed coyly. "But I'm alive, aren't I? And I have been driving for twenty years!"

"For who?" the officer asked. "The Keystone Kops? Driving license."

"Oh—that's in my pocketbook . . ." She was about to open the door again; the dog looked as if it were licking its lips at the prospect of his succulent calves.

"All right already," the officer said. "I'll look at that later. First I need some information. Name?"

"Martin—Baker. Dorothy Hepzibah."

The dog, behind her, began to roar and bang its head against the window.

"Would you spell that middle name, please?"

"H-E-P-Z . . ."

"All right," the officer said. "Profession?"

"Administrator of the Mordechai Monk Institute for the Blind. Sally is a Seeing-Eye dog, you know. It's a Christian charity . . ."

"Christian charity?" the officer said. "That animal looks as if it fed on Christians! It belongs in a Roman circus, not loose in a station wagon in New York traffic."

She saw her chance, with feminine canniness. "Oh, please, please," she begged. "My son and daughter-in-law are about to arrive from Europe! I was told only this morning that they—"

"Save your breath, lady," the officer said. "I'm not interested in a bunch of rationalizations. Address?"

"Really, truly!" the woman cried, her eyes suddenly full of tears. "Look! There they come!" She pointed at a gray passenger ship with three funnels, sailing up the Hudson.

"That's the *Queen Mary*," the officer said suspiciously. "How come you knew she'd arrive this morning? You have a Pennsylvania license plate, you must have left early."

"Oh, yes, very early!"

"Then how did you know about the ship? Ship movements are classified."

"I know. The lighthouse keeper of Sandy Hook is a Friend—a Quaker, you know. He promised me he would telephone the moment he saw the ship. Well, he did. Now, please may I go?"

The officer refused to be mollified. It took ten minutes before she was allowed to continue; she drove, very slowly, underneath the arches of the West Side Highway to the pier where the *Queen Mary* would be mooring. She parked the station wagon, a bit untidily because there were an awful lot of cars, then ran to join the crowd on the pier, leaving Sally inside having a fit.

* * *

It was impossible to find a spot on any of the decks where they did not have to fight for a glimpse of the Hudson. The troopship was filled to overflowing with American servicemen who, now they were approaching New York, cheered themselves to a frenzy. In the end, Laura and Boniface managed to squeeze through to a rail on the foredeck, and there she caught her first glimpse of the Statue of Liberty.

It should have been a moment of gratitude and joy; he looked at her with religious eyes and said, with emotion, "Well, Laura, we made it! You are home. Let's thank the Lord."

He looked as if he wanted to go into meeting then and there, but all he did was look moist-eyed at the statue. She noticed tiny people among the teeth of its crown, like lice, and was surprised at her own lack of elation or even gratitude. Instead, she had a feeling of unreality, as if the whole thing were a concoction of her imagination.

All the way, from Germany to Manhattan, she had managed to keep up the illusion that she was starting a new life, in a country where no one had ever heard of Schwalbenbach or Heinzl or nuns among the ruins, where she could start afresh as Laura, an American girl. Yeah, yeah; she had had no problem with the language, for although she didn't remember her American mother at all, English had come back to her like a never-forgotten native language. But the slang was new; she had picked up phrases from movies shown on board ship: Bogart saying, 'Park your pants,' and 'She was tryin' to sit on my lap while I was standin' up.' GI life was also new, and very different from Quaker life or life among the nuns. She had guzzled Coke and eaten Moron's Delight, stared at incomprehensible jokes about mule-skinners and the mattress business, and dutifully hooted with the rest of the audience when Mae West asked on the dance floor, 'Is that your gun, officer, or are you just pleased to see me?'

Bonny had told her about his mother and the Institute for the Blind and about her grandmother's school; there had been a time, three days before they were due to arrive, when she had really thought she had swung it, babe: she was word perfect about her own past in preparation of meeting her so-called grandmother, and she had managed to stick to the crucial decision not to think about Heinzl any more, not ever. Heinzl was dead, so was the girl who had become part of him, the way he had become part of her. Finished. Look away, look away, look away, Dixieland. Turn toward the westering sun. Hi ya, schnozzola! A scream in a secret passage: 'What was that?'—'The ghost just saw *me!*' A new world for a new Laura: Jimmy Durante, Bogey, Betty Grable, hi ya sarge, creep into my tent tonight, don't be gloomy honey, God's own country, some of my best friends are niggers, America the Beautiful, the pledge, tears at the first glimpse of the Nantucket light ship, boy, I'm goin' to kiss the ground.

But now, as she stood watching the lice on the head of the Stat
of Lib, the whole edifice suddenly collapsed like a house of
cards; in its stead, there was Heinzl, right behind her, alive,
more real than the yelling crowd around her, more real than
Bonny with his perpetual smile.

'*Liebes, lass' mich 'mal . . .* ' His hands cupped her breasts.
'*Endlich! Da sind sie, die Hollandische Käsen!*' The hallucination was so compelling that she turned around and saw, with a
jarring sense of awakening, a grinning GI smoking a cigar. The
smell had brought him back to life, for one bewildering moment.

It shot her down in flames. In one second, all she had achieved
exploded in her face. Without Heinzl, she did not have the foggiest idea who she was, what she was; what she had achieved was
merely negative. Instead of feeling, as she had with Heinzl, she
felt nothing; instead of laughing as with Heinzl, she just laughed
whenever everyone else did; instead of being loving, excited,
hungry for his embrace, she was frigid, nonloving, a dead duck, a
Quaker duck in battle dress, as sexless as Mother Goose. But she
should not think this way; even if it was true, she should not allow herself to admit it. She must, come what may, cling to the
carefully constructed Laura Baker, go through the right motions, use the right phrases, pretend the right feelings, kiss the
ground, America the Beautiful, hi ya Granny, remember the
Alamo. If only underneath it all there weren't that odd rage,
that subterranean fury against the new Laura, Bonny, the Glen
Miller sound, Smoochin' Frankie, Red Cross donuts, French
perfoom that rocks the room, Red Roses for a Blue Lady, were
you there when they crucified our Lord, cha-cha-cha?

She wished that the creep with the cigar would take off; then,
suddenly, Bonny took her hand and kissed it. "I'm so happy,
Laura," he said, "for thee."

Thee for two and two for thee. Here comes the bride. "I owe it
all to you, Bonny . . ." Nauseated by her own duplicity, she said,
"I'll be right back," and made off, plowing through the ranks of
bellowing GI's back to the stairwell where the candy machines
were. He let her go because he assumed, good boy, that she was
on her way to the ladies' room.

Finally she managed to fight her way to the one shrine where
she could worship without feeling she was a fake: the candy machine. All her worries were momentarily lifted as she asked herself, 'What shall it be? Baby Ruth, Life Savers, or gum?' She

ended up, as she always did, sometimes in the middle of the
night, with one of each. She had become inordinately dependent
on candy; it was soothing to crunch a Life Saver or chew gum
when things suddenly got too much and she felt, crazily, like
screaming wildly about nothing, nothing at all, just let it rip and
scream.

Above her, on the deck, tear-choked voices started to bellow
"America the Beautiful." Okay, babe, here it comes: hitch up
your girdle and say tweet-tweet. Greet Granny on the quayside
with a hearty hug, and ask, 'Do you remember Daddy?' without
adding, 'I sure as hell don't.' I remember Heinzl, damn him; until I shake that man, I'll never be at home among the ghosts.

"Howdy, toots, why aren't you up on deck, blowing kisses at
Manhattan?"

She grinned at the Pfc and replied, "You'd better behave,
buster. Out there your mommy is waiting."

It seemed to depress him. "Yeah," he said. "Wonder if she
still loves me."

She had a sudden sense of kinship and held out the roll of Life
Savers. "Here. Help yourself. That way, she will at least love
your breath."

"Gee, thanks. Doing anything special tonight?"

"You bet."

"Who's the lucky guy?"

"My granny."

"Ouch! She on the quay?"

"Unless old rocking chair got her."

He laughed, took a card from his breast pocket and scribbled
something on the back of it. "Here. If she's gone AWOL, call
this number. Like spaghetti?"

"What's your name?"

"Butch. It isn't, but that's what they call me. Make sure you
call me that when you phone. Will you? Let's get away from it
all."

For some reason, she felt her eyes fill with tears. "I'd love to
do just that. But your mommy will eat you, and so will my
granny."

"What's your name? Little Red Riding Hood?"

"Laura," she said. "Glad to meet you, Butch. Now we'd better go and face the music."

"Sure thing," he said. "Thanks for the Life Saver. I needed
that."

* * *

The rusty flank of the troopship was house-high. Above it were tiers of decks, and everywhere, from the portholes, over the railings, between the lifeboats, soldiers were cheering and calling and waving their caps. None of them seemed to realize that they all looked exactly alike in their uniforms, and that it was impossible to spot among those thousands of identical boys the one for whom a mother waited. The only thing Dorothy Baker could do was wave, like everyone else on the dock, and call, "Hurrah! Hurrah! Welcome, welcome!" Her eyes filled with tears, with the result that she no longer could discern anybody. For days she had been a nervous wreck at the prospect of meeting her daughter-in-law; she was sorry now that Stella Best, whom she had telephoned the moment she knew the *Queen Mary* was on its way, would not arrive until the day after tomorrow and could not share this trial with her. What would the girl look like? What should she say? What could she do to put her at her ease? She had seen photographs of those concentration camps, people so famished and tortured that they no longer looked like human beings but apparitions. Bonny had written to her, telling her all about Laura Martens, but, like all men, the thought had not occurred to him to describe her looks. Was she short, tall, fat, skinny? Of course, skinny, after three years spent in one of those monstrous camps as the concubine of Nazi . . . She should not think about it! The moment she thought about that she lost her last vestige of confidence. She should meet the girl as if nothing had happened. She had simply arrived from abroad. But that would be difficult, if not impossible. The child must be emaciated, with those hollow eyes she had seen on the photographs.

The first servicemen started to run down the gangways. All about her, mothers and girlfriends were swept up in bear hugs, all from the same boy in the same uniform and the same hat, carrying the same duffel bag.

"Mother!"

Her heart stopped; there he was! But no, it was another boy. He laughed sheepishly and said, "Sorry, ma'am, you look exactly like her! You didn't happen to see her, did you? Somebody just like you? I—Mom!" He ran off. In the eyes of the boys who were now pouring down the gangways, all the mothers on the quayside must look alike.

"Mother!"

She called, with a lump in her throat, "Yes, Bonny! Here!" Again it was somebody else, not as nice as the previous one; this one looked at her as if she had fooled him on purpose, said, "Well, I'll be damned!" and turned his back on her. What if she took off her hat? Perhaps that—

"Mom!"

She stared stonily ahead, with a fixed smile, this time on her guard; then arms were thrown around her neck, and her darling cried, "Oh Mother, Mother, Mother, how marvelous! Oh, Mother!"

They stood swaying in an embrace; tears ran down her face, she kissed him and stroked his hair and felt that he had gained weight and kissed his hands. Then both at the same time, they realized that they had forgotten the girl. He let go of her, and said, "Well, Mother: this is she. This is Laura . . ."

There she stood, on the fringe of the milling crowd. She did not look at all as Dorothy had imagined. She was plump, fair-haired, of medium height, and had oddly cold blue eyes. Well, no wonder, maybe, after all she had gone through; yet it seemed incongruous that this well-fed, gum-chewing girl had indeed experienced all those terrible things. But this was not the time to reflect on all that. Dorothy approached her, arms outstretched, and said, as warmly as she could, "Laura, darling child, how *wonderful* to see you!" and kissed her cheeks. The girl did not move. She just stood there, stone-faced, like a rock. Oh what a cold, sinister— No, she must not think like that! This was the first step on a road that might be God knew how long. "Come," she said, taking the girl's arm. "Let's go to the car. On the way home you must tell me everything, everything." That, of course, was a stupid remark. Imagine if she were to do so!

As they approached the mass of parked cars, she heard a deafening hooting and bleating of Klaxons and saw to her horror another policeman standing near her station wagon, kept at a distance by Sally, who was howling with rage. Behind her car, a row of trucks honked and hooted in angry frustration.

She approached the policeman warily and saw to her relief that it was a different one. "I'm so terribly sorry," she said. "I can't tell you how sorry I am! You know, my son has just returned from the war and . . . "

He had already written out a ticket and only asked to see her driving license. She had to sign the ticket, and when finally she was done he said, "Congratulations, and have a nice day, mother. If I were you I'd give these boys a wide berth. They've been leaning on their horns for twenty minutes."

She got in and had to hit Sally with her pocketbook to calm her down. Then she said, hurriedly, "Come, Laura! Get in beside me! And you too, Bonny! Quick, quick! Those men . . ." Behind her, the chorus of Klaxons increased in volume. She could not start the miserable car, the engine would not take. Men appeared beside her, obviously the drivers of the trucks, for they started to bang on the roof and shout invectives; Sally went berserk and barked so furiously that it deafened her. At last the car started, she drove off in third with a jolt that made the men jump back; bucking, she headed in the direction of the Holland Tunnel.

The policeman had been right: a huge truck followed right behind her, bumper to bumper. She wished she could pull off the road somewhere and let Bonny drive, but it was impossible. There were so many cars that she couldn't move into the right-hand lane. To stop in the tunnel was altogether impossible; all the time the truck was right behind her, honking its horn and flashing its headlights. But at last she managed to swerve into a toll gate that was banned to trucks. She paid hastily, through a crack of the side window, while Sally put her front paws on the back of the seat, yowled at the collector and snapped at his hand. She had to take her pocketbook again and clout Sally and cry, "Go away! Down! Down! Sit!" She began to lose control; her face was screwed up in a grimace of nerves and tears. She started off again in third, but thank God, this time the ghastly truck was gone. At last she could drive normally, relax . . . Only then did she become aware of the girl by her side. What a reception for the poor child! She glanced at her, fearing the worst. But the girl sat there, stony-faced, staring ahead as if the whole business had nothing to do with her.

"Well," she said. "Well, Laura, thank God we have that behind us! How are you, Bonny?"

"Just fine," Bonny said behind her. "Take it easy, you don't have to talk. Shall I drive?"

"No, no," she said, "it's really not necessary, thank you. I'm all right now. Well, Laura, let me tell you where we are going. First we go through New Jersey, then—" Sally, who had nothing left to do, put her front paws on the back of the seat and stuck her head between the two of them, to watch the road.

"You know what, Bonny?" Dorothy said, suddenly exhausted. "Why don't *you* tell Laura? Tell her where we're going."

"Yes, Mother," he said, in the tone of tired resignation that she knew so well and that gave her, suddenly, a feeling of loneliness.

* * *

Laura knew she should have spoken up, the moment she saw the car with that dog inside, snarling behind the window, teeth bared. She should have said, 'Please, don't put me in there, not with that dog!' But it had been impossible. All those honking trucks, the policeman, the chaos, the stifling crowd, the mounting tension . . . Now she sat rigid, hands tightly folded, staring fixedly ahead, saying to herself, 'Stay calm! It's nothing! He's harmless! Forget about him!' But she couldn't. The animal put his head right beside hers, panting, tongue lolling, growling at cars. She could not stand it. They must stop. She had to get out. She had to get away.

'Calm down, calm down!' she said to herself. 'Calm down, it's only a dog, he is harmless, calm down!'

But she could not help herself. The dog panted beside her, she felt within her a mounting terror, some image that was unbearable, a horror she could not face.

"Well, all right then," Bonny said, cheerful once more. "That bridge was the Pulaski Skyway. Soon we'll be on the Garden State Parkway, and then . . . "

'God,' she prayed, 'God, God.'

But it was too late.

* * *

"Halt! Hilfe! HILFE!" The scream took Boniface totally by surprise. Tires squealed, the station wagon yawed wildly, the dog roared; they bounced onto the shoulder of the road. A door was thrown open, Laura tumbled out, landing on all fours in the grass. Before he could get to her, she scrambled to her feet and ran, screaming, toward a barbed-wire fence around a field that skirted the freeway, the barking dog at her heels.

Boniface ran after her; suddenly she came to a jerky halt: arms wide, struggling, screaming, screaming. When he got to her, he saw that she was caught in the barbed wire. "Laura! What happened? What's wrong? Calm down, please . . ." He tried to free her clothes from the vicious barbs; she fought and struggled. When finally he managed to pull her loose, her battle dress was torn, her hands were bleeding, her face was scratched; all the time she went on screaming, screaming. Around them pranced the idiotic dog, barking its head off. He tried to kick it, cried, "Go away! Shoosh!" Then he said, "Laura, please, what happened? All is well, it's all right, honest, there's nothing wrong, come, calm down; come, please, please . . ." He managed in the end to put an arm around her and half carried, half dragged her back to the station wagon, the dog barking at their heels. Inside, Mother sat behind the wheel, her head in her hands.

"Come, Laura . . ." He eased her onto the back seat; she slumped in the corner, moaning. Blood from the scratches on her face mingled with tears.

"Mother!" Mother did not move. "Mother! Where is the first-aid kit?"

Mother took her hands off her face, groped under the front seat and handed him the box.

While one car after the other whooshed past, making the station wagon shudder, he bandaged Laura's hands, dabbed her face, and finally said, "Come Mother, you sit next to her; I'll drive. Please."

Mother stared at him as if she had not registered what he was saying, but when she spoke her voice was calm. "What if you two went to stay on Eden Island for a few days?"

"Why?"

"There are a lot of people at home who'll want to see you. She needs rest, and Eden Island is very quiet right now. All the cottages are empty, there are no conferences or retreats. Why don't you two go there for a while? She needs a chance to—to adjust. Once she has settled down, Stella Best and you and I should discuss what to do next."

"All right," he said, "but can we just turn up there?"

"At the next gas station I'll give them a call. I'm sure Hannah Muggeridge will be helpful. She is a very understanding and experienced woman."

"All right. Come, you sit beside her. I'll drive." He gently let go of Laura, who now had gone as limp as a rag doll, and propped her up in the corner; then he got out and opened the front door.

"Laura?" Mother asked, stooping to climb into the back seat. "Would you mind moving over a little? I'd like to sit beside you."

It looked as if the poor girl had lost all her strength, or maybe she did not hear. Mother put her arm around her; when the dog sniffed at them and licked Laura's ear, she screamed suddenly, *"Nein, nein! Um Gotteswillen!"*

"Oh, my God," Mother said, "please, Bonny, please! Tie the animal up!"

Boniface opened the tailgate, crawled inside the station wagon, grabbed the dog's collar and took off his belt. He tied it to the handle of the tire compartment; the animal yowled and struggled, but the belt seemed to hold. He closed the back, got behind the wheel, started the car and stuck out his hand. Slowly, as if it were an ambulance full of wounded, he eased the station wagon off the shoulder of the road, back onto the freeway.

Only when the shock had worn off and he began to ask himself what on earth could be the matter with her did it penetrate to him that she had cried out in German. He remembered Dr. Wassermann's warning, 'The moment you arrive in America, take her to a psychiatrist and flee.' But that would be impossible right now. The one she needed for the moment, more than anyone else, was himself. To deliver her into the hands of an impersonal doctor who had no experience of the reality of destroyed Europe, let alone Camp Schwalbenbach, would be cruel. He would have to see it through for a little while longer. After all, her grandmother was on her way.

*   *   *

When they drew up at the small dock, the island ferry was waiting for them, with on board a fair-haired boy in green coveralls and gum boots, chewing a cigar.

"Hi," the boy said, without taking the cigar out of his mouth; he reached out to help Mother into the boat. "Careful, put your foot in the center. That's right."

Once Mother had sat down, Laura let herself be lowered into

the boat. Boniface sat down beside her; when the moorings were
cast off and the little boat nosed into the current, outboard engine snarling, he put an arm around her and said, as to a child,
"We're on our way now to a Quaker island. It's a retreat. They'll
let us have a cottage where we can take it easy for a few days.
My family used to own the island. It's where my great-great-
great-grandfather lived when he liberated his slaves and left with
his two daughters to go west. It's under the care of Philadelphia
Yearly Meeting now." He didn't know if the words penetrated to
her. "You'll see, it's very quiet. Usually there are a lot of people,
as there's always something going on, but right now there's nobody, only the caretaker and her helper. You need not see a
soul." She did not respond.

He looked up at the green island ahead, the red brick mansion
with the white-pillared porch. On the dock a stocky woman in a
muu-muu was waiting. He remembered her from some Young
Friends' conference: Hannah Muggeridge. During singsongs her
voice used to soar out, high and strident. When the boat moored
and she welcomed them, she was solicitous. "Good morning,
Dorothy Baker," she said, as in a sickroom. "Good morning,
Boniface. Is this your wife?"

"Yes, this is Laura. Laura, Hannah Muggeridge."

"Well," Hannah Muggeridge said as Laura did not react, "I
opened up *Caleb Martin* for you, you can go there straight away.
The beds are made, there are no groceries yet, but there is tea
and coffee."

"Good," Mother said curtly. "Where is that cottage?"

"At the far end of the island. You can either take the golf cart
or walk, whatever you like."

"I'd say let's take the cart," Boniface said.

"Well, it's right here, ready to go. It only has room for two,
though. Dorothy Baker, would you mind coming with me to the
main house?" Hannah Muggeridge continued to Laura, "The
buildings on this island are all named after members of the Baker family in the eighteenth century. The main house is called
after Ann Baker Traylor, who—"

"Here you are," the boy in the coveralls said. "Have you driv-
en one of these before?"

At the top of the steps stood a golf cart with a bright orange
canopy.

"There's only one forward speed, isn't there?"

"That's right," the boy said, "it's as easy as falling off a log. You know where *Caleb Martin* is? Just follow this path past the tennis courts and the old ruins, then there's a few hundred yards of open field and straight ahead a double row of cottages among the trees. Yours is the last on the right. I turned on the gas, and there are matches, but be careful: it's all wood and very old. Now, what about your luggage? There's no room for it with the two of you inside, only for the two grips."

"That's all right. I'll just take my wife there, I'll come back for the rest." He helped Laura onto the narrow seat, joined her, and with a hum and a smell of battery acid the golf cart waddled down the path. The moment they had passed the main building they entered the silence and the wide-open space that he remembered from previous visits. It took them ten minutes to reach the small wood at the southernmost tip of the island. The cottages, hidden among the trees, were all shuttered. On each of them was a sign with a name: *Boniface Baker, Abigail Baker, Rebekah Baker, Joshua Baker, Cleopatra Baker.* He drew up in front of the somber little bungalow under a canopy of old chestnut trees; when he stopped the engine he could hear the leaves lisp massively overhead. *Caleb Martin* said the sign over the porch. "Come, Laura." He helped her down.

She walked unsteadily to the steps and stood still. Something made her hesitate. No wonder, in that green underwater light it looked a gloomy little place. The inside turned out to be gloomier still; despite the modern furniture and the colorful posters on the wall it had the atmosphere of a funeral parlor. During the summer, full of jolly young Friends, it was different; now it was chilly and dark. Would it be better to stay with her, instead of going for the baggage? She stood motionless in the center of the room, without looking around. Suddenly a bicycle bell tinkled outside. It was the boy with the cigar, who climbed onto the porch, gum boots squelching. "You want me to explain the lights?"

"No, thank you, we'll manage."

"I came to take the cart back. I'll get your luggage. You stay here."

"That's very kind of you."

"You're welcome." He was about to turn around, then he said, "Let me turn on the icebox for you." He squelched to the kitchenette and opened the door of the refrigerator. After doing something to the insides, he muttered, "Damn! The old story!"

He put his cigar on the draining board, knelt down and took the bottom panel off the icebox.

"Come, Laura, sit down. Relax."

She let herself be guided toward one of the rattan chairs and sat down.

"Okie-doke, there she goes! I'll be right back." The boy left.

"Now, how are you feeling? Tell me." Outside, the golf cart hummed and waddled off, orange canopy swaying.

She did not reply. Her face was expressionless, she seemed calm and composed.

"Look, Laura," he said, taking her hand; it was cold. "What you should do now is rest. Why don't we have a look at the bedroom? The woman said the beds were made, so why don't you lie down and take it easy for a while? It was too much pressure for you. I understand."

She turned her head and looked at him; her eyes were cold and remote.

"Would you like to lie down and rest?"

"I'm sorry," she said.

"Don't be silly. There's no need to be sorry, for heaven's sake! If anybody has to be sorry, it's me. I didn't know Mother would turn up with that miserable dog. She's a dear woman, but a bit of a ninny at times." It wasn't fair, but he had to say something. "Come on, lie down for a while."

"I'd like to just sit here."

"All right, as you like. Would you rather be alone?"

"That's all right."

"Tell you what, I'll take the boy's bike to the main house. I have to register anyhow, and say goodbye to Mother. Will you be all right? I won't be long."

"I'll be all right," she said.

He left her sitting there in that cold little room with her bandaged hands, her torn battle dress, her face full of scratches. He should have put her to bed, made a fuss; but he got onto the bike and rode off, past the blind cottages among the trees, haunted by the image of her crucified on the barbed wire.

*   *   *

The moment she was sure he was out of sight, she went to the veranda and sat on the steps, listening to the birds, the wind in the leaves. What had made her lose control like that? It had been the dog, but why? Because it looked like Siegfried? Siegfried had never done her any harm, only prisoners who tried to run away. She remembered being afraid of him in the very beginning, but later she hadn't minded having him around. It had been a safe feeling at times, having him there. No inmate would dare enter the bungalow while Siegfried was inside. She had seen him bring down the man in the striped suit, and that had upset her. But enough to make her behave like that? Fly off the handle like that? Go into hysterics, with the mad compulsion to flee screaming? It was strange. She didn't like it one bit. It made her feel insecure, because she had upset Bonny. It was not something a Quakerly person would do. It didn't please him, and she wanted to please him. Could she make up for it? Should she allow him to make love to her? She had the impression, more often of late, that he secretly wanted that, although he would never say so. But there was no doubt that if she gave him any encouragement at all, he would, like Heinzl—

She couldn't stand the thought. It made her physically sick. And yet, it might have to come to that. To be a Quakerly person was not going to be enough, in the long run. She remembered the first time with Heinzl, how she had lain staring at the ceiling with a sense of triumph and thought: 'Now I have him, now he is mine.' It would be the same with Bonny; the moment she enticed him to make love to her, the moment he had penetrated her and cried *'Laura! Now!'* he would be hers. But she couldn't.

She was a mess. Her heart was with Heinzl and her head with Bonny. She owed everything to Bonny and was terrified at the thought of his leaving her. Looking at it soberly, she must be prepared to let him make love to her if that was the price for tying him to her until she was independent enough to let go. For she didn't believe in the grandmother; the mere idea of an old woman, any old woman forcing the past on her was terrifying. She didn't need a past, she needed a present that was stable and reliable. It began to look as if, in order to ensure that present, she would have to let Bonny in where Heinzl had been. And that she could not do. It was stronger than reason, stronger than the dark, faceless terror that awaited her if she should find herself cast off. What other means did she have of making him hang on to her, now they actually were in America? He had promised to take her to her grandmother, period. Then he would be through. What else could she do to stop him? She rose and went back inside to make herself a cup of tea; anything to take her mind off it.

But the thoughts followed her. Girl, you had better be prepared for it. One more scene like the one you made today, and he is going to wash his hands of you. And you never know when it's going to hit you again; it came out of the blue, just like that, because of a dog. Who knows what may trigger it next time. So, get with it. Catch him before it is too late. 'Bonny, darling, could you scratch my back for me? Lower—no—lower . . .' God, never! Never, never in a thousand years. She'd rather—what? Let's hear that, now: rather what? Be deserted again, left hanging in the air in a blind panic, just because for the second time the man who was the center of your life is gone?

For God's sake! Tea!

Then, as she stood by the stove, waiting for the water to boil, there Heinzl was again, right behind her. *'Laurachen? Tasschen Tee? Ach, wie nett!'*

It was spooky. Again it was as if he were really there, sneaking up on her as he had done so often. *'Boo!'* And he'd hold her breasts, and kiss her neck, and she would—

Suddenly she was overcome by a wild, surging desire for him. His kisses, his embrace— "Heinzl! Go away! *Kscht!* Heinzl!"

Then she saw the cigar stub on the edge of the sink. The smell had done it, just as it had on board ship. How did a cigar get here? Oh, the boy in the green coveralls. He must have left it there when he checked on the icebox.

She felt Heinzl draw away. Suddenly she was so lonely, so lost and rudderless without him, that on an impulse she put the filthy thing in her mouth, struck a match and lit it. The first mouthful of smoke made her heave, but she persevered. After a few mouthfuls the smell got to her, despite the foul taste in her mouth. There he was, large as life. *'Now, Laura! Now!'*

She realized once again that she should have done what he had asked: kept that capsule in her mouth. They would have made love one last time, passionately; she would have let him sweep her up in those wild spirals of color and joy, and then, as he cried out, *'Laura! Now!'* she would have crunched the capsule, and spiraled down in his arms, into nothingness.

Oh, well. She threw out the cigar; it made her sick. She poured herself a cup of tea and took it to the veranda. She sat down again on the steps and accepted without hysterics the fact that she had made a mistake. It simply was a fact of life. What now lay ahead of her, as the price for survival, was to let Bonny— She gulped the tea. It was too hot, it burned her tongue, but it helped chase the vision of Bonny with an erection, which she had occasionally glimpsed when he got up in the morning, in hotels in Europe where they had been forced to share a room. Poor guy. So prudish, always with his back to her . . . Why mess it up? Why couldn't she go on the way she had so far: be good, do good deeds, be a good Quaker wife to a truly good man?

The answer was simple: he was going to stick to the deal. Here comes grandmother, bye bye Laura. 'Well, Laura, child, let me tell thee about thy Daddy.' It didn't bear thinking about. She had to find a way to hang on to him, and there was only one— but that was out. So she was damned if she did and damned if she didn't.

She sipped her tea and suddenly had a vision of the grandmother, racing across America at that very moment in some train, on her way to this island. She had rehearsed all the answers she would give about her past as a child in Westerdam; it had been like a game. 'Where did you live?'—'A house at the end of a street.'—'What was the name of your dog?' 'Caesar.' Bonny had known the answers and she had learned them by heart. Bonny had talked about her father, but never set eyes on him, so it had all been hearsay; now here came a woman who had really known him. The thought of having a real father forced on her was terrifying. Dammit, she didn't need a father, didn't want a father, didn't want a past! All she wanted was to be left alone, with Bonny somewhere in the background, and to emerge, cautiously, bit by little bit, as the Laura she was meant to be. The Laura she could feel occasionally right inside her, like an unborn child. Was that what it was like? Heinzl had never allowed her to wait long enough to find that out. The moment she thought she was pregnant, he had forced her onto that operating table in the consulting-room. God! The fear, the sadness, the sense of loss . . . Well, right now the threat was Grandmother. She had been able to write Granny creepy little letters, *dada* and *baba* and *oo-ooh,* like a child; but those had just been little notes to Santa Claus, dropped in a mailbox. Now the real woman was on her way here; tonight, tomorrow there she would be, as large as life, coming for her with open arms, 'Laura! Darling!' and the questioning would start. Do you remember this? Do you remember that? As your Daddy used to say—

She got up and went to meet Bonny. She met him at the end of the row of cottages; he came plowing toward her on a bicycle, holding a paper bag. She waved, he waved and came a cropper, spilling groceries. "Bonny! Did you hurt yourself?!" She ran to him, helped him to his feet; he hadn't hurt himself, but he was shaken. She made a fuss over him, hugged him protectively all the way home to the bungalow, plied him with tea, frankfurters, made sandwiches, peeled an apple for him. Sweet guy, he had worried about her being hungry; he had even brought her a couple of Hershey Bars.

When finally he sat there, wide-eyed, getting a good taste of being spoiled by a doting Quaker wifie, he sniffed and said, "It stinks in here. Of cigars."

"Yes," she said, "the boy in the frog suit left his on the sink. Can you still smell it?"

"I sure can," he said. "How about another sandwich?"

"Okay, Bonny-bear. Coming up."

It was enough to make a cat sick. But he was all she had to defend herself against Grandmother. How on earth was she going to cope with the woman?

That night, after meeting, he could have had her. She would have let him, out of sheer blue funk. But he wasn't very bright. Or maybe she had been wrong, maybe she left him cold. Maybe he really wanted to dump her as soon as he had kept his promise. Anyhow, they ended up in separate rooms; he on the couch in the living-room, she on one of the narrow twins in the bedroom.

She didn't sleep much; there were frogs croaking right outside the window, there were boats on the river, hooting in the night, there were ghosts. *'Laura, Liebes, du machst mich ja verrückt, du!'*

She went through the whole thing with Heinzl in her mind, lonely as hell, terrified of tomorrow.

CHAPTER THREE

TWO days later, a taxi rattled down the cobbled road that followed the river from Philadelphia to Eden Island. The road was little used; the driver cursed under his breath most of the way, muttering about springs.

The frail old lady in the back seat, dressed in gray with long skirt and Quaker bonnet—Pendle Hill Monthly Meeting being one of the last adhering to plain dress—was unaware of the driver's irritation and the rattling of the vehicle. She held on to the strap on the left and gazed unseeingly at the river, preoccupied with anxious thoughts about her granddaughter.

Dorothy Martin Baker had told her of Laura's outburst in the car; it could only be explained as a symptom of total disorientation. Oh, how she could identify with the child! How long it had been before she herself had been able to function! She knew exactly how the child must feel toward the thugs who had defiled her. She must be consumed by hatred, beset by visions in which— She opened her eyes and looked at the river.

She must suppress these destructive thoughts, think positively: of herself as a child, how she had come down this same road in a four-in-hand, when this had still been open country. She forced herself to remember those carefree gatherings of young women Friends, but hatred went on quivering right underneath the thin membrane of the faded images of girlhood. Forty years, and still a trembling wreck, still, deep inside— She tapped on the glass partition. The driver opened the window. "Yes, ma'am?"

"Friend, we're almost there. It's such a lovely day, I'd like to walk the rest of the way. Would you mind letting me out here?"

She paid; the moment the taxi had turned around and driven off she was sorry. She still had a long way to go, and she had the grip with her night-things to carry. She walked hurriedly, on the shoulder of the road, under the trees that must date back to the years when the first Bakers came driving this way in their sulkies. Dorothy Baker had been of the opinion that Laura should receive psychiatric care. If only that had existed forty years ago! But at that time, if anyone had lived through a horror like hers and suffered a shock from which she could not recover, all there was in the way of help was faith in God. No Quaker would have dreamed of consulting an analyst, or whatever they were called then. Who could tell, she herself might have turned into a different person if, immediately after it happened, an experienced, caring doctor had listened to her, encouraged her to tell it all, helped her see things in their true perspective. But, dear God, *what* true perspective?

She walked faster; in the end, she jogged along under those trees, a quaint old lady in gray carrying an old-fashioned grip.

When finally she arrived at the little dock opposite the island, she asked herself: could it be that her own experience was a bridge between herself and Laura? Could it be that here was a chance to turn the disaster that had destroyed her life into a positive force? She rang the bell for the ferry. Putting down the grip, she watched a little motorboat detach itself from the wooded shore of the island. It came foaming toward her, made a wide, fast sweep; the boy inside moored it and held out his hand. "Please step down into the center of the boat."

She was glad when she was sitting safely on the seat. The little boat took off; when it approached the dock on the other side, she saw a woman waiting for them. For a moment, her heart in her throat, she thought it was Laura, then she realized that it was an older woman in a shapeless dress with a choker of wooden beads.

"Welcome, Friend, welcome! Thee must be Stella Best? I am Hannah Muggeridge, administrator of the island. Welcome, welcome."

She looked up at the imposing house with the white pillars and asked, "Is my—are they inside?"

"No, no. They have a cottage at the other end of the island. Harry will take thee there in the golf cart."

"Careful now," the boy said, "mind you don't trip. There's a lot of current today."

Fearfully, Stella Best clambered onto the dock. Ridiculous to force people her age to go through an athletic exercise like this, but probably not too many people her age came to the island. In her time everybody had seemed so young.

"Lovely day, isn't it?" the woman with the beads said. "Has it been a long time since thee last saw thy granddaughter?"

Ah, a gossip. "It has," she said. "How did you say I'd get there?"

"This way, please," said the boy carrying her grip.

She followed him past a hedge of aromatic shrubs that suddenly dislodged vague memories of a young girl's first love. The boy led her to a little cart with an orange canopy; she sat down beside him. With a whining noise, the cart started down a road that she vaguely remembered. Old buildings? Factory? Something to do with indigo? They rounded a bend and met an overweight young man on a bicycle, who waved to stop the cart. He was wearing a lumber-jacket of red and blue squares and green pants. Color-blind, obviously.

"Stella Best?" the young man asked, panting from the effort of pedaling.

This must be he! "Boniface . . . ?"

"So glad to meet you." He reached across the handlebars to shake hands. "Listen, Harry, let me take Stella Best to the cottage. You take the bike, I'll see to it that the cart is returned."

"Fair enough," the boy beside her said. He climbed out, the fat one climbed in. She should not judge hastily, but after his letter and his report she had expected someone more mature.

He fiddled with a lever, the little cart continued on its way. "I thought maybe you and I could have a word before you meet Laura."

"Very well," she said. "Your mother told me what happened in the car after you arrived. I'd like to hear your version. Does Laura know I'm here, by the way?"

"Yes, Hannah Muggeridge called from the main house." He made a left-hand turn, toward a group of trees near the river. Only when she saw the gravestones in the high grass did she remember the burial ground of the Bakers. Here John and she, one summer night . . .

It was tranquil in the graveyard. He stopped the cart and they sat for a while, side by side, listening to the sound of water rippling in the reeds. Then she asked, "How is she now?"

"Not too bad."

"Your mother mentioned the urgent need for psychiatric treatment."

"I believe she needs someone who loves her. That might be more important to her than some psychiatrist on whose couch she'd be allowed to unburden herself an hour at a time."

"No need to be delicate about this. You mean I am the one to provide that love?"

"Well, you read my report. She was in desperate shape until she was told about the possibility of going to America, to you. This whole expedition has been a pilgrimage to you."

"You are eager to hand over the responsibility, is that it?" It was a catty thing to say, but it was out before she knew it.

He didn't mind. He was sturdier than she had thought. "Yes," he said. "As you well know, it was a marriage of convenience, just to get her a visa that she otherwise would never have gotten. I have taken care of her as best I could, in Germany and on the way over; this is where the arrangement ends."

"Sorry," she said. "I know that, of course. I'm ready to take her back with me, tomorrow."

He picked up the edge in her voice. "It's not as cold-blooded as it sounds, Stella Best. I am sure that for Laura also the moment has come to go our separate ways. You will be able to do for her what I cannot do: tell her who she is. She is still suffering from amnesia. She has managed to patch things together, she knows who she is supposed to be. But my guess is that, so far, she has it all second hand. She doesn't really want to talk about herself, she never asks any questions about her past; the moment it's forced on her, she shows signs of anger. Otherwise, she is quite even-tempered, really. She can be very sweet. Explosions like the one in the car— I had never known her to fly off the handle like that. It was quite scary."

"She has never shown any signs of instability before?"

"Not that I know of."

"But you have been married to her for months!"

"I didn't get to see much of her, really. The unit I belonged to moved on with the Army; she was taken care of by nuns in Schwalbenbach, they later put her to work among the displaced children. I visited her there occasionally, on a weekend pass. It was a joy to see her turn into a normal person, jolly, pleasant and very popular among the children. Then, when we crossed the Atlantic on the *Queen Mary,* she was again very popular, this time among the GI's. She had adapted beautifully, it seemed. An irrational act like this is totally out of character."

"Well," she said, "let's go and see her. She must be wondering where we are."

He started the cart and they wobbled back to the path through the fields. She gazed at the white cottages and prayed for strength; as they approached the last one in the row, she saw a girl waiting on the porch.

"Here we are!" the boy cried with forced jollity. He jumped out of the cart, helped her down. She walked slowly toward the porch. Then she saw the child's face and froze with shock. It was Lily!

Tears welled up in her eyes, but she managed to say, "Hello, child. How is thee?"

"Fine, Grandmother," the girl said. "How are you?"

"Laura..." She stumbled up the steps, embraced the child, tightly; it was as if she were holding Lily, given back all that had been taken away from her. But she must get a grip on herself! She must! Then it penetrated to her that the girl she was hugging so fiercely was totally unresponsive. It was as if she were embracing a stranger. Of course she was! This wasn't Lily Best, this was Laura Martens, a stranger who had gone through terrible experiences in a concentration camp.

"My goodness, how thee has grown! I'm so happy to see thee, Laura!"

"I'm happy to be here, Grandmother," the stranger said politely.

*   *   *

To her astonishment and enormous relief, Laura discovered that the quaint old lady, advancing on her like a vision from another century in her long gray dress and Quaker bonnet, presented no threat at all. She turned out to be as weak as dishwater, almost pathetically so; all it would need for the apparition from a wax museum to evaporate was to give her the cold eye and, maybe, say 'Boo!' Boy, what a relief! There she had been, worrying herself sick...

Even so, she wished the old woman would stop drooling over her. The embrace had been hateful; after Heinzl, no one had forced himself on her physically like this. Ugh! She smelled, too.

Of old age, probably. One thing was absolutely certain: she had never set eyes on this person in her life, whatever her life might have been. It was sheer convention on the old woman's part; they could have showed her any girl of roughly the same age and she wouldn't have known the difference. But convention demanded that she embrace her so-called granddaughter as a long lost love and stagger around with tears in her eyes, making poopie-doopie noises, or she'd be considered degenerate, heartless. Well, forget it, lady; I'm not about to join you in that game.

Bonny and the old lady tootled into the cottage and, after opening closets, began to lay the table for three, Grandmother uttering cries like "What do you think this is?" holding up a perfectly normal pepper-mill. She obviously expected her granddaughter to join in the charade, but the hell with it. She was going to lock herself in the bathroom for a while, just to be rid of the spectacle of those two getting jumpier and jumpier. Bonny must indeed be jumpy, for when she passed him and put her hand on the nape of his neck as he was peering into the closet under the sink, he dropped a colander with a clatter that made Grandmother squeal.

As she sat in the bathroom, enjoying her moment of solitude, she could hear the mumble-mumble in the living-room. Obviously they were discussing, in low voices, what to do with the villain when she came back. Wrestle her to the ground? Crown her with the colander? What had Bonny wanted with a colander anyhow?

To her amazement she realized again that instead of being a bundle of nerves as she had foreseen, she was bored to the back teeth. One hell of a long evening stretched ahead. They would have meeting for worship, of course, on the veranda, and be stung by mosquitoes while ministering to the frogs. Never mind, Laura, she told herself, never mind. Just go on acting like a good Quaker wifie. You'll live through the boring night. You've lived through worse.

She stood up, braced herself and, to lend credibility to her own performance, flushed the toilet. Why it happened she had no idea, but suddenly there she stood, dazed with shock and numb with terror, in a torn dress flushing the toilet in the bungalow for the first time. What had happened to her? She remembered asking herself that over and over again: What happened to me? What happened?

Funny thing was, she still didn't know. The only difference

was that at the time she had been desperate to find out; now, what she would like to know was not who she had been but who she was going to be. Who was the Laura she could feel stirring within her? Time would tell. One person who sure as death could not tell her was Grandmother. Or Bonny, for that matter. But as she went back into the living-room, she somehow knew that she was just about through with Limp Laura the Quaker Leech. So, let's give her a send-off that will be remembered.

'Easy now, girl,' she thought, 'easy.' For she went back to her nearest and dearest with a feeling that she could eat them alive.

* * *

During the meal and the washing-up that followed, the girl's silent, motionless presence began to weigh so heavily that Stella Best became thoroughly rattled. The girl said nothing, did nothing; she let them do all the work and observed them as if they were two hamsters on a treadmill. She answered all questions with mumbled evasions, showed no interest, no sign of affection, let her husband wait on her hand and foot; all he got in the way of thanks was a smile that would have scared away a child, and one little pat on his neck as she passed behind him. It must have been a rare demonstration indeed, for the boy nearly jumped a mile, as if scared out of his wits. That became clear as the hours went by: the girl scared people. She scared her own grandmother, let alone that big, humorless innocent. Stella began to appreciate what the boy had done, it was nothing short of heroic.

But when, after the meal, they had meeting on the porch in the gathering dusk, she felt guilty. Was this a way to approach a child who had gone through a hell that no one could possibly imagine—except she herself? Again she felt the hope she had felt earlier, that her own experience might turn out to be the bridge between them. If anyone could, she should be able to identify with the child. Their experiences were hauntingly similar. And as the silence deepened, it occurred to her that maybe it worked both ways: maybe the child was the only one who would be able to identify with *her,* the first one in forty years. The thought brought about such a sudden, dazzling burst of joy that she was about to speak, overflowing with gratitude, when the boy himself broke the silence.

He spoke about "the joy of reunion," thanked God that they

had arrived safely and could now start with a clean slate. He even begged God to write the first words on that clean slate, and she had the irreverent impulse to furnish those words as she read them in the young man's mind: two tickets to Indiana for both women, and good riddance. But she could understand his eagerness to shake the girl. She was full of confidence now that all this was part of God's plan; that she was the only one in the world able to identify with the girl and what she had gone through. It was not something to bring up in a sentimental fashion, but soberly, matter-of-factly. Pathos would scare the child away. The most difficult part was going to be the feelings of guilt. Totally ridiculous, monstrously unfair, but there it was: guilt. The first year after it happened she had felt guilty. Of what? It had been a bizarre, involuted sense of guilt, as if being punished in such a monstrous fashion meant she must be guilty of a monstrous sin, even if she couldn't figure out what it could have been. She had managed to shake that guilty feeling eventually, or, rather, it had worked itself out. But if the child and she were to talk about it, that was one of the first things she should speak to. She would! She felt certain once more, as she sat there, eyes closed, that she had been sent by God to help the child carry her cross, because she herself carried the same. She opened her eyes and looked at her lovingly.

The girl sat staring ahead, hands in her lap, knees together, in an oddly stiff immobility, like an angel on a tomb. The chill she felt, seeing that marble face, was sobering. But she had to be firm now, and brave, and loving; she should not let herself be intimidated by the child's manner. It was a defense, obviously; she herself must have looked like that when she came home from Africa and everyone started to commiserate ... Again she was struck by the similarity. Even this morning, in the taxi, she had not dreamed that this would be the gift, the priceless gift at the end of her road to Calvary: that the monstrousness would one day serve a purpose, make sense.

She herself broke meeting by shaking hands, first with the perspiring boy, then with the icy child. They sat on the porch for another half hour or so, drinking a late night cup of cocoa. They didn't say much; they watched the bats gambol in the falling night, listened to the frogs starting to roll their dice in the reeds and the foghorns of the freighters braying on the river. They talked about the slaves who once had lived here, although probably these cottages were not the original ones. "Well, Stella Best, I don't know, this particular one looks very old. What would you say? Two hundred years?"

"Just about, Boniface. Must have been the middle seventeen hundreds. Your ancestor, wasn't he—Boniface Baker of Eden Island?"

"Yes."

"Which branch are you?"

"His son Joshua's."

"Ah, yes. I think I remember. Didn't he marry a Woodhouse girl?"

"No, he married an English Friend called Foot."

"Ah! That's right. She was one of the Birmingham Feet."

And so they slipped, safely, into the standard Quaker pastime: genealogy.

At last it was time to go to bed. The boy slept on the couch in the living-room, Laura and she in the twin beds in the bedroom. Each undressed modestly while the other was in the bathroom; the child got into bed last.

"Shall we turn off the light, Grandmother? The mosquitoes—"

"Of course, child, of course."

After the light was out, they lay silent for a while, gazing at the slatted blinds showing slivers of night. The frogs croaked, monotonously, a primeval sound. The freighters had fallen silent. Finally Stella mustered the courage to say, "All right, child. Tell me."

There was a silence; then the voice from the bed next to hers asked warily, "Tell you what?"

"Everything. Not only am I thy grandmother, but I understand. Oh, how I understand!"

"What?"

"Exactly the same thing happened to me, child. I lived through exactly the same nightmare . . ."

She had been so sure that she could handle it calmly, but to her dismay she felt herself go to pieces at once. Instead of coolly stating the facts, she already had tears in her voice when she began, "It happened in Africa, forty-one years ago . . ." And there it came, in a torrent: everything, every ghastly detail, things she thought she had forgotten, sounds, faces, pain, terror, panic, and an inexpressible sorrow, even as it was happening, the sorrow of knowing that she was being destroyed forever, never to rise again as a whole person, only as a cripple for the rest of her life. Out it came, all of it, and she could do nothing to stop herself, she spilled it all, sobbing, choking, making a ghastly fool of herself, but even though she was overcome by a feeling of disaster, she clung to the thought: She will understand, of all the people in this world she is the one who will understand, she must, she cannot help but understand, she has been through it herself. Oh God, she was supposed to be telling all this to help the child, not to unburden herself for the first time in forty years! She must help her, help her . . .

"Darling, dearest, dearest Laura, one thing thee must tell thyself over and over again: thee is not guilty! I know that's what thee feels, right now: guilt. Terrible guilt. And why? Thee doesn't know, but there it is, the idiotic self-accusation: 'Guilty. I am guilty.' Of what? It is ridiculous! If anyone is free of guilt, it is thee. Thee must tell thyself, over and over again, it was against thy will! Thee was the victim of a catastrophe, a disaster. I know thee will not be able to convince thyself. Thee can reason as much as thee likes, but thee will go on believing, despite it all, that thee *is* guilty. Thee *must* be, to be given this shattering punishment, to be banished like this to the outer regions of hell . . . "

*   *   *

At first, Laura listened with an interest that bordered on sympathy. Poor woman! Her story was unintelligible because of the tears, but obviously the old dear had to tell somebody and never dared. Now the sight of her own flesh and blood had been too much for her. But as the old woman lay there, snottering and blubbering and started crowing at her 'Thee is not guilty!' she was overcome by a terrible anger. Guilty of *what,* you old hag? What the hell do you mean, putting words in my mouth that have nothing to do with me?

She stopped listening and lay there, shaking with fury. The hell with the maudlin, snottering old bitch! She wanted to shriek, 'Stop! For God's sake, *stop!*' But Bonny was in the next room; she must be careful. Everything depended on her keeping cool, not rising to the bait, not letting herself be swept along by that crazy, terrifying rage. Shut up, Laura, for God's sake, *shut up!*

It was difficult, surprisingly so; she ended by having to fight back the impulse to grab the old woman by the throat and throttle her, just to make *her* shut up; but she managed, admirably really, considering the provocation. She lay staring at the ceiling, thinking beautiful thoughts, like: cherry pie, Hershey Bar, Baby Ruth, Oh Henry. It worked. It always worked.

"Remember, darling, darling child, it has nothing to do with sin! Sin is when we violate God's laws by obeying our basest instincts, like animals; not when we are the victims . . . "

Well, well, fancy that. 'Obeying our basest instincts' must be Quakerese for loving it, hungering for it, giving everything, everything for it, for just one glorious, howling ecstasy under his bucking body, his sweat-slick, panting . . .

Oh, no! There we go again. But really: 'sin'! No one here in America would ever understand; if any of them should ever suspect that she had enjoyed what Heinzl did to her, with her, on her . . .

Oh, for God's sake, stop it! If she were to divulge as much as a glimpse of the truth, she'd be 'out! No more sympathy, no more patience, no more divine concern to succor the suffering—*out!* Bonny would come to the conclusion that he had been hoodwinked all these months: instead of saving a violated virgin, he had been tricked into importing a camp-follower. 'Sin,' to them, is obeying all your basest instincts, hear? All she should have been was a side of beef. All she should have felt was shame, and horror, and—what had she called it, the old slobberer? *Destroyed forever.*

Okay, here she was, destroyed forever. Suddenly the woman grabbed her hand and she couldn't help it, she pulled it away as if she had been stung. Ah, what a pity! How stupid! What had she done . . . ?

She listened, holding her breath. Grandmother lay stock still, as if she wasn't breathing either. Oh Lord . . . What could she do? What could she say?

"Laura . . . ?"

"Huh?"

"Would thee—would you like to come and live with me for a while? I—I would enjoy that . . . "

"I'd sooner—"

"What . . . dear?"

"No, thanks." She had to say more. She had to. "It's very kind of you, Grandmother, but I—I'd rather not."

"But, Laura, why not? Isn't that why thee's here? Have I said something—"

And then, despite all her firm decisions, that rage tore loose within her. "Because I hate you! You and your sob stories! Leave me alone! Leave me alone, you hear?! Beat it!"

She lay trembling, and, sure enough, there it came, dammit: the old woman started to cry in the darkness. She should say something, make some gesture, but she'd be damned if she would. The hell with her! So she wouldn't take her—

All of a sudden, there it was: the answer! The solution to the whole thing! She *need* not allow Bonny to make love to her! All she need do was to make sure the old woman would not have her at any price! She knew Bonny well enough by now; he'd never abandon her if Grandmother turned her down. He would stick by her, no matter what.

She lay listening to the sobs in the darkness, wondering how to really scare the old creep. Attack her? No, she'd scream for help. But she could threaten her and she had better do it now, before the old woman had a chance to recover.

With her heart in her mouth, she leaned over the vague shape in the bed next to her and whispered, as fiercely as she could, "Listen, don't you *dare* try and take me with you tomorrow! If you do, God help me, I'll kill you. Do you hear me? You'll end up with a knife in your belly, or strangled in—"

"For God's sake!" The shape leaped out of bed. Then there was the sound of strangled sobs, somewhere in a corner.

Poor old soul . . . No! She shouldn't go soft now! If she let up now, tomorrow the old lady might think it had all been a nightmare. She crawled onto the other bed and hissed at the dark shape huddled in the corner, "Stop it! Stop blubbering! You leave me alone, do you hear? Leave me alone, you old bitch, or you'll end up in a green bag! Do you hear me? Answer! Answer, or I'll—"

"I—I—I hear thee—you . . . " the poor woman whispered, choking with terror.

"Okay!" She crawled back into her own bed. "You can lie down now. Lie down and go to sleep! But shut up!"

It took a while, but the old woman finally obeyed and got back into bed. There were no more sobs; she had brought it off. No fear; now Granny dear would sooner take home a rattlesnake. She felt sorry for the old soul, but not enough to spoil things by taking her hand, or just touching her; she might scream the place down, thinking her hour had struck already. Suddenly, despite the grimness of it all, she was overcome by giggles and lay shaking with suppressed laughter. She didn't know what exactly there was to laugh about, other than that she felt free—free, and full of irrepressible joy. She had done it! Bonny, baby, you're stuck with me!

* * *

At first, Boniface had tried to listen to the voices behind the thin partition, but could not make out what they were saying; and the croaking of the frogs soon lulled him to sleep. At breakfast the next morning he realized that something must have gone wrong between Laura and her grandmother.

The old lady made an effort to hide it by chatting with forced gaiety; Laura sat stonily between them, her face as closed and hostile as it had been the night before. No wonder that, when breakfast was over, Stella said, "Sorry, but I'm afraid I'm going to have to leave."

"So soon, Stella Best? We had hoped—"

"Sorry, I have no choice. I have a meeting with Ethan Woodhouse of Meeting for Sufferings, and I must see a man about a legacy he wants to make to the school. It's too bad, but that's the way it has to be."

Boniface called the main house; Harry brought down the golf cart.

"Okay, Harry," he said, "I'll take Stella Best to the ferry, if it's all right with you."

Stella and Laura took leave of each other as if they were mere acquaintances. It was bewildering and distressing. The old lady took her seat beside him in the cart, her hands on the grip on her lap. The moment they reached the open field he asked, "Stella, what on earth happened? What's the matter with Laura?"

"Not here!" she whispered.

"Shall we go back to the graveyard, where we were yesterday?"

She nodded.

They drove in silence to the little burial ground under the trees. Morning mist still shrouded the river; in the reeds, birds chirped and twittered.

"What happened?"

"Never mind that," the old lady replied brusquely. "What matters is that she is a very sick girl. Your mother was right, she needs psychiatric treatment. Urgently."

"But Stella—"

"I know! She's my granddaughter. Of course I'm prepared to take her on. But not while she is in her present state. I'm sorry, I cannot handle that."

"Stella, I—"

"Let me finish, please! I will not burden you with a responsibility you had clearly not intended to take upon yourself. But I have been dealing with adolescents all my life; I recognize schizophrenia when I see it. She must receive professional care, as soon as possible. No, let me finish! Under the law, you are her husband. Should it come to having her committed, your permission is required. You will have to instigate it. I—"

He could hold back no longer. "Stella Best! I'm sorry, but this is outrageous! I know she has problems, but she most definitely is *not* a schizo who needs to be committed! She needs—"

"Love! I know! But I refuse to be the one who—"

"I wasn't talking about grandmotherly love, I was talking about the love we speak of in meeting, the kind—"

"The kind you spell *lurve.*"

He looked at her, flabbergasted. "I—I thought you were a Friend!"

"Let's go back to the beginning, shall we? I know that I am supposed—"

"You are not supposed to do anything! As far as I'm concerned, you need never set eyes on her again! But I will not have her committed!"

"That may have been too strongly put. I meant: receive professional treatment."

"I don't want to hand her over to some stranger who hasn't the foggiest idea what she's been through!"

"Make no mistake, young man. There *are* people around who know exactly what she's been through."

"Here in the States? I'd like to know them."

She took a deep breath. "All right," she said, "take me. I saw my own husband put to death, the way she saw her father. I too was raped, and not by one brute, by a score of them. I was beaten and kicked and left for dead. And when I came to, I found myself in hell. Children massacred in the arms of their raped mothers, unborn babies hacked out of the bellies of dead women. So, forget the adolescent notion that every horror is a new one on earth."

"I—I'm sorry."

"Good for you. What I mean to say is: when you think that all she needs is someone who can identify with her experiences, forget it. That's not what she needs, or she would have availed herself of that last night. No, what she needs is a professional, to get to the bottom of her problem. That's the crux of it: she has a problem, a big one, and neither you nor I have the foggiest notion what it is. So don't you mess with it, leave her to the experts. That girl has more violence inside her than a mad lion. She is dangerous."

He sat there, shaken. Dr. Wassermann had used virtually the same words. "All right, Stella," he said finally, "I see why you can't take her on yourself. But I do maintain that what she needs is love . . . "

"Dear boy." She put a hand on his. "Don't fool yourself. There is no such thing as abstract love. If you love a woman, you don't love that of God in her, you love her like any man loves a woman: carnal love, spiritual love, love of her beautiful character, her beautiful legs, it's all one immensely powerful, overwhelming emotion. The emotion that created not the world, but *you.*"

He looked at her for a moment, then his shoulders drooped. "Okay," he said. "Where do we go from here?"

"You decide. I have had my say. And don't worry about the expense. At least I can take care of that."

Decide? What could he decide, out of the blue? He had lived toward this moment, never looked beyond it; it had gone without saying that Laura would go to her grandmother the moment they arrived in America. This was totally unexpected, he could not possibly decide anything right now. Except that Laura must not be locked up—that was out of the question. But what now? "Well," he said, "I need time to think this over. Offhand, I'd say we should go somewhere, she and I, where she can do the same kind of work she did in Germany. Somewhere, work with Indians. She has a thing about Indians . . . "

He had just been thinking aloud, trying to find his bearings, but Stella took him up on it at once. "All right," she said, "I'll ask Ethan Woodhouse. Meeting for Sufferings carries concerns like that, maybe he has an opening for the two of you on a reservation. But I want it understood that I do not agree with you, that you are acting on your own responsibility entirely."

"Don't worry, Stella. You made that clear, all right. I won't come running to you for—"

"Don't be a fool! I am an experienced educator, with more knowledge of adolescents and their problems than you know. I want you to realize, clearly, that you are deciding on this course of action not because you have sought professional advice, but because—well, God knows why. Someday you'll explain it to me."

"Stella, I—"

"Not now. I've had about as much as I can take right now. Let's go."

There was a silence.

"Do I go to see Ethan Woodhouse now," he asked, "or do I wait to hear from you?"

"Wait. Let me handle him. He's a great one for all the Quaker arguments you may have on tap. But he wouldn't be where he is if he didn't make sure first that he is on solid ground. Quaker mandarins like Ethan are no fools, you know. They are as level-headed and as canny as they come. They had better be; if you can't have violence, you must have canniness."

He didn't say what he would have liked to say. He took her to the dock, put her on the ferry and watched her leave. Only on the way back to the cottage, as it began to dawn on him what he had taken on, did the possibility occur to him that this might well be what Laura had wanted all along, that she had engineered the whole thing because she balked at the prospect of having to move in with her grandmother. 'Bonny? Why can't you and I stay together a little while longer?' She had said that a couple of times in the past and he had felt flattered. Had she done this deliberately? In that case . . .

He swung the wheel and steered the golf cart into the graveyard. There, under the soughing trees, with wavelets sloshing softly in the bullrushes, he surveyed the situation. The more he thought about it, the more he realized that crafty Laura, if this was indeed her doing, had him over a barrel. The idea of taking her to an Indian reservation was, of course, nonsense. That would be asking for trouble, if Wassermann's predictions were accurate. What he should do was follow Wassermann's instructions: 'See that she gets to a good psychiatrist as soon as she is with her grandmother.' He would have to take the place of the grandmother, that was all. He had to do what she would have done: take Laura to a doctor, sit in the waiting-room while she was being treated, read six-month-old copies of the *Saturday Evening Post* and *Reader's Digest,* day after day, until she could make it on her own.

Not a very happy prospect. And it would cost a lot of money, just their board and keep, not to mention the treatment, surely more than Stella Best could afford. Luckily, he had the bonds his father had left him. He had planned to use the money differently—a trip around the world, a sports car—well, whatever. Not in a thousand years could he have foreseen that he would be condemned to blow it all on . . . well. That, probably, was what *lurve* was all about. He had taken her on as a concern, now he was stuck with it and had to see it through to the bitter end.

He should have known! Whenever some starry-eyed Quaker in the power of the Lord presented his Meeting with a "concern," saying, 'We must do this! This is what the Lord asks us to do!' the answer had always been: 'Wonderful, Friend. How does thee plan to go about it?'

He sat in the little cart in the graveyard, listening to the wind and the rippling water for quite a while, then he turned on the engine and headed for the cottage, where Laura, crafty Laura, was waiting for him.

* * *

She watched him coming down the road between the cottages. She had decided the best thing for her to do would be to run out, greet him effusively, forestall any protestations on his part. She had no idea how he would react, but one thing was certain: he would never cast her off the way her grandmother had done.

As it turned out, he was quite tough. Not panicky, not angry, tough. "Darling!" was her cry as she ran to greet him; "No, Laura," he replied instantly, "don't 'darling' me. You and I are going to have a talk. Let's sit on the porch and have this out."

He confused her; her feeling of triumph collapsed. Good God, he was going to do it! He was going to cast her off after all! She sat down beside him on the veranda, wary, suspicious, scared. "Okay," she said, brazening it out, trying to sound as tough as he did. "What do you want to talk about?"

"Did you deliberately see to it that your grandmother would refuse to take you on?"

There seemed to be no point in denying it, he obviously saw through her. He was not as goody-goody as she had thought. He *was* tough. Like a stranger, almost. But although that frightened her, it gave her a sense of security at the same time.

"Well? Are you going to answer my question or aren't you?"

"Okay," she said, "I did."

"Why?"

"Because I was not about to move in with a total stranger."

"Would you tell me what alternative you had in mind?"

"I didn't have anything in mind," she replied. "I just didn't want to move in with a total stranger, period."

But he was having none of that. "Laura, you engineered this deliberately; you *must* have thought about the consequences."

"No, what are they?"

"That I am left holding the bag."

"The bag being me?"

"Yes."

"Thanks."

But no. "Laura," he said, completely in control of the situation, "you knew it, you deliberately arranged it that you are now my responsibility. I will take it on, on one condition."

"And that is?" She loved it, the way he suddenly had turned from sweetie-pie into tough guy. Okay, whatever he said. She could relax. He could handle her. Good old Bonny. Nice, tough Bonny.

"That you have psychiatric treatment until you are able to look after yourself. Once you are, you're on your own. Until then, I'll stand by you. Take it or leave it, that's the way it is going to be."

Her blood ran cold. "Psychiatric treatment? What for?"

"To cure your amnesia, find out who you are and send you off on your own."

"But they tried that! Hei—Dr. Schmidt tried it for years! It's no good!"

"We'll see. We start tomorrow."

"I don't want to!"

"I don't care what you want. That's the way it's going to be. You and I are going to see a psychiatrist, and we'll take it from there. If you think I'm going to let myself be saddled with you for the rest of my days, you have a surprise coming."

My God—he really scared her! Psychiatric treatment? Somebody strange, a doctor she had never seen before, putting her through the same ordeal Heinzl had put her through? "I won't do it," she said, trembling.

"You know my answer to that. Tomorrow."

"I'd sooner shoot myself!" she cried, in real panic now.

"With what?" he asked, eyebrows raised. "A popgun?"

Oh, my God . . . She had to keep hold of herself, or she'd run off, screaming. And if she did, next thing she knew he'd stick her in some asylum. "I am not kidding, Bonny. I'd sooner drown myself, throw myself out the window—"

"All right," he said, pointing behind them. "There's a window. Throw yourself out of it. Then come and make lunch. I'm hungry." He got up and went inside.

She put out a hand and caught his sleeve. But for her trembling, which was uncontrollable, she was quite calm. "You can't," she said.

"Can't what?"

"Force me to have psychiatric treatment against my will."

"All right. In that case: march. You're on your own."

"I'll kill myself!"

"Go ahead."

My God—he was going to do it! He turned away and went into the cottage. She had to—what? What could she do? Anything, anything at all, lovemaking, anything, but no psychiatric treatment, no probing . . . She ran inside and found him at the sink, where he stood filling a glass with water.

"Let's—let's talk about it! Let me explain why not! Listen to me! For God's sake! Listen!"

"I'm listening. Drink of water?"

"No!"

He drank, and wiped his lips. "Okay. I'm listening. But if you think you'll make me change my mind, save your breath. I won't. We're going to see a —"

"Listen!" Without thinking, she grabbed him by the shoulders, shook him, and saw a flicker of fear in his eyes. Was that the way? Scare him into it? But then he would pack her off to an

asylum! She had to reason with him. Seduce him. Anything. She was fighting for her life.

"All right," he said, "why not? Let's sit out there; you talk, I listen."

She followed him, back to the veranda where they sat down in the deck chairs, side by side. He looked away, at the trees, the cottages. Suddenly, crazily, she was overcome by longing for a cigar. Why? For God's sake, why?

"Okay, shoot."

"I don't want any psychiatric treatment." When he took a breath to reply, she put a hand on his arm. "Not *now*. Later."

"That's what they all say, sweetheart. I've worked in the Friends' Hospital in Philadelphia as a volunteer. Nobody wants psychiatric treatment, somebody has to tell them to get it. And I'm telling you, now."

"That business in the car? Anybody would have cracked up after that reception! With a huge dog slavering right next to me? And those trucks, and—no, that I can explain to any doctor! The miracle is that I didn't start screaming sooner. My God!"

"All right," he said. "What did you do to your grandmother?"

"That's my business."

"You must have done something to scare her away. What?"

"As I say—"

"Sweetheart," he put his hand on her knee, "knock it off." The two things didn't go together, the hand and the tough tone. He puzzled her. He took his hand away. "Okay, let's have it. What did you do?"

"I—I told her I'd kill her if she took me away."

"Away where?"

"From you." She looked at him sideways.

Well, there it was. It didn't seem to surprise him; he smiled wryly. "What a dirty thing to do," he said.

"To whom?"

"Me."

"You—you don't want me to stay with you? Just a little while longer? Until I'm ready for—"

"You'll never be ready," he said brutally. "You won't be ready until you get the screaming heebie-jeebies. And I'm not going to wait around for *that*."

There was only one way left. "Let's—let's go to bed," she said suddenly.

He turned to face her. "My God," he said, "you *must* be desperate. No, Laura. Don't talk nonsense." Then he added, "But don't be scared. I'll be there, right through it all, beside you."

She cried, "Oh, Bonny—!" slid out of her chair and burst into sobs, her head on his knees.

It took an eternity before she felt his hand, stroking her hair.

CHAPTER FOUR

M R. Baker?" the receptionist asked.

Boniface put the six-month-old copy of *Reader's Digest* back on the table. "Yes?"

"The doctor will see you now." She held the door open for him.

The consulting-room looked like an executive's office; the silver-haired man who welcomed him and waved at a chair in front of his desk looked like an executive.

"Mr.—Baker, is it? What can I do for you?"

"I'm here on behalf of my wife."

The doctor frowned. "Is she a patient of mine?"

"No, but she should be. So far, she refuses to come and see you."

The attentive gray eyes expressed nothing. "Tell me about her, Mr. Baker."

Boniface told him the whole story, from the moment the QAS had entered Camp Schwalbenbach. The gray eyes remained attentive, expressionless, until he came to the reason for his visit: "I wonder if you would take her on as a patient."

"If she comes here voluntarily, with pleasure."

"She won't."

"In that case, we'll have to wait until she changes her mind."

"Couldn't I—couldn't we do something to make her? Gently, I mean? Couldn't she be in some way committed? I would stay with her, all the time. I would share a room with her, if necessary."

The doctor now looked at him with a different attentiveness. "Let me clear up a few misconceptions of yours, Mr. Baker, before we go any further. To begin with, forcing a patient into therapy is impossible. Unless she seeks treatment of her own free will there is nothing I or any other psychiatrist can or will do. As to having her committed, that is not only a medical but a legal matter. I would not touch it unless she was clearly a danger to others or herself."

"She threatened to kill her grandmother!"

"I'm not prepared to take that at face value, Mr. Baker. It sounds, as you suggested yourself, like a means to an end. Indubitably, she wants to stay with you. And I see no reason why she shouldn't."

"The psychiatrist in Germany—"

The doctor's gaze became glacial. "I am not about to dispute either the diagnosis or the prognosis of a German colleague. Not until I have had an opportunity to work with the patient myself."

"He warned me that she might turn violent. She has begun to do so, only verbally, so far. Wouldn't it be sensible to put her in a safe place before—"

"Mr. Baker!" The doctor's voice was sharp now. "The mental patient's rights are well protected in this state, in order to avoid situations such as the one you are suggesting."

"I—I don't understand . . . "

"You married your wife as a formality, to help her acquire a visa for the United States, expecting to hand her over to her grandmother on arrival. Her grandmother refuses. Now you come to me and ask that she be committed. It was to prevent this kind of thing from happening that the law was changed recently. Too many people managed, in the past, to have their aged parents or tiresome wives committed, just to be rid of the responsibility. From what you tell me, your wife is not insane in the legal sense of the word. Until she is, no psychiatrist will consider committing her."

"But what about her amnesia?"

"Amnesia is not a committable offense, Mr. Baker. Does it render her unable to function? Or to be a useful, productive member of society? What she needs after her recent experiences is rest. Mental and emotional rest. Give her that. Take a job together with her, in some institution having to do with children, as you yourself suggested at one point. Stop fussing over her, give her something to do, something she has proved herself capable of doing, and allow time to do its work."

"But the German psychiatrist—"

"Mr. Baker, as I said before: I will not discuss my colleagues. But I may point out that our opinions may differ. From what you tell me, the gentleman in question is a Freudian from before the war. Psychiatry has moved on since then. Nowadays, in a case like hers, we start by looking for physical trauma, then for any chemical imbalance, and then we commence the appropriate treatment, psychotherapy or otherwise, as the case dictates. That, I'm afraid, is all I can do for you at this point." He rose behind his desk and went toward the door.

"But what do I do in case she does turn violent?"

"See a doctor, who may put her on some mild sedative. Let him be the judge as to whether or not she needs psychiatric treatment. And, if I may give you some advice: don't speak of committing her unless she becomes a real danger to herself or to others. Until then, you'd only land yourself in trouble." He smiled, opened the door. "Goodbye, Mr. Baker."

As he entered the waiting-room, the receptionist called, "Mrs. Evers?" A huge woman rose and sailed in through the open door.

"Do you want us to send you a bill, or would you like to settle now?" the receptionist asked.

"I'll pay now, thank you."

"That will be twenty-five dollars. Would you like a receipt?"

While he stood waiting for her to write out the receipt, he decided he had better go to Meeting for Sufferings after all, to find out about the assignment Stella Best had mentioned on the phone that morning. This was not what he had had in mind, but if no psychiatrist would take her on unless she went of her own accord, all he could do was wait.

Before going to see the Assistant Secretary for Indian Affairs of Meeting for Sufferings, he had a cup of coffee and a Danish in a small, dainty Snack Shoppe opposite the offices of MFS. There, on the spur of the moment, he asked for some paper and an envelope and wrote a letter to Dr. Wassermann, telling him of his predicament and asking him for any advice he might care to give. He addressed the letter to UNRRA Camp, Schwalbenbach, British Zone, Western Germany. As a return address he gave Meeting for Sufferings, Philadelphia.

The letter was like a cry for help stuck in a bottle and dropped in the ocean. Given the chaotic conditions in Occupied Germany, it was unlikely ever to get to Dr. Wassermann who had probably moved on by now. Even if it were to reach him eventually, how long would it take for a reply to get back to Philadelphia? By that time matters would have been decided anyhow, one way or another.

But the writing of it helped; it was a solace just to unburden himself to the one man who would understand. It had all seemed so simple, so straightforward: marry her, take her to her grandmother and flee. By now they should have gone their separate ways, he should have started to pick up a life of his own—postwar life, full of romantic adventure and realized dreams. But she had cheated him out of that by refusing to play the role assigned to her, and now here he sat, sipping foul coffee in Ye Olde Snack Shoppe, opposite the gloomy red-brick building of Meeting for Sufferings, massive and severe in its monumental Quaker humility. Ethan Woodhouse lurked in there with some worthy concern for the both of them, one of those weighty Friends who always made him feel like a large dog bursting into their office, wagging a table-brushing tail. Plain language, plain clothes, plain living might have become things of the past, but the Quaker personality had not changed, neither had the elementary Testimony: 'All He has is thee.' At that moment, he wished with all his heart and all his soul that God would now choose some other instrument to transmit His love to Laura, for he himself felt like giving her a sharp kick up the butt. But well, these were just idle thoughts, while the prune-mouthed proprietress of Ye Olde Home of Heartburn sliced miniature sandwiches at the counter, a canary somewhere behind a bead curtain tried to pierce the sound barrier, and the radio gave vent to the Mormon Tabernacle Choir singing "Trees." God knew for how long he would have to go on carrying her, in sickness and in health. Stuffy old George Weatherby's misgivings about the wedding vows had not been so spinsterish after all—*'For richer, for poorer, to love and to cherish, until death do us part.'*

Well, he'd better go and see the guy across the street.

The moment Boniface confronted Herbert Haring III, Assistant Secretary for Indian Affairs, one thing instantly became obvious: the little man behind the untidy desk did not consider his visitor to be a gift from the gods. Haring, glowering at him from behind piles of files, IN- and OUT-baskets and stacks of reference books like a squirrel guarding its hoard, made no bones about the fact that he considered Boniface Baker and the ludicrous assignment set aside for him a nuisance and an outrage.

The little man, who, apart from a boy's soprano and a foul disposition, also turned out to have the vocabulary of a stevedore, told Boniface Baker with startling frankness that if Ethan Woodhouse and the Steering Committee wanted to appoint him and his wife to that retirement home in the sky called the Huni Pueblo Lazaret, there was nothing he could do to stop them. But he, Herbert Haring, would be triple goddamned if he'd go through the charade of briefing them or in any other way pretending that he took this scandalous piece of nepotism seriously. "Your appointment as custodians of the Huni Lazaret, Baker, is a purely political one. It's handed to you on a platter because of your ancestry, or because your family made a large contribution, or God knows what; anywhere but here the so-called assignment would be called featherbedding. You and your wife are going to be as useful in that pueblo as a couple of firemen on an electric locomotive. So, go and see Ethan Woodhouse, let him enlighten you; I am too busy with real concerns to fritter away my time with this kind of boondoggle. Goodbye."

The reception was so startling and the man's hostility so insulting, that Boniface was tempted to take him on. But he was battle-weary; so he meekly went to see Ethan Woodhouse, who made him wait three quarters of an hour before his spindly secretary finally said, "Ah! I think he's off the phone now. You may go in, Boniface Baker."

The office into which she ushered him was high-ceilinged, cool and patrician. Tall windows overlooked the trees in the courtyard, the walls were decorated with somber oil portraits of previous Clerks of Meeting for Sufferings—all of them after 1900, as before that time it had been considered 'creaturely activity' among Friends to have your portrait painted. Ethan Woodhouse rose to his full gangling height to welcome young Boniface, he even came out from behind his desk to greet him and shake him by the hand with a paw the size of a small frying pan. He was a giant in his sixties, stoop-shouldered and rumpled, his suit a sample chart of past meals, his tie awry, his hair tousled: the unlooked-after bachelor personified. But his eyes were as shrewd as an old badger's and his mild manner highly deceptive, as Boniface had occasion to remember. If there was one weighty Friend in Philadelphia Yearly Meeting for whom he felt a holy respect, it was benevolent, absent-minded Ethan Woodhouse.

"Sit down, sit down, Boniface," the old man said, pointing at a sagging leather armchair in front of his desk. He himself loped back to the one behind his desk, slumped down, leaned back and put his enormous feet on the desk between himself and his visitor. "Well, well," he said, "that was quite a surprise to hear from Stella Best that you and your wife are available to do some work for us. Did you meet with Herbert Haring of our Indian Section?"

Boniface told him he had and what course the interview had taken. It did not seem to surprise the old man, at least not his shoes which were all Boniface could see of him. Their heels were worn down and the elastic straps of his spats were frayed. The voice behind the shoes said, "Yes, that sounds like Herbert. He's not a Friend, you know, but a humanistic social worker. To non-Quaker social workers, the Huni Lazaret is an anathema."

"Why?"

"It's one of the oldest spiritual concerns we carry. It's funded by a grant made in the seventeen-hundreds by a colorful Friend called Buffalo McHair, as a memorial to a girlfriend of his called Gulielma Woodhouse, a great-great-great-aunt of mine. She was a medical missionary among the Indians, an eccentric woman known among the trappers and the buffalo hunters as 'Pissing Gulie.' " The shoes separated for a moment to show the old badger's face, peering at him. "You may have heard of her?"

Boniface said he had; the shoes joined together again.

"Matter of fact, she was quite an Amazon. Became blood-sister to the Huni Chief, after he took her prisoner. Interesting ceremony, that." The shoes separated. "Familiar with it?" the old badger inquired impishly.

"Can't say I am."

"Well, books containing descriptions of it were handed out to faculty only, until recently. Even nowadays it needs a declaration signed by the Dean of the Department that the student needs the information for scientific purposes."

Boniface wondered what the old man was leading up to. The thing about Ethan Woodhouse was that you never knew what went on behind those canny, twinkling eyes. "Was this Gulielma the one who started the lazaret, Ethan Woodhouse?"

"No, no; that was Buffalo McHair. The first custodians were a natural daughter of his, a Shawnee Indian girl, and her husband, an idealistic great-great-uncle of mine, of whom there were a few. So there were in your case; I recall an Indian girl called Himsha who—this was a hundred years or so later—married a namesake of yours, another idealist. They tried to start a school among the Hunis at the time of the Civil War or thereabouts. He was shot for his pains. Your branch of the family?"

"No, he was a descendant of Moses Baker. The son of Cleopatra, our common ancestor's black slave."

The shoes separated again for a moment of contemplation. "Rum lot, those ancestors of ours."

"You could say that."

"Well, don't let's get any ideas about ourselves. We're a bunch of eccentrics too, to denizens of the world like Herbert Haring. And that's exactly what the lazaret in the Huni Pueblo needs: a constant supply of eccentrics. Haring sparks from all orifices at the mere mention of the place. Did he call it 'Potemkin's Village?' "

"No."

"Well, in his eyes, that's exactly what it is."

"I don't understand."

The shoes swung off the desk; the old badger now eyed him full face. "It's a monument of love. A sort of Quaker Taj Mahal. There never was a practical point to its existence. It was useless and a waste of money from the day it was built, two centuries ago. It's a monstrous Valentine, from a God-smitten old rogue to a mischievous saint."

"Why is it useless?"

"Because the Hunis never needed a lazaret, never wanted one, and decided from the word go that they would never set foot inside it. To the Huni, sickness is the result of a spell thrown over a person by a witch, who prolongs his or her own life at the expense of others. Smaller ailments are supposed to be caused by quarreling, by having bad thoughts, by sacrilege; in order to cure those, a confession must be made to the mother's brother. You can understand why, according to our records, not one single patient ever presented him- or herself to us for treatment. To keep that sort of enterprise going is not sane to professional social workers. That's why Buffalo McHair stipulated in his grant that the place must be staffed by active members of the Society. His aim was, obviously, to maintain a Quaker presence among the people Gulielma loved, so that her spirit might remain alive among them. It has been our custom from the beginning to staff the lazaret with older members of the Society: widows, widowers, Friends whose lives had spoken and who found solace and purpose in spending their last years among the Huni Indians to maintain a Quaker presence."

"Sounds reasonable enough."

"Yes, but the most eccentric aspect of the whole undertaking is that the Hunis totally ignore the Quakers in residence. They treat them as if they didn't exist. It needs a peculiar kind of Friend to be able to live in cheerful invisibility among people who would step over him if he dropped dead at their feet. The last one was a tender old Friend called Parry Winkler. He lived in the lazaret for a number of years. His hobby was cliff-dwelling birds. One nest he wanted to investigate was too far from the edge; he dropped off the cliff at the age of eighty-seven. It was a great loss. He was a truly luminous Friend."

The old badger swung his chair around and, humming tunelessly, gazed for a few moments out of the window at the trees in the courtyard, which were alive with riotous blackbirds, a first hint of fall. "What most infuriates the Harings among us," he continued, "is that, after pretending all the time that the resident Friend does not exist, the Hunis pick clean the lazaret the moment he's gone. They steal everything: drugs, medications, bandages, stores, the lot. So each time a new custodian moves in we have to fit out the place from scratch. The grant pays for it, but our Harings want the money to be spent on a worthier cause, not waste it on"—he swung back his chair—"What did he call it this time?"

"He called it a lot of things. Featherbedding, among others."

Ethan Woodhouse sighed. "Ah," he said. "How little they understand the real function of the place!"

Boniface did not comment. As far as he was concerned, Herbert Haring was right. It sounded like a nonsensical undertaking, and the idea of Laura and he becoming the custodians of an old rogue's Quaker Taj Mahal failed to attract him. Yet the atmosphere of the office, this ancient building that had once been a Meeting House, the somber portraits on the wall contrived to convey an impression of mystical purpose, a reality of which Herbert Haring knew nothing and which he himself could only sense. "Well, Ethan Woodhouse," he said finally, "I appreciate your kindness, but I wonder—well, I just don't think this is quite what my wife needs, in her present condition."

The old badger's eyes peered at him with unsettling perspicacity. "Let me be the judge of that when I meet her," he said. "Speak for yourself."

"But she is an unstable—"

"In other words: you don't see the point of it either. Well, let me explain. The Hunis are among the most secretive and xenophobic Indians in America. Because of their almost total isolation, they are also the most primitive. They still live in the same darkness and fear in which Stone Age people lived. Thunder, wind, rain, drought—to them they are all brought about by demonic forces. The only ones who can exorcise the demons are their shamans, who also tell the future, read thoughts, perform miracles, relieve fear. But the shamans can no longer hold back the tide. Less than thirty miles from the pueblo, in the Alamogordo Desert, the first atom bomb was exploded six months ago. The pueblo must have been shaken to its foundations. I don't know how the shamans explained it to the people, but it must be obvious to them that time is running out. In a few years, the twentieth century will have overwhelmed that last stronghold of the Stone Age. This is our concern: Friends have been involved with the Hunis for two centuries. We cannot, at this critical moment in their history, desert them. We must try to help them make the transition from the Stone Age to the Atom Age without destroying their identity in the process."

"But how can we, if they ignore us?"

"They pretend not to see, but they see. They don't acknowledge the Friendly presence in their midst, but it is there. Our duty, as always, is to be available if needed."

"But my wife—"

"Your wife spent three years in a concentration camp, after going through an unspeakable experience. If anyone knows the terror of the Stone Age first hand, it is she."

"But she is an amnesiac who needs help herself!"

The old man rose. "Boniface Baker," he said, "stop hiding behind thy wife's skirts. I will see for myself whether she is fit to take on the assignment. Make an appointment with my secretary for her to come to see me, tomorrow." He held out his hand. "Goodbye, Boniface."

Fuming, but incapable of expressing his feelings under the

stare of all those weighty Friends who had gone before, he let himself be ushered out. The spindly secretary smiled when he asked her for an appointment for his wife. "Ethan Woodhouse is a hard man to resist," she said. "I'm sure your wife and you will be quite happy in the Huni Pueblo. And very useful."

"Someday, I'd like you to explain to me why."

"I can't," she said. "But I have unlimited confidence in his judgment. He has held this post for a long time, you know. What he doesn't know about human character by now isn't worth knowing."

"I'm happy for him he has such a loyal assistant," Boniface said. "I wish I shared your confidence. My wife—"

"You'll see," she said blithely. "He'll tell you more about your wife after meeting with her for five minutes than—well—anyone else."

He smiled wanly and took his leave. One thing he did not need at that moment was a woman Friend with a chronic case of hero worship.

*　*　*

When Laura Baker was shown in by his secretary the following day, Ethan Woodhouse saw to his irritation that young Boniface accompanied her with the obvious intention of remaining present during the interview. "Good afternoon, Laura Baker," he said, shaking her hand. "Please have a seat."

Boniface pulled up a second chair.

"If you don't mind, I'd like to labor with your wife in private."

The boy glowered at him, the girl observed him coolly. She was quite a surprise; his first impression of her was one of power. He had expected a fey, vacillating creature; she turned out to be one of the strongest personalities that had ever entered his office.

"I think I should be present," the boy said.

Ethan smiled at the girl who sat sizing him up. "Laura? It's up to you."

She hesitated for a moment, then she turned to the boy and said, "It's all right, Bonny. I don't mind seeing him alone."

The boy rose and went to the door without a word; the effectiveness of a Quaker education was demonstrated by the fact that he did not slam it as he left the room.

"Well, I'm happy to see you, Laura. Did your husband describe the nature of the assignment I have in mind for you?"

"Yes," she said indifferently.

"And how does it strike you?"

She shrugged her shoulders. "Sounds okay to me."

"Well, let's talk about you for a moment. I read the report on your experiences, and there is one aspect that particularly interests me."

She seemed to stiffen. It was as if a door closed.

"How did you manage, as a child of fifteen, to make your way to that camp on your bicycle, under the noses of the Germans? Quite a feat at any age. Was it mostly luck, or did you plan it meticulously?"

"I don't remember. I don't remember anything before I arrived in the camp."

"Ah yes, of course. When do your memories start?"

She looked at him sullenly. "When I woke up in the doctor's office."

"Do you have any idea what caused your amnesia?"

"Emotional trauma," she replied promptly.

"Did you receive treatment?"

"Yes."

"Where?"

"In the camp."

"What kind of treatment?"

"Psychotherapy and hypnotherapy." It came out pat, an old record.

During the silence that followed, he observed her over his folded hands. She did not look at him, but he sensed that she was observing him too. She was as watchful and as wary as a wolverine. Yet there was about her a strange radiance that he could not define. Beautiful child, very strong. Fascinating.

"Tell me, Laura: how do you feel about going to live among the pueblo Indians?"

She looked him straight in the eye and said, "I'm ready to go wherever way opens."

Et ta soeur, he found himself thinking. It sounded better than the English equivalent, which was fairly coarse. Maybe the French was too, you never really knew. "Tell me about the work you did in Germany, how you feel about that."

"I worked with children and babies in a *Hospiz*," she replied, bored. "I had no problems with them. I'll work with any children: Indian, Chinese, Zulus, it's all the same to me. Wherever my husband wants to go, I go. If he doesn't, I don't."

She certainly was a surly young woman, but that radiance she had brought into the room made him decide to labor with her at a deeper level. "Your father was killed because he had been trying to save the lives of Jewish babies. We don't know if he ever succeeded. Sounds like a senseless sacrifice, doesn't it? Do you think you should leave it at that?"

"What do you mean?" She was openly hostile now.

"Let me read you something." He got up and went to the bookcase. "One of the ancestors of your husband, the first Boniface Baker, was a stableboy in Swarthmoor Hall. You know about Swarthmoor, Margaret Fell? The first Boniface died in a dungeon in Lancaster Castle, where he was imprisoned because he was a Quaker, together with his young wife, Ann Traylor. His widow described his death in her journal. Here it is." He took the book back to his desk, found the page and read aloud.

"Although he was by far the most cheerful and loving among us, Bonny became rapidly weaker, and on Christmas Eve of the year of our Lord 1663 he died. He was lucid and at peace until the end, whispering to us he had no fear or pain, because of his knowledge that it was so ordained by the Lord in His infinite love and mercy. I, from my mortality, cried out, 'Why? What could be God's purpose in letting thee die so young?' He looked at me as if he were already drawing away; I thought it was the light of the candle shining in his eyes and I begged Thomas Woodhouse to remove it. I heard him whisper, 'It is the seed of the future.'

"I did not want to disturb his last moments, yet I could not help but cry, 'What seed? Bonny, what dost thou mean?'

"He was silent for so long that I thought he had passed. But then his voice came, quietly and with a strange joy which at that moment seemed, to me, demented. 'Remember me, and do not rest until . . .'

" 'Until what, Bonny? What?'

" 'Until, by thy labor, the seed has grown a harvest of light and love.' "

He closed the book. "In your father's apparently senseless death also there is contained, somewhere, a seed waiting to grow a harvest of light and love. What happens to that seed is up to you now."

She looked at him with barely contained fury; then she rose.

He was tempted to press on, but experience had taught him when to leave well enough alone. "Tell your husband he may take up an advance on your salaries," he said matter-of-factly. "Let him come back tomorrow to see me and we'll settle the details."

She turned without a word, strode to the door and slammed herself out.

He sat for a while looking at the door, trying to put into words what it was that had impressed him so about her. In the end, he concluded that it had to do with a sense of the presence of God. Of all unlikely people, the troubled, hostile child had brought in with her a light that he had experienced but rarely. The word 'light' was a hyperbole by now; it had been used too glibly for too long among Friends to have kept its reality. There was only the poet's description left for her tormented state of grace: the Hound of Heaven was on her traces.

Well, one thing was obvious: young Boniface Baker was going to have his hands full.

*   *   *

Laura had controlled herself with difficulty. To speak her mind to the old buzzard might have tricked her onto treacherous ground. She must put that man resolutely out of her mind; he spelled danger.

Bonny sat waiting for her on a bench in the corridor; he looked up as if she were coming out of the consulting room of a doctor.

"Well?" he asked.

"Well what?"

"What do you think of his proposal?"

"Okay with me."

"It's a bizarre assignment. Think you can handle it?"

She almost gave him a snotty reply, but she should watch it now. She had to get away by herself for a bit. "Sure," she said curtly.

They went down the stairs and entered the courtyard. Halfway to the gate she said, "Look, I need some money."

"Why?"

"I want to go shopping."

"Now, just a moment," he said, grasping her arm. "Don't give me that! This is an important decision and I want a clear answer. Do you want to go to the Huni pueblo? Yes or no."

"Yes," she said.

"Do you know enough about it to say that, or is this just one of your moods? I must know because there are risks involved. There are benefits too, but the risks worry me. Do you think you can handle it?"

She smiled.

"Laura, if you can't carry on a sensible conversation at this point, I'm going to call the whole thing off!"

"Take it easy," she said. "Give me some money and I'll shop for the Far West. I promise you I won't come back with a corset on my head."

He gave her a searching look. "I'm the one who must be crazy," he said.

She grinned.

"How much do you need? Ten?"

"Let's say fifty."

That really threw him.

"Before you say anything," she continued, "Ethan Woodhouse said you can get an advance on our salary."

Muttering, he emptied his wallet.

"That's the spirit," she said. "So long, old buddy." She strode toward the gate.

"Hey!" he called after her. "Shall we meet back here? How long do you need?"

"Oh," she said, "whatever it takes to dress for a new life. Say fiveish?"

"Okay. Five o'clock, here in the courtyard. Are you sure you can manage?"

She turned her back on him without a word, marched out the gate and walked briskly away. But when she reached a busy street full of people, she panicked. An intense feeling of insecurity made her want to turn around and run back to him. She had never been on her own like this, in a strange city. But what the hell! She had fifty dollars. If she got lost, or it became too much for her, she could always hail a taxi and say 'Meeting for Suckers, please.' What kept her going was her rage at the old man. She wondered how far it would carry her, for she was shaking like a leaf. Come on, halfwit! Move!

She moved, uncertainly. People stared at her in passing. It

nearly undid her, until she realized what they were staring at: her battle dress. Ridiculous to go on walking about in British Army fatigues! At the first department store she spotted, she fled inside. It was full of people, but she felt safer indoors. She wouldn't mind spending a lot of time in here. And she should! On second thought, she needed loads of stuff. Summer dress, underwear, boots, jeans... Where was she going to put it all? Maybe best to get a suitcase first, a cheap one.

She found the luggage department and asked a girl who hung around there, "Would you have a cheap, large suitcase?"

The haughty creature sized her up and replied, "Depends what you call cheap."

"Why don't you show me some?"

"Well," the girl said, "what about this one? Very spacious, very strong."

"How much?"

"Twenty-three dollars."

"You call that cheap?"

Again the girl sized her up, as if she were measuring her for a coffin. "What you want is cardboard. You won't find that here; try a drugstore. Or the sports department. Get yourself a duffel bag."

"That's an idea. Where do I find that?"

"Second floor, right."

"Thank you very much," she said sweetly.

The girl turned away.

Maybe it would be best to buy a dress first. Or just walk around for a while. She roamed through the department store. It was incredible, Aladdin's cave. Just to buy a simple dress turned out to be impossible. There were hundreds of simple dresses; she rummaged through them helplessly, incapable of making a decision. The riches were overwhelming; she was glad they weren't planning to stay in Philadelphia. One thing was certain: they would not have a hundred simple summer dresses in the trading post of the pueblo.

Suddenly she couldn't bear it any longer, walked away and found herself in front of a counter full of boxes of cigars. One, labeled *Virgen de la Habana*, showed a Spanish beauty on the lid, peeping over a fan. "Could I help you, madam?" The man sounded polite, but he was another coffin-maker sizing her up.

"I'm looking for a box of cigars—for my husband." She was

mad! What on earth was she going to do with them?

"What does he usually smoke, madam?"

"Well, he has been smoking—what's the name?—_Schimmel-penninck._ You don't have those, do you? They're Dutch."

"No, I'm afraid we haven't had Dutch cigars for a long time, madam. How did your husband manage to lay his hands on them, may I ask? Oh, of course: a member of the Services. No, now he is back home again, he'll have to get used to our cigars. I have something similar though . . ." He opened a sliding door underneath the counter, rummaged inside and produced a box large enough to bury a cat in.

"Look, these are real Havanas, similar to Dutch cigars. _Río de Oro._ Your husband is sure to like these. Here—smell." He opened the box, breaking the seal, and held it out to her.

She sniffed. They did not smell like Heinzl's cigars. "Show me some others," she said.

"Well, let me see . . . How about these? These aren't as close to the Dutch as _Río de Oro,_ but—smell." He opened another box; the picture on the lid showed a cowboy on a bucking horse, losing his hat. _Bronco-buster, the ol'-fashioned stogie of the Far West._ She sniffed, but the label had already seduced her. "How many in this box?"

"Fifty, madam." The man looked at the bottom of the box. "Two dollars and forty-nine cents. You can't do better than that. Less than five cents a cigar."

"Okay," she said, "I'll take them."

She left the store an hour later with a yellow duffel bag hanging from her shoulder. The moment she stepped out into the crowded street, she was hit by that unnerving feeling of insecurity again. She felt like going back inside, but somehow the cigars in the duffel bag helped. They suddenly seemed less crazy; if it all became too much for her she would light one. That would make them stop and stare all right! Manfully, with an exaggerated swagger, she sauntered down the street, attracted by a sign over a shop window: WESTERN WEAR FOR GUYS AND GALS.

The window was full of ten-gallon hats, leather aprons with fringes, high-heeled riding boots with pointed toes. In a corner stood a life-size female mannequin, her hair in a red bandana, wearing T-shirt and blue jeans; what captivated her was the motto printed on the T-shirt: IF YOU CAN READ THIS YOU ARE TOO DAMN CLOSE. She had seen that sign on the backs of cars,

when they were driving to town from the Island; to have it printed on a T-shirt was a terrific idea. She should have worn that
when she went in to see Ethan Woodhouse! That would have
taken care of him all right. On an impulse, she went inside.

A quarter of an hour later, she reappeared as the replica of the
mannequin in the window: red bandana, blue jeans, T-shirt with
motto. In her duffel bag she carried, as well as her cigars and her
battle dress, another T-shirt with the legend TO HELL WITH
HOUSEWORK. This time she had no problem venturing out
into the open and mingling with the crowd. It gave her a heady
feeling of freedom. Ah, how she would love to light a cigar! She
didn't quite dare, not yet. But maybe she could find some candy.

At four-thirty she was sitting on one of the wooden benches in
the courtyard of Meeting for Sufferings, with, beside her on the
seat, the yellow duffel bag full of cigars and candy. She had
spread her arms across the back of the seat, displaying the legend on her T-shirt to the Quakers who were beginning to emerge
from the building in droves at the end of their working day.
Their startled looks provoked her into lighting a cigar, even if it
did make her feel sick. She was puffing away when Ethan
Woodhouse came out. He showed more self-control than the rest
of them and did not bat an eye as he approached her. She had
not realized that he wore spats.

"Well, Laura? Waiting for your husband?"

She took the cigar out of her mouth. "Park your pants," she
said, and made room for him on the seat.

He called her bluff, sat down, took off his hat and put it between them on the bench. "Been shopping?"

"Yes. Cigar?"

"No, thanks. I smoke only after supper."

Suddenly she began to feel insecure. "I smoke all day, myself," she said, puffing at her cigar.

"Would you mind writing to me after your arrival? To tell me
how things are among the Hunis?"

"No," she said. "I'll leave that to my husband."

"Do you want to go to the pueblo?"

"Yep."

"All right, then." He rose and held out his hand. "Goodbye,
Laura. Good luck."

She shook his hand. Only after he left did she begin to have
the shivers.

When Bonny hurried into the courtyard, a quarter of an hour late, he caught sight of her and stopped short. Suddenly she saw herself through his eyes: yellow duffel bag, cigar, IF YOU CAN READ THIS YOU ARE TOO DAMN CLOSE. She knew exactly what he was thinking: stark, raving mad. She could not possibly explain the cigar; he must never find out about Heinzl.

"Did you buy that . . . ?" He asked it so cautiously that she felt like saying 'Cuckoo!' and sticking out her tongue, but her ebullience and her self-confidence had gone. What was she doing, for God's sake? Who was she?

"Yes," she said. "I bought that." She tried to hide the cigar in her hand.

"That's all right, then," he said with forced jocularity. "Well, shall we go?"

"Okay."

He picked up the duffel bag and was startled by its weight. "What on earth have you got in here?"

"Nothing. Woman's things. If it's too heavy for you, I'll carry it."

"No, no!"

He led the way to the street. When she thought nobody was watching she threw the cigar away.

CHAPTER FIVE

THE desert west of the small town of Kissing Tree was arid and infinitely lonely. The dark mountains on the horizon were already capped with snow; the lion-colored hills of the Llano Estacado were mottled with desert cactus and juniper bushes, indistinguishable from the black cattle roaming in the solitude.

The old Chevrolet Bonny had bought in Pennsylvania, with which Laura and he had crossed the country, trailed a house-high cloud of dust as it bounced down the rutted cart track that, according to a sign on the highway, would take them to the McHair ranch. They would have to leave the car behind when they set out from there; at the diner where Bonny had telephoned ahead, a man in a ten-gallon hat had said, "Yore headin' for some mighty rugged country; better get yosself and the missus some leather pants. Desert cactus can be right prickly, if yore hoss gits spooked by tumble weed."

After driving for over an hour across the desolate plain, they arrived at a gate where two people with horses stood waiting. A huge dog came loping toward the car, barking. The two people turned out to be a young Indian squaw of about Laura's age, with a closed face and two long black braids; the other was a man with a sombrero, a face like old leather and a dazzling smile. "*Señor* Baker?" he asked, after Bonny had wound down the window.

"*Sí, amigo.*"

"*Doña* Ana send me show you way. Shall I steer?"

"Steer? Ah, yes. No, that won't be necessary. Why don't you hop in beside me? Laura, would you mind sitting in the back?"

She got out and climbed into the back, between their overnight bags. The Mexican slid into the front seat and slammed the door. *"Oké, señor, vamos! Par aqui . . . "*

The car bounced on, slowly so as not to raise too much dust for the Indian girl who rode behind them, leading the Mexican's horse. The Great Dane loped along beside her, barking, looking gigantic in the swirling dust. The beautiful black-haired squaw with the two horses was the first wild Indian Laura had ever seen. She watched her through the rear window as they drove along; the girl rode beautifully, with unselfconscious grace. Suddenly the image was exactly like the picture of herself in the Far West that had sustained her these past months: the real America, where cowboys galloped across the prairie with their blood brother, the Indian Chief.

As she watched the girl riding that magnificent stallion she suddenly knew: 'We are going to be friends. Tomorrow, I'll be riding that other horse, and we'll go galloping across the desert together, that huge dog bounding along with us.' She wondered what tribe the girl belonged to. Apache? Or was she a Huni? The whole thing suddenly took on a different aspect. It came as such a relief that she couldn't help herself: she waved to the girl on the horse.

But the young squaw, although looking straight at her, did not respond. Her contempt was unmistakable.

Hurt, bewildered, Laura turned away and looked at the road ahead. Of course it was childish to feel hurt; it took a long time for an Indian to trust you. Even so, she could at least have smiled. Well, so much for dreams.

*　*　*

They approached a dark cluster of trees around another of those silver water towers on spidery legs that were typical of the desert. "The ranch?" Boniface asked.

The Mexican said, *"Sí, Señor. La hacienda."*

As they drove into the coolness of the oasis, the first thing Boniface noticed was the spicy scent of woodsmoke. "Is that cedar you are burning?"

"No, Señor, piñon."

Spanish spruce. He had read in the library book that the slopes of the Sacramento Mountains were covered with piñon. But the oasis was made up of cottonwood, huge, scaly gray trees, barren and wintry, garlanded with mistletoe, their branches overhanging the cart track. A passel of dogs came to meet them and ran along with them, yapping. The car rounded a bend in the dirt road and Boniface saw a cluster of adobe buildings. The largest must be the main house, the others stables. All were shaded by the giant trees; during the summer it must be broiling hot here. Beyond the buildings, behind a white plank fence, a number of horses watched them curiously. There were tractors, a pump shed, a tall mast with a radio antenna; as they drew up in front of the house he spotted a small building in a grove of greener trees with a bell tower and a cross on its steeple.

He stopped the car in front of the central archway of the main building and saw it led to a patio. *"Gracias, amigo,"* he said to the ranch hand, and got out to open the door for Laura. The girl with the horses drew up and slid out of the saddle. "Hi," she said. "I'm Gulielma McHair."

"Oh, hello!" Boniface was surprised; he had taken the girl to be an Indian servant. "I'm Boniface Baker, and this is my wife, Laura."

They shook hands.

"I'd better warn you," the girl said abruptly, "before I take you to see my grandmother. In case you weren't told, she's a dwarf. Not a midget; she never grew beyond the age of five. But, as you will discover, she is by no means a child. Juancho! *Hazme el favor de secar a Hidalgo y llevarlo al establo."* Without waiting for a reply she turned back to them, said, "This way, please," and led the way into the patio.

It was ancient and closed, with a stillness that made it appear to belong to another world. An old apricot tree shaded a glass door, bougainvillea covered the walls, there were miniature orange trees in wooden barrels. Their footsteps echoed off the walls as they walked down the flagstone path to the glass door; the girl opened it for them, but the dog got in first. Inside, a high-pitched voice cried, "Gulielma! Keep that creature out of here! How often must I tell you? Take him out! Quick, quick!" The girl hurried inside; Boniface and Laura waited. They heard, inside, the sounds of a scuffle, a smack, a puppyish yelp; the girl appeared again, dragging the Great Dane by its collar. Boniface glanced at Laura, worried about the dog, but she seemed unaffected by it. "Would you go in, please? Grandmother is expecting you."

They entered a dark, vaulted room full of oversized Spanish furniture. There was a large fireplace with burning logs smelling of piñon smoke. A child came to meet them in the dim light. "Welcome, Mr. and Mrs. Baker, I'm pleased to see you here. How do you do?"

It was *Doña* Ana. She did indeed look like a child of five. But her eyes were shrewd and her face, babyish in its proportions, was wizened like an old apple. She held out a wrinkled hand, so small and fragile that Boniface shook it gingerly. "Won't you sit down?" She indicated a pair of uncomfortable-looking chairs, hopped onto a settee and wriggled backward into the cushions. Her feet in tiny high-button shoes did not reach the edge of the couch. She clapped her hands; a maid appeared in the doorway. "*Holandés para cuatro.*"

"*Sí, Señora . . .*" The maid disappeared.

"You must have done a great deal of research on the Hunis, Mr. Baker?"

"We heard about this assignment only a couple of weeks ago. I have some books—"

"Books? Don't be ridiculous," the old lady said. "Gulie will tell you about them. She has been in and out of the pueblo ever since she was a child."

The Mexican servant shuffled into the room, put down a tray with six small glasses and left.

"Gulie!"

The girl rose and seemed to grope on the table before she found the tray. The old lady said sharply, "Where are your glasses, child? You'll have an accident."

With a surly look the girl took a pair of spectacles out of her shirt pocket and put them on; they transformed her instantly from an exotic Indian beauty into a Jewish intellectual.

"Well," the old lady said, "welcome to the ranch. *Salud!*" She tossed back her drink and held the empty glass out to the girl, who replaced it with a full one.

"All right, Gulielma. Tell them about the Hunis."

"Everything?" The girl smiled.

"Everything. *Salud!*" There went the second glass; it was promptly replaced with a third one.

"All right: the Hunis!"

"Well," the girl said, "they are Pueblo Indians, and rather similar to other—"

"Nonsense. They are totally different, for the simple reason that they never see anybody except you, Father Alvarez and occasionally me. And of course whatever Quakers are in residence. The pueblo wasn't discovered by the Spanish until—"

"It wasn't discovered by the Spanish at all, but by the Quakers."

"Pah! You mean that woman? Well, she may have been a Quaker in name, but the way she carried on did not exactly bring the Glad Tidings."

"Grandmother means that Gulielma Woodhouse ministered to the sick and the injured without proselytizing—"

"That's exactly what I mean! She was made a prisoner and became a blood sister, and we all know what kind of ceremony *that* entails."

"I was named after her," the girl said, smiling.

"Nonsense! You were named after your great-aunt. Anyhow: the Hunis had no contact with any Christian missionaries until 1870—"

"Catholic missionaries."

"Now who is telling this story? You or I?"

"I thought I was."

"All right. Go ahead. But don't start writing your own history. Mrs. Baker, you are not drinking."

"I don't drink," Laura said curtly.

"Ah, but you should try this! Excellent against the vapors. Gulie!"

The girl obediently offered the last remaining glass of gin to Laura; when it was refused, she handed it to her grandmother who swiftly tossed it off. "Well," the old lady said, "why are you dithering? Tell them about the Hunis."

"As I said, they were not occupied by the Spanish during the invasion of 1598 under Juan de Ornado because they were simply never discovered. When you go there yourselves, tomorrow, you will see that the pueblo is on top of a mesa and invisible from the valley. The Gulielma Woodhouse lazaret was started in 1758 and it's been continually operated by Quakers—"

"Pah!" the old lady said. "A fat lot of good it's done!"

The maid appeared in the doorway and mumbled something.

"Supper is served," the old lady said. "Let's go; we don't want it to get cold. You tell them during supper, Gulie. Help me, please." She stretched out her hands and the girl helped her off the couch.

"I'd rather not eat, if you don't mind," Laura said.

"You don't feel well?" The old lady peered up at her.

"I'm tired. Would it be all right if I went straight to bed?"

"As you wish. Dolores will take you to your room. Dolores! *Acompaña a esta señora a su cuarto.*"

"I'll see my wife to her room," Boniface said.

"Nonsense!" the old lady cried. "You come in to supper! My dear, the woman will take you there. If you need anything, let her know. Dolores!"

Everybody obeyed, without demur. Boniface realized that this was not a visit but an audience.

The dining room was another dark vault, full of enormous furniture. The table was lit by candles in ornate silver candelabra. The old lady was lifted into her chair by Gulielma. She imperiously clapped her hands, two Mexican servants appeared carrying dishes. They served the old lady first, Boniface second and Gulielma last.

"Frijoles y chile." The high child's voice echoed in the vault of the room. "What I should have ordered today is dried buffalo meat. That was the menu of the first Franciscan missionaries in this part of the world. Are you familiar with New Mexico, young man?"

"I visited Sante Fé when—"

"The Llano Estacado has remained unchanged since those days. No wagon roads, no cart tracks beyond this hacienda. All trade with the Hunis is still carried on by pack mule, only mules can clamber up those trails, and down, which is worse. Can you imagine how the early Franciscan fraters must have felt, when they first penetrated this inhospitable country? . . . "

She carried on about the early Franciscan monks during the rest of the meal; she had forgotten that her granddaughter was supposed to be telling him about the Hunis. Boniface found his attention wandering. What was the matter with Laura this time? What was she doing, all alone in a strange bedroom in this strange household? He stared at the girl across the table while the grandmother carried on and on. At first, the girl had seemed remote and odd; now, patiently listening in the candlelight to the dwarf's interminable monologue, she looked quite charming in an original, exotic way. Poor girl! What a life to be at the beck and call of a screaming, gin-swilling ... Well, never mind.

They were on to the dessert now: lugubrious, ear-shaped bagels, or something, covered with what had to be eighty-proof vanilla sauce. At last, the meal was over; but the imperious dwarf clapped her hands commandingly and said, "Wait! I have something special for you."

The Mexican maid appeared, carrying a box of cigars; she opened it for the old lady to select one. *Doña* Ana lit it and leaned back, letting the smoke trickle from her mouth with obvious relish. "Try one," she said to Boniface. "I promise you, you have never tasted anything like it."

"I'm sorry. I don't smoke."

She was not listening. She rarely listened, it seemed. "During the Civil War, when the Union troops conquered the pueblo, they stole the treasure from the bat cave that must have been there since the Mayas. But it was my father-in-law, Jesse McHair, who discovered the real treasure: guano. Dung, thousands of years old, from prehistoric bats. He made a fortune by growing the tobacco for these cigars on soil fertilized with guano from the bat cave. Taste one. Come on!"

"I'm sorry, I'm sure they're excellent but I really am a nonsmoker."

The old lady looked at him with distaste and clapped her hands again. The Mexican maid reappeared.

"Acompaña al señor a su cuarto."

"Sí, Señora."

The woman was obviously waiting for him to move; he realized he had been dismissed. He thanked *Doña* Ana for the meal, wished her and the girl good night. He was about to follow the maid into the corridor when the shrill child's voice shrieked after him, "If your wife isn't fit to travel tomorrow, you're welcome to stay!"

"Thank you, *Doña* Ana."

He followed the maid. What the devil had he done, for the little old tartar to dismiss him so unceremoniously? Just because he didn't happen to smoke, let alone foot-long stinkers raised on bat-droppings? Boy! After this evening, the Hunis would come as a relief. He couldn't wait for someone to give him the silent treatment and look right through him. Guano from prehistoric bats! It was a wonder she and her family of desert barons hadn't started a still with it.

The maid led the way into a patio, then through a low archway into another patio. The pungent odor of wood smoke was everywhere. Cicadas chirped with loud, monotonous grating; the sky was full of stars. They were about to enter a third patio when, out of nowhere, the huge dog hurled itself between them. The maid squealed with fright; he himself needed a moment to recover. A girl's voice called, "Boomer! Here! Come here!"

There she was, a dark shape in the starlight. "I'm so sorry," she said. "He's very young still, and— " The dog came racing back and nearly threw the maid off her feet as he stormed by. In the dark, he looked the size of a calf. *"Gracias, Dolores, gracias."*

"No hay de que, Señorita. Buenas noches, Señor."

"Buenas noches, amiga," he said.

When they were alone, the girl asked, "Would you like to see the stables? I have to walk Boomer, and I want to have a look at the horses."

He thought of Laura waiting for him, but let himself be tempted. The girl was like a breath of fresh air after the past few weeks. Only now did he realize the stress he had been under. "I'd love to," he said.

She took him back through the two dark patios, opened a door in a wall and suddenly they found themselves in the open. The dog came storming from the darkness and hurtled through the doorway; this time Boniface was prepared for it. "Lovely night," he said, as they walked side by side across an open space toward the stables.

"Yes, the nights are lovely." She opened a door in the dark, low building, lit by a soft golden glow. "Come in," she said.

He followed her inside. A row of oil lamps lined the rough stone wall of a long passage, lighting up a series of stalls, each with a horse in it. There was a continuous sound of munching; each horse had its nose in a feeding bin.

"By the way," she said, "I've been waiting for a chance to give you this." She pulled a crumpled letter out of a pocket in her jeans. "Sorry it got messed up, but as it was marked 'Private and Personal' I thought it best to hang on to it. Here you are."

The envelope was covered with exotic stamps from Western Germany, British Zone, forwarded from Philadelphia. *'Dr. Al-*

fred Wassermann, D.P. Camp, Schwalbenbach.' "Well, what d'you know!" he said, astounded. "I wrote the man only a couple of weeks ago, and here's his reply! I thought it would take months."

"Well, I hope it's good news," she said. Then she added, "Do you mind if I ask you something—?"

His instant reaction was one of withdrawal. Goddammit, he might have known. Another curiosity seeker.

She sensed his reaction, and blushed so deeply that it was visible in the dim light. "I—I just wondered if I could have the stamps . . . "

"Of course!" he said contritely. "I'll give them to you now . . ." He tore open the letter. "Here, take the whole envelope."

"But I didn't want— You may need the return address . . . "

"It's on the letter," he said, and put it in his pocket. "Now tell me about the horses."

She gave him a searching look, then she said, "Well, this is Hidalgo, my stallion. You saw him this afternoon."

"He's lovely."

"Thank you."

"Must be quite a handful."

"That he is."

As they moved on to the next stall, he felt as if a load were being lifted from his shoulders. The innocent request for the stamps, the munching horses, the smell of manure and sawdust, the scent of ammonia, the lamplight—it was a world of peace and youth, evoking a sense of nostalgia, as if he had known a world like this, once upon a time. But he hadn't, it was the world where he would have been now if he had come home from the war like the others: relieved, free—ready for life, adventure, romance. He had a feeling of bitterness at the thought of Laura, waiting for him in a bedroom they would share, filled with gloom and moodiness and the menace of things to come.

"Your wife is quite lovely," the girl said.

"Ah? Yes."

"Unbelievable to us, with our sheltered lives out here, what she must have gone through. All I have ever known is horses, and stablehands, and Indians. And Grandmother, of course."

"A remarkable person."

She laughed. "You can say *that* again!"

The horses munched in the silence; one of them banged

against a partition with a hollow sound. In one of the stalls, a chicken cackled briefly.

"You keep chickens in here too?"

"No, that's just one of the bantams. We let them run wild; the horses make friends with them. Horses get lonely very quickly."

"I never knew that."

"They're like people. Each of them has a distinct personality, different from the others. Some of them are very bright. Here— this one. His name is Chester. He drinks beer, eats pizza and smokes cigarettes."

"Hi, Chester," he said, rubbing the hard forehead of a black horse that stared at him with startling awareness.

"The only thing he doesn't do," she said by his side, "is talk. Sometimes he almost does. Don't you, Chester?"

The horse threw its head back alarmingly and whinnied. Boniface stepped back.

She laughed. "Don't let him bully you. He's a lamb to ride, the moment he realizes you are as bright as he is. He tries you out first, though. If you like, you can ride him tomorrow, to the pueblo. Do you ride?"

"I used to as a boy."

"In that case, you won't have any problem. It's like skating, they say. Once you've learned how to do it, you never forget."

"Let's hope so."

"Does your wife ride?"

"She doesn't remember anything about her life before the camp. But she occasionally talks about a horse she had once, called Winnetou."

"That's an Apache name."

"It is?"

"Odd, for a Dutch horse. I wonder if she rides English or Western."

"I wouldn't know."

They walked as far as the wall at the end of the passage. There was a score of horses. The munching seemed to get louder, until it sounded like the churning of a large machine. Somewhere a horse sloshed the water in its bucket as it drank.

"About the Hunis—I gather you go there quite often?" he asked.

"Oh, yes. At least once every two weeks. Why?"

"You know them well?"

"As well as anyone, I guess."

"They don't ostracize you, the way they do the Quakers?"

"Oh, no! But they don't ostracize the Quakers either. Who told you that?"

"It's what they believe in Philadelphia. How about old Parry Winkler, our predecessor? Didn't they send him to Coventry?"

"Pardon?"

"Didn't they give him the silent treatment? That's what I was told."

She smiled. "People don't understand. To the Hunis, looking someone straight in the eye is bad magic. Mr. Winkler surely knew that. I once saw an old squaw called Lucille sitting next to him on the edge of the mesa, looking out over the valley for hours without exchanging a word, as if they were having Quaker meeting for worship. Lucille was not her real name, of course. They don't like giving us their real names. It's like their fear of being looked straight in the eye. It takes something away from them, they believe. You have to accept them as they are, and in the end they will accept you."

"Will they? Philadelphia is convinced they won't."

"They won't in our sense. It may take weeks, or months, then suddenly one of them will sit down beside you, as Lucille did in the case of old Mr. Winkler. Yet they probably never exchanged a single word."

"And you? Do they ever talk to you?"

"A few of them do. There's a young couple, a potter and his wife. He makes little ceramic figures of animals and bowls and vases. They're called Atu and Morga. That's to say, that's what they want to be called. We're quite friendly, especially since she is expecting her first baby. I think that, secretly, she'd like to go to the hospital in Kissing Tree to have it. She doesn't dare, of course, it would be bad magic. But she's scared."

"Why?"

"Well, the infant mortality in the pueblo is very high, right now. It always has been, but the last six months or so it has been very serious. Mr. Winkler worried about it. He told me he would write to Philadelphia. Did he?"

"Not that I know. I'm sure they would have told me if he had."

"He must have left it too late. But it is worrying. Since last May or so, there have been nothing but stillbirths."

"Shouldn't that be investigated?"

She shrugged her shoulders. "The brujos wouldn't allow it. They want to deal with that sort of thing themselves, without interference."

"Brujos?"

"Sorry—shamans, you would call them. Medicine men. There are two of them in the pueblo; the chief shaman is called Anagonga, to the outside world, that is."

"But what about the Catholic priest?"

"Father Alvarez? He's a sweetie, but totally lost to the world. All he ever does is sit in his cloister and paint parrots."

"Parrots?"

"It's an old tradition, some arrangement between the brujos and the Catholic church that goes back to God knows when. The priest takes care of the sacred parrots in his cloister. They're anything but sacred, let me warn you. Poor Father Alvarez—whenever his back is turned, Huni urchins climb over the wall and teach the parrots dirty words. You'll be in for a shock when you visit him the first time. If you speak Spanish, that is."

There was a silence, then he said, "About that infant mortality. Why doesn't he bring in a Catholic medical mission?"

"Look," she said patiently. "You have to understand that, to the Hunis, anything to do with the outside world is bad magic. You are, I am, everyone is. They tolerate us only on condition that none of us interfere in what they consider to be their internal affairs. If Father Alvarez were to bring in outsiders to examine their women, the men would dance him off the rock."

"What do you mean?"

"That's their ancient way of execution. It's quite involved and I'll tell you all about it one of these days."

"What do we do about food?" he asked, after a moment.

"You'll find plenty of canned food among your stores tomorrow. Their staple diet is beans, and a sort of matzos they bake themselves. If you are lucky and after a month or so they have taken a liking to you, you may find a pot of beans or a stack of matzos outside your door one morning. But you'll probably never find out who put them there. So, just make out as best you can and hope for the best. My guess is that you'll do all right. Now, shouldn't you go and see how your wife is doing?"

He would have liked to go on talking with her, here in the stables, for hours. "Yes," he said. "Thanks. I'd forgotten the time."

They walked to the door. "Don't you bother," he said. "I'll find my way."

"I don't think you can. The old house is like a maze, with all those patios. Careful, here he comes!"

The dog threw itself at them the moment they stepped outside into the starry night. "Boomer! Down! Quiet!" The Great Dane barked, a deep, sonorous sound. Other dogs started to yap all around them, invisible in the darkness. Suddenly she asked, "Are you going to have meeting tonight? You and your wife, I mean?"

"Pardon?"

"Don't you have meeting for worship every night?"

"Well, yes . . . "

"I asked because I would have loved to join you. I'm a Quaker too, but I've never had meeting with anyone." She laughed self-consciously; he couldn't see her face in the dark. "I think I'm the only Friend in the Llano Estacado. Certainly in Kissing Tree."

He hated to disappoint her, but the idea of her and her dog turning up in their bedroom, with Laura in her present mood . . . "Maybe sometime soon," he said. "I'd love to, but my wife is probably in bed by now. You don't mind?"

"Not at all," she said easily. "I just thought I'd ask. This way."

She took him back through the two little patios, or maybe they were different ones. At the entrance to the third one she stopped and said, her voice low, "Here you are. The door with the light inside."

"I enjoyed our talk. Very much."

"So did I," she replied in the darkness. "Good night." Then she was gone.

He stood for a moment in the archway, mustering his courage. Then he walked to the lighted glass door, framed by bougainvillea. He knocked.

Laura's voice shouted, "Come in!"

It turned out to be yet another room full of outsize Spanish furniture, lit by candles. It was dominated by two colossal beds on one of which Laura was lying, staring at the ceiling, her hands under her head. Something about the way she lay there made him ask warily, "How are you feeling?"

"I'm fine."

"What was the matter with you?"

"When?"

"Why didn't you stay for supper?"

"Because I'd had a bellyful."

"Of what?"

"Of yak!" She sat up and swung her legs off the bed. She looked as if she were spoiling for a fight.

"I thought what the old lady had to say was quite interesting."

"I thought she was a crashing bore, and the girl with the pimples a pain in the ass!"

He felt an uprush of anger at her pointless animosity. "Knock it off, Laura!"

"Oh-ho!" she cried in a phony voice. "Strong-arm stuff! Aren't you ashamed of being unkind to the victim of the concentration camp? The poor wretch who has gone through so much? Enough to make her go cuckoo?"

"Laura, take it easy!"

"Mad!" she cried. "Nuts! Crazy! Cuckoo! Want to see? Llll!" She stuck out her tongue at him, made horns with her hands and cried, "Cuckoo! Cuckoo!"

"Don't try that act on me," he said, "you're as sane as I am, as you damn well know. You have a problem, but it has nothing to do with insanity. This is just one of your foul moods. What triggered it this time?"

"You really want to know? Really?"

"Sure."

"Okay. Before I start—do you mind?" She went to her duffel bag, rummaged inside and took out a cigar. She bit off the tip, spat it into the room and went to the candle on the bedside table to light it. As she stood there, bent over, hands on her knees, sucking the flame into the obscene thing, she looked coarse, lewd, almost as if she were turning back into the SS monster's moll. But he shouldn't exaggerate. She was just under stress, like himself. It was time they got to that pueblo. If anything, it sounded like a restful place.

She straightened up. "Sit down," she said, the cigar between her teeth, "and I'll tell you what's bothering me."

"Are you sure this is the moment? Hadn't we better wait until—"

"Until I am docile again? Little Nutcake with the clammy hands? Is that what you want?"

"Oh, for Pete's sake!"

"All right. Sit down and brace yourself. You're going to get an earful." She turned away and sat down on the bed.

Should she be allowed to do this? She sounded overwrought. She must have been lying there, staring at the ceiling for hours, with hysteria building up inside her. He should stop her before it got out of hand. But he felt weary; not tonight, not tonight. He closed his eyes.

"What are you standing there for? Are you praying, or is it the booze?"

"If you must know: yes, I was praying."

"For what?" She was waiting for a chance to let it rip.

"For strength."

"To wrestle with a nut? Relax. I'm not going to attack you. I'm not *that* far gone."

"How far *are* you gone, Laura?"

She stared at him through the smoke of her cigar, and he saw her go through another transformation, right in front of his eyes. Slowly the coarseness in her face seemed to dissipate. She stared at him with eyes that became haunted. The cigar became incongruous. She looked at him pleadingly, and said, "I—I don't know . . . Oh, Bonny—" She burst into tears.

He took her cigar away and put it on the candle-holder on the bedside table. He sat down on the edge of the bed and put an arm around her.

"Don't worry, Laura," he said, "don't be afraid. I'm with you. I'm with you all the way, don't worry."

She hid her face in his shoulder, weeping.

"Tell me. Hush now, hush. Tell me, what is it?"

"Would you—would you—" She sobbed louder.

"Would I what?" He asked it gently, filled with tenderness and pity. "Come, out with it. Would I—what?"

She buried her face deeper in his shoulder, and said something in a muffled voice.

"I can't hear what you're saying."

She lifted her head. Her face was wet with tears. Her eyes looked—impossible to say. 'Horses get lonely very quickly.' But how was it possible? He had been with her every hour of every day . . .

"I—I know I shouldn't say this, but I . . .you . . . "

"Come, Laura. Say it. That's what I'm for: to say things to. Everything."

"Everything?" She searched his eyes for the truth.

"Every single thing. Believe me, nothing will frighten me. I—" He had been about to say 'I love you.' But he did not love her. She moved him deeply, he would never desert her as long as she needed him, but he had to believe his future lay elsewhere, especially after that walk through the stables.

She looked at him as if she read his every thought. Her face became resigned.

"What is it, Laura? Come, tell me."

She gave him an odd look: tender, sad. "I know I shouldn't ask you this, but would you mind not looking at others before—before I'm able to make it on my own?"

"Others?"

"Other women." She smiled ruefully. "I'm a mess, aren't I?"

"But *who?*"

"That girl with—the glasses. I know it's silly. I just . . . It just made me feel—I don't know. Scared."

"My God. Of what?"

"Your leaving me."

He sighed. "Laura, look, I—"

She put her hand on his mouth. "Don't. Don't say anything. I know it's crazy. I know you didn't know it yourself."

He wanted to say something, but she wouldn't let him. "I know it didn't mean a thing. It's just that—well—she's a normal person. Young, healthy, bright—a normal woman. It made me feel scared when you looked at her. So please don't; don't look at any of them. Not until I'm over the fear of death at the thought 'He's going to leave me.' " She took her hand away from his mouth.

"Laura, I honestly—"

She kissed him on the lips, to shut him up.

It wasn't anything, the kiss. It just meant 'Don't talk about it,' in sign language. But it made him feel lonely too.

"All right," he said. "Let's go to bed."

They undressed, as usual, with their backs to each other. He didn't turn around until he heard her get into her bed; she always took the one on the right. "Aren't you going to wash first?" he asked.

She beamed at him from the huge, exotic bed. "Try the pitcher," she said. "It's empty. A thousand Spanish servants, and no water to pour into the basin."

He told her the joke about the Australian schoolboy who, when asked what a bison was answered, 'A thing to wash your fice in.'

She laughed. One more storm weathered. One more for the road.

"I need to go to the bathroom," he said. "Know where it is?"

"Sure—the woman showed me. It's outside, second door to the left. But you'll have to take a candle. And depending on what you have in mind, it's crouchers."

"You mean, just a hole in the floor?"

"Yep. We're in Old Spain now."

He took the candle, found the alien and uninviting toilet, put the candle on the sill of the little window and took Wassermann's letter out of his pocket.

"Schwalbenbach, BZ APO 6 Reg 473/a." This explained the speed with which the reply had reached him: it had been sent by Army Mail. *"Dear Mr. Baker, It was an unexpected pleasure to hear from you. You would find Camp Schwalbenbach very different from the last time you saw it. It is now used for Displaced Persons (refugees from the Russian zone, mostly East Prussia). It is quite civilized and pleasant, I am the resident physician and live in Dr. Schmidt's bungalow where I also have my office. Of course, I hope, as we all do, that soon I will be able to get out of here and start a normal life, preferably in America. My dream is to brush up on my particular field of medicine in Harvard or Yale, and to open a practice in New York, not as a regular psychiatrist but as a specialist in the post-concentration-camp syndrome. Many of us survivors will end up eventually in the United States, and I am certain that all of them (myself included) will continue to carry the psychological scars of these past years. Any suggestions you might have to offer as to how I should go about applying to Yale, Harvard or any other first-class medical school, given my highly specialized and unique knowledge, would be much appreciated. Maybe someone among the Quaker hierarchy in Philadelphia might be willing to sponsor me? But this is all very self-centered in view of your request for advice re Laura Martens Baker.*

"It is, of course, extremely regrettable that her grandmother proved unequal to her and that the psychiatrist you consulted was obviously unfamiliar with the syndrome and therefore underestimated its destructive potential. I must say to you again

that you are in no way qualified or equipped to handle a person in her situation other than on a first-aid basis, but I assume that you have indeed explored all possibilities and found yourself faced with a 'fait accompli.' My advice is: avoid any confrontation. She may indeed become violent, especially toward you. Let me explain why: in order to shake her false identity, imposed (be it involuntarily) by you, she will, like any adolescent, obey the irresistible impulse to break away from parental domination in order to find her own identity. Even as late as the recent past, it was extremely important to her to conform to your idea of her, one that, judging from your letter, was both idealistic and unworldly, but her survival depended on her living up to it. Now, in order to free the way for her true identity to re-emerge, she MUST eliminate you and will act with great hostility toward you, something she will rationalize in her own way. (This is, of course, a simplified version of what is a most complex process.) So do not be disturbed by her animosity or even any physical aggressiveness. It is reassuring to know that you are not emotionally involved with her, otherwise it would be difficult, if not impossible, for you to deal with the situation. If she becomes too much for you to handle, simply remove yourself from the scene and call on professional help. Don't accept any evasiveness on the part of the professionals or any shirking of their responsibility. Show them this letter if you wish and tell them that she MUST be isolated for her own good, because she may turn self-destructive. Tell whoever the consulting psychiatrist may be to write to me at this address or, should luck be with me, at the medical school in the United States. As to warning signs, the symptoms cannot be generalized. In her case, my guess would be that she would return—at times—to speaking the languages associated with her previous identities: German and Dutch. Also, coarse and offensive behavior may become prevalent. I would expect the onset of her violent phase to be quite evident.

"*Again, I deeply regret that the course of events (and Laura's deliberate scheming) prolonged your being responsible for her beyond the limit that we all expected. As I said in our hasty conversation that night in Schwalbenbach, on the eve of your wedding: you are a noble young man. I am happy to conclude from your letter that you are also a wise young man. But I impress upon you, with the utmost urgency, that you must keep the bridge with the so-called civilized world open wherever you may ultimately go with her and call for professional help before she does irreparable damage to you and herself.*

"Recommending myself to your kind attention re the matter briefly mentioned at the beginning of this letter, and with my best wishes for both of you, Yours truly, Alfred Wassermann, M.D." At the bottom of the letter was a P.S. *"Best to keep this letter from Laura. Sleeping dogs, you know! W."*

Well, it was all very interesting, but it didn't help much. One thing was obvious: he was in for a hairy time. Damn those doctors! Why wouldn't they accept her as a patient, even if she did refuse to submit herself voluntarily? Should he take this letter to the nearest psychiatrist—Santa Fé? Albuquerque? But the experience with the one in Philadelphia told him what the result would be: 'Unless she becomes a clear danger to herself or others . . . ' Hopefully, the stores they were taking with them to the pueblo would contain some sedative.

He thought of keeping the letter to show to a psychiatrist should it prove necessary, but Wassermann was right, it was too risky. She was sure to find it, sooner or later. He rolled it into a ball and dropped it into the hole in the floor, took the candle off the windowsill and ventured back into the night where the cicadas were chirping and the ranch dogs yapping.

He now wished he had had meeting for worship with Gulielma, as she had suggested. For if he was in need of anything right now, it was the power that had saved Laura once before.

*   *   *

When Gulielma entered the room from the patio, Gran's bedtime ritual was in full swing. The two maids had already helped her undress and put on her nightgown, one of them was now brushing her mousey hair in front of the mirror, the other opening the bed and arranging the pillows. There was a smell of incense; in front of the statue of St. Mary in the corner, the votive light flickered in its little red vase. The only other light was shed by two candles, one in front of the mirror and one on the bedside table.

"Well?" Gran asked, giving Gulie a searching look in the mirror; the maid, impassively, went on brushing her hair. "Have they gone to bed?"

"Yes. Did they bring your milk?" It was a superfluous question; a glass of milk stood, white and large, next to the candle on the bedside table.

Suddenly, Gran had had enough. *"Basta, basta!"* she snapped at the maid who was brushing her hair. To the other she cried, *"Esta bien! Buenas noches!"*

The two hastily made their getaway.

Gran stretched out her little arms; Gulie lifted her off her stool and carried her to the bed.

"My book," Gran said, when she was settled in the pillows and had pulled up the eiderdown. "By the mirror."

Gulie went to fetch the book, lying open among the combs and the brushes. "What are you reading?"

"Never mind," Gran said. "What do you have to tell me?"

"Nothing! I just came in to say good night."

"And what else?"

"Tomorrow morning at five, Juancho and three of the men will take them and their stores to the pueblo. I'll go along as far as the pass and be back in time for supper."

Gran, her face set in a scowl, gazed at her fixedly, a sign that she was about to say something unpleasant. "Why don't you leave those people alone? Mind your own business! Let them stew in their own juice."

"But, Granny, I just want—"

"Mind your own business!" the old woman cried. "Can't you see, you stupid child, that she hates his guts? And so, may the Virgin forgive me, would I!"

"Good God! Why?"

"Because a man either marries for love, or because his parents have arranged the match. No man should marry as a good deed. That's an unforgivable insult to any woman."

"But, Gran!" Gulie cried. "He's a Quaker! To him 'love' is something higher!" How could she explain to a seventy-year-old Catholic from Latin America what a 'concern' was?

"You are young and foolish," Gran said sternly. "You have a head full of romantic notions. Life is not like that. It is less of an insult to a woman to be violated than to be married as a good deed. Poor girl!"

"You can't be serious! You mean that it is better to be *raped?"*

"I did not use that word! You keep a civil tongue in your head,

young woman! I did not say: it is better; I said: less of an insult.
A woman who is assaulted at least knows she is not repulsive,
that she has made a man forget about chivalry, civilization, the
church, prison and, in my country, the hangman's tree. No! It is
preferable to be assaulted, although I would not look forward to
it, than to receive matrimony as a gift bestowed on me by a
saintly husband. And then to see him make a play for another
woman! Ugh!" She slapped the eiderdown into place so that the
outline of her little legs became visible. "My book!"

Gulie handed it to her, outraged and bewildered. "What on
earth do you mean?" she asked.

"Don't be ridiculous! Either you're stupid or you need stronger glasses. Didn't you notice the sheep's eyes he made at you all
through supper? You stay away! Let them cut each other's
throats in private." She put the book on her lap, it suddenly
looked big.

"Well! I *must* say!" Gulielma felt like telling her what she
thought of her, but knew better. Despite her size, Gran had a
crushing superiority once she cut loose. "I'm going to bed," she
said tartly.

"Good night, Gulielma."

By the time Gulie closed the door to the patio, the old lady
was immersed in her book, or pretended to be.

This time, Boomer startled her when he licked her hand in the
darkness. "Oh, stop it!" The night was restless with the sound of
crickets and spiced with the scent of piñon smoke. There was no
moon, the patios were dark, but she found the door to her room
without registering the fact that she could barely see where she
was going. As always, Boomer pressed his snout against the door
before she opened it, in a terrible hurry to enter, as if something
exciting was waiting for him on the other side. Normally it
amused her, tonight she found it irritating. "Take it easy, *easy!*"
As she opened the door, the animal burst into the room, creating
such turbulence that the candle flame by her bed flickered and
nearly went out. "Down!" she cried. "Down, I say! Boomer,
down!" She had to push down his powerful haunches before he
obeyed; he crashed to the floor with a thud, put his head on his
paws and looked up at her, his ears half-cocked in covert antici-
pation.

Gulie undressed slowly, deep in thought. What on earth had
made Gran say that, about Boniface Baker 'making sheep's eyes'

at her? She must be right, she observed people like a lynx. Not a glance, not a flicker of an eyelid escaped her. And she was an unnervingly astute judge of character. At least, Gulie had always thought so. But in this case? Surely, she herself would have noticed? Out there in the stables he had been very friendly, but there had been no hint of anything more.

She sat down at her dressing table and looked in the mirror. Awful! Her face was bad enough without them, but those glasses made her look even more ghoulish. And her hair! She could shampoo it every day and still it looked oily. She picked up a strand and let it drop. Yuck! Ah—to be blonde, to have a decent bosom . . . What was it really like, to be raped? *Not nearly as bad as being married out of pity.*

Would there ever come a man who would marry her out of pity? It would be the only reason. That, or her money. So far, only mangy old Huni brujos had lusted after her; Anagonga could leer at her with eyes that would make a goat flee. But nobody remotely like Boniface Baker had ever given her a second look. Even that unpleasant little man called Herbert Haring had turned up his nose at her. Gran must have been drunk.

She did not read, but blew out the candle and lay staring in the darkness. Beyond the wall of the patio, the stable dogs were yapping, they must hear a coyote. Boomer growled, she sensed that he lifted his head in the darkness.

"Down," she said. There was a thud.

In the far distance, the coyote howled. The ranch dogs yapped monotonously. The crickets chirped. Night deepened over the desert.

CHAPTER SIX

THE small caravan of mules crawled, ant-like, across the Llano Estacado under a mottled sky, lit from below by the sun which had not yet risen. The desert was a vast expanse of yellowish-gray, dotted here and there with cactus and juniper bushes.

Toward sunrise the wind began to blow and the tumbleweeds began to bounce across the plain, fleeing ghosts of the night. The sky became lighter, but on the horizon a dark bank of cloud remained. Trails criss-crossing the plain became visible; here and there the conical tips of foothills loomed above the cloud.

Then the sun rose and suddenly the desert was flooded with color. The shrouds dropped away from the hills; the dark cloud was revealed as a mountain range, capped with snow. The higher the sun rose, the smaller the caravan appeared in the vastness of the desert.

Boniface reined his horse and waited for Laura to overtake him. "Well," he asked, "how are you doing?"

"Fine," she replied. She looked as if she had been on horseback all her life. She seemed in high spirits, once again the charming companion he had come to know in the months before the episode with the dog in the station wagon.

It took them the better part of the morning to reach the snow border. The bridle path up the mountainside was strewn with rocks; parts of it were so steep that the horses' hoofs, scrabbling, dislodged cascades of rolling stones. It was amazing, though, how nimbly the horses and the mules climbed the almost perpendicular trail; most amazing was Gulie's stallion, which sprinted up the steepest incline like a goat. Boniface discovered it was best to just let himself be carried along; no need to do anything but hang on for dear life, the horse did the rest.

The higher they climbed, the colder it became. The sun now stood high in the sky, veiled by a thin cloud layer. The filtered light seemed to bleach all color from the landscape again until the mountainside was as gray as ashes. There was no sign of life anywhere until, finally, they reached the first fir trees. The narrow trail vanished into a thin forest.

At that point Gulie McHair took her leave. "This is as far as I go today," she said, patting the neck of her restless horse. "Juancho will take you the rest of the way. I'll be up to the peublo myself in a few days. See you then." She swung her horse around, then she said, as an afterthought, "If you want a message sent to the ranch, give it to the priest, Father Alvarez; he and Grandmother are in daily contact by radio. And ever since Mr. Winkler's accident, if there is an emergency and the priest wants to contact her, it's arranged that he'll send up a flare. The ranch hands will see it, or someone will. Good luck now. Be seeing you."

Her stallion reared nervously; she calmed him down by patting his neck and whispering to him. She was a romantic sight, silhouetted against the white sky; then she plunged over the edge and vanished from view.

"Well," Boniface said, "let's carry on, Juancho. How far have we left to go?"

"Four hours, *Señor,* maybe five. It depends on the snow." The Mexican sounded pleasant enough, but there was a difference in his attitude now Gulie had gone. He seemed less respectful, and suddenly in a hurry. *"Anda! Vámonos! Vámonos!"* The rancheros yelled at the mules; the caravan moved, clanking and creaking, into the forest. At first the trees were sparse and the snow thin and dirty; gradually the forest became thicker. It was made up of fir trees of a kind that Boniface had never seen before, with needles as thick as twigs; these must be the piñons. The trail became steeper as it wound its way between the trees; after a long, scrambling climb they reached the point where it seemed to end in the sky, at a huge red rock like the ruin of a watch-tower. The first mule with its bulky load climbed the crest and sank, skidding, out of sight. One after another dipped over the edge; when it was Boniface's turn, his mouth fell open.

He found himself on the rim of the mesa; at his feet lay a valley. It must be ten miles wide, and was surrounded by red cliffs. The colors were incredible. The bottom of the valley was yellow, strewn with orange boulders looking like the ruins of a prehistoric city, with heavy black shadows cast by the sun. In the distance, above the red cliffs, rose a range of snow-capped mountains, behind it another range, and another; white peaks floated above the horizon as far as the eye could reach. He looked back, saw that Laura was close behind him and called, "Well, here we go!"

He started down the trail, and as he did so the view changed. The boulders in the valley now looked like a Moorish town. The hallucination became so strong that he thought he saw people moving among the houses; but it was a mirage. He had entered a ghostly region in which nature deceived the eye and created the illusion of human settlements where there was nothing but lifeless emptiness.

As he descended lower and lower, the shadows began to lengthen. The bottom of the valley turned from yellow to ocher, to brown. The Moorish settlement changed into the ruins of a Roman city; what from above had looked like boulders turned out to be colossal orange towers, standing in pairs like the remnants of triumphal arches. They dwarfed the small caravan as it passed among them, and cast a spell of stillness and death.

It was unlike any landscape Boniface had ever seen; he had not known that such a place existed. The valley seemed not only millions of miles but millions of years removed from the world they had left behind. Even the rancheros appeared to be subdued by the somber majesty of the necropolis as they slowly made their way among the colossal towers. At the top of some of them he occasionally saw what looked like Indian sentinels—another mirage, for they were impossible to climb; their flanks were perpendicular, some slanted outward.

After he passed the last of them the valley dipped to a deeper level. In the center of a vast, concave dell stood the biggest rock of all, higher and more massive than any of those they had left behind. It rose, stark and orange, from the ocher plain. Juancho stopped by the side of the trail and let the caravan pass until Boniface caught up with him. Then he pointed at the rock in the distance and said, "The pueblo, *Señor.*"

"Where?"

"Right on top. If you look sharply, you'll see the church: two little towers."

Boniface looked, shielding his eyes with his hand, but he saw nothing. The rock seemed as barren and inhospitable as the moon.

"Do you see it, *Señor?*"

Peering hard, he thought that indeed he discerned some minuscule buildings on the top, but it might be another mirage.

"We should move on now, *Señor,* or it will be dark by the time we get up there. The path to the pueblo is very dangerous."

"By all means," Boniface said, "let's go."

"Vámos! Vámos! Anda!"

The caravan trotted on, a thin line of ants, surrounded by battlements of the Gods.

*   *   *

The ride was so long and the landscape so monotonous that Laura dozed off, despite her aching limbs. She awoke with a start when they reached the foot of the gigantic, rust-colored sugarloaf on top of which, the foreman said, was the pueblo.

"Let's catch our breath before we carry on," Boniface said.

The rancheros dismounted and walked about, stretching their legs, patting their steaming horses. The mules, heads hanging low, seemed to fall asleep where they stood.

"Does anything grow up there?" she asked the foreman.

"*No, Señora, nada.* There is no soil. Only in the churchyard and in the patio of the priest. It was carried up in baskets."

"And water?"

"*Sí, Señora.* There are cisterns that catch the rain."

"Does it ever rain here?" Everything seemed so arid, so dead.

"Oh, yes! Thunder, gales, sandstorms. Not *divertido* up there when gale blows."

"Are the Indians nice?" she asked childishly.

"No," the man replied promptly. "Not nice. *Silenciosos, muy silenciosos.*" Then he shouted, "Antonio! Pancho!" The rancheros lashed the mules awake. "*Anda! Anda!*" As if they were sleepwalking, the beasts lined up in a single file and started to climb the steep, narrow path that wound its tortuous way up the rock. The rancheros followed; when Boniface went to join them,

Juancho held him back. "No, no, *Señor,*" he said. "Wait!
Stones, many stones. Boom boom! Ouch!" He acted out a panto-
mime of being bombarded with falling rocks.

They waited; finally Juancho said, "*Oké!* You first, *Señor,*
then the *Señora.* I'll follow; if any stones, me ouch."

Boniface moved ahead, Laura followed. The path they had to
climb was so scary that she didn't believe her horse could make
it. It was not really a path but a crevice between sheer walls of
rock, very steep and very slippery. She could hear the hoofs of
the mules scrabbling above; showers of stones skittered down the
path.

It took them an hour to reach a small plateau, no more than a
narrow shelf in front of a dark cave, with on its other side a dizzying precipice. The rancheros and the mules stood together in a
huddle, as far away from the edge as possible.

"This is the bat cave," the foreman said. "In summertime millions of bats come out, this time of day."

"Where are they now?" Boniface asked.

"Mexico."

"Is this the cave from which the guano was mined?"

"Yes, *Señor.*"

"How did they manage to carry their baskets down that steep
trail?"

The foreman grinned. "Indians have tricks," he said. "Full of
tricks, they are."

The sun had set; it was getting cold. The bottom of the valley
had vanished in a lake of darkness from which the tips of the
buttes in the distance rose like islands. The snowcapped mountains on the horizon were dazzling white in the deep blue sky.

"Pardon, *Señor,*" the foreman said, "but from here you have
to go alone. We unload the mules, tomorrow you come and collect the packs."

"Why won't you come with us?" Boniface asked, surprised.

"Pueblo out of bounds for *chicanos.* You just follow the path;
when you get to the top, you cross the square and straight ahead
is the lazaret. You can walk; if the *Señora* wants to ride, you'll
have to bring the horse back at once."

"Do you want to ride?" Boniface asked her.

"I'd better," she replied. "My legs are so stiff I don't think I
can walk that far."

"All right." They shook hands with the foreman and all the

other rancheros who first wiped their hands on the seats of their pants. Ten times they mumbled *"Gracias, adiós";* at last Boniface took her horse's reins and led it up the narrow crevice. She heard the foreman call behind her, *"Señora!* Look up and you'll see the tumble rock!"

She looked up and saw a round orange boulder outlined against the blue sky. She would not have realized how huge it was if she hadn't seen, at the bottom of it, two little heads peering over the edge.

"Tumble rock!" the Mexican repeated, behind her. "One blow with hammer and *boom boom!* Everybody down here, finish! That's how they kept out the Spaniards, the Apaches, the Navahos, the BIA. Ha-ha!" His laughter echoed in the crevasse.

Stumbling and falling, Boniface led her horse. The trail was even steeper than it had been before the plateau; she clutched the pommel of her saddle. At one moment her horse slithered back a full length, dragging Boniface with it; stones cascaded down with a frightening rumble. But the horse gamely scrabbled on, past the next bend. There, something white came fluttering down. She ducked, thinking it to be a bird; it landed against the wall and hung suspended for a second before continuing down; she saw it was a piece of newspaper. She looked up and caught a glimpse of a sheer wall, with on top of it, a row of gray wooden structures.

They scrambled on for another five minutes; suddenly they emerged in limitless space. The vastness of the sky in which she seemed to float made Laura's head reel. The first thing she saw was the row of gray buildings, much smaller than she had expected, lined up on the edge of the precipice. They looked like privies; it seemed a desecration of the infinity in which they floated. Yet, the idea that bare-buttocked people squatted backward over this dizzying view of the first day of creation was comforting, somehow. Ahead of her lay the village: a welter of adobe dwellings, two- and three-storied, built one against the other as if they were one edifice. Behind them rose the two squat towers of a church. There was a sweet, spicy scent in the air, the same as in the hacienda.

Boniface led her horse into the village. Here and there, in the middle of the street, were stacks of white, bleached tree trunks. There was not a soul in sight, neither behind the windows nor on the flat roofs of the randomly stacked houses. The only thing that moved was smoke from the chimneys, otherwise the village seemed deserted.

The hoofbeats of her horse echoed in the narrow street. The absence of life was eerie; there was not even a dog to be seen. No tree, no blade of grass, nothing seemed to live on top of this huge rock. They crossed a square, with in its center a squat tower with a wooden roof which must be a water cistern. On the opposite side of the square was another narrow street, with at its far end a low adobe building with barred windows and a heavy door. It opened as they approached, and there was the first human being: an old Indian woman with a flat face, high cheekbones and black eyes like pebbles. She wore a dirty green pullover, a long brown skirt and carpet slippers.

"I am Mrs. Sanchez," the woman said, when they reached her. "I am your housekeeper."

Laura dismounted painfully, tied her horse to a hook in the wall and waddled toward the woman. *"Buenas noches,* Mrs. Sanchez."

"Good evening. Supper ready." She turned away and they followed her inside.

The doorway was low and the interior dark, after the brilliant sunlight; Laura almost fell because the floor was a step down. The room was long and narrow; the windows had opaque panes, blue in the evening light, that looked like paper. The ceiling was supported by dark, heavy beams; the walls, which must have been whitewashed at one time, were covered with rows of empty shelves. In a hearth a fire was smoldering, over it hung a black pot. At the other end of the room was a bed covered with a quilt, a huge wooden structure with flowers painted on it. There was a wardrobe, a table with two chairs, and two chairs by the fireside.

"Stew and beans in there." Mrs. Sanchez pointed at the pot. "Back in the morning if you want."

"Oh, yes, please, Mrs. Sanchez." It was all very alien, but exciting at the same time. She was going to like it here.

"Señora . . . " The woman made a little bow and vanished.

"Well, Bonny," she said, "here we are. Welcome."

But he hadn't heard her. He stood looking at the door through which Mrs. Sanchez had vanished with a strange look on his face.

"Hey! What's the matter?"

He gazed at her as if he were miles away. "That's funny," he said.

"What is?"

"For us to be welcomed by a housekeeper."

"Why? She probably goes with the place. Not that there's much for her to do," she added, looking around.

"Everybody has been telling me that we would be ignored, that we would have to open cans, that we shouldn't look them in the eye—and first thing we know, here's a housekeeper, cooking supper."

"Well," she said, exasperated. "Don't knock it! Next time, don't look at the poor woman as if she was a ghost. Kid the help, old buddy! I'm not about to start scrubbing this floor myself. What are you planning to do with my duffel bag?"

"Huh? Oh, yes . . . " He took it off his shoulder. "Where do you want me to put it?"

"Oh, anywhere. I don't know where to put things yet."

He went to the bed. "I'd better get the candles. They're in one of the saddlebags we left below. I have to take the horse back anyway." He dumped the duffel bag on the bed and went to the door. "I'll be back soon. You don't mind being left alone, do you?"

"Not at all. If I'm not here when you come back, I'll be in the saloon."

"Ah? Ah—yes. Ha-ha."

When he left, she suddenly had the feeling of having been here before. She had no idea why; the room was totally alien, as was the village. The feeling itself was familiar; her past was gradually being pieced together by association. Yet this time it was different, like a memory from a previous incarnation. Heinzl had often talked about his previous incarnation: a Roman physician. 'Have you ever been kissed by a Roman surgeon, *Schatzrl?* Let me show you. This is how the Romans do it.'—'Heinzl! The door. . . . !'

She sat down on the edge of the bed. It was the only one; she would have to share it with Boniface. It would be the first time; so far, there had always been two beds, or he had slept on a sofa as he had done in that motel on the road. She could not expect him to sleep on the floor; it was bare rock and looked filthy. The bed had plenty of room, it was the biggest bed she had ever seen.

Even so, the thought of having him close beside her . . .

Well, never mind. Here she was, among the Indians. That Mrs. Sanchez did not look like the Indians she had imagined. *Winnetou.* She had told Heinzl that was the name of her horse. But it hadn't been; when she climbed into the saddle this morning she had instantly known it was not so. Winnetou was the name of an Indian. Where had she picked it up? Never mind. Stick with the present. No more visions, no more memories. Down, Heinzl.

Look at those windows. What were they made of? Parchment? And there was another smell, apart from the smoke; something sweet, sickly. The pot on the fire? She went to check and dropped the lid, for it was as hot as a poker. Dammit! Where was Bonny? He took an awfully long time, getting a couple of candles. He probably was shaking hands again, all round. *'Gracias, amigos, adiós, amigos.'* Why did he irritate her so? He was good, he was—well, good. Goody-goody Two-shoes. They were all good. Grandma, old Ethan Woodhouse and his spats, the lot. So good that at times she felt like being sick on the carpet. Well, no carpet here, baby. You'll have to be sick in one of those privies on the brink of the precipice and read the bits of newspaper. What did Indians do with newspapers? Could they read? What language? She was overcome by curiosity; what was printed on those square pieces of newspaper? *'Kissing Tree Meeting had a covered dish luncheon at which Friends from—'* No, it sure as heck wouldn't be pages from *Friends Journal.* Why did Boniface read that before going to sleep, turning the pages as if he were tearing down a building? Never a detective novel, or a *Schundroman.* 'Hush now, Laura, let me read! *"Baroness von Scholle opened her thighs, and the valet . . ."* '

She got up and walked around the room. As grim as a morgue; but at least it wasn't humid, the patches on the walls—

"Hi there! That was quick!"

He came in, puffing, lugging one of the saddlebags, which he dumped on the table. "Oof! It's heavy! I hope it's the one with the candles." He began to dig around in it. "By the way, the rancheros have decided to make camp in the cave; the foreman said it was getting too dark for the trip home."

"Have you seen any more Indians, apart from Mrs. Sanchez?"

"No."

"Odd, don't you think?"

"They'll come out tomorrow."

"Okay. Now I'm going out, for a breath of fresh air."

"I'll come with you!"

"Sorry. There's no toilet in this place, only the public facilities on the edge of the cliff. So, see you in a minute."

She ducked out through the low doorway. Night was falling, very high up some light lingered. The silence in the empty village was ghostly. Having to walk all the way to those dark privies on the edge of a nine hundred foot drop scared her. All she wanted was to have a pee. She found a dark corner nearby and squatted there. Suddenly she heard a faint, nasal singing of high-pitched, tinny voices. It gave her the shivers; then she realized it came from inside their house. When she entered the room, she found Boniface, like a magician who had produced a rabbit, standing by the table with a portable gramophone on it. The high-pitched voices whined, *"I was dancing, with my darling, to the Tennessee Wa-haltz . . ."*

"Where on earth did you find that?"

"In the wardrobe. There's only this one record: the Andrews Sisters, with 'Roll Out the Barrel' on the flip side."

"So I lost my little darling, the night they were playing, the beautiful Tennessee Waltz . . ."

The record finished with a sanding sound and a click.

"Strange, they didn't filch this one," he said. "Ethan Woodhouse told me that each time a resident Quaker left, the Indians came and picked the place clean."

"Well, maybe it's not their taste in music. But so far the information you've been given seems a lot of bull."

She went to the bed, took a Mars bar from her duffel bag and held it out to him. "Here, have one."

"No, thanks, I'll wait until after supper. By the way, our plates are not in this bag. We'll have to eat from the pot."

"Why not? We'll have to sleep in the same bed."

"Oh—yes. Er—sorry about that."

She shrugged her shoulders. "We'll get used to it. Do we have knives and forks?"

"Only spoons." He produced them from the saddlebag.

"All right, let's eat."

He handed her a pair of gloves from the bag. "Use these, or you'll burn your fingers. The handle must be red hot."

"It sure is." She put the gloves on and lifted the pot off the hook over the fire. It weighed a ton. "Have we got anything to put it on? I don't want to mess up the table."

"No, we— Wait!" He rummaged in the bag and pulled out an issue of *Friends Journal.* "Use this."

"It's going to be black with soot."

"Better that than the table." He opened up the paper. "Here."

She put the pot down and lifted the lid.

He sniffed. "H'm! Mexican beans."

"That's going to be fun."

"Why?"

"Jedes Bönchen gibt sein Tönchen."

"What's that?"

"A coarse German joke." She sat down opposite him on one of the chairs; they weren't as solid as they looked. "Take it easy," she warned, "or you'll end up *Beine in die Luft.*"

He held out his hand. "Let's have grace."

They joined hands, bent their heads and sat in silence for a while; suddenly it struck her why she had that feeling of having been here before. Ever since they arrived in the village she had been thinking in German, as if Heinzl and she had been here together.

He pressed her hand and said, "Well, let's find out what Mrs. Sanchez has prepared for us. How did she know we were coming, by the way?"

"That's a thought."

"Could she have seen the caravan coming?"

"It takes hours to prepare a pot of beans. She must have started them early this morning."

"Spooky place." He blew on a spoonful of beans. "Hot. Watch it."

"They probably have lookouts. All Indians have."

"How do you know?"

"I just know. One of them was called Old Shatterhand. No, he was a white man."

"Who was that?"

"Don't know. Can't remember."

He tasted the beans. "Delicious. Try them."

She did. "Very good. Not too *würzig* for you?"

He looked at her. "What is *würzig?*"

"Oh, sorry. Hot, peppery. Too hot for you?"

"No, I like them this way."

They ate for a while in silence, then he said, "I don't think we'll have too hard a time here. I'll start by paying a visit to the priest, tomorrow morning. Just to show the flag."

"Don't forget we have to lug all those saddlebags up the trail from the cave. Over thirty of them."

"Oh, together we'll do that in no time."

"We also have to unpack them, store everything: bottles, pots, packages of cotton wool, bandages . . . It's going to take at least a day."

"Don't worry. One thing we have plenty of is time."

She looked at him as he sat there, munching. Well, here they were, all alone in the cold. Two sparrows on a rock on the moon.

*   *   *

It was a real bore, there being only one bed; Boniface took as long as he could, unpacking his one bag; but it was getting colder and the fire was going out; in the end he bit the bullet and said, "How about bed? I'm getting cold."

"Okay with me."

They undressed with their backs to each other; at a given moment he looked around and saw her standing with her back to him in front of the fire, stark naked, warming her nightdress.

"That's a good idea! I think I'll do the same." He unpacked a pair of pajamas he had bought in an Army surplus store in Philadelphia the day before leaving. He waited until she had put on her nightgown; to stand side by side in front of the fire stark naked didn't seem a good idea.

She pulled back the quilt and said, "Oof! This bed stinks!"

"Of what?"

"Dust, cobwebs, feet—somebody with sweaty feet has been sleeping in it. Maybe that old Mr. Winkler."

He heard the bed creak behind him; then she said, "Brr! Come, get in! It's an icebox!"

"I'm coming." He put on his pajamas.

"Boy," she said, "you're lucky there aren't any bulls up here."

"Excuse me?"

"If you showed yourself in those pajamas you'd be gored. Who chose them for you?"

"I did."

"Well, congratulations."

Although he agreed the red and white stripes were a little loud, it irritated him. "Sorry, we can't all have exquisite taste. And they were the only ones I could get in my size."

"Oh, I don't care a rap. As long as you hop into bed now; my teeth are chattering. Come!"

He put on the jacket and went to the bed, feeling like a walking beach ball.

She was sitting upright, shivering, her arms crossed in front of her chest, her hands on her shoulders, looking very young with her hair up.

"What's the mattress like?"

"You'll find out."

He lay down and discovered that there was no mattress, but a pallet, full of straw. "Well, it's going to be a comfortable night!"

"We'll get used to it. Perhaps the thing will adjust to our shape."

"Boy, it's cold!" he cried.

"All right if we keep each other warm? Would you like to lie behind me?"

"No, I prefer you at my back, otherwise— well, I prefer it."

She pressed herself against his back, was silent for a while; then she said, "Sorry I was beastly last night." He felt her breath on his neck. "There was a reason for it, though—wasn't there, this time?"

"Can I blow out the candle?"

"Sure."

He did; the embers in the hearth shed a reddish glow.

"Well," he said, "I wonder how many couples have lain like this, over the past two hundred years."

"Cozy thought," she said behind his ear.

"You find it sinister here?"

"Don't you?"

"Let's try and make it more cheerful, tomorrow."

"That isn't going to be easy. It's like lying in your grave, remembering. *'Oft in der stillen Nacht . . . '* "

"What's that?"

"A poem. By a man called Otto Julius Bierbaum, who stole it from an English poet called Moore. *'Oft in the stilly night, ere slumber's chain has bound me.'* "

"Go on."

" 'Fond memory brings the light of other days around me.' "
"And?"

" 'The smiles, the tears of boyhood's years, the words of love then spoken, the eyes that shone, now dimmed and gone, the cheerful hearts now broken.' "

"That's good! Is there more?"

She was silent for a while, then she said, "There is, but I don't remember."

He stared at the dying fire. A log cracked and shot sparks into the room. "We didn't have meeting tonight. Would you like to have meeting?"

She said drowsily, "Can we have it lying down? It's so cold."

"I don't see why not."

"That Mrs. Sanchez," she said, "do you think her real name is Sanchez? Or would she have an Indian name? Like Silver Rain, or Hopping Squirrel?"

"When Dr. Gulielma Woodhouse first arrived here in the seventeen-hundreds, I'm sure they didn't have Spanish names. I wonder if she built this lazaret. No, that was Buffalo McHair." Suddenly he was overcome by a feeling of gratitude. Here they were: from Camp Schwalbenbach to the Huni pueblo in the Sacramento Mountains. It had been quite a journey, but they had made it.

Another log cracked, showering sparks. He felt her twitch behind his back; she was falling asleep. It wasn't long before he followed suit.

* * *

She woke up to the sound of dance music; Heinzl had turned on the radio. She waited for the time signal, followed by the voice of the announcer: *"Guten Morgen, meine Damen und Herren. Hier sind die Nachrichten. Das Oberkommando der Wehrmacht macht bekannt . . .'* Then the words of the music got through to her. *"I was dancing, with my darling, to the Tennessee Wa-haltz, when an old friend I happened to see."* She opened her eyes.

"Morning." He was sitting at the table, fully dressed, "I wanted to let you sleep while I went to see the priest, but I was afraid you'd be alarmed if you woke up and found me gone."

"To tell you the truth, I was alarmed to find it was you," she said, drowsily.

"Excuse me?"

"What's the time?"

"Half past seven. Who did you think I was?"

"Mrs. Sanchez," she lied.

"She's been and gone. She brought bread for our breakfast, if you want to call it bread."

"Was gibt's? Knüsperische Brötchen?"

"I wish you'd stop that."

"Sorry. What did she bring? Hard rolls?"

"No, sort of matzos. Here—try one."

She opened her eyes. He held what looked like a piece of old pancake in front of her nose. She sniffed; it smelled like the bed. "No, thanks. I think I'll wait. What time did you say it was?"

"Seven-thirty."

She stretched under the quilt, yawned and sat up. It was still cold, she covered her bare shoulders with her hands. "How come you're dressed already?" He was wearing his sheepskin vest and his ten-gallon hat. He looked ridiculous.

". . . the beautiful Tennessee Waltz . . ." The tinny voices stopped, the record grated, click.

"What did you say was on the other side?"

" 'Roll out the Barrel.' "

"Oh, I know that one! The Dutch sang it before the war. *'Rats, kuch en bonen'* it was called." Another piece of the jigsaw puzzle of the past.

"Do you want to hear it?"

"No, thanks. Did she bring any coffee?"

"No, but I made some."

"How? Did you unpack the stove?"

"I heated water in the iron pot."

She looked at the hearth; a new fire was burning briskly. "Goodness! You *have* been active! Did you wash the pot first?"

"Of course."

She lay down and pulled up the quilt; it was too cold. She looked at the ceiling. "Pretty filthy, but at least there are no cobwebs."

"What's that?"

"The ceiling. It could do with a coat of whitewash, though."

Suddenly she remembered a joke. "Do you know what wives of three different nationalities say while they are being . . . " No, better not.

"There are no cobwebs here," he said ingenuously, "because there are no spiders. You find spiders only where there are mosquitoes. We're too high, and the nights are too cold."

She yawned; halfway through the yawn she was suddenly overcome by longing for Heinzl. Oh, what a cold, lonely business! There was no fun left, life wasn't worth living any more. She asked curtly, "What about that coffee?"

"Sorry." He hurried to the fireplace and fussed with the iron pot.

She dozed off again *'Das Oberkommando der Wehrmacht macht bekannt dass die Truppen des Generals Paulus—'* She awoke, startled. He must never find out about Heinzl. He was a sweet guy, but he'd never understand. Nobody would.

"If a person has two sides to his character, it doesn't mean he is mad," she mused aloud.

"What was that?"

"Some people are angels at home and wolves outside." Now, *why* had she said that? Only to bring Heinzl into the conversation? "I mean, our nextdoor neighbor was a policeman, very sweet to his wife, bringing home flowers and that kind of thing; you could hear them sing in descant while they were doing the washing up. But the moment he put his uniform on to go on duty, first thing you knew he pulled out his blackjack."

"Was that van Loon?"

"No—the neighbor on the other side."

He was silent for a moment, standing in front of the fire with his back to her, then he said, "Laura?"

"Yes?"

"Your house was the last one on the street."

"Oh. Yes, that's right."

"You don't really remember, do you?"

"What? The policeman and his wife?"

"The street where you lived. The people called van Loon."

She decided to own up. "I don't know. Honestly I don't. Sometimes I can't sort out what I was told and what I really remember."

"Such as?"

"Well, you have talked so often about the street and the

neighbors called van Loon that I can picture the whole thing. But do I see what you told me, or is it a real memory? I wish sometimes that you'd stop telling me bits of my past. Hein—Dr. Schmidt did the same thing. My father's death, for instance. That I really don't remember. But tell me that my father was beaten to death by the Kapos, and I see it, because one time I looked out of the window and watched them do it to some other man."

He kept his back turned, and looked at the flames. "Laura . . ."

"What?"

He turned to face her. "I wish you would trust me."

But she had had enough. "Hell! There's nothing to tell! It's just—well, not now. It's too soon." She had got out of that rather neatly.

"I understand," he said. "Well, I'd better be going. I suppose the priest will be awake by now."

"Okay. Have fun."

"See you." There he went, with his ten-gallon hat. She waited until he had left, swung her legs out of bed and got up. Ouch, that stone floor was cold! She hopped to the hearth, pulled up a chair, stretched out her bare feet to the fire to warm them and looked at the flames. Suddenly she was back on board a houseboat, of which she occasionally had caught a fleeting glimpse. She had no idea why it should be a houseboat, for she never saw water. But there it was: a fireplace, a log fire; this time a dog was asleep in front of it, a brown and white dog; and a man's legs in green tweed trousers, stretched out toward the flames. Brown shoes. Brown socks. A man's voice said, *'No, thank you, sir, those things are too dainty for me. I prefer my Old Stinker. We have shared so many hazardous adventures, like the time I was captured by the Black Feet in the prairie west of . . . '* Gone.

Who was the girl in front of the fire on board the houseboat? And who was the man who had been captured by the Black Feet? Time would tell. Well, as Bonny had said, time was the only thing they had plenty of. And she wasn't all that interested, anyhow. She had enough memories as it was. Enough to last her a lifetime.

To sit like this, with her legs stretched out, was a strain; she pulled up her duffel bag and put her feet on top of it. Time. Time to sit, and close your eyes, and remember. To go through a whole morning with Heinzl. First, she felt him stir behind her in her sleep, stroke her thigh, rub her stomach, fondle her breasts. She was too drowsy to react. Then he kissed the nape of her neck, and she felt him get out of bed, leaving a cold emptiness. But he'd tuck in the blankets, he always did; then she heard him pad away on his bare feet to the lab, and put the water on for tea; on his way he'd turn on the radio. *'Das Oberkommando der Wehrmacht macht bekannt . . . '* Behind the voice of the announcer she heard the tinkling of spoons in mugs, and the hiss of the gas ring. Then his footsteps came padding back, she heard the tray being put down on the bedside table, and there he was, climbing back into bed. This time she was awake and waited for him to kiss her neck, as she knew he would. Warm, soft lips, his breath warm on her skin. There was his hand, stroking her thigh. She turned on her back, eyes closed; there was his mouth, on hers. The radio started to blare music with a brassy beat. It blared, blared . . . Shivers of ecstasy—

Dammit! She jumped to her feet. He was dead, dead and gone! She must tear him out by the roots and fling him into the fire!

But he wouldn't go. As she stood there, watching the flames, she thought about hell, and what happened to the soul of a man who had become a murderer out of love. Well, whatever his fate, eventually she would share it. For whatever happened to such a man must also happen to his girl, who had cried out in ecstasy while outside, behind the glass curtains, old men were being beaten to death and mothers were robbed of their children.

* * *

The adobe church with the two plump towers was set in a burial ground at the edge of the precipice. Its heavy doors, braced with iron straps, made it look like a fortress rather than a house of God. From one of its towers sprouted, incongruously, a radio mast. The doors were reached by way of the churchyard, a bleak plot surrounded by a low wall. The crosses on the graves carried Spanish names, some were decorated with paper flowers that rustled eerily in the wind. Beyond the wall of the churchyard was the valley, still steeped in darkness, for the light of the rising sun had not yet touched the bottom. In the far distance the dark mass of the snowcapped mountains seemed to float in mist. It was the loneliest place Boniface had ever been to.

As he turned to go into the church, he saw that, in the few minutes he had been gazing at the valley and the mountains, the colorless building had turned a soft pink in the rising sun. The houses of the pueblo had gained color too: beige, soft yellow; last night they had been red. That probably was the reason why the pueblo had not been discovered for centuries: like the mesa itself, the village changed color, making it indistinguishable from the rock.

In the silence deepened by the rustling of the paper flowers, he walked to the steps and pushed open the church door. The screech of the hinges echoed in the dark cavern beyond. It was ice cold in there, the walls were four feet thick. Once his eyes had adjusted to the darkness, he saw, at the far end, an altar with behind it a mural: a smiling sun, a weeping moon, three primitive saints without perspective, grouped around a crucifix that was three-dimensional: an emaciated Christ, slumped forward, hanging by his torn hands, his long hair dangling in ragged tresses. The pain expressed by the emaciated body could almost be felt; it was the most realistic image of the crucifixion he had ever seen. There could be no doubt that Christ was an Indian.

He looked around. There were a few rows of benches, a wooden confession booth, gaily painted, with colorful curtains. The walls were covered with a fresco that, as far as he could make out, represented episodes from Huni history, parts of which were obliterated by soot from the oil lamps below. A row of gory pictures, none of them approaching the realism of the crucifix. Each time he looked at it, he felt as if he were actually standing at the foot of the real cross on an Indian Golgotha. Here and there, higher up on the walls, rainbows had been painted, arched over a series of exotic birds, green and blue with red heads and yellow beaks, each standing on two crossed roses. Higher still were long, low windows with rose gauze curtains which seemed more suitable for the House of the Rising Sun in New Orleans than a church; they billowed slowly in the wind.

At the side of the altar was a door, presumably leading to the vestry. He knocked and opened it to find it led to the cloister, a small, verdant garden full of vividly colored flowers, surrounded by a vaulted walkway with carved pillars. In the center of the garden a priest in a black habit sat in front of an easel with a half-finished painting. He appeared to be completely immersed in his work; Boniface coughed to attract his attention. The man gave a start; suddenly all the vividly colored flowers sprang to life and came fluttering toward him, shrieking, *"Masturba, padre! Puta tu madre! No cojones! No cojones!"*

He backed away as the parrots, fluttering and skidding, landed at his feet.

"Good morning!"

Boniface did not know quite what he had expected, but the big, blond, baby-faced priest came as a surprise. His complexion was pink, his hands, protruding from the coarse black cassock, were covered with boyish down. His eyes were so pale as to be almost white; he looked about fifty, but could be much older. "Good morning, I am Father Alvarez," he said, with a heavy Spanish accent. "I heard you arrived last night. You are Señor . . . ?"

"Baker, Boniface Baker. My wife's name is Laura. How do you do?"

"Oh, fine, fine, very fine," the priest said with a shyness incongruous for someone so large. "I hope my parrots do not bother you?"

The creatures scrabbled around their feet, cursing; Boniface was glad he was wearing boots. "Oh, no, not at all," he replied. "They are very interesting birds."

"Oh, yes, yes!" The priest seemed relieved they had found a subject for conversation so quickly. "The parrot is a sacred bird to the Hunis. You must have come through the church so you have, of course, seen the murals. Parrots are still used in ceremonies. I mean their feathers. Did you notice the carving on the beams supporting the roof?"

"No, not yet." The birds were now scratching and pecking at his boots.

"The shamans paint the faces of the dead before they are buried, cut their hair and braid parrots' feathers into it. The faces of the males are decorated with figures, the faces of the women painted with pollen."

"And the children?"

The priest gave him a startled look. "How—what—ah, yes! The children! No—"

"Ha-ha-ha! No cojones!" The leader of the parrots headed for Boniface, its stubby wings spread; it made a dive-bombing run, shrieked, *"Masturba!"* and attacked his left foot.

"Push him aside!" the priest cried. "Please, please, just give him a little push with your foot!"

"Don't worry," Boniface said. "He doesn't bother me."

"Maybe we had better go to my loggia. Come."

The priest walked toward a corner of the cloisters; Boniface followed him with, at his heels, the pack of parrots, shrieking and cursing. The priest opened a door a crack and said, "It's best if you go first, please. Then I can hold them back, or they will follow us up the stairs. They never see anybody, so they're very excited. Now! Quick!" Boniface slipped inside, behind him he heard the priest shout some words in Spanish that did not convey devotion, then the door slammed. "Please go up, up the stairs."

Boniface climbed a dark spiral staircase; after the third turn he reached a loggia. It was open to three sides, with a whitewashed ceiling. There were two wicker armchairs and a rickety table; the balustrade was made of wood, the banisters were decorated with primitive carving, bleached by the sun.

"Sit down, sit down, please."

Boniface lowered himself cautiously into one of the chairs; it sagged to one side, creaking. The priest sat down in the other one; it sagged the opposite way. "Well? What do you think of my view?"

It was breathtaking. Now the sun had risen higher, the rim of the valley had turned red, the Moorish town was bright orange, with long black shadows. The snowy peaks on the horizon floated disembodied in the dazzling blue sky. The houses of the pueblo were ocher now, with deep blue shadows. The loggia being high, he could look down on the flat roofs; there still was no one to be seen. "Could you tell me why we haven't seen any Indians except Mrs. Sanchez? Are they hiding from us?"

"Who? Oh, no, no, that doesn't mean a thing," the priest said, startled for some reason. "They bide their time, you know. You mustn't forget, they never see anybody. I mean, only the McHair girl, and she is . . . You know the history of the McHairs?"

"I know that a man called Jesse McHair started the guano mine in the pueblo at the time of the Civil War."

"But do you know what happened to him after? How he died? Do you know what happened to William, his son?"

"No."

"Well," the priest said, settling back in his sagging chair. "I don't think I'm being indiscreet when I tell you. William McHair was a dwarf; when he was twenty-five years old, his father, Jesse, ordered a midget bride for him from an agency in South America. She is the present *Doña* Ana McHair. She was very young then; the agency specialized in—well—freaks for circuses. Not exactly a promising beginning, one would say, but, oddly enough, it became an excellent marriage. Idyllic. They were always walking hand in hand, very sweet to one another, really touching. You know that William was blind as well?"

"No, I don't know anything about them."

"Well, eventually they had a son, whom they called Absalom. He was normal in size and in sight. A beautiful boy, very artistic. He was to inherit the hacienda and all that goes with it, this valley, the pueblo, the tobacco plantations—in short: the McHair empire. His parents had arranged a marriage to the daughter of a landowner, Montoya, almost as rich as the McHairs. But the boy fell in love with a member of the kitchen staff, a young Mexican girl, a little wetback about whom nothing is known. Absalom wanted to marry her, his parents refused permission, but a child was born, a girl. After the birth of the child the mother disappeared, the rumor goes that *Doña* Ana had her picked up by the Feds and deported. In any case, she disappeared. The wedding date with the daughter of Montoya was set. The night before the wedding Absalom hanged himself. Odd, don't you think: Absalom? As if the two dwarfs, at his birth, had determined his fate by giving him that name. Oh, well, a fanciful thought. William, the father, died soon thereafter, they say of a broken heart. *Doña* Ana inherited the hacienda and all the rest. She took in the little girl and treated her, somewhat belatedly, as her grandchild. They have been living together, just the two of them, ever since. The girl will inherit the empire in her turn, her grandmother appointed her as a sort of ambassador to the Hunis. That's why she turns up here so often, you understand?"

"Yes, I see."

"What hobbies do you have, may I ask?"

The question was so unexpected that Boniface looked at him, amazed. "Hobbies?"

"Well, nothing ever happens here, you know. Except for the McHair girl, nobody ever comes. I myself have taken up painting, and I must say it gives me tremendous satisfaction. That's why I say, if you have a hobby, cultivate it. If you don't have one, think of something. It needn't be oil painting, something else will do just as well: weaving, pottery, water colors. This landscape asks for watercolors. I have tried, but I'm no good at it. They all turn into a sort of sunset. Why don't you try? You don't have any paints with you, do you?"

"No, I don't."

"What about bird-watching like dear old Mr. Winkler? H'm, perhaps not. Well, we must think of something. Believe me, it's a tedious life up here if you have nothing to do. You could, of course, study Huni history. If you're interested, I'll be happy to lend you a book that you should read. It will give you an excellent insight into what's going on here. I mean: the traditions. It will tell you how Jesse McHair died. I wish your predecessor had read it. I believe it would have made a difference."

"Which book, may I ask? I've read everything the Swarthmore library had on the Hunis."

"This is a manuscript. Never been printed, handwritten. I hope you can read old-fashioned handwriting? Well, old-fashioned; it's fifty years old. My predecessor, Father Foglia, was the writer. A god-fearing man. He knew the Hunis better than anyone else, before or after. His manuscript should be of interest to you. As I said, it's a pity Mr. Winkler was not interested. I loaned it to him, but he was preoccupied with birds' nests. I have it downstairs and I suggest you read it, then we'll have another conversation. I'd enjoy talking to you about it. Did you see the crucifix in the church?"

"I did."

"Did you notice the neck was broken?"

"I thought it was intentional."

"No, no! It was broken at the time of the atom bomb. You know of course that they exploded the atom bomb in the Alamogordo desert, behind those mountains." He pointed at the floating snowy peaks, an eternity away. "When the shock wave hit us, we thought it was an earthquake. We all got the fright of our lives; the crucifix fell off the wall and broke its neck. I left it like that, for, well, it is an antique."

"I think it is very impressive as it is."

"Yes," the priest said. "Yes, I often stand in front of it. There always comes a moment when I am forced to kneel." He rose from his creaking chair. "Let me lead the way this time, because of our little boys downstairs."

They went down the spiral staircase. As the priest opened the door the parrots shrieked. Boniface followed him down the walkway to the door of the church, the cockatoos pecking at his heels.

When they reached the door, the priest said, "If you'd wait one second, I'll get that book. One second!" He ran off at a trot; the parrots hesitated, then decided to follow his slapping sandals. *"No cojones! Masturba, padre!"* The priest slipped through a little door and closed it on them; the birds cursed and scolded. He reappeared with an exercise book in his hand. The parrots hurled themselves on his toes, pecking, but he didn't seem to notice.

"Here," he said. "I hope you'll be careful with it, it's very old. Read it thoroughly. Please. It's important to you. Well, Mr. Baker, I enjoyed your visit very much. Please give my regards to your wife, I hope that both of you will have a splendid time here. And, by the way, on your way out, do look at those murals again, you'll find them very interesting. Very." He opened the door to the church, holding back the parrots with his foot. "Quick!" he cried. "Goodbye, goodbye!"

"Goodbye . . . "

Boniface stepped into the murky vault; after giving his eyes time to adjust, he strolled past the murals and stood still in front of the painting of a white man chased by nightmarish monsters; the man, arms spread wide, was jumping off the mesa. It was reminiscent of Brueghel's painting of the death of Icarus, for life in the pueblo went on, unconcerned. On the roofs sat women, wrapped in blankets; in front of the squat tower in the village square a group of Indians in colorful costumes with feather headdresses were dancing a ballet, at least that was what it looked like. The next painting was of a female dwarf, holding a baby, who came riding into the square on a mule, a sort of deformed virgin Mary; all the Indians were kneeling to honor her.

The last of the series was the most fascinating. In the background rose a tall white mushroom cloud in an empty blue sky. It had, like a fist, knocked the Holy Trinity off their thrones; the dove of the Holy Spirit flew away; God the Father, with a white beard, was falling to earth upside down, losing His crown; the Son, His gown fluttering, was falling backward, as from a window, His halo sailing off into the blue. In the foreground a huge black vulture came winging up from the pueblo, its claws full of infants, its beak dripping with blood, while in the square terrified Indians were fleeing, hiding their faces in their hands. It was a curious picture; it clearly represented the explosion of the atom bomb, but what did the Holy Trinity have to do with it?

What was the meaning of the vulture? Boniface turned and walked toward the doors, past the crucifix with the broken neck and the dangling hair. High above him the adulterous gauze curtains billowed in the wind.

When he returned to the lazaret and called "Laura!" there was no answer. He frowned, then realized she must have gone to one of the little privies at the other end of the village. If she wasn't home in ten minutes, he'd go to meet her. He put the book the priest had given him on the table, pulled up a chair and opened it. *"A Case of Witchery Among the Huni Indians, Sept. 1895, by Alfonso Foglia, S.J."* It was written in an old-fashioned hand.

He turned the page. *"Contents. I: The historical background of the conflict between the McHair family and the Huni Indians. II: The acts of Jesse McHair that caused his execution by Huni witchery. III: The execution of Jesse McHair. IV: The importance of these occurrences to the H. Church."*

* * *

The Indians had finally begun to show themselves. As Laura walked down the narrow streets she spotted squatting figures on the rooftops, wrapped in blankets; squaws with closed faces walked past her as if she were thin air.

She walked awkwardly because of her saddle-soreness, and crossed the square with the cistern. At the foot of it sat an Indian, staring straight ahead. He gave no sign of life as she passed. She was wearing her T-shirt with *"If you can read this you are too damn close,"* perhaps he took it literally.

She had never visited the latrines in camp Schwalbenbach, but had smelled them in summertime, especially in the evening after a hot day; the privies on the edge of the precipice smelled the same. She didn't know whether the things were privately owned, but she opened the rickety door of one of them and instantly stepped back. The inside had no floor, all it contained was a beam, worn smooth, with below it a dizzying drop. A wad of torn-up newspaper was nailed to the wall; she wondered whether she should put a few pieces on the beam, but decided not to fool around or she would not dare sit down at all.

When she came out of the little cubicle she found herself muttering, *"Nanu, gehen wir mal wieder nach Hause."* She really should try to stop this. For months she had thought in English, now she not only dreamed in German, she thought in it. Why? Because something in the atmosphere was reminiscent of the camp? As she walked back through the narrow streets, she did what she hadn't dared to do before: she peered through a few of the windows. Most of them had glass curtains, yet she could catch glimpses of interiors: old-fashioned chairs, tables with vases of paper flowers, on one of the sills a white china shepherd and shepherdess, ogling each other on a white log. 'Come on,' she thought, 'there's work to be done! All those stores stacked up in the cave!'

As she crossed the square, she glanced in passing at the cistern with its wooden roof and caught sight of the Indian again. He now had spread a blanket in front of him, on which was displayed a number of jugs in various sizes and little statuettes made of pottery. Animals, birds, a woman carrying a child on her back, all in the sandy color of the village itself, with brown geometric figures painted on them. The Indian looked young; he sat there with his outlandish face like a manikin in a wax museum. In her imagination, Indians had noses like eagles' beaks, feather headdresses, tomahawks, wampum and pipes of peace. This one looked more like an Eskimo.

She was about to limp on when the thought hit her: he must be sitting there waiting for her. Who else was likely to buy that stuff? She stopped in front of him, squatted painfully and looked at the statuettes on the blanket. There was one among them, a little dog or fox with two puppies, that she liked. She picked it up. "Is this for sale?"

At first she thought he wasn't going to answer, for he went on staring straight ahead; then he shook his head and said, without looking at her, "Take it. Quick. It's for you." She looked around. On the roof of one of the houses behind her, two old Indians wrapped in blankets sat peering down at them.

"Quick!" the Indian whispered. "It's a gift! It costs nothing! Take it! Quick!"

"Thanks. That's very nice of you." She got up, it was obvious he wanted her to move on because of the two old men on the roof. She hobbled down the street eager to escape their field of vision.

When she entered the lazaret, she found Bonny sitting at the table, reading, and the sight of him was so reassuring that she said happily, "Hi there!"

He looked up. "Where were you?"

"I went to the john. They're pretty scary. A nine-hundred-foot drop, and only one beam to hang on to." She sat down at the table. "I was given a present." She put the little figure in front of him.

He picked it up. "Who gave you this?"

"The artist himself, I suppose. In the square. Near the cistern."

"That's not a cistern. It's the kiva, a sort of city hall, for men only."

"Well, whatever it is. He had a whole lot of stuff displayed on a blanket, I presumed it was for sale, but when I asked him how much, he whispered, 'Quick! Take it! It's for you!' He seemed very nervous about two old men sitting on one of the roofs. Very old, looking like Chinese mandarins. The only thing lacking were thin little beards. They had their eyes on me, all right. Who could they be?"

"Shamans, probably. Priests. Here they call them brujos."

"Well, they certainly didn't look at me as if they were priests."

"Why?"

"Well, it was the undressing look men give you."

It was the kind of remark he hated. He put the figure back on the table. "Well, this is at least a beginning."

"Let's hope so. What are you reading?"

"A Case of Witchery Among the Huni Indians."

"I'm not surprised. If they go in for witchcraft anywhere, it must be here."

"To start with—"

She put her hand on his arm. "To start with: let's collect those packs in the cave. Maybe we can finish fitting out this place before nightfall. Then we'll light the fire and you can tell me all about witchcraft."

"All right. Are you fit enough to carry one of those packs?"

She laughed. "Let's try. You walk behind me. Then, if I crash on my back, it'll be a soft drop."

He laughed, but it sounded forced. Obviously, he didn't trust her present jolly mood. Who could blame him? But that was going to change. From now on, she was going to be sweetness and light. "Come," she said, and added, "dear."

It came out in a way that made her decide it was a little early. Yet she felt more kindly disposed toward him than at any other time since they had set out for New Mexico. He had stuck with her through thick and thin. If anyone deserved kindness, it was Boniface Baker the fifteenth, or whatever his serial number was.

"Come on," she said, taking his arm. "A docker's work is never done."

"Ha-ha," he said, trying.

*   *   *

For three hours they slaved and sweated, lugging packs up the trail. There were more than thirty; the day before Boniface had wondered why the stores for the hospital had been divided up into such a multitude of small parcels, now he understood. He was glad they were small, for toward the end each one of them seemed to weigh a ton. Once or twice he saw heads peer down at them from beside the huge orange ball of the tumble rock.

Laura perspired heavily; no wonder, she was getting quite plump. But she seemed to enjoy the physical labor; she started to sing as she climbed, a German song of some sort. She worked like a horse; when she dropped the last pack in front of the door of the lazaret, she said, panting, "Well, that's it. Now I'm going to take a shower; I smell like a goat."

"What water are you going to use?"

"That's a thought. So it's not a cistern, that thing in the square?"

"No. The only water we have is the bucket Mrs. Sanchez brought in this morning. And that's as good as empty, just enough left for a pot of tea."

"Okay, tea. Let's hope she comes back today. Shall we start unpacking?"

They spent the afternoon arranging the medical stores on the shelves of the lazaret. According to the list Meeting for Sufferings had enclosed, they were equipped for all eventualities from *"abscesses"* to *"zymotic diseases."* It was like the pharmacy in the ambulance convoy, only more complete and in greater quantities. At the bottom of the list was a note: *"The preceding drugs were donated by the Gulielma Woodhouse M.D. Memorial Fund, founded in 1758 by James 'Buffalo' McHair."*

They were almost through when Mrs. Sanchez turned up, carrying a yoke with two buckets of water. He hurried to relieve her of the load and she dourly mumbled something in Spanish.

"What was that?" Laura asked.

"Something about bringing in the meal."

"Would there be time for me to clean up? I've got to the point where I can't stand myself. And what about you? You aren't exactly a bunch of roses either."

"I'll wait until after supper."

"Never swim after a meal," she said, and without further ado pulled her soaked T-shirt over her head.

"Mrs. Sanchez may turn up any moment," he said nervously.

But there she stood, in brassiere and panties. "Mrs. Sanchez is a woman too," she said, throwing the soggy T-shirt on the floor. "Maybe it's time she found me stark naked, it may convince her that we are indeed man and wife. She'd never know it from the bedsheets."

What the devil did she say that for? He turned away angrily and lit the fire. He heard her clang with the buckets and splash and snort. He didn't carry any matches, but there was a box on the table. When he turned around, he caught a glimpse of her naked body, lathered with soap. He hastily lit the fire. Then he heard the door open and there stood Mrs. Sanchez, gaping at Laura open-mouthed. She slowly came in, without taking her eyes off the pink, soapy body, and put the iron pot down on the table with a bang.

"Gracias, Friend. That is extremely kind . . ."

She had no eyes for him, only for Laura as she slowly made her way back to the door. It became too much for Laura, for she turned her back on the woman. *"Buenas noches,"* Mrs. Sanchez snarled, then she shut the door behind her with a slam.

"Well, you can dry yourself now," he said. "There won't be any more spectators tonight."

She took it in her stride. She rinsed off the soap, dried herself with a towel, went to the bed, turned back the quilt and pulled out her nightgown, which she put on. He lifted the lid of the iron pot and sniffed. "H'm!" he said, "I'm sure it'll be as hot as blazes again, but it smells delicious."

She came to the table and sat down, but obviously she was not listening. "Hey!" he said. "Wake up!"

She looked at him. "Do you know what?"

"What?"

"That Mrs. Sanchez."

"Well?"

"That's not a woman. That's a man."

"Don't be ridiculous!"

"Even if she was a lesbian, only a man looks at a woman that way. An old man, at that."

"For Pete's sake, Laura!"

"She looked at me the way those two old goats on the roof did, this morning. Who knows, she may be a priest pretending to be a woman in order to spy on us."

He laughed but felt suddenly uneasy.

"Well, let's keep an eye on her, or him." She lifted the lid of the pot to sniff in her turn. "Boy, that does smell like a blast. Let's hope he didn't put any rat poison in it."

"Laura, don't talk rubbish! It's spooky enough up here without your imagining things. Let's eat."

She looked at him, surprised. "What's spooky about it? A man is a man; I'd rather discover it now than wake up one morning and find Mrs. Sanchez rutting behind me instead of you."

He didn't know what to say to that. Her changes of mood bewildered him. She really was turning into a dingbat.

"Mrs. Sanchez leering at me gives me the shivers, but I have no problem with a Mr. Sanchez in skirts," she said. "Shall we have grace?" She held out her hands.

He took them, bent his head and closed his eyes, but he could not pray. Mrs. Sanchez a man? Ludicrous. Must be another symptom of her instability, and that alarmed him more than the idea of Mr. Sanchez. He must take care not to be drawn into her crazy world.

"Amen," she said and pressed his hands. "Sorry if I cut you short, but I'm hungry. Boy, that was quite a job, lugging those packs. Well, anything to get into shape. Have you seen how fat I'm getting?"

"Yes."

"I should be doing exercises every morning. I'll wait until Mrs. Sanchez turns up, then I'll hop up and down with a skipping rope. While I do that, you watch her. I wouldn't be surprised if she had to leave on all fours."

He suppressed his irritation. First, walking around naked; now the way she was eating: like a pig at the trough. He felt a sudden revulsion against the cigar-chomping battle-axe with her jailhouse language; but that was the tragic thing: she—

She belched like a dog's bark. "Sorry. Did I startle you?"

"Yes," he said. "Look, even though we are locked up here, just the two of us, and eating from the same pot, we should try to retain a semblance of civilization, however tenuous."

She gave him a searching look. "You'd prefer me to shut up, wouldn't you? To get back into the sweet little girl who was afraid of everything, leaned on you every step of the way? You enjoyed that, didn't you? Sorry, boy; I left her behind."

"When?"

"Oh, somewhere along the road. Maybe when I was called on the mat by that old headmaster with spats. What's his name? Mr. Quakerism."

"Ethan Woodhouse?"

She pushed back her chair. " 'Laura Martens,' " she intoned, wickedly, " ' "you must try to discover the seed of light and love in your father's death. Shall I read you something, Laura Martens, from the history of the Society of Friends? *Boniface Baker the stableboy lay dying in a dungeon in Lancaster Castle, and his last words were, Seed! Seed! I am the Seed!* ' "

She looked at him the way she had done that night in the hacienda, with a hostility that shocked him. "Well," she continued, "shall I tell you my reaction?" Without waiting for him to answer, she went on, "I was mad as hell. I have no recollection of how my father died; I don't remember the man at all. He's nothing to me, just nothing. But from what I was told he died the way I saw other old men die, a way nobody who hasn't seen it could possibly imagine, least of all a Quaker creep in spats, with heavenly eyes and his ears full of hair, who spent the war years sitting on his ass in an office in Philadelphia. I'm game to join you in being sanctimonious about that of God in Mrs. Sanchez' pants, but I'll be damned if I let you turn the beating to death of helpless old men into the martyrdom of plaster saints! Do you hear me? I'll be damned, Bonny Baker, and damn your long-suffering *Fratz!* Do you hear me?"

"I hear you," he said.

"All right. Then don't forget it. I don't care if you sneak up behind me at dead of night. I don't mind if you pretend to sleep and lift my nightie, I'll just give you a wallop and it'll pass. But don't you ever try to sprinkle the death of my father and those other old men with powdered sugar! Understood? That's what he tried to do, that creep in Philadelphia, and I'll be damned if I'll let him get away with it! Never, never, never! There was no 'light and love' in the way that old man was beaten to death by the Kapos! Anyone who dares to say that deserves to have his balls cut off and stuffed down his throat! Oh, yes, look shocked! How terrible that a sweet Quaker girl can say such things! Honey baby ... " She put her hand on his. "That's what they did. Oh, yes. People do things to other people that you could never imagine, not in your darkest nightmare. Man is not good, Bonny. Man is a rabid beast. And God save our soul." She continued to eat like a pig.

He sat looking at her, aghast; only when she fell silent did he realize he was trembling like a reed. My God! What had got into him when he said to Stella Best that love could liberate this girl? He didn't know her at all. She was obsessed. It was obvious now, she was obsessed by an evil spirit, full of hatred. How long would he be able to put up with this? He should have listened to Wassermann ...

"Don't look so glum," she said. "I'm sorry if I frightened you. But, you know, it's like the case of Mrs. Sanchez: as long as I know. So Mrs. Sanchez is a man, okay. That I can handle. So I carry a rabid beast within me. All right, that I can handle. As long as I know. Can't you understand? The spookiness starts, the fear starts the moment I try to convince myself that I'm different from what I am. I've decided not to pretend any longer. So I belch. So I walk around without a stitch on. So I use unquakerly language, stuff myself with candy, get fat, and love a good cigar. Well, Bonny boy, you'll have to get used to it. Next time you fumble behind me in bed, don't expect me to lie there trembling with fear. That time is past. The virgin with the clammy hands is dead."

"So I gather."

"What's that supposed to mean?"

"It means that I've had enough!" He was unable to contain himself any longer. "Now eat your food, and shut up!"

"I see," she said laconically. "You refuse to accept this one. You'll only put up with the scared little sweetie with the clammy hands, the poor girl who went mute as a result of her experiences in the concentration camp. Well, buddy, you can stuff that one up your asshole."

"I said *enough!*"

"Okay, okay. Don't think it's for want of trying. I've tried to stuff the genie back into the bottle, but no go. Your friend with the spats let it out, and I can't get it back in. What's more, I'll be damned if I will." She picked up her spoon again. "By the way, this stuff is delicious. There's something to the Frogs' theory about a man being a better cook than a woman." She got up, went to the hearth, tossed a couple of logs onto the fire, dusted her hands and said, "Tell you what: you have meeting by yourself, I'm going to bed. Pray for me, and you'll see: you'll recover in no time." She went to the bed, plumped the pillows, propped them up against the headboard, climbed in, and glared at him, blue eyes blazing.

Wassermann had been wrong. It was not like the explosion of a time bomb at all; it was like the slow uncoiling of a snake. And she had only just begun.

*   *   *

She wanted a cigar, but the way he sat staring at her made her decide against it; she had raised enough hell. She could read his thoughts: 'Stark raving mad. Dangerous. One of these days she'll slit my throat.'

Suddenly her sense of release dimmed. The feeling of freedom, of waking up as a new Laura, turned sour. Was this the true Laura? She had no idea. She saw herself in the mirror of his face: shrieking whore with rolls of fat and a mouth that stank like an ashtray. What would Heinzl think of her if he could see her now, and hear her? Would he be as shocked as the boy sitting there as if he had watched the genie come out of the bottle? That had been a marvelous fairytale, the genie in the bottle. *Tasschen Tee,* and those delicious bonbons the Belgians made only for the *Wehrmacht.* What had been the name of those yummy chocolates? *Lady Godiva.* That's how the evenings of fairytale-telling had started. How delighted Heinzl had been when he realized that she didn't know a single one of them. 'I thought every child knew the story of Cinderella?' 'But, *Schatzrl,* I never was a child, remember?'

Suddenly she felt such homesickness for Heinzl and the world they had shared that she almost asked Bonny to let the true genie out of the bottle. She had it in her duffel bag: an earthenware bottle of Bols Dutch Geneva which she had picked up on an impulse in the last town before the hacienda, when Bonny had been off on a search for a ten-gallon hat. She had wandered off, window-shopping, and suddenly spotted a notice behind the yellow glass of a liquor store: "*Buy your Dutch Geneva here and remember your friends and relatives around the globe. Send them a bottle via our unique and efficient* GLOBOLS *service. We send your* BOLS *all over the world. Just say* GLOBOLS!" She had bought a bottle out of sheer nostalgia; Heinzl always had tossed back two small glasses of the stuff before meals, sometimes three. To her, at the time, it had tasted like kerosene straight from the lamp, but he had rolled tiny mouthfuls of it on his tongue, groaning with delight. She was ready for a swig herself right now. But no, poor Bonny! A cigar was bad enough, now to start swilling Dutch gin as well . . . "I know," she said. "Why don't you read me something? That priest's story. Never mind the washing up, we'll leave that for Mr. Sanchez. If it had been Mrs. Sanchez I'd have done it, but now that it's Mr. Sanchez, I'll leave it to him."

"It's not exactly a bedtime story."

"I don't want to sleep. I want to be read to. It's *gezellig.* Sorry, I know that's Dutch, but I just don't know the English word. Snug. Cosy."

"All right," he said. "But I warn you, it's a horror story."

A horror story. That would take some doing. "If I find it's getting too much for me, I'll tell you," she said sweetly.

He got up, fetched the book and sat down by the fire. Again she felt like having a cigar. "Go on," she said, "Read."

He read, "*'Before I begin my report on the occurrences which are the subject of this treatise, it is necessary to give the reader an insight into the relationship between the McHair family and the Huni Indians. In the year 1862, during the Civil War, the Huni pueblo was invaded by Union troops . . .'* "

The similarity with Heinzl reading to her was so strong that, before she knew what was happening, her eyes filled with tears. Oh Heinzl, Heinzl . . .

She was miles away when she heard him say, "I warned you it was gruesome. Are you sure you want to hear the rest?"

She could only nod, hoping he hadn't seen her tears. Suppose he should ask her what was the matter? She could stand it no longer. She managed a smile and said casually, "Hey, listen, I suddenly feel like a cigar. Get one for me, there's a dear. They're in the duffel bag."

He put the book on the floor, picked up the candle, went to the bag and took a cigar out of the box. He helped her light it with the candle flame.

"Thanks."

"Are you sure you want to hear the rest?"

"Yes, quite sure." She felt better now. But at the first whiff of smoke he was back. *'Mach mal Platz, mein Liebchen, dann steige ich in die Kutsche . . . '*

"Go on," she said.

" 'Jesse McHair managed to become owner of the entire valley, the pueblo, and thousands of acres of the Llano Estacado; even the U.S. government could no longer dislodge him . . . ' "

The voice droned on. Smoking, gazing at the fire, she daydreamed about Heinzl.

*   *   *

" 'In 1868, when Jesse began to show the symptoms of insanity that resulted from his unmentionable disease, he started to mistreat the Hunis. The Mexican drovers forced them with whips to carry more and more baskets of guano down the steep, hazardous trail to the bottom of the mesa, where one mule train after another was loaded with the precious dung. Never before had the tribe been so degraded. They were not prepared for an armed conflict; any form of violence was against their beliefs. They had always put their trust in the tumble rock. But the Army had shattered the original rock with gunpowder; now they were helpless in the power of the insane Jesse McHair. There remained no way out for them but to put an end to their own existence. After meeting in secret conclave, the brujos decided to put an end to the tribe, without waiting for the white cloud that, according to legend, would foretell the end of man. During a solemn meeting in the kiva, the men resolved that no more children were to be conceived; those that were, would be killed at birth. Jesse McHair discovered this plan, and his reaction was that of a madman. He ordered his Mexican slave-drivers to rape all the women in the pueblo, repeatedly; he himself raped the uncrowned Queen of the Hunis, the Quaker widow Himsha . . . ' "

This was going too far. He looked up warily, but Laura was lying on the bed, smoking, a picture of contentment. He read on.

" 'When, despite her advanced age, Himsha gave birth to a male

child, Jesse took his son down to the hacienda. He sent to Indiana for his sister Lucretia to look after the child. But the wrath of the Lord smote him. After a short while Lucretia discovered that the child was blind; the sins of its father were visited upon it. But the Lord had not finished punishing Jesse yet. When the child became older and started to walk, it soon stopped growing. After five years it became clear that the little boy, christened William, was not only blind: he was a dwarf.'"

"Well," she said, puffing at her cigar. "Fancy that."

He closed the book. "I'll read the rest tomorrow night. Let's go to sleep."

"Okay," she said. "Do we have meeting first? In that case I'll put away my cigar."

He sat down, bent his head and closed his eyes.

"Don't you want to undress first?" she asked.

"No. Now be quiet for a moment, please."

"Sorry."

He smelled the cigar. She had not put it away. He tried to center down, but it was difficult. Suddenly she asked, out of the blue, "Do you ever pray for somebody else's soul?"

Now what had brought that up, all of a sudden? "Yes, I do."

"In that case, pray for the soul of that blind dwarf," she said. "How can a man who calls himself a priest explain that as punishment for the guy who raped the widow? How about giving some thought to the child itself? How would you feel if you were condemned to live whatever life a blind dwarf lives, and be told you are somebody else's punishment?"

He thought for a moment. "You are right. The priest's conclusion was brittle."

"Would you translate that for me, please?"

"It's an old Quaker expression for insensitive, running out of virtue."

"Running out of virtue! Boy, you Quakers are really something else!"

"What do you mean, you Quakers?" he asked. "You're one yourself!"

"Ha! For all I know, I may have been a Holy Roller. Or a fire-worshipper. Quakerism? It doesn't mean a thing to me."

Obviously she was trying to get a rise out of him; he had had enough. "Let's go to sleep," he said. "Would you mind putting that stinker away?"

But she was not listening. "Do you know what I don't understand? How you can have an open fireplace on board a houseboat. Do they, in Holland? Do you know?"

"Why? Do you remember a houseboat?"

"No—just something that crossed my mind. As I sat looking at the fire." She held out to him what was left of her cigar.

He took the unsavory stub and threw it into the flames. He undressed with his back to her; dammit, he didn't have his pajamas! It bothered him, but there was nothing else he could do: although stark naked, he started to look for them. He could feel her eyes on him. Where were the damn things? What had he done with them this morning?

Then he heard her laugh. "Okay," she said. "Here you are." She held the pajama jacket out to him.

"Where the devil—"

"I warmed it for you. Between my legs. Surprise, eh? Good little wifie, what?"

He took a breath, then let it out in a sigh. She was completely out of whack right now. "Thanks," he said and took the jacket from her.

"Sorry, I didn't warm your pants." She produced them from under the blankets. "I would have, but I forgot about them once I sat here, day—listening to you, reading. You needn't put them on, as far as I'm concerned."

"Laura," he said, determined to put a stop to this, "I don't know what your game is, but knock it off! Give them here!"

"Game? I have no—"

"Knock it off, I said!" He grabbed the pants and put them on. "Sorry. I shouldn't lose my temper. All right, move over."

She opened the quilt for him; he climbed into bed. "What the devil is inside this pallet?" he asked. "Straw?"

"Dried seaweed, I think. That's how it feels. Exactly like my mattress at the farm."

"Which farm?"

"One I must have stayed at, as a child. I remember a toy stove. And a picture of a little boy, praying. And the sound of sparrows under the eaves. I remember feeding calves; they drank so greedily that when they got to the end of the bucket of milk they sounded just like an emptying bath."

He stretched out, relaxing. "Any more memories of that farm?"

"A truck. Very old, with a blond boy in it. It was so rickety, he had to tie the door shut with a strap."

"What was the boy's name?"

"That's the odd thing about him. He never would tell me. Why wouldn't he, I wonder? Just one of those childish things, I suppose. We had one like that in the *Hospiz*. Whenever I asked her what her name was, she stuck out her tongue and gave me a raspberry."

"The boy could hardly have been a child," he said, "if you remember him driving a truck."

"That's true . . ."

"Can you describe him more fully?"

"Blond hair, blue eyes. Yes, very blue, sort of cold. Blue coveralls. He must have been a farm hand."

"Maybe," he said. "I think I know who he was. I think I met him."

The way she looked at him was ominous, but he decided to risk it. "I think he was the one who placed you on that farm."

"As a child?"

"No. He was a member of the same cell in the underground resistance your father belonged to, the one that tried to find homes for Jewish babies before they were deported. When your father was arrested, the boy took you to that farm to hide you from the Germans. He was afraid that the Gestapo would get hold of you. He works for the city of Westerdam now, but still wears blue coveralls. They all do, the ex-members of the underground. It's a uniform to them. He told me that your father—"

"Stop it!" she cried fiercely. He might have known. She looked as if she were about to attack him physically and he braced himself for the onslaught, but she simmered down and said dourly, "I don't need any more memories, thank you. I have enough to last me a lifetime. I'm not interested in where I come from, not any longer. There was a time when I felt I had to know or I'd never be able to put myself back together. I no longer feel that way. I no longer feel I can't be anybody without knowing what my father was like, how we lived before the war, what happened to the horse called Winnetou. They're all dead. Let the dead rest in peace."

It sounded like progress, but something was wrong. Something was terribly wrong.

Suddenly she said, "Poor guy. Poor, poor guy."

"Who?"

"He thought he could take on the tide, all by himself. He thought our sand castle was really going to last."

Her voice sounded strained, as if she was trying to hold back tears. Better not press her. They lay for a while in silence, side by side, gazing at the ceiling. In the flickering firelight, the beams seemed alive. Ghosts of Himsha the widow, who must have lain in this same bed with her husband, and later, after his death . . . Could it have happened right here? Had Jesse McHair raped her on this same bed—?

Suddenly she rose on her elbow beside him and looked down at his face. "I'm sorry," she said softly. "I *know* I'm giving you a hard time. Don't let me hurt you. I never want to hurt you. Just—well, let me work it out. It has nothing to do with you. You've done a wonderful thing, and one day I will thank you for it." She kissed him on the mouth.

He was taken unawares, and she bewildered him utterly. For her lips had been warm and soft, but her eyes were full of pity.

*   *   *

She had kissed him on an impulse, because she suddenly felt sorry for him; now, as she lay with her back to him, pretending to be asleep, she knew from the way he lay there rigidly, staring at the ceiling, that she had done something she had never intended to do. She sensed his sudden hunger for closeness, tenderness, love. Then he put out a hand and touched her. She snapped, "Don't *do* that!"

He mumbled something and turned his back to her.

Poor guy! If anyone understood how he felt, it was she. How could she have done that, kiss him and then turn away? What had got into her? Maybe she shouldn't have turned him down? No, she still could not bear the thought of his touching her, of anyone touching her. It was stronger than her will, her reason; it threw her into a fury of sorrow and revulsion. That's how that Indian widow must have felt. She felt close to that woman, right now. "Good night, Bonny," she said. "Thank you for reading to me. It was very helpful. I mean—it was really *gezellig*."

Nonsense. She only said it because she wanted to make amends. She lay wide awake, looking at the flickering light of the flames on the ceiling. This spooky room with its dancing shadows was full of ghosts. Well, she was not afraid of ghosts. She was afraid of nothing except memories, jumping her from the dark when she wasn't prepared for them.

She must try to sleep. What should she think about to make herself sleepy? Waving wheatfields, Heinzl used to say. No. What about Indians? Real ones, with feathers and deerskin suits with fringes and mustangs and inscrutable eyes? But it didn't work; instead, she found herself thinking about odd names she remembered: 'Old Shatterhand,' 'Old Firehand.' And endless plains of grass with herds of wild buffalo that, so far, were still a pie in the sky.

Pie! That did it. A succulent, luscious, gooey cherry pie. How she would eat it: slowly, sensuously, with sinful rapture . . .

* * *

He was lying in the grass at the bottom of a dike with a girl called Clara, a wild, reckless girl he had made love to in the reeds somewhere in Holland, the night after her hometown had been liberated. Clara had her hand inside his trousers and whispered hotly, *'Liebes, liebes, Liebchen, liebe mich!'*

Suddenly he was wide awake.

'Um Gotteswillen! Liebe mich, liebe mich! Komm . . .'

He tore himself free and tumbled out of bed.

He sat on the floor, his head in his hands; slowly, the meaning of it penetrated to him. Getting to his feet he looked down at her in the faint glow of the embers. She lay quite still, evidently asleep.

He went to the chair by the fireplace and sat down to gaze at the dying fire. It could not be true. It could not be! She just thought in German, that was all. It was part of her illness. But it was no good. It was true. Inconceivable, but true. She had been in love with that ghoul.

Suddenly her voice asked in the stillness. "Did I say anything?"

"Yes."

"Did I—do anything?"

"Yes."

"So now you know."

"Yes."

"I'm sorry."

"It's all right. Go back to sleep."

But it wasn't. This was more than he could handle. He needed help. Now he needed help. Not from a psychiatrist, but a Friend, a weighty Quaker who could tell him where to go from here, how to carry on. For this was unimaginable, repulsive, words failed him. She had not been the slave of that mass-murderer, but his lovesick mistress. It explained everything: the German, everything. The unspeakable part was: if she had been sexually aroused by that butcher, lived with him not as a serf but as his passionate mistress, then the whore with the cigar was the true Laura. The charming, easygoing girl of the *Hospiz* had been a sham, the temporary result of the shock of the monster's death, from which she was now recovering.

Dear God! How could he overcome his revulsion from the woman who lay there, haunted by desire for that thug, a murderer who had set his dog on fleeing prisoners? A ghoul who had selected women and children to be gassed?

Everything became clear now. The constant correction of "Hei—" into "Dr. Schmidt." The German she spoke. Words failed him. It was total damnation; she was a damned soul. He simply was not equipped to handle her, yet he would have to, alone. He must cling to what he had within himself, what he had been taught, the Christian approach to this monstrousness. The approach to conflict after the manner of Friends. Step one: identify with thy adversary . . .

Impossible. The very first step was an impossibility. He would not be able to identify with her in a thousand years. Amnesia, disorientation, fear of death—he had explained her living with the ghoul in numerous ways. Wassermann had explained it to him. It made sense. Even Wassermann, obviously, had had no idea that she had been in love with the mass-murderer.

He could not see it through. He must leave. He might say things he would regret; worse, do things. He barely dared face it, but there was inside him a rage, a growing rage at having been betrayed. There he sat, the pacifist, the conscientious objector, the apostle of non-violence, fists clenched, arms taut, ready to beat the hell out of her for her betrayal of his trust, his faith. Oh! He would love to take this very chair, swing it, beat—

Suddenly he realized how serious this was. He was no longer protecting her with the sheltering arms of the Society of Friends. He was tainted himself now; the virus of violence had found its way into his very soul. Beat, kick, pummel, rape . . . *Rape?!*

My God! Dear God! He must leave! But he could not desert her—or could he? He did not know! He needed help! He could not carry this load alone any longer! But who? Who? Dear God, please, please: who? Christ, dear Christ . . .

Suddenly there was an answer: the oldest testimony of the Society of Friends. George Fox himself had said it, *'There is one: Christ Jesus, who can speak to thy condition.'*

In the darkness he found his pants, his jacket, his boots. He heard her call his name as he stumbled to the door, but he ripped it open and fled into the night.

*   *   *

The door slammed; he was gone.

For a moment she was panic-stricken. She leaped out of bed, ran to the door, then stopped and walked over to the fire.

Wherever he might be running, he was running away from *her.* Baby, you're on your own now. Run after him? No. No more fear, no more panic, no more sickening terror at the mere thought of being left alone. He had left, for good. And she had only herself to blame. This is it, baby. You've asked for it, now you've got it—bye-bye, Bonny. Bye-bye, saint.

She had observed him as he sat there, head in his hands, shaking until she could hear the chair creak. The shoe was on the other foot now. The one sick with terror was he, the innocent, horrified boy. And why? Because he had discovered, she still didn't quite know how, that she had loved Heinzl instead of having been a cold side of beef, a virgin clutching her pure soul, eyes upturned, while she let the monster have his way with her. What the hell had been the good of all Bonny's praying, if it made him bolt like a stag the moment he was faced with real, live sin? He was no better than her grandmother. There had been nothing to forgive as long as she had been an abused young girl, who had gone off her rocker with fright when the commandant raped her. She didn't remember the rape at all, but Heinzl had made such a production of it over the years that in the end she had come to feel guilty because she didn't. The sanctimonious Quaker creep! The cowardly shit! *"Shit!"* She screamed it at the door, so loudly that she hurt her throat.

Take it easy, baby. Calm down. Have a cigar.

She did and sat down by the fire, in the chair where he had been sitting before he streaked out like a bat out of hell. She threw a couple of logs onto the glowing embers; they caught fire at once. The fires of hell. That's where Heinzl was: in hell, screaming his heart out as the eternal fire refused to consume him, but tortured him, in terror and loneliness, for all eternity. Bah! The sanctimonious Quaker creep! What would *he* have done, in Heinzl's place? What if not Heinzl, but St. Bonny had ended up as Schwalbenbach's SS doctor? All it had needed to turn Bonny into a saint and Heinzl into a fallen angel was a caprice of fortune. How often had Heinzl used those words! 'Caprice of fortune' this, 'caprice of fortune' that; and he had been right. What would St. Bonny have done, faced with the choice between setting the dog on that old man and having her tossed into the truck to the gas oven? Would he have sacrificed *her?* What do you mean, you shit, running out on Heinzl in horror when only the roll of the dice of chance has saved you from being forced to serve in a concentration camp, from being saddled with a dazed girl who had nobody else in the world except you? Ha! I'd like to see *you* faced with the choice: either she, or an old geezer I don't know from Adam! *"Shit!"* She shouted it again, but not as loudly this time, for she *had* hurt her throat. She tried to clear it, spat in the fire; it hissed. *'Ich spucke nicht auf dir, liebes, liebes . . .'* No, never. Never would she spit on poor Heinzl, screaming in the fires of hell. She'd join him there, when her time came.

Why not now? What did she have to lose? Bonny had run off into the night. At the speed he had cannonballed out of here, he should be halfway to that ranch by now. For of course that was where he was headed: the titless creature with the acne and the binoculars! He had spent hours with her, the evening before they left for the pueblo. 'I visited the stables.' God knows, he had probably screwed her right there in the hay. Bah! She threw the cigar into the fire. It sent up a shower of sparks, glowed briefly and was gone.

But not Heinzl. Not poor, tormented, star-crossed Heinzl. *'Two households, both alike in dignity, in fair Verona, where we lay our scene.'* Verona, hell: Zweibrücken, Rheinpfalz, and Media, Pennsylvania. Two households, both alike in dignity; one had produced a devil, the other a saint. Why? The dice had rolled; one was damned, the other saved.

Well, there he went, the shitless saint, galloping across the plains on his way to the girl, the dwarf, the thousand Spanish servants, and no water in the bison to wash your fice in. And if he knew what was good for him, he'd stay gone, or the dice might roll once more.

She gazed at the flames. Suddenly, something told her—instinct, intuition, or just the fact that she knew him so well—that he was not running away at all. He was not in the valley, but somewhere in the pueblo, God knew where. He would be back. All she could do was wait.

Nursing her fury, savoring it, she waited, watching the flames, and thought about the rolling dice.

*   *   *

The church was a haven of stillness and peace. Votive lights were burning underneath the paintings on the wall. On the altar, a row of candles shed a tranquil light, illuminating from below the figure of the crucified Christ, slumped forward, hanging by His torn hands, His dangling hair hiding His face.

Alone in the church, Boniface sat on a bench halfway down the aisle, gazing at the figure on the cross. He tried to tie in the tormented, alien figure with his own concept of Christ; it was impossible. All the crucifix conveyed was the savagery of the execution, the suffering, the despair: *'My God, my God, why hast Thou forsaken me?'* The Indian Christ still had to go through endless, unbearable torment before finally, in the ninth hour, He could whisper, 'It is finished,' and release the Spirit that had become man's hope and consolation. Facing that crucifix, it was impossible to empty himself of all thoughts and turn himself into an empty vessel to be filled with the spirit of Christ.

But the stillness of the place, the gently flickering candles brought him a sense of peace. The violence within subsided. He could not forget it was there. He would never forget. But it receded, until all was calm and still, and his thoughts became rational once more.

Laura had been, and still was, in love with one of her father's murderers. Judged by human standards, she was depraved beyond redemption. But how would Christ have judged her, had her guilty secret been revealed to Him?

There was an answer to that: the woman taken in adultery.

'He that is without sin among you, let him cast the first stone.'
How glibly he had quoted that passage to the general! It had
been the beginning of the whole thing; if he had not quoted those
words at that moment, Laura and he would never have married,
he would not be sitting here, at the end of his tether. *'Those who
heard it, convicted by their own conscience, went out one by one.
"Where are thy accusers, woman? Has no man condemned
thee?" "No, Lord." "Neither do I condemn thee. Go, and sin no
more." '* Jesus had asked no questions. To Him, Laura would
have been a victim of circumstance, a shell-shocked waif, carried
off by a man who had proceeded to abuse her. But she had fallen
in love with the man! *Neither do I condemn thee. Go, and sin no
more.*

Was he the one to go and sin no more? Boniface the Quaker,
who had in turn carried off the shell-shocked waif and turned
her into a creature of his own making? Neither he nor the ghoul
had cared who she really was; the ghoul had turned her into a
creature of his own making too: *'Eine nette kleine Hausfrau.'*
Some *Hausfrau!* But she had only been fifteen when she fell in
love with the man, still a child . . .

He was in no position to cast any stone, let alone the first. In
spite of Wassermann's warning, he had become emotionally involved with her; *that* was the reason why he was now so full of
moral outrage. What price his ululating about 'faith' and 'love'?
What about that high-falutin Quaker sermon he had treated
Stella Best to, after she had found Laura to be too much for her?
What about 'the power of the Presence' that had saved her from
the camp? If he failed her now, it was not only she that would be
lost. By God, he had better see it through!

It took another hour before he could bring himself to move.
Day was breaking; the windows high up in the wall were turning
blue. As he walked up the aisle toward the doors, he saw a dark
figure kneeling behind the last bench. It was the priest.

He went out into the graveyard, to the corner overlooking the
valley, and watched the dawn break over the moonscape. He was
so absorbed in the spectacle before him that he only noticed the
priest when the man suddenly appeared beside him. For a long
time, neither of them spoke; then the priest said, "It's a sight one
never tires of."

Boniface nodded, gazing at the sky.

After a long silence the priest continued, "Do come here

whenever you feel the need. I would be very happy if you would join me in prayer, whenever you wish. Mr. Winkler used to. Praying can be a lonely business, sometimes."

"Yes," he said. Then, after a while, "I think I'd better go and join my wife. Good day, Father."

"Thank you, Mr. Baker. Strength."

It was an odd thing to say. As Boniface slowly walked home, he wondered how much the priest knew, or had guessed. Maybe it was simply that men didn't usually pray in empty churches at dead of night if all was well with their marriages. There were eyes and ears everywhere in this place, watching, listening, as Laura and he wrestled with their demons in the midnight of the soul.

*   *   *

"Had a nice walk?" She knocked back her third little glass of Dutch gin and put it on the mantle, beside the stone bottle. He had been gone for hours; meanwhile, she had unearthed the bottle and opened it. Now she stood with the taste of Heinzl's five-o'clock kisses in her mouth, the smell of his breath in her nostrils. *'Ach, wie herrlich!'* We send your Bols all over the world.

"Wonderful!" He came toward the fire rubbing his hands. "I must say, this place isn't so bad after all. The view over that valley, incredible! I found a marvelous spot for watching the sunrise. It's in the graveyard, where it overlooks the valley . . . "

On and on he jabbered. There was about him a lightheartedness, a well-being that made her watch him like a lynx, ready to pounce on the slightest rustle of the hidden mouse of his secret. It could be no more than a mouse, of that she was certain.

Watching him, she felt her mouth go sour with hatred. Maybe it was the gin, or the cigar. She shot the butt into the fire and wandered over to the table. They still had the rest of the stores to sort out; she might as well get on with it. There obviously was no chance of stopping him talking, he paced up and down, driveling on and on. He had fled in panic; all of a sudden he was cock of the walk. What had brought this about? What the devil had he been up to? Something had happened during that walk of his. He had seen somebody. Done something—

There was a banging on the door. Interrupted in mid-crow, the cock of the walk strode over to see who was there. It turned out to be Sanchez of the beady eyes.

"Ah, good morning, Mrs. Sanchez! Lovely morning, isn't it? Laura, do we need Mrs. Sanchez this morning?"

She had a remark on the tip of her tongue, but she should watch it, that gin was wicked stuff. "No," she answered. "Not this morning. But I'd like another pot of beans tonight."

He asked the leering Indian about the pot of beans as if he were asking for a big favor, like dropping her skirt to settle it once and for all: do we say Mr. or Mrs. Sanchez? The old Indian, while staring at her with beady eyes, agreed, then asked in that croaking voice, "Will you send message to Missie Gulie? Message from Atu?"

"Father Alvarez is the one to send messages to the ranch, Mrs. Sanchez," he said primly.

"You tell Missie Gulie," Mrs. Sanchez said aggressively. *"You* talk to her, on priest machine. You say: Atu not want see her. Morga not want see her. She must *not* come tomorrow. Okay? Atu no. Morga no. Nobody want see her. She stay home."

"Why should *I* be the one to tell her?"

The double-crossing bastard! So that's where he had been all these hours: at the priest's talking to that bitch with the glasses, over the radio! He had been telling her to send a bunch of goons with a strait-jacket, to take mad wifie to the bin!

"You tell Missie Gulie," the old Indian said, leering. "She must not come. She stay away. *Comprende?"* Without waiting for an answer, the old creep turned and walked away.

Laura went back to the hearth, poured herself another glass of Bols and tossed it straight back.

*   *   *

"Well, how about that! I wonder why she doesn't want the priest to do it."

"Because priests don't screw," her voice said behind him.

She was standing by the fireplace, taut with tension; he had never seen her look at him like that before. "So *that's* why," she said.

"Why what?"

"Why you came back full of *Klatsch.* You fucked her once, you're going to fuck her again tomorrow."

My God, she *was* insane!

"Oh, yes," she said, closing in on him. "I knew it the moment you came in that night. Don't think you can fool me, you sneaky bastard. I knew, but kept my trap shut, saying to myself: 'Don't wipe your ass with your meal ticket, sweetheart!' "

The power. He had to call on the power. She was coming for him with those mad, blazing eyes. What could he do? What—

"Yes, you creep!" she shouted. Her breath stank of alcohol. "You banged that slut, didn't you? You fucked her, you double-crossing shit! You screwed her in the hay!"

There was only one thing he could do: he slapped her face, hard. "Sorry," he said. "What have you been drinking?"

She did not reply. The effect of the slap was totally unexpected. The fury drained out of her eyes, a smile transformed her face; it was as if she were shedding an ugly mask, revealing the gentle, charming girl who had worked with such dedication among the children in the *Hospiz*. Then she cried "So *that's* how it happened! He hit me. *'Bitch!'* then again, *'Bitch! Bitch!'* and again! And do you know *why?* Because of the little pillow! He saw the pillow with *'God is love!' That's* where it came from!" She threw her arms round his neck, kissed his cheeks, his nose; then she held him at arm's length. "Bonny!" she cried. *"I remember!"*

"Good for you," he said unsteadily. "Now will you tell me what all this is about?"

"The rape! I remember the rape! The commandant! I remember how it happened! It *is* a memory, Bonny, nobody can have told me this! I went in, he closed the door, somebody cried *'No!'* or *'Ho!'* I turned around and saw him put the key in his pocket; then he took off his tunic and started to unbutton his fly. Somebody cried *'No!'* again. He grabbed my shoulder, said something about Christian arrogance, grabbed the top of my dress and ripped it open! And then I saw his face turn to a snarl, he tore that little pillow off my stomach, looked at it, and slapped my face, *'Bitch! Bitch!'* That's where it came from! All these years I have racked my brains over that little pillow, now I know! I wore it strapped to my stomach with surgical tape, to make people think I was pregnant! That's what caused the burns! I had burns—here, on my sides, for days—it was where he tore off the skin! Come, come on! Bounce me off the wall some more! Shake the piggy bank!"

"Laura," he said, collected now, "calm down. Take it easy."

But she went on hysterically, "He didn't really rape me, he

just pretended to! Heinzl did tell me that, and he was right. The only pain was on my sides, a burning . . . "

Now he must face her with the truth. She might go completely out of control, but he must risk it; a chance like this might never come again. "And your father?" he asked.

Her joy darkened; her face became hard. "What about him?"

"Where was he during all this?"

"How should I know?"

"The man, crying *'No!'* Who do you think it was?"

"Don't ask *me!*"

"Do you want me to tell you?"

"How would *you* know?"

"It was your father. Kroll raped you in front of him; or went through the motions."

She exploded. "Holy shit! Here we go again! Don't you guys ever tire of that sob story?"

"It's true, Laura! The commandant did it out of revenge! That reference to Christian arrogance, who do you think he was talking to?"

"To me! Who else?"

"You? A fifteen-year-old girl he had never set eyes on before? What Christian arrogance could you have taunted him with, to the point where he decided to rape you?"

"For God's sake, will you stop carrying on about my father? I don't know what you're talking about!"

"Laura, listen. Now you have remembered this much, you must accept, at last, that your father was a Quaker who—"

"For Christ's sake!" She walked over to her duffel bag. "Don't *you* start now! Heinzl bored the living daylights out of me with that crap!" She took a cigar, bit off the tip, spat it into the room; Laura the camp-follower was back. She lit it with a match she struck on the seat of her jeans.

"Look, buster," she said, puffing, "don't *you* start using my past as a coloring book!" She shook out the match. "I told Heinzl to can it and he did, finally. Until then, every time he had had a glass too many he would carry on about my saintly father and how lucky he had been to have been allowed to embody the Spirit of Christ. Every time he had loaded a truck full of Jews for the gas ovens he would start hitting the jug and weep over my saintly father, and he always ended up sobbing, *'Christ has no body now on earth but ours, no hands but ours, no feet but ours.'* By the time he got to the eyes, he became mixed up in the anatomy and that was the sign I had to lug him to bed or he'd throw up on the couch. I had to wrestle him into the bedroom—"

"Laura, all I meant—"

"Listen! You may learn something! After taking his boots off, undressing him, heaving his dead weight back on the bed, I would get in with him, and take him in my arms, and do you know why? Because I loved him. Yes, I loved a murderer with the soul of a little boy! You will never understand that! None of you will! I loved him, and he loved me! *Me,* not a victim of the concentration camp, *me!* With all his heart, and all his soul, forever and ever, until death did us part. You people don't know what love is. All you've ever been in love with is yourselves. Oh, Heinzl! Heinzl . . . "

She went to the bed and fell onto it, her face in the quilt.

It took a while before he could sit down beside her, stroke her hair, say soothing words. Once he did it, it was easy; he had done it so often before.

* * *

She was weeping not for Heinzl but with rage and frustration. Couldn't he see, the saintly creep, now stroking her hair as if he were counting the strokes, how extraordinary that was? To do a thoughtful, sensitive thing like hiding that little pillow under the sink, so as not to upset her with a memory? Of course he would never understand. He would never have thought of doing it himself, let alone recognize sensitivity in Heinzl. 'Oh, you wait! you just wait, you arrogant bastard! I may have blown one chance but there will be another. Oh yes, there will be another! You wait!' Afraid that he might sense her hatred, she moaned, "Oh Bonny, Bonny—I'm so sorry—so terribly sorry . . . " Rather good, for a drunk.

But he didn't buy it. His hand stopped stroking her hair and he said, in that calm, tough voice she had at one time loved to hear, "Laura, turn over. I want to talk to you."

"Oh Bonny . . . Bonny . . . "

"Laura, turn over."

She obeyed. Whooee—was she *drunk!* She lay on her back and looked at the ceiling. Transparent worms wriggled in front of her eyes; the bed heaved. She was going to throw up . . . ! His voice came and went; then he said something that caught her attention: " . . . no longer possible, we must go."

"Go where?" She tried to focus on him; he was a blur behind the wriggling worms.

"You said at the time that you weren't ready. Well, I'm not going to put it off any longer."

"Put what off?"

"I'm going to take you to a doctor."

Oh-oh, she was going to throw up . . .

"Tomorrow."

She vomited on the floor beside the bed. Luckily, it was made of stone.

He put an arm around her, a hand on her forehead. He had done that before, sometime. Yuck! That stuff stank. "Sorry," she said, as she sank back into the pillow.

There was the clatter of a bucket. She said, "Don't do that, I'll do it. Just give me a minute . . . "

But the bucket went on clattering and clanking, ear-splitting noises. "Stop that, for God's sake! Stop it!"

"You see?" His voice had echoes. "You see why I have to get you to a doctor?"

"Oh, Bonny . . . "

"No, Laura. Enough is enough; you need treatment and I'm going to see that you get it. Now."

"You're *hurting* me! With that goddam racket!"

"Laura, you *are* going to see a doctor!"

"A medicine man? Mr. Sanchez?"

"Tomorrow we're going to Kissing Tree."

That sobered her. "You're kidding!" She opened her eyes. There he stood, or swam, among the worms. "Leave the pueblo?"

"I can't handle you any longer. I'm not a psychiatrist, I'm a medic. Whatever your problem is, it's beyond me. You *shall* go and see a doctor. I'll take you there."

"You're crazy! Have you never seen a drunk before? Jesus, I must have knocked back half a bottle of that stuff! I've never been so stinko in my life!"

"No, Laura. Tomorrow we go to the ranch, the day after: Kissing Tree, or Albuquerque, or Santa Fe, wherever the best man is."

"The best man? Who are you marrying?"

"Laura, stop it! You are a good actress, but real drunks don't act like that."

"Oh no? What do you think I puked? Dishwater?"

"Don't worry, I'll go with you. I'll stay with you until the end."

"The end? What are they going to do, hang me?"

"Don't talk nonsense. Sleep it off."

"Nonsense? You're speaking to me as if—if—" She couldn't remember. The hell with him. She would think when she could think.

She turned over on her stomach, maybe that would help. Sick as a cat. Could there be more Bols inside?

"There's no need for you to start snoring," his voice said, echoing. "I believe you."

He believed me. Boy-oh-boy-oh-boy. 'Blessed are the . . . Blessed are . . . '

She fell into oblivion.

*   *   *

There she lay, poor soul. It might not be what Jesus would have done, but the slap in her face had been the only solution. Only, he had slapped her too hard, with feeling; he was losing control, despite all his good intentions.

Take her to a doctor, fast—he should have done so long ago; now it was almost too late. Not for her, for himself. He would go to see the priest as soon as she was really asleep, not just lying there hamming it up.

But why should he wait? She couldn't go far, and it was urgent. Was there a key to the front door? He could lock her in . . .

There was no key; if there was, Mrs. Sanchez must have it. There were bolts, but on the inside. But there *was* something outside, a bar . . . He opened the door and there it was: a length of two-by-four, bleached by the sun, that fitted into large wooden hooks, two on the door, one on the jamb. He looked at her; she still lay on her stomach, out like a light. He went out, closed the door and put the bar in place. He felt a pang of guilt, but had no choice. He could not risk her staggering outside and hurting herself.

On his way to the church he noticed a strange odor, the kind you would find in an old attic that hadn't been opened for a long time. The sun, fierce now, drained the adobe walls of all color; but the view was hazy. If this had been the coast, he would have said a sea mist was rolling in.

He knew of no other way to the priest's quarters than through the graveyard and the church. The paper flowers on the tombstones hung motionless, there was no wind. The church doors screeched on their hinges; inside, it was dark and cool. The curtains in front of the windows hung motionless too; not a breath of air. He opened the door to the cloister; there he was, Father Alvarez, painting away among the flowers.

He had forgotten about the parrots; once again they startled him as they fluttered, screaming, from their perches and went straight for his feet. The priest looked up. "Mr. Baker! Welcome! What an unexpected pleasure!"

"I'm afraid it's an emergency, Father Alvarez. Would you be kind enough to send a message to the ranch for me? It concerns my wife."

"Ah?" The priest looked concerned. "Nothing serious, I hope?"

"It is, I'm afraid. We must leave tomorrow. I must get her to a doctor."

"Oh—I'm so sorry . . . " The priest looked shifty, afraid of confidences. But he need not worry. There was no question of discussing Laura with him.

"Thank you. Would you send the message, or talk to *Doña* Ana?"

"Ah," the priest said, spreading his large, pale hands in a gesture of regret. "She and I have already had our daily chat."

"When will you be talking to her again?"

"Tomorrow morning, eight o'clock. Can it wait until then?"

"Frankly, I don't think so."

"In that case, I would have to send up a rocket. Is your wife's condition serious enough for that? I have never done it before." Now he looked shiftier than ever.

"Miss McHair seems to be planning to come tomorrow, I want her to bring two horses for us. My wife should not remain here any longer."

The priest frowned. "Miss McHair, tomorrow? How do you know that?"

"Mrs. Sanchez came to ask me if I would pass on a message to *Doña* Ana, telling her granddaughter not to come."

"Did Mrs. Sanchez say why Miss McHair should not come tomorrow?"

The parrots were screaming and pecking at their feet. Boniface felt his patience wear thin. "Father Alvarez, please! My wife—"

"One second, Mr. Baker!" The priest was getting agitated, although he tried not to show it. "Forgive me, *why* should Miss McHair not come here tomorrow? Please, tell me."

"Because somebody called Atu and somebody called Morgan—"

"Morga, yes, yes?"

"Mrs. Sanchez said that Atu and Morga do not want to see Miss McHair tomorrow, that was all." One of the parrots was now unlacing his left boot and he shoved it away irritably with his foot.

"The priest said suddenly, "In that case . . . Do you know how to fire a rocket?"

"I've never done it before either. Don't the instructions come with it?"

"Oh! That's a thought. I'll go and get it." He shuffled away, followed by some of the parrots. Those that remained were soon sorry; they had never been kicked like that in their lives. They screamed blue murder as they sailed through the air, fluttering, landing messily among the sunflowers. They started to curse him with shrieked obscenities, but stayed under cover.

The priest came back, carrying a large, oblong black box in his arms. He put it down gently between them; his escort of parrots began to investigate it. But the others, screaming in the greenery, somehow got the message across; cursing, the birds waddled off and joined the rest among the sunflowers.

The priest opened the box and took out a sheet of instructions. "Here," he said, "you read it, I am no good at technical things. What does it say?"

"There should be a rocket stand to go with this package."

"Ah! *That's* what it is! One second . . . " He shuffled off again.

The instructions warned against firing the thing from an enclosed space like this one. The priest came back with the stand, which was meant to hold the rocket and aim it at the sky. "Here you are . . ! " He was out of breath. "Is this what you meant?"

"Looks like it. But we shouldn't fire the rocket here in the cloister."

"Why not?"

"According to the instructions, it must be fired in the open, because of the noise and the gases."

"Gases?"

"Well, you know, the fumes, when it blasts off."

"Oh, never mind, never mind. Let's do it here, quickly!"

"But—"

"I don't mind a bit of smell, not at all! And we can hurry indoors after the fuse is lit, can't we?"

"Your parrots are going to have a fit. And they may be gassed."

"Never mind, Mr. Baker, please! Let's fire the thing and have done with it! Then we'll hurry to the radio and listen. Will you do the firing? Please?"

"All right," Boniface said. "You'd better go inside. Hold the door for me."

"Right. I'll be in my study, over there . . . " He trotted off in his flopping sandals, then stopped and asked, "Do you have matches?"

"It's a trigger mechanism. All I have to do is pull a cord."

"Well—you know best," the priest said, doubtfully. When he saw Boniface pull a long, evil-looking rocket out of the box, he scurried toward a door in the walkway, opened it and cried, "Will you be all right?"

"Yes sir, as long as you keep that door open. Here we go. Ready?"

"Madre de Dios," the priest mumbled, and sprang inside. "Yes!" he called, invisible, from the dark room.

Boniface pulled the cord as instructed, only half believing that the thing would actually go off; he had seen fireworks misfire too often. But this was a thing intended for shipwrecked vessels; it took off instantly, with an alarming shriek and billowing clouds of white and orange fumes. He made a dash for the room and stumbled inside. It was pitch dark; the priest closed the door on the hellish racket in the cloister. The shrieks, though diminished, continued; the priest, peering through one of the little windows, muttered, "Oh, my poor children . . ! " The man's regret was somewhat belated; probably all the birds would be dead in a matter of minutes. If the priest and he had stayed outside, they would have been gassed too. At least, that's what it looked like.

Yet the shrieks not only continued, they became angry. There was a loud bang overhead; blurry objects began to career through the cloud and the shrieks became curses. It would take more than the fumes of a rocket to exterminate that lot.

Behind him, Boniface heard the crackling of a loudspeaker and electronic squeals, rising and falling. The priest was sitting at a table, fiddling with an old-fashioned transmitter crowned with coils. There was a stench of battery acid, but that might be the fumes seeping in. The priest adjusted the dials until the squeals ceased; then he said, "Now all we can do is wait. Do sit down, Mr. Baker. It's apt to take a while. I hope they will see it from down there."

"According to the instructions, they should be able to see it in Kissing Tree."

"Ah?"

"They may even send the fire brigade," Boniface joked lamely.

"Well, I hope they will! Let them send the National Guard, as far as I'm concerned! The fat is in the fire now, we might as well go the whole hog." The priest's agitation seemed to have passed; he looked calm and collected.

"I don't think we need go that far," Boniface said. "Just a few men with a couple of horses for us will do. Or is there something else I should know?"

"Pardon? No, no . . . " The priest looked shifty again.

The loudspeaker began, secretively, to build up a squeal. But the priest caught it by tapping one of the coils. Obviously, the old wireless transmitter was the one technical thing he could handle, though it seemed doubtful that he understood how it worked. "Look, Mr. Baker," he said, "let *me* do the rest. I mean, I have a message for *Doña* Ana too, so I will kill two birds with one stone. I mean—" The loudspeaker crackled, hissed and said, with a high, metallic voice like a mechanical parrot, *"Allo, allo, Padre, Doña Ana par aqui, over, over."*

"That was quick!" the priest cried, pressing a button on a microphone the size of a Ping-Pong paddle. He began to speak, a torrent of Spanish; Boniface understood only the words *"Doña Ana," "pronto, pronto,"* and *"pueblo."* "Baker" was not mentioned. He thought he heard the words *"recién nacidos,"* which he remembered having read on a box among the stores.

The priest released the button, the loudspeaker crackled, the parrot voice started a long answer in Spanish that seemed to disappoint the priest; suddenly there was a high-pitched squeal on one shrill note. The priest banged on the set, tapped and wriggled the coils, the squeal remained. "Something's the matter!" he shouted, slapping the set much too hard for so delicate an instrument.

"Turn the sound down!" Boniface cried.

The priest obeyed; it became silent. "I'm afraid something went wrong. I can't understand why. It always works, always!"

"How much of your message did you manage to get across?"

"Oh, the essence—but there is a disappointing circumstance."

"What is that?"

"She can't come, because of high winds. Seems we are about to have one of those gales. Most unfortunate."

"I don't understand. Why would a gale stop them coming to the pueblo?"

"I thought I noticed it an hour ago. Didn't you? The smell of dust? The haze out there? A gale in this valley means a sandstorm. No one could make his way through that. Alas, we'll have to sit it out. Poor—er—Mrs. Baker. Do you think you can handle her alone for twenty-four, maybe forty-eight hours longer?"

"I hope so," he said soberly.

"You might try some bromide, perhaps?"

Boniface looked at the innocuous face, the bland eyes. "That's a thought," he said. It was indeed: the sedative. "I should have thought of that. You are supposed to be the priest and I the medic."

"Oh, well," Father Alvarez mumbled, "I occasionally take it myself, that's why. It's beneficial for minor episodes of—well—excitement."

"Thank you, Father." He rose. "You are right: all we can do is sit it out." He went to the door.

"Mr. Baker!" The priest sounded surprisingly forceful; he had risen and moved to bar his way. "This is very important. You have never lived through one of these sandstorms before. You must go home, close door and windows tightly and seal up all the cracks. You must also close the damper in your chimney."

"Why?"

"The sand penetrates everything. It will find its way inside even so, but that way you will keep most of it out. Read, go to bed, but under no circumstances open your door."

"All right, Father," he said. "How long do these storms usually last?"

"No more than twenty-four hours. But they always excite the Indians; the rocket must already have done so, chances are they'll start eating peyote and, believe me, that's no joking matter. They'll go on making mischief until they drop by the wayside; that may take another twenty-four hours. So, all in all, you and your wife had better settle in for a two-day siege. Come, I think you'd better go back now." He opened the door.

Boniface was welcomed to the cloister by shrieking parrots and a stench of gunpowder. The sunflowers drooped, obviously dying; the parrots looked ruffled, but screamed as loudly as before, cursing his mother, urging him to commit the sin of Onan, until he had locked the door of the church on them. The stillness inside appeared unchanged, but there was some wind now, outside; the bordello curtains in front of the windows billowed.

In the graveyard, the paper flowers rustled and the smell of dust was stronger. The sun was veiled, a sea mist was indeed rolling in. As he stood looking at the sky, his eye was caught by a movement beside one of the church towers, the one with the radio mast on it. A small movement, almost invisible in the glare of the sky: a loose wire swinging in the wind. It was the cable to the antenna.

He stared at the swinging wire with alarm. The cable had been cut deliberately; there was no other explanation, there was hardly any wind as yet. That was the reason why the transmitter had gone dead in the middle of *Doña* Ana's answer: somebody had cut that cable; it could only have been an Indian.

Hurriedly, he opened the gate of the graveyard and ran home. There was no one to be seen in the village; it looked as deserted as it had on the day they arrived. It had seemed merely eerie then; now the air was full of menace.

He lifted the bar and opened the door to the lazaret. There she lay, as he had left her: on her stomach, lost to the world.

He closed the door, bolted it and looked for a roll of surgical tape wide enough to cover the cracks around the door and the windows.

* * *

As she woke up, Laura heard a monotonous hooting, accompanied by whistling.

She opened her eyes and saw Boniface, in his lumber-jacket, standing on a chair, doing something to the door. What was he doing? Surgical tape? "Hey!" she shouted, but he did not hear her; the hooting and the whistling were too loud. *"Hey!"*

This time he heard. He turned around, climbed off the chair and came toward her, a roll of surgical tape in his hand. "How are you feeling?"

"What *are* you doing?"

"I'm taping up the door and the windows. There's a sandstorm blowing up out there."

That's what the hooting was: the wind in the chimney. And the whistling came through the cracks of the door. "Why?" she asked. "Why tape them up?"

"Because if I don't, this room is going to be full of flying sand." He sounded firm and calm.

"Who told you to do that?"

"The priest. Now, if it's all right with you, I'll finish the job before it hits full force." He climbed back on the chair and was about to resume his activity when he turned back to her and asked, "Want some coffee?"

"No, thanks." What she wanted was a gun, to shoot her way out of this prison! He was not taping the door to keep out any sand, but to make sure she couldn't rip it open while his back was turned and run away. He had done it! He had sent a message to the ranch for them to come and cart her off to a madhouse!

For a few moments she felt sick with panic. Then common sense returned. No point in running away anyhow; they would catch up with her. And who could she run to? Grandmother? She'd sooner slit her throat. The ranch? They'd lock her up until the ambulance came with the strait jacket. There was no other solution but to bring him down. Stomp on his arrogance until he lay sobbing his heart out. Then let them come to take her away—they would find two patients instead of one.

Her hatred for him returned, not as it had been, not with the shakes and a mouth full of bile, but cold and calculating. Once she got over her revulsion, it would be easy. A pushover, kid stuff. If that beanstalk with the glasses could make him roll over,

Laura the Broncobuster would drive him straight up the wall.

Now think, baby, think. Don't lie there bragging, expecting your tits to do all the work. This thing has to be planned carefully, carried out without a slipup, like surgery. Surgery! Ha! *'Little Kitty has been altered.'* Now who the hell's voice was that? A woman's; and there was that cat again, the one she had seen before: black and white, in a basket. But the white was a bandage: the cat, huge and black, glared at her with motionless fury— gone. Those patchwork-quilt memories were coming hard and fast, these days. She'd have to live with them; as long as they didn't begin to make sense, what the hell. If they didn't hit her at the wrong moment, and trip her up while she was altering little kitty . . . Ah-ah! No violent thoughts! But this was meant as a joke! No violent jokes, even; cool, collected, steady, calm. She would have to slip him the axe in one swift— No, goddammit! No rage, no surges of hate! Calm, sweet, deadly. Well, get with it. Start by unveiling the ironing board. Ironing board, my foot! The only reason she might have to work at it was that she was too fat. Just cooing, 'Come into my parlor, sweetheart' was not going to do it, not with her Bantu buttocks and two bobbing piglets. Boy, the GI jokes also were coming thick and fast today. Seriously now. Step number one: undress. Or put more logs on the fire first?

She considered it, watching him as he stood on his chair, playing with his tape. Suddenly she was hit by a wave of sadness, a moment near tears, of— Knock it off! St. Boniface, here we come.

She swung her legs out of bed and pulled her T-shirt over her head. Off with the bra. Down with the jeans. Off with the panties. Off with the football socks. Ouch! That floor was *cold.*

Come on, soldier, rise and shine! One more battle and he'll be eating out of your hand.

Noiselessly she padded across the room and tossed two logs on the fire. The wind roared in the chimney; they burst into flames at once.

* * *

"Well," he said, "that ought to do it! Now all we can do is sit it out." He climbed down off the chair and picked it up to put it

back by the fireplace. "From what I hear, these sandstorms—"
His mouth fell open. There stood Laura, without a stitch on, in
front of the blazing fire.

It took him a moment before he could ask casually, "Why the
tropical costume, dear?"

She turned to face him. Despite the fact that she was too
plump, she took his breath away. She answered laconically, "Because of the heat, dear."

Indeed, it was stiflingly hot. More logs had been piled on the
fire and were roaring away; she must have done it while his back
was turned. "Why did you push the fire?"

"Because I was cold."

"Well, now it's too hot! And dammit, I'm supposed to close
the damper!"

"If you think it's too hot," she said, "do what I did: strip."

She heaved on another log; it burst into flame with a gushing
sound and a shower of sparks. Bent over in front of the fire,
breasts dangling, lit by the flames, she looked like a painting by
Rubens. He had never seen her naked body except for that time
Mrs. Sanchez came in, then she had been covered with soap;
now the sight of her sleek, silken plumpness made his mouth go
dry. Why was she doing this? Why had she taken her clothes
off? Had he become so much like a piece of furniture in her life
that she no longer considered him normal?

"Look, Laura, stop this nonsense! If you're cold, go back to
bed!"

"You go to bed, dear," she said sweetly. "I'll just sit here by
the fire and warm my little feet." She sat down in the chair and
stretched out her legs. The fire roared; the wind thundered in the
chimney.

This was it! She had gone off the deep end! Only an insane
person would do such a thing. Now what? Force her to put some
clothes on? Force her back into bed? That would only make her
violent. He mustn't touch her, certainly not wrestle her to the
bed. My God, what was he to do?

He went to the wardrobe and took out his pajama jacket.
"Here," he said. "At least put this on, before you catch your
death."

"Thanks, but no thanks. I'm fine as I am. Why don't you go to
bed?"

"I don't want to."

"Well, go sit and read or something. Don't hang around me like that. It makes me nervous."

He put the pajama jacket over the back of her chair, went to pick up the priest's manuscript, took it to the table and sat down, pretending to read. Then it occurred to him that he had done exactly what he was told. She was in control of this game, if it was a game and not a bout of out-and-out madness, like sitting in the courtyard of Meeting for Sufferings in that brazen T-shirt, smoking a cigar, taunting the Friends as they came out of the building. He should have known then, he should have told the psychiatrist—

She rose, and started to wander around the room. Provocatively? He did not look at her, but he was conscious of her every movement, and, dammit, yes, was beginning to get aroused. He had felt no sexual desire since that night with Clara on the dike; apart from an occasional vague dream, those urges had gone into hibernation. Now, suddenly, they came surging back with a vengeance. What frightened him was that the rage came back at the same time; lust for that sleek, sweat-slick body, taunting him, beguiling him, and rage against the slut who was doing this to him, deliberately, the camp-follower and her easy tricks, the Nazi whore, who deserved to be— No! He, at least, must keep sane, not let himself be engulfed by that sickening mixture of violence and lust again, he must keep sight at all costs of Laura, the unique, irreplaceable— Bullshit! He didn't care a damn about her precious soul right now; he wanted to feel her naked body under his, penetrate her, rape— My God! Gone, it was all gone, all the strength and the power he'd thought he had regained last night in church! He was back at the point where, last time, he had managed to flee before— God damn her! What kind of woman was this? What sick, sick game was she playing? Did she have any idea what she was doing to him, what she unleashed—?

She pulled up a chair and sat down, facing him, thighs parted, hair loose, eyes heavy-lidded with some mad, snakey, reptilian lust. There could be no doubt any more, she *was* deliberately trying to arouse him. Yet her eyes were not amorous, but cold, calculating, sizing him up with that half-lidded look like a snake sizing up a goat. Well, she had better watch it! She was playing with something that scared even him . . .

The logs crackled and hissed. The words on the page danced in front of his eyes. Sweat ran down his forehead, his nose; he wiped it off with the back of his hand. The storm shrieked and thundered, shaking the building. The fire roared. He should close that damper! But he couldn't take any logs off the fire; he had taped the door and the windows, they would be overcome by smoke. She had him over a barrel, the wily bitch! He could feel her mocking cold stare as she watched him squirm.

Should he do what she had said: take off his clothes and the hell with it? No, no—that would mean—God, he must not panic!

He got up and went over to the fire, just to get away from her unblinking, mad stare. She was mad, mad; she was a mental patient; he must not allow himself to be drawn into her mad world. God only knew what she would be up to next; she might take a knife and plunge it into his chest, she was staring at him as if she would like to do that right now. He must keep calm, still at the center, tranquil, hold on to that of God in her, think of other things, the stables, Gulie McHair; he must approach her with unsensual, sublimated love, with . . . Words, words, meaningless words. The wind seemed to be increasing by the minute; the windowpanes bulged and flapped, pushed in by gusts, lashed by sand. He must concentrate . . .

She rose, and joined him by the fire. No, not another log! He was about to cry out, but to see her bending over made his blood surge. He closed his eyes, tried to remember what she had looked like when she slipped from his grip in the ambulance and slumped onto the bunk: skull black with tar, breasts tarred, pubic hair . . . He shook his head to clear it, took a deep breath and said, "Laura, for God's sake! Let's—let's have meeting!"

She grinned. "Like hell we will." She picked up another log.

"No!" he cried, aghast. "Don't! You'll set the place on fire!"

She threw the log into the flames; it virtually exploded, sending a wave of heat into the room like the blast from a furnace.

She bent over to pick up yet another; he pulled her back; the touch of her flesh undid him. Suddenly they stood very close, her mad eyes were very close; he could hold on no longer. He grabbed her, pressed her against him, her skin was slippery with sweat, he grabbed her hair, pulled back her head and ground his mouth onto hers.

She was like a pillar of ice, totally unresponsive. He faltered, stepped back; she gave him a look full of loathing and asked, with a sneer, "Well? What was all that in aid of?"

Unnerved, confused, he cried, "Goddammit, Laura! Stop behaving like a whore! And no more logs on the damn fire! Stop it!" He turned away, went back to the table, beset by that frightening, growing rage. It was as if the Nazi sadist who still held her in bondage even after his death was in the room with them, sneering, saying, *'You don't know what to do, boy; you don't know how to handle whores like her; stop the gentle stuff!* He was beset by an evil impulse to outdo the taunting ghost, knock her to the ground, kick her, drag her to the bed— God, dear God . . . !

He sat down at the table, his head in his hands. There she came, flaunting her breasts, her sleek belly, her silky thighs. He closed his eyes and tried to center down on Christ, peace, love, anything, anything at all to protect him from the violence within; then he felt her behind him, bending over him. "Well?" she whispered. "What does He say? Or are you getting a busy signal?"

"God damn you!" He jumped up; the chair crashed on its back. "What the hell are you up to? What do you want? What—" She grabbed his genitals.

For one moment he stood stunned, then, with a roar, he tore off his clothes, tried to grab her, she slipped away, he got hold of her hair; roaring, he hurled her at the bed. She hit it with a thud, fell to her knees; he dragged her back on her feet, threw her backward on the bed; she tried to escape, but he threw himself on top of her, forced her knees apart, mounted her like a beast—

But it was pointless. She was closed, dry, inaccessible. *"You bitch!"* he cried, as he realized he had been tricked. *"You—"* Then she spat in his face.

The rage within tore itself free. Blind with fury, he grabbed her by the throat, banged her head on the bed, banged it, banged it, shrieking, *"Bitch! Bitch! Goddam bitch!"* Then it penetrated to him what he was doing, what he was screaming, and his blood ran cold. Horrified, he let her drop on the bed, and stared at her, speechless.

"There! You see?" Her voice was hoarse but triumphant. "See, you sanctimonious shit?! You're no better than that Nazi after all! Look at my throat, Quaker saint! Look! You tried to strangle me!"

Aghast at the evil she had unleashed in him, he stammered, "But why? Why?!"

"To teach you not to go holy on Heinzl, you arrogant bastard! Pious creep! You're not a patch on him! He was a *man!* You are nothing but a slimy toad! Look at that limp little prick! Go find yourself a Quaker mouse! Go fuck pissed-up Gulie McHair! Fuck off, you goddamn eunuch! Yes! That's what you are! A castrated, impotent—"

"Laura!" he shouted, feeling himself slipping. "Shut up, do you hear? You can't see straight for your own madness! Look at me! Look! I am Bonny! Bonny Baker! I'm the one who reached out to you when—" He stopped, aghast.

"Oh yes, we all know!" she cried triumphantly. "I should be grateful to you, right? Right! Thank you, St. Boniface!" Again she spat in his face.

Spittle dribbling down his cheek, he could no longer hold out. "Yes!" he roared. "Yes, you filthy, insane whore! How many men do you think would have done what I did? Saved your miserable life for you, saved you from hell, after you had yourself screwed, for three fucking years, by your father's fucking murderer?!"

He saw on her face how low he had fallen.

"That's it, baby," she said calmly. "Now you know who you *really* are."

He sank to his knees, slumped forward on the bed, his head in his hands.

*   *   *

She got up and looked down on him, rubbing her throat. There he lay, poor bastard, weeping like a baby. The beautiful, pure, godly Bonny, God's own little baby, was crushed. He was in hell now, poor bastard. Well, welcome to the club.

She was not sorry she had done it. Somebody had to do it. Yet she felt as if she had been cheated out of something. It had been too easy, too cheaply easy, to destroy his virtue, like stepping on a beetle. Maybe virtue was indeed like a beetle: a small marvel of God. And she had crushed it, just like that.

She went to her duffel bag, took out a cigar, bit off the tip and went to the fire. She found a sliver of kindling, held it in the flames and lit the cigar. Then she went to get the kerosene stove

and the kettle, carried them to the table, the cigar between her
teeth. She lit the stove; as she sat down to wait for the water to
boil, she watched him. He still lay there, sobbing. It was time he
pulled himself together.

She made up a mug of instant coffee, took it to him and
nudged him with her foot. "Hey!" she said. "Here, drink this."

He looked up; his face was bloated and wet with tears.

"Drink this, and stop bawling over your lost virginity. It happens to the best of us. One thing is sure as hell, boy: you never
get it back. So—here. Have some coffee."

"We're lost, Laura . . . lost . . . "

He was worse than Heinzl after loading a truck.

"Boniface, you don't know what 'lost' means. The way I see it,
all you did was use naughty language and shake up a teasing
broad. If that meant a one-way ticket to hell for a man, it would
be a crowded place. Well, maybe it is. Cheers!" She took a sip
herself for, truth be told, she too was a little shaky. She held out
the mug to him again. "Come, drink this. Don't be an ass. Take
it!"

But he didn't want any coffee. He just lay there, bawling. Boy,
the one thing lacking was *'Christ has no body now on earth but
ours.'* "Okay," she said, with a sigh. "Here we go again." She
put the mug away and bent over him. "Put your arms around my
neck and hang on." She tried to lug him to his feet; Heinzl had
been lighter. "Look, Bonny, I know women aren't supposed to
get a hernia, but don't try me! Come on, up you get! Up!"

No, she might as well try to uproot the Statue of Liberty. 'The
Stat of Lib,' the GI's had called it. She had felt at home with the
GI's. They were all the same, men at war. Holy or unholy, men
at war were a breed apart. "Come on, you lug! Hang on!"

No. Well, let's try the pulling trick. She pulled his legs, his
knees slipped from under him, he scrambled to his feet. Good.
"Komm, Schatzrl, inn's Bett! Hoppla!"

As if she had found the magic word, he toppled into bed himself. Now what? Cover him up? No. In this heat, it would be like
covering up a soul in hell.

She lay down in front of the fire. The heat was ferocious, the
stone floor almost too hot to lie on. Smoking, her head on her
arm, she gazed at the flames. The wind thundered in the chimney like a passing train, the fire flickered, flared, fanned by the

gusts. High up on the back wall of the fireplace, the flames revealed some old, blackened scribblings. A fish, some Roman numerals. Someone, long ago, must have chiseled or scratched them there. Seeing those primitive squiggles, made by a forgotten predecessor in this godforsaken place, gave her a sudden sense of evanescence: here today, gone tomorrow. It brought back the melancholy, that old, old sadness. God, dear God, she thought, let tomorrow come soon.

*   *   *

She did not know how long she had been lying there when she was awakened by banging. She must have dropped off, for her cigar lay on the floor in front of her nose; she looked up, the fire had burned down to a dark red glow.

There it was again: *Bang! Bang!* A loose shutter? The place had no shutters. The wind seemed to have died down anyhow. The banging persisted; she thought she heard a voice calling. There was someone at the door. Who the hell could that be? In this weather? There was another round of bangs; she now distinctly heard a voice cry, "Open up!" She went to the door, remembered in time she was naked, picked up Bonny's lumberjacket off the floor and slipped it on. "Yes! *Yes!* Just a minute!" It reached down to her knees. She zipped it up hurriedly, pulled the quilt over Bonny and ran to the door; whoever it was went on hammering. She stubbed her toe on the step, cursed, lifted the latch to open up, but the tape held firm.

"Push!" she called. "Give it a push!"

The door opened abruptly and nearly knocked her over. An Indian came stumbling in, a whirling gust of wind blew out the candle. He put something on the table, shouted, "You keep! No give away! You keep! *Keep!*" and turned to run off.

"Hey, wait a minute!" She barred his way. "What *is* this? Who are you?"

"Atu, Atu!" the Indian cried, "I gave you statue! You keep! Don't let them kill! My wife—" He ran off, pulling the door shut behind him.

She stood staring at it, flabbergasted, when Bonny asked behind her, in the voice of a child who had just awakened, "What was that?"

She recovered. "The mail just came," she said. "Parcel post."

The bundle on the table stirred and made a small, plaintive noise. She went to look at it, lit the candle.

It was wrapped in a shawl. It squealed again. She opened it. "Oh, no . . ."

It was a newborn infant, covered with blood, umbilical cord and all.

"What is it, Laura?"

"We have a baby," she said. "Have a cigar."

*   *   *

The moment Boniface heard the child's anguished squeals, the trained medic took over. He shook off his sense of damnation, forgot about his soul, and went over to the infant on the table. It was an Indian baby girl, with a flat little nose, tightly shut eyes and a black tuft of hair that was wet with blood. The umbilical cord had not been tied and was bleeding profusely. "Quick!" he said. "One of the stack on the second shelf to your right, in a sterile wrapper; *'Suture Tray'* it says. And some half-inch bandage."

While she fetched the tray and the bandage, he gently spread the buttery substance that still covered part of the skin around the tiny body with his hands; then, by the light of the candle which she held for him, he tied and trimmed the umbilical cord. "Whose baby can this be?" he asked.

"The potter brought it. The guy who gave me the little figure."

"Gauze, please."

She picked up the gauze with the forceps. He had just finished when someone banged on the door again. She hastily covered the child with the shawl; he pulled on his pants and went to open up. It was Sanchez; the wind hurled itself into the room, blew out the candle again, knocked over a chair; smoke was sucked into the room. Laura cried, "Close that door!" Together with Sanchez, Boniface forced the door shut in the dark; the only light came from the glowing embers. Sanchez said, breathless with the effort, "I—come—for—child," and went toward the table.

Laura barred his way. "Oh, no, you don't!"

The old Indian looked at the girl through narrowed eyes, then cried commandingly, "My nephew! Mother died in birth! I come for child!" He tried to force his way past her, but Laura stopped him.

"This is a hospital! Get out!"

Boniface came to her aid. "Look, Sanchez," he said, "you can't take the child away in this weather. We are taking good care of it, we have everything here to look after a newborn baby. Later today—"

Laura interrupted him. "Later today the father may take it away! But he must come himself!"

Sanchez cried, "No father! Mother dead! I take child! Now!"

"Bonny," Laura said, "stop him! He's going to hurt the baby!"

Bonny held Sanchez back; the old Indian was feeble, it really was no contest. "No, Sanchez," he said calmly, "go home. We'll look after the child; once the storm is over, the father may come, and if the child is fit to be moved, he may have it."

"You will regret!" The old Indian looked dangerous now. "You will, *mucho, mucho!*"

Boniface opened the door, it was nearly ripped out of his hands by the wind. When he pushed Sanchez out, he felt guilty, it was like releasing a bird during a hurricane. The sand still blew too thickly for him to keep his eyes open; "Help!" he groaned, as he found he could not close the door by himself. Laura put the baby on the bed and went to help; together they managed and he bolted the door. "Well," he said, panting, "that's that."

She went to the bed and looked at the child. It lay shrieking with a huge, wide mouth, waving its little arms, legs feebly kicking. "Hush, beastie, hush!" She picked it up, took it in her arms, kissed the dirty little head, but the child went on struggling and screaming.

"Support her head!" he warned.

"Let's try to give her a bottle. Would you light the stove?"

"Too early," he said. "She shouldn't be fed straight away. The most important thing is to get her calmed down."

She tried to calm the child, cradling it in her arms, but the shrieking became more desperate. "I know what," she said, "the gramophone. Maybe that'll work. Here, you take her for a moment." She handed him the struggling little creature and went to wind the gramophone.

Boniface took the tiny, almost weightless body in his arms; it was like trying to hold a wriggling fish. "Hush," he said, "hush, hush now . . ." But it made no difference. The child was going into a fit.

'I was dancing, with my darling, to the Ten-nessee Wa-haltz . . .'

He moved in time with the music, waltzing slowly around the little room.

'When an old friend I happened to see . . .'

He danced, the baby's head on his shoulder, supporting it with his hand. It still shuddered convulsively, but gradually the screaming stopped. Then the record screeched to a finish.

"Start it up again!"

'I was dancing, with my darling, to the Ten-nessee Wa-haltz . . .'

He waltzed, and waltzed. The baby calmed down.

* * *

The moment he stopped dancing, the little creature started to bellow again. Whatever was wrong with it, it sure was not respiratory trouble.

"You'd better hand her to me," Laura said. "I'll take her for a while." When he went to the gramophone, she stopped him. "No— I think I'll get into bed with her. You make up some formula. Know where it is?"

"Believe me," he said, "it's too soon. This child has just gone through the trauma of birth. God knows what went on over there before the father took it and carried it through the sandstorm. Let it come to rest."

"But wouldn't at least a pacifier help?"

"If it will take it, sure."

He went to the shelves; she plumped up the pillows, put them against the headboard and climbed into bed. By the time she was settled, the baby was turning purple with screaming. Bonny found a pacifier; together they tried to make the desperate little thing take it. "No good," she said, after a while. "She'll choke on it. I wish we had some honey."

"Try putting it against your skin. I think all it's looking for is motherly warmth."

She unzipped the lumber-jacket and put the baby close to her body; no sooner had she done so than the child calmed down.

"How about that?" he said.

"Put the quilt over us, there's a dear. And some more wood on the fire, it's getting chilly."

He tucked them in so that only the baby's head showed above the covers. "Want something around your shoulders?"

"No, thanks."

Well, there she sat, a child at her breast. She thought of the babies she had not been allowed to have, the nights she had spent in secret tears. Heinzl's arguments had been conclusive, but the sadness, the lonely despair . . .

"What do you know?" she said. "A baby, at last." She looked up and added impulsively, "I could have had two, you know, but he wouldn't let me." Then, seeing the look on his face, she said, "Sorry . . ."

*   *   *

It was as if in those few words the whole tragedy was contained: the fifteen-year-old child looking for her father, the violence of war that had overwhelmed her, the slaughter of the lamb. He had no words for his own downfall into violence; all he felt was heartbreak.

He looked at the little Indian baby, brown against her white breast. "What do you think Sanchez was planning to do with it?" he asked.

"Kill it," she said, calmly.

"Why?"

"I don't know. But that's what the father cried when he brought it in: 'Don't let them kill.'"

"What did you say his name was?"

"I forget. It was the potter."

"Atu, or Morga?"

"Atu, maybe. Yes. Atu. Why?"

"That time Sanchez came to ask me to send a message to the ranch on the priest's radio. 'Miss Gulie must not come to see Atu or Morga.' Morga was the name of Gulie's friend, the one who was so terrified of having her baby in the pueblo."

"She sure had reason to be. I wonder what's going on in this village. Something is. I felt it the moment we arrived: something evil, like the camp. Maybe that was why I started to talk German again."

"It seems that in the last few months all the children have been stillborn, that's why Morga was so scared. Gulie told me that Parry Winkler, the Friend who lived here before we came, was going to write about it to Phildelphia."

"Well, didn't he?"

"No, he had his accident before he could get around to it."

"Maybe it wasn't an accident after all."

He looked at her, stunned. Suddenly he too had a sense of evil. He had never met Parry Winkler, but had heard about the gentle, elderly Friend, the kind of old Quaker that radiated kindliness and understanding. If the Indians had indeed planned to do away with him because he had discovered something was wrong, he would not have been afraid. He would have known a letter would never reach Philadelphia. He would have tried to transmit a warning in some other way, left something behind—a note in a language the Indians didn't understand. "If Parry Winkler was on to something," he said, "he would have left some message. But the Indians cleaned out this place after he died. They must have taken everything, every scrap of paper."

"Hey . . ." she said.

"What?"

"The fireplace—there's something scratched on the back of the chimney! You can't see it unless you lie down. When I was lying in front of the fire last night, I saw some scribbles, high up. They looked very old, though . . ."

He went to the fireplace, lay down in front of it and peered up the chimney.

"See them?" she asked.

"A fish? Some Roman numerals?"

"Yes! Looks like a rebus."

"The fish is the sign of the early Christians. The numerals— one, three, sixteen . . . Could be a quotation from the Bible. But then why three numbers?"

"Maybe it's something else entirely."

"Fish—one . . ." He scrambled to his feet and went over to his rucksack.

"What are you looking for?"

He brought out his Bible, started to leaf through it. "Christians means the New Testament. One must be Matthew . . . Chapter Three . . . Verse sixteen . . . *Then King Herod, when he*

*saw that he was mocked by the wise men, was exceeding wroth
and sent forth and slew all the children that were in Bethlehem,
from two years old and under . . .' "*

"So they *are* killing their newborn children!"

"It looks like it. It all begins to make sense, now."

"What does?"

"The fact that we were received by a housekeeper when everyone before us had been ostracized. The priest's alarm when he
heard that Sanchez wanted to keep Gulie away. The white
cloud."

She stared at him, frowning.

"The one that's painted on the wall of the church, with a big
black bird stealing the children. The one that's mentioned in Father Foglia's manuscript. Remember? I read it to you; at the
time of Jesse McHair, the Hunis murdered all infants at birth
because they wanted to put an end to the tribe, 'despite the fact
that no tall white cloud had been seen above the mountains to
the west, foretelling the end of man.' The atom bomb must have
been that cloud. They are convinced the world is coming to an
end. Their legend tells them it's time to put an end to their
tribe."

*   *   *

She looked down at the infant in her arm. It was dozing off,
its little fists by the side of its head. Incredible, that anyone
could want to kill this little thing because of some prehistoric belief. But then, the Nazis had killed not just Jewish babies; they
had tried to kill off a whole people. "If that's true," she said,
"they'll come for the child as soon as the gale is over."

"Yes, I'm afraid they might."

She thought for a moment. "Well, the door is bolted. As long
as we sit tight . . ."

"Don't let's kid ourselves," he said. "If they want her, they
aren't going to stop at a bolted door. They'll turn up with a bat-
tering ram."

"We could push the wardrobe in front of it. And the bed."

"They'll blast us out of here. Or blow us up, together with the
baby. We should get out, quick."

She climbed out of bed. "Where are we going?"

The baby woke up and started to scream once more.

"The church. Let's get out while the gale is still blowing and join the priest."

"But they would come for her there too, wouldn't they?"

"Anything's better than staying here like sitting ducks! You take the baby, I'll open the door. But first put some clothes on! The sand must be fierce . . ."

She hastily pulled on her jeans and picked up the shawl. He put on his sheepskin jacket, and went to open the door.

"Okay," she said, the child in her arms, "I'm ready."

He pulled at the door; it would not budge. He tried pushing it.

"It opens inward!"

"I know," he said. "But it's locked."

"By the tape?"

"From the outside."

She looked at him, stunned. "How? There's no key!"

"There's a bar. I used it this afternoon, when I left you to go to the priest. They've put it back on."

"You mean—we're trapped?"

"Yes."

For a few seconds, she stood motionless, looking at the door. Then she said, "Okay, back to bed." She climbed back into the bed, bared her breast and silenced the baby by pressing it against her skin. "Well," she said, when the child had settled down, "what do we do now?"

He sat down on the edge of the bed. "Let's have meeting."

He really was exasperating. "You have meeting," she said.

"Don't knock it, Laura," he said quietly. "It worked before, remember?"

"All right," she said, sighing. "Let's."

He closed his eyes and bent his head. She tried to join him in worship, but all she could do was listen to the wind hooting in the chimney, the windowpanes plopping, the lashes of sand on the parchment. If only she could find peace, serenity, but it was impossible. Also, the baby was beginning to smell something fearful. When at last he took her hand to end meeting, she said, "What if you tried to sneak up on her now?"

"Excuse me?"

"Give her a bath. She's quiet now, and seems fast asleep. Wash her gently, with warm water and cotton wool. She does need it."

"She doesn't," he said. "The natural grease she's covered in is called the vernix and has a function: it prevents heat loss. We're planning to take her out of here soon, so, really, the best we can do is leave her undisturbed."

"Well, that's not what Sister Theresa told me. Or the book 'Feeding and Care of Babies' that she made me learn by rote."

"Did the book have a chapter on birth during battles or air attacks?"

"No . . ."

"Well, that's what *I* was taught: how to handle and care for babies born on the battlefront. Don't try to feed them during the first twenty-four hours, don't bathe them, just keep them warm and if possible have someone carry the child in his arms. Don't leave it alone in an ambulance, not even in a bassinet; let someone hang on to it, hug it, establish bodily contact. Well, that's what we are doing."

"But what about the blood in its hair? It's going to be the devil of a job to get it out later . . ."

"Okay," he said. "I suppose that wouldn't hurt."

He got up, warmed the water, brought the basin and the cotton wool to the bed and began to clean up the baby's head. As a medic, he was the gentlest of men. That's how he had salvaged her: as a medic. He had even gone so far as to marry the screaming nut, just to carry her to safety and put her in a clean bed somewhere, though he had to cross the ocean to do it. Of course he had wanted to hand her over to the doctors, after carrying her on his back through hell and high water, for that was his function. But instead of saying, 'Thanks, doc, I'll see you around,' she had clung to him and driven him to the point where he betrayed his basic impulse: to help the helpless. Well, it had to be, somehow. Now, for the first time, she felt she could make it on her own—if ever they got out of this place alive. How strange: when she had lain in front of the fire after bringing him to his knees, she had done with life; now, with that little mite with the screwed-up face and the tiny fists in her arms, she wanted desperately to stay alive.

He wiped the baby's head carefully with damp cotton, then patted it dry and produced a comb.

"No, Bonny!"

"Why not? Might as well." He started to comb the infant's silky hair, parting it in the middle.

"You're making her look like part of a barber-shop quartet!"

He stood back, his head on one side, and said, "No, she looks like H. L. Mencken."

"Who's that?"

"An essayist."

"Give here!" She took the comb and gently parted the baby's hair on the side, making a little curl on its forehead, then looked up at him and smiled.

"All you've got to do now is stick it to her forehead with spit and you have it made."

"Ha-ha."

He gave her a lopsided grin. "An old soldier's saying: if you've got to go, you might as well go laughing."

"Do you think we have a chance?"

"I don't know how much the priest got across. If he managed to tell them enough before the transmitter went dead, they'll be here as soon as the storm blows over."

"Will they come in time?"

He shrugged his shoulders.

"What do you think the Indians will do to us if . . ."

"First, I think they'll ask us to hand over the baby."

"And when we don't?"

"Need we go into all this now?"

"Yes," she said. "Have you any idea?"

He hesitated. "Well . . . Gulie McHair said something that came back to me when I read the priest's manuscript. She talked about someone being 'danced off the rock.' I didn't understand it at the time, but the manuscript says that, to the Indians, it's bad magic to use physical violence on people. So they execute their victims by forcing them to commit suicide."

"How?"

"The priest didn't know how exactly. The one time it happened while he was here, in the case of Jesse McHair, the Indians kept him locked in his cloister. It involved a long ceremony of some kind, he heard banging and hooting and wild screams in the square. But he remained convinced that although Jesse was executed, no actual violence was involved. Maybe drugs, which they mixed through Jesse McHair's food, or made him inhale by smoke."

"If, to the Hunis, it's bad magic to commit violence, then why would they try to kill the baby?"

"This time, they must have some rationale for killing newborn infants. Maybe as an act of mercy, to spare them the horror of having to live through the end of the world. It must be a pretty gruesome event in their mythology."

She was silent for a while, then she asked, "Do you think this is what they did to old Mr. Winkler?"

"I have no idea," he said. "But when Father Alvarez gave me this to read, he said he wished Parry Winkler had read it, as it might have made a difference."

"How?"

He shrugged his shoulders. "Let's hope we're lucky and the McHairs arrive in time."

"What about drugs? Those beans, for instance? You don't think . . ."

"It might explain a few things."

"But what about tonight and tomorrow?"

"Well, we've plenty of stores ourselves. But let's watch the fire. Maybe put the bucket of water ready, just in case they sprinkle something on it, down the chimney. Or let it go out altogether."

"Why don't we do both? Tell you what: why don't you put the bucket by the fire and try to get some sleep? I'll keep an eye on it; when I get tired you take over."

"Okay," he said. He went to fetch the bucket and put it by the side of the fireplace.

"Come and lie down with us," she said.

"No, I think I'll just sit in the chair, here, and doze. Are you sure you're all right?"

"Sure. Go and have a snooze."

"No cup of chocolate, or anything. Nothing to eat?"

"No, thanks, doc." When he grinned and turned to go to his chair, she added, "You're one hell of a guy. And I'm sorry."

He gave her a wistful look. "So am I."

"Go to sleep," she said.

He did, leaving her listening to the wind and the sand, holding the fragile little body that now felt as if it were part of her. Gazing at the fire, it struck her that neither of them considered for a moment giving up the child.

She looked down at the baby with the little curl on its forehead. So tiny, so vulnerable, so utterly dependent on her for its very life. Odd, this will to live; a couple of hours ago she couldn't have cared less; now she did not want to give up her life. Yet she would, for a baby. Well, plenty of people had . . .

It wasn't that she was curious about her father, but it would just be interesting to know if the baby he had tried to save when they arrested him had been killed in some other camp. Maybe she had better think about him a little.

But she couldn't, not even now. She closed her eyes, felt she was nodding off and decided that just a few minutes wouldn't hurt. Just a few minutes . . .

'It's a concern about babies.'

She jerked awake. Had Bonny said that? It had been a man's voice. She wanted to look up, but couldn't be bothered. But she should keep watch!

She opened her eyes. The world had become still, the logs turned to glowing embers; Bonny sat slumped in the chair, his chin on his chest. It couldn't have been he; maybe she'd dreamed it.

All seemed tranquil and at peace out there. She kissed the baby's silky head and nodded off again. A man in a tweed suit, standing with his back to her in front of the fireplace, said, *'It's an ecumenical thing. A priest, a Protestant clergyman, a doctor and a young farmer who says he's an atheist.'*

She looked up; but it had been another fireplace, smaller. That houseboat again.

Could it have been a real memory? Or just something she had been told over and over until she thought she remembered it? But who could have told her about 'an ecumenical thing' with a priest, a young farmer who was an atheist? Bonny had mentioned talking to that young farmer later. Could he have mentioned the man being an atheist? Possibly. She couldn't remember.

So she had had a father who had lost his life trying to save babies, and it had been an ecumenical thing. God knew that was no news. But as she looked down at the baby sleeping in the crook of her arm with its little fists by the side of its head, she thought of him, of what he had done. Then maybe the man in front of the fireplace had not been her father at all.

'Man,' she thought, 'whoever you are, wherever you are, help us tonight.'

When she opened her eyes again, groggy with sleep, she saw that the windows had turned red. It must be dawn already. Bonny was still slumped in his chair, head back, mouth open. The fire was still alive; it crackled and hissed, spitting small showers of sparks. There was a spicy scent in the room. The baby lay asleep in the crook of her arm. She gazed somnolently at the embers spurting sparks, the small puffs of smoke playfully escaping from the hearth and drifting into the room. It was a peaceful sight and she closed her eyes to doze off again, but there was a strange, jarring sound somewhere. She tried to ignore it, but could not. She opened her eyes and gazed drowsily at the showers of sparks, the room filling with smoke. Why wasn't the smoke going up the chimney? Suddenly she was wide awake: they had closed off the chimney! She must douse the fire, at once!

"Bonny!" she called, and tried to jump out of bed, but found she could not move. Good God, the baby! It lay in her arm, its little fists no longer by the side of its head, mouth open, eyes closed, limp as a doll. The smoke was drugged! They were trying to kill the baby!

She laid the child down beside her, strained, cursed, and managed to roll out of bed. She crawled to the bucket by the hearth, tipped it onto the fire; steam exploded with a hiss, instantly filling the room and making her cough. Choking, she grabbed the poker, crawled toward one of the little windows, clawed herself up the wall, onto her feet, and managed to get hold of one of the bars. Swinging the poker with an awful feeling of weakness, she feebly hit the parchment pane, crying with frustration. In despair, she stabbed at it and the poker went through.

With renewed strength, she pulled herself up at the bars and drank in the fresh air. It revived her; she tore the parchment with both hands. Outside, she heard a loud noise, banging and hooting, but it was not the wind.

She stumbled to the bed, picked up the baby; it was limp, little arms dangling. She carried it to the window. "Come, sweetie, come," she pleaded, "breathe, breathe! For God's sake, breathe!"

She put her mouth to the child's and breathed into its lungs; suddenly, the little body sucked in her breath. When she let go of its mouth, it whimpered.

Holding the baby with one arm, she stumbled to Bonny and shook him. "Bonny, wake up! Wake up!" His head lolled, he made no move to rise. She picked up the poker and smashed the

parchment in the other windows to admit more outside air, the
baby crying in her arm. Bonny stared at her with glazed eyes, his
mouth slack. He mumbled, but could not speak.

"Come on! Bonny!" she urged. "On your feet!" She only had
one hand free; he was too heavy for her. She put the baby back
on the bed, it started to scream. She returned to Bonny, feeling
as if she were skating. "Come! On your feet! On your feet!"

He rose to his feet, swaying. "To the window! Breathe! They
are trying to drug us!" He made it to the window, reeling like a
drunk, grabbed the bars, tried to pull himself up. "Come on!"
She helped him, he managed to stick his face between the bars
and drank in the outside air. The banging and the hooting were
very loud now, fear overwhelmed her. They were going to kill the
baby! She stood for a moment, eyes closed; then she rallied. This
was ridiculous! It just couldn't happen! Not after Schwalbenbach! Nothing could be worse than Schwalbenbach!

She picked up the baby and took it back to the window, to let
it breathe the outside air once more. They stood there, the baby
and she, drinking in the air, when somebody rattled the latch of
the door. A voice called nervously, "Quick! Mr. Baker! It's Father Alvarez! Quick! *Doña* Ana has arrived!"

She staggered to the door and shoved the bolts aside; a priest
in black cassock came in. She closed the door and bolted it
again.

"Quick!" the priest said. *"Doña* Ana has arrived in front of
the bat cave! We must go to her! If she tries to come up herself,
they'll drop the tumble rock. What's the matter with Mr. Baker?" He went over to Bonny, now leaning against the wall, too
groggy to move. The priest lifted Bonny's head, looked at his
eyes, sniffed the air. "Did they drop drugs on the fire?"

"Yes."

"Madre de Dios! Your husband is in bad shape! Can you
walk?"

"Yes. I'll take the child, you help him." The priest put his arm
around Bonny, helping him to the door; she pulled it open, the
screaming baby in her arm. "Calm down, beastie," she whispered, "nothing is going to happen." But she knew that, in her
present shape, she'd be too weak to hold on to the baby if someone were to grab hold of it. She looked around for something she
could use to attach it to her, and saw the duffel bag. She picked
it up, dumped the contents on the table and put the baby inside.

The priest called from outside, "Mrs. Baker! Please!"
She picked up a cigar and put it into the bag with the baby.
"Mrs. Baker! *Please!*"
She zipped up the bag and joined the men outside.

*   *   *

Like a swimmer under water, Boniface watched Laura put the strap of her duffel bag around her neck and tie it around her waist. "Come on, Laura!" he cried drunkenly, his arm round the priest's neck. It was a pleasant drunkenness that made him feel lighthearted, weightless. "Now, Padre," he asked, "Where's the fair?" A steam calliope with drums and cymbals banged in the distance, with monotonous hoots.

The priest, supporting him, looked up with frightened eyes. "There is a chance that we'll be attacked by mudheads as we pass the kiva," he said.

"Mum—mudheads?"

"They are clowns, but very unpleasant. They will try to side-track us. You must hold on to me. Come!" The priest started to lead him in the direction of the village square. "Come, Mr. Baker, *please! Doña* Ana is waiting for us!"

"Tum-de-dum!" Bonny sang, swaying to the beat of the music; it became louder as they approached the square.

The priest looked up at the roofs. Women wrapped in blankets sat staring down at them like the audience in a circus. "Hi, ladies!" Bonny called. "How's your knitting?" He giggled; it was irresistibly funny. He wanted to repeat it, to make sure they had heard it.

"Think he'll make it?" the priest asked anxiously.

Laura's voice replied, "We may have to pull him across together."

They entered the square. To his amazement, Boniface saw smoke rising from the squat tower of the kiva. The hooting and thudding of the calliope seemed to be coming from inside. The square was empty, but on the roofs women wrapped in blankets sat watching. "Ladies!" he called, elated, "how about some applause as we enter the ring?" He was still laughing at his own joke when the priest pulled him across a white ledge that barred his way. "Here comes the bull!" he cried, lifting his foot to step over it, but it was just a white stripe painted on the cobbles of the square. Suddenly a cheering crowd of Mardi Gras creatures came tumbling from the cistern—birds, animals, weird apparitions with masks. As they came closer he saw the masks were covered with warts and disfigured by welts; the Mardi Gras crowd turned out to be a herd of monsters from a nightmare.

He wanted to break into a run, but the priest held him back. "Don't, Mr. Baker! Pretend you do not see them! They are clowns! Remember: clowns!"

But the creatures that came tumbling toward them were no ordinary clowns. A monstrous priest, a disfigured old woman, dogs, birds, pigs, freaks with long beaks on stilts. They all came hopping, tumbling, forming a ring around the three of them, and began a solemn dance that Boniface, after a few moments of bewildered fright, recognized as a parody of prayer. The dancers beat their breasts, one of them bawled *"Pater Noster,"* the rest mimicked reciting the Rosary. Father Alvarez cried, "Please, please, my children! In the name of God! This is blasphemy! Please!" In response, the clowns singled him out. The drums and hooters quickened their rhythm, the shrilling of flutes became more strident, the clowns went into a frenzy. They began to eat their filthy rags, one pretended to relieve himself, another picked it up and started to eat it. Another of them mimicked urinating into a beaker, handed it to a wing-flapping bird, which drank it, smacked its beak and rubbed its stomach. Then two giant creatures emerged from the kiva, two parrots with colored feathers, huge yellow beaks, massive claws. They came waddling toward the priest with stumbling hops, like the parrots in the cloister. *"No cojones!"* they shrieked. *"Masturba, padre!"* The priest let go of Boniface and ran in the direction of the church. Shrieking, the crowd ran after him, hopping, flailing, tumbling. The two parrots overtook him, started to chase him back and forth between them, shrieking obscenities, pecking at him, tripping him with their claws, pushing him over with their beaks. The priest fell to his knees, protecting the back of his head with his hands; the birds continued to attack him.

"Bonny, come on!" Laura pulled him by the arm; he understood, dazedly, that she wanted to make a run for it while they had the chance. He stumbled a few steps; then, with massive shrieking, the kiva spewed out a new herd of creatures. Their masks were as repulsive as those of the others, but they were wearing Quaker bonnets, wide-brimmed black hats, shadbelly coats. The coats were green with mildew, the gray dresses ragged and torn; where had the monsters found them? They must have belonged to Friends . . . The clowns began to prance around him in a circle, bellowing, wailing, their arms stretched out to the sky. They were singling him out as they had the priest; but they did not frighten him, not this time, because those clothes were real; they had been worn, long ago, by real Friends. Then the males with the black hats grabbed the females with the bonnets and started to ape the act of copulation.

He tried to tell himself they were clowns, clowns, that he must not take their antics seriously, that they were trying to scare him with their hocus-pocus. He should calmly walk to the other side of the square, where he would be safe. "Excuse me, Friends," he said. "This is very amusing, but allow me . . ."

One of the male creatures, his face a repulsive mass of sores and boils, holding a struggling female, advanced on him like a crab, but he managed to remain calm and said, "I'd like to get through, thank thee, Friend . . ." Suddenly the circle opened; from the direction of the kiva a crowd of pink, toad-like creatures advanced on him, hopping. As they came closer he saw they were naked women, leering witches with blond wigs, slavering mouths, white fangs. They came, long flaccid breasts flapping, toward him. He knew he was falling under a spell, but there was something about the approaching monsters, something so terrifying that he did what the priest had done: he turned and fled, back toward the lazaret. He heard Laura cry, "Bonny! Don't! Come back!" The crowd lit out after him, shrieking; the naked women overtook and encircled him, taunted him with obscene gestures, the nightmarish males booed and hooted as he stumbled, now terrified out of his wits, around the square, trying to escape from them. Faster, faster they hounded him, until he fell, scrambled to his feet, ran, howling with fear. Around and around the square he ran, falling, scrambling to his feet, falling; suddenly he saw a way out: a narrow alley opened before him. He ran down the alley as fast as he could, the jeering crowd at his heels; he jumped onto a flat rock at the far end; with a cry of terror, he found himself on the edge of a precipice. He turned around and faced the crowd. The ghoulish females were flapping their breasts, jerking their pelvises, yowling, screaming; the men had dropped their women and now stretched out their hands toward him, shrieking. He closed his eyes for a moment, suddenly composed. 'They won't touch me,' he said to himself, 'they never use violence, it's against their beliefs.' He advanced on them, their ranks opened, he knew a brief moment of hope; then he froze.

Down the narrow alley a strange apparition came slowly stumbling toward him. A man? A bird? Wings spread, head down, black beak trailing . . . As it approached, he recognized it. It was the crucifix from the church, Christ stumbling under the cross, long black hair dangling. Closer He came, closer; as He reached the rock He slowly lifted His head, His hair parted; for one moment it was Sanchez, then the face changed into that of a white boy sick with terror. The boy slowly straightened up. Boniface's stomach rose to his throat when he saw what the boy's hands tried to contain: a dangling mass of glistening, bloody loops of intestine. The boy looked at him with such terrified eyes that he wanted to cover his own with his hands, but he could not. As they stood facing each other, the boy's eyes staring into his with a dying look, he knew who it was: the boy who had been drafted into the Army instead of him, the dumb boy with the fallen arches, whom he had seen wading through the surf on D-day. He was guilty of the boy's gruesome death because he had decided to plant little trees instead of joining the others of his generation. "No!" he cried. "No, no! I didn't mean it that way! It is our Peace Testimony, our ancient witness!" Then the boy on the cross, trying to contain his dangling guts, clumsily climbed the rock.

Boniface could not hold out any longer. Again he seemed to hear Laura's voice, "Bonny, wait! Bonny!" But the encroaching horror of the crucified boy made him turn around to flee—and there was the precipice at his feet. He turned back.

The boy, eyes closed, slowly bent forward, his hands trying to contain his guts. The naked women took the cross off his shoulders. They laid it on the rock at Boniface's feet, then, wailing, they watched the boy collapse and die.

"God, dear God!" he prayed. "Forgive me! It's not my fault! I—" All the Quakers around him started to bleat, to whinny, to squeal with laughter.

"God!" he shrieked. "Christ! Save me!"

As if the Quakers had waited for that cry, they grabbed hold of him. While he screamed in terror, they threw him on his back, spread his arms, sat on them, straightened his legs and sat on them, crossed his feet. Over him, like a giant hawk in the sky, loomed Sanchez, holding a hammer in one hand and three long nails in the other. He tried to tear himself free, felt hands grab his ankles. There was a sharp, horrendous pain, the sound of hammer blows on iron.

'God! God . . .'

Life oozed out of him in unbearable agony.

He died slowly, as they nailed him to the cross.

*   *   *

When Bonny disappeared down the alley, surrounded by carnival figures, Laura stood for a moment at a loss. Should she go after him or head for the other side of the square, the street to the trail? It would be her turn next; first they had isolated the priest and finished him off; the poor man still lay where he had fallen; now they'd gone after Bonny; it could only be a matter of time before they came for the prize: the baby. Hesitating no longer, she left Bonny to his fate and ran across the square as fast as she could.

But before she reached the street on the other side she was assailed by a shrieking band of masked Indians. She had no idea where they came from, but they gave her no time to rally. They formed a circle around her, screaming, jeering. She pressed the duffel bag with the baby tightly against her, prepared for someone to make a dash for it; suddenly one of the huge parrots that had attacked the priest bore down upon her.

"Shoosh!" she shouted. *"Kscht!* Scat!" realizing too late she had chased him as if he were a real bird. 'They are people like me,' she told herself, 'remember, they are people!' She went on repeating it as the creatures hopped around her, screaming, bleating, crowing, barking, in a narrow circle. 'They are people,' she kept thinking, 'remember: people!' As long as she could remain aware of that, she could face down the monsters tumbling around her, birds, dogs, sheep. 'They are people! Don't fall for it! Remember, they're just people!'

There came another attack. A pig, its swinish snout full of warts and boils, advanced on her and reached for the baby. She wavered; this animal was more frightening than the idiotic parrot had been. 'A man! A man! It's only a man!' This could not be happening to her, not after Schwalbenbach. Yes, that was it!

Schwalbenbach! Nothing could be worse than Schwalbenbach! Compared to the horror of the crowd that had dragged her through the camp and shorn and tarred her and lashed her to the stake, these clowns were nothing, carnival puppets. The pig made another dash for the baby; she advanced on him, crying, "Schwalbenbach! Get out of my way! Scat! Schwalbenbach!"

The pig and his crowd drew back but went on prancing around her; the shrieks and bleats increased in intensity. Suddenly their ranks opened and a bird-like creature came storming straight at her, brandishing a flaming torch. She realized what it was up to, grabbed hold of the torch, wrenched it out of the creature's claw and swung it around her in a circle, yelling, "Schwalbenbach! Schwalbenbach!"

They drew back, and she knew she had a momentary advantage. But what now? She unzipped the duffel bag, groped inside, felt the small warm legs of the baby, found the cigar, stuck it between her teeth; she closed the bag and lit the cigar with the torch, searing her eyebrows. She blew a cloud of smoke into the face of the beaked monster as it made a dash for her; then, in a mad gesture of defiance, she gave it back the torch. "Bye-bye, birdie," she said. "Why don't you hop off and set fire to some of your little friends? Scat! *Move!*" She advanced on it, it backed away, turned and ran off, torch and all. Puffing on her cigar, she strode forcefully across the square, surrounded by prancing and tumbling monsters.

Then, behind the pounding of the drum and the lowing of the hooters, another sound grew: a formal, rhythmic music. It seemed to come from the direction of the kiva; there she saw, beyond the prancing demons, a row of disciplined dancers, dressed in blue and orange with feathered headdresses. The clowns went on prancing around her, yelling and howling, but she began to discern the discipline in their antics. While they gave the impression of chaos, they were in fact responding to the pounding of the drum as rigidly as the row of dancers to the music from the kiva.

The cigar clamped between her teeth, she strode on, full of self-confidence, until she realized, with a sudden cramp in her stomach, that instead of being on her left, the kiva was now to her right. She was headed back toward the lazaret.

She stopped. The circle of tumbling clowns opened. The row of stately, disciplined dancers slowly advanced on her. Suddenly her cigar seemed no longer a token of supremacy, but a hollow gesture in the face of the discipline of those dancers. The herd of demons began to close in once more, forcing her to turn and walk in the opposite direction, clutching her duffel bag. It was clear what their purpose was: to drive her around and around the square, as they had Bonny, until she lost her sense of direction.

But she found that by keeping an eye on the tower of the kiva, she could maintain her sense of direction. With new determination, she headed for the street that led to freedom. But the dancers followed, the monsters moved in and when they once more reached for the baby, she cried again, "Schwalbenbach! Schwalbenbach!"

Silence fell so suddenly that it confused her. She stood still. The whole crowd of parrots, pigs, priests, Quakers, naked women ran off and disappeared in the side alleys of the square. The pounding of the drum ceased. The hooters stopped blowing. The dancers froze in mid-movement. The rhythmic music stopped, and she knew: this is it.

She found herself in the center of the square, exposed, alone. The women on the roofs gazed down at her. In the silence, she heard the baby crying inside the duffel bag. The sound cast out her fear. She opened the bag and took the baby out; its thin screams rang in the silence. She cradled it against her chest, kissed its head, then one of the dancers stepped out of the frozen ranks and advanced on her with measured steps. As he came closer she recognized the face underneath the feathered headdress. It was Sanchez.

"Hi, San—" Her voice stuck in her throat, for the image of the slowly advancing man in the colorful costume changed into a man in a prisoner's suit, chained to a wall, staring at her in horror. *'Laura! No! For God's sake!'* A fist struck her face, she reeled under the blow. *'Bitch! Bitch!'* She was thrown across a bed, her dress was torn, her knees were forced apart, but all the time she was conscious of the desperate man chained to the wall as she heard him scream, *'No! No!'* A body forced itself upon her, but she cried, with her last strength, *"It's all right, Daddy! I'm all right!"* She saw Kroll's grinning face above her, and spat.

Instantly she was back on her feet in the square. The man with the feathered headdress was standing right in front of her, wiping his face. She clutched the baby and said, "Never! You got my father's, you won't get *mine!*"

The eyes of the man bored into hers. She was lifted off the

ground; the square, the buildings keeled over, she floated horizontally in the air. Someone was carrying her away in his arms. She heard a scream behind her, *'Laura!'* She cried *'Daddy!'* The man who was carrying her turned around, and she saw Daddy stagger toward her, arms outstretched. *'Laura!'* A black and yellow streak flashed at him and lunged at his throat. He screamed, a voice above her called *'Siegfried! Fuss!'* The dog let go of him, he staggered, his hands at his throat, blood spurted between his fingers, he sank slowly to his knees. Two men in striped suits came running with sticks and started to beat him, beat him, crying, *'Judengeziefer! Schwein! Venerisches Judenschwein!'*

She wanted to hide her face in her hands, but she could not; she was holding something. She saw a wide-open little mouth, tiny fists waving frantically, a brown hand taking the baby from her grasp. She cried, "Heinzl! Put me down!" Heinzl set her on her feet, leaving her to face the vision from hell: the Kapos beating, her father cringing on the ground, howling, howling. She wanted to go to him, but something held her back—the awareness of her own culpability. She had fought her way into the camp to find him; now there he lay, being beaten to death. She felt the desperate need to undo what she had done, to ask his forgiveness, but the baby was being taken away from her, the baby he had tried to save and for which he was now paying with his life. She broke the spell by crying, "I'll do it, Dad! I'll do it for you! Look, look, here it is—" She slapped the hand that tried to take the baby away from her. "Here, Dad! Look!" But he was gone. There was nothing but the empty cobbles at her feet.

She looked up at the Indian with the feathered headdress waiting for her. "No, Sanchez," she said. "Not this time." She wanted to pass him, but he stepped in front of her, barring her way. "Schwalbenbach! Schwalbenbach!" She spat at him.

The Indian refused to budge.

Summoning all her strength, she cried in desperation, *"Heinzl! Daddy! Kapos! Wassermann! Rabbi Hirsch! Kroll! Frau Rosenbach! Siegfried! Annelieschen! Schwalbenbach! Schwalbenbach! Help me!"*

The Indian stepped aside.

Filled with a new strength that was not hers, holding the baby she walked past him to the street that led to freedom. She walked under the protection of all who had died in Schwalbenbach, henchmen and victims alike, all welded together into one irresistible force.

She crossed the white line of the circle at the other side of the square; suddenly, with a roar that froze her with fright, the crowd came rushing toward her. She swung around and pressed the baby against her, knowing she could hold out no longer. All the monsters that had tormented her came running for her; she closed her eyes, waiting to be trampled underfoot; then she felt them pass her. She looked up and saw them enter the street, shouting as they ran. She thought they were making for the trail to bar her way, but they ran past it to the huge round rock that loomed against the sky. They reached it, cheering, and lined up beside it.

That was it. The tumble rock. With a sudden feeling of exhaustion, she kissed the baby's head. "We've had it, sweetie," she whispered. "Well, we tried." She looked up and saw the motionless women on the roofs. She had the feeling of standing all alone in an arena; she wanted to call out to them, cry for their help, for mercy for the child, but her voice failed her. In desperation, she held up the crying baby, slowly turning around, showing it to all the women on the roofs around the square. There was no sound, only the child's thin, high cries. Then she gathered the tiny body to her breast and walked aimlessly along the edge of the square.

Suddenly there came the crowd again; not screaming this time, but in silent ranks, from all sides. She was about to sink to her knees, for the silence in which they advanced on her was more terrifying than their wild shrieks had been. Then she looked round and found they were all women, wrapped in blankets, smiling at her. She realized these were the women from the roofs; they had come to join her, not to bar her way.

Silently, massively, they surrounded her. Overpowered by their alien closeness, the strangeness of their scent, she gave in to their pressure and walked slowly in their midst toward the street that led to the trail. No longer able to think coherently, she let herself be carried forward by their silent, slow-moving mass. They stopped when they reached the entrance to the trail.

She was immured in a mass of bodies, but how could they protect her on the way down? The path was much too narrow. The women left her standing alone, and started to form a single file; when they were lined up, they bent forward and each woman took hold of the waist band of the one in front. Two women went down the line to pull everyone's blanket over her head so it covered the one in front, turning them into a long snake of blankets.

One of the women who had helped cover up the row came to fetch her. A space was made for her in the line. She joined it, bent over, grabbed hold of the waistband of the woman in front, felt the one behind her grab hold of the top of her jeans; then she too was covered by a blanket. The baby started to yell blue murder; she knew she must silence it, or it would give its presence away. She pulled up her T-shirt and pushed a breast into the baby's face; it chomped its jaws on her nipple at once. Holding it like a mother monkey her young, she shuffled along in the row, hanging on to the one in front with her free hand.

Her feet felt the beginning of the steep incline of the trail. She wanted to straighten up because she was pitching forward, but the woman behind her held on to the top of her jeans and she understood she could let herself go and leave it to the one behind to keep her from falling.

She shuffled on in a daze, interminably, overwhelmed by their alien scent, pitched forward, secure in the grip of the woman behind her, hanging on to the one in front. She had no idea how far down they were, whether they had passed the tumble rock yet, how much longer she would have to go on like this. Suddenly the one in front of her straightened up.

The blanket slid off her. Dazzled by blinding light, she found herself standing on the plateau in front of the bat cave, surrounded by women. Someone grabbed her, shook her, a voice cried, "Where is he? Where *is* he?" It was the McHair girl.

She had no notion of anything other than the baby at her breast.

"Your husband! Where is he?"

She felt suddenly faint. "Up there, somewhere," she said.

"Where? *Where?*"

She had to sit down.

"Please! Please! Is he all right?

She had no idea, but to be rid of the girl she said, "I guess so." She should do something now: cry, pray, but she was utterly drained. Then a child appeared beside her with a small glass in its hand.

"Here," the child said, "drink this."

She looked at the old little face, the black eyes, the gray doll's hair. "Thanks, *Doña* Ana," she said, and tossed it back.

Well, what do you know! *'We send your Bols all over the world.'* An unworthy ending to a miracle, but there it was: Dutch gin.

*   *   *

As if responding to a call, the women turned around, all in one movement, and headed back for the trail. Gulielma realized that if she wanted to get up there before they blocked her way, she should make a run for it.

Ever since the Indians had barred Gran's way to the pueblo, earlier this morning, Gulie had known that something terrible was going on up there; now she was certain Boniface Baker had fallen victim to it. There was only one place where that could have happened.

With a sickening feeling of disaster, she scrambled up the trail to the pueblo as fast as she could; when she reached the top she ran toward the square. An alley branched off to the left opposite the kiva, at its far end was the execution rock from which, according to legend, past victims of the brujos had fallen to their deaths. If Boniface was still alive, that was where she would find him.

The square was crowded with Indians in weird costumes, clustered around wooden tubs, washing mud off their faces; she pushed her way through the throng to the alley. At the far end, she saw a body lying on the rock. A figure in black squatted beside it. Mustering her courage, she ran toward them.

As she came closer she recognized Father Alvarez. The body on the ground was Boniface Baker. He lay, arms spread, on top of a flat cardboard cross, his face turned away. "Is he—dead?" she asked.

Father Alvarez looked up, dazed. "No, no," he said. "Just drugged."

She knelt down and touched his shoulder. "Boniface? Boniface, are you all right?"

To her immense relief, he rolled his head. His eyes were upturned, only the whites were showing. He was deathly pale, his mouth hung slack and open. "What happened?"

Father Alvarez slowly turned his head and gazed at her with a dazed look. He too must be drugged, or under some spell. She knew Indian magic, but had never seen anything as frightening as this. Father Alvarez stared at her, then slowly rose to his feet and staggered down the alley.

Boniface groaned. She touched his forehead; it was damp with sweat. She didn't know what made her think so, but she felt sure he was caught in some nightmare from which he couldn't free himself. What was it his wife had called him? "Bonny," she said, "you're all right now. All is well, Bonny, you're safe. It is all over, you are fine. I'm Gulielma. Gulie McHair. Remember the stables? Remember Chester, the horse that drinks beer and eats pizza? He's here, in front of the cave, waiting to take you home."

He did not move. If only there were something she could slip under his head! He obviously wouldn't be ready to go for some time.

After a moment's indecision, she sat down and lifted his head onto her lap. On the cardboard cross on which he had been lying was printed in blue, "PET CONDENSED MILK, ONE PINT, CASE OF TWENTY-FOUR."

*　　*　　*

In the darkness in which he lay drowned, a silvery shimmer flickered briefly, like a fish flashing in the deep. It seemed an added torment, a brief hint of life, of all that was lost forever. He hoped he would not see it again, not again be tortured by despair. The darkness, the immobility of death were eternal and therefore, somehow, bearable.

But there it was again: brighter this time, a silver flash, twisting, flitting away. Despite the knowledge that this was another stage of the torture, he waited for it to reappear, the brief flash of light in the heart of darkness.

After a long time, there it was again. A fish? A star? A sword? The thought gave him a sudden stabbing pain, and the awareness of what had happened to him. Nailed to the cross. He lay at the bottom of a black pit, in eternal damnation, nailed to a cross.

There it was once again, brighter this time; clearly not a fish. A star? Above him, clouds were breaking, revealing briefly the heartbreaking fullness of life that was lost forever. Suddenly, the hunger to experience life once more became overwhelming. He would give everything, everything he still had, for just one more taste of life, just to know that it existed, even in the depths of damnation, just to believe.

'The devils also believe, and tremble.' Where did that come from? The Bible? Where, where? His consciousness groped in the darkness. James. The Epistle of St. James. *'Thou believest*

that there is one God, thou doest well: the devils also believe, and tremble.'

He lay, motionless, on the brink of awareness. Was he dead? Was his body dead? Was this what lay beyond death, for those who had sinned?

'Then, when lust hath conceived, it bringeth forth sin; and sin, when it is finished, bringeth forth death.'

Laura. He had failed Laura. He was damned forever, because sin had brought forth death.

But there the silver shimmer flashed again in the darkness, this time almost within reach. There was a sound; the first sound in the dead silence of the ocean of darkness. Music? A lovely sound. It became clearer. Singing. It was singing. A choir. A slow, beautiful choir that brought tears to his eyes. What were they singing?

"Bonny . . . Bonny . . . Safe . . . Safe . . ."

The choir fell silent. No, this was just part of the torture. He would never return to life. He was damned forever. Yet somehow damnation had lost its sting. The utter despair in which he had lain there had lifted. Somewhere, an infinity away, there still was life.

The darkness cleared. There was blueness now. In the blueness appeared, above him, a shadow. An infinitely comforting shadow.

"Oh God, dear God," he whispered. "God . . . I love thee . . . I give my all to thee . . ." He had spoken those words aloud. But how could that be? How could he speak from death?

"Bonny," the voice called, from the vast blue stillness. *"Bonny . . ."*

With a rush of terror, panic, he tried to tear his body free from the cross to which he was nailed.

"Bonny, Bonny, you are all right . . . You are all right, I'm here, all is well, I'm here . . ."

"God!" he cried, rising on his elbows. "Help me! Mercy! Mercy!"

"You're all right, Bonny, all right." The shadow above him exuded such compassion and tenderness that his body filled with life again, his consciousness with the light of a radiant blue sky. He tried, with terror still on the horizon of this blinding glory, to rise on his arms, expecting to feel the hurt of the nails. But there were no nails.

Miraculously, he was free. Reborn in a blinding light, a new day. Swaying, he felt an arm around his shoulders. "You are safe, safe, you are safe; come . . . let me take you down . . ."

"Laura," he said, trying to rise to his feet. "Laura . . . must find Laura . . ."

"She's safe too," the voice said. "So is the baby."

Baby. Dancing. *'I was dancing with my darling.'* He closed his eyes, feeling so light-headed that he was afraid he would fall. Giddy, half conscious, he let himself be guided away from the beach of the ocean of darkness.

"Can you make it? Can you walk?"

"Yes . . ."

"Lean on me."

He opened his eyes and saw beside him an exotic being, inhabitant of another planet, with flashing round mirrors for eyes.

Was this another planet?

Orange. Blue.

Infinity, and the "Tennessee Waltz."

CHAPTER SEVEN

WHEN Herbert Haring, head of the Indian Desk of Meeting for Sufferings, arrived at the ranch in his Rent-a-Ford, he was told by a grinning chicano that an expedition to bring back the Bakers from the pueblo had set out the day before. *Doña* Ana had left instructions for him to go after them as soon as he arrived.

The message irritated Herbert. Not only was it the high-handedness of the command, but he was an execrable horseman and the desert scared him. Grimly, he set out alone, on a horse the size of a small elephant which, the grinning ranchero assured him, was not fast, but *'muy simpatico.'*

The flanks of the horse forced his legs farther apart than seemed humanly possible, and as he cataplonked down the desert trail toward the mountains he reflected grimly that this would probably result in physical damage, maybe irreparable.

As the horse began to heave itself up the mountainside, straining and farting, his thighs were rubbed raw on the hellishly uncomfortable saddle. Why did *Doña* McHair insist that he be there, if all she intended to do was to get the Bakers out of the pueblo? It was sheer malevolence on her part, she must have known how miserable, frightened and sore he would be atop the largest horse in the Far West, scrambling up the mountainside at an angle of forty-five degrees. The ranchero had told him before he left that he would be able to find the bridle path easily, it was clearly marked by centuries of wear. But in order to discern the signs of centuries of wear you had to have a rudimentary knowledge of tracking, a moronic Boy Scout activity he had avoided like the plague in his time. Now he regretted his refusal to join the pack of obese Wolf Cubs crawling around the city park, tracking their pack leader to the public conveniences by following a trail of bits of newspaper.

By the time he approached the snow border, his legs were twisted out of their sockets, his thighs and buttocks were on fire, and the thought occurred to him that he might have to spend the night in the open. For the sun was setting behind the mountains; the sky, which had been a dazzling blue, was turning that particular shade of cobalt he remembered from his previous visit as heralding the fall of the axe of darkness. The mere thought sent him into a panic. He couldn't possibly! How would he go about it? Just sit down among the holly, or whatever it was, halfway up the mountain? How in the name of God did these people think he was going to survive? What about coyotes? Already he saw himself lying on his back, following the lugubrious circling of vultures, waiting. The infernal dwarf! She had done this to him on purpose! He should have had the sense to say, 'She wants me to join her? Well, guess what: I'm going to sit right here in her living-room, in front of the fire, waited on hand and foot by her flunkeys, and when she comes down from the mountain I'll be there, applauding.' Why had he not thought? Just *thought?* Anyone else with— A stone came rolling down the trail.

He looked up; there was one of the chicano bandits from the ranch, peering down at him with a grin. *"Señora! Doña Ana!"*

There came *Doña* Ana, on a dust-covered beast, like a monkey in a circus astride a giraffe. She was followed by her granddaughter with the bottle-bottom glasses, on her Arabian stallion. And there came another woman, stone-faced and blowsy, a yellow duffel bag on her back, who must be Mrs. Baker, and Baker himself, looking drunk, lurching on top of a mule. The small band came trudging down the bridle path; when *Doña* Ana reached him, she said, "You're too late, as usual."

He would have loved to wring her scraggy little neck, but he greeted her effusively. "Hi, *Doña* Ana, hi, Miss McHair! Hi, Mrs. Baker! How are you, Mr. Baker? All right?"

None of them made much of an effort to return his greeting; they all looked completely done in. What on earth could have happened? The caravan moved on down the mountain, he had to turn his horse around. A scary operation at that angle; there came a moment when he felt he was about to fall off, for the whole world tilted with a swoop. But he managed, or rather the horse did; he had better stay near the Baker woman or he would end up among the bandits. He trotted along behind her, and thought he heard a thin squealing; it seemed to come from the duffel bag bouncing on her back. Presently she swung it round, opened it and brought out a squalling baby. The caravan stopped and *Doña* McHair said, "We'll camp here. Build a fire! *Pronto! Pronto!"*

Everyone dismounted, except Baker and himself. Baker was too groggy; he himself felt as if he could only be lifted off, legs spread, and deposited on the ground in a permanent *grand jeté.* One thing was sure: after this trip was over, never again would he ride a horse.

One of the rancheros grinned at him and helped him down with such efficiency that he found himself deposited beside *Doña* Ana who sat on a little wicker throne. The infernal midget shrilled, with the force of an army trumpet, *"Juancho! Holandés para seis!"* Then she turned to him and asked, "How are you to-day?"

He was about to tell her, when the Baker female, squatting on the other side of the fire, calmly lifted a T-shirt saying "TO HELL WITH HOUSEWORK," bared a breast and proceeded to feed the screaming infant, which, to his utter bafflement, instantly battened on to her and started to suck with a vengeance, pummeling her breast as if it were a punching bag. Had she had a child?

"Give the *Señora* a blanket, please," *Doña* Ana said, "and prepare some warm water and honey for the child."

Two rancheros fell over each other to drape an Indian shawl around the Baker woman's shoulders; Baker himself came staggering to the fireside, dropped on his haunches and was fussed over by the McHair girl, who propped him up against some saddle packs. What the devil was going on?

A tiny hand holding a tiny glass appeared in front of his nose, and the dwarf said, "Here's mud in your eye." She knocked back her own little glass with the speed of a snake catching a fly; he said, "Cheers," followed her example and sat, for minutes on end, mouth tightly closed, cheeks blown out, eyes like saucers. Then, slowly, cautiously, he downed the firewater in the smallest swallows he could manage.

The dwarf asked, "Cigar?"

He was about to shake his head when he realized that she had not been addressing him, but the Baker female across the fire, who said, "Thanks."

"Juancho!" the midget shrieked. The foreman came running, took a foot-long stogie from her and obediently carried it over to the woman squatting behind the flames. The woman bit the tip off, spat it into the fire, lit the cigar, blew the first smoke onto the glowing end and said to the dwarf, "That's no Bronco-buster."

"I should think not," the dwarf replied smugly. "This is the McHair brand, grown for my private use only. Still manured with guano from the bat cave. How would you like to take a box with you?"

The woman said, "Sure would."

The midget lit one of the Groucho Marx stinkers herself; Herbert contemplated them both with incredulous distaste. No wonder he basically detested women. This was an image he would nurture in years to come: a glimpse of the naked truth, hidden behind all the feminine folderol of helplessness, vapors and delicate sensibilities. They sat there like two cohorts of Attila the Hun, resting from the rape of Europe.

"Juancho!" the dwarf shrieked. *"Holandés!"*

Suddenly she turned on him. "I'd like to have a word in private with Mrs. Baker," she said. "Why don't you join the men? They are making your bed now. Over there."

"Oh. Excuse me . . ." He scrambled painfully to his feet, debating with himself whether he would wring her neck now or wait until morning.

"This way, *Señor.*"

He let himself be taken to another fire, half a mile up the slope; when he finally got there, his behind aflame, his ego bruised, he eased himself slowly onto his back on the pallet spread out for him, let himself be covered with a blanket smelling of horse and gazed up at the stars flashing overhead in the great void. Around him he heard the low voices of the rancheros; the smell of cheap cigarette smoke drifted past. No foot-long cigars of the house brand for them; he was bedded down in the slave quarters, part of the spoils of war of Attila the Hun. God help civilized man. God help *men.*

* * *

"Well," the old lady persisted, "how *did* you do it?"

Laura shrugged. "I didn't do anything."

Doña Ana gave her a low-lidded look and tossed off another of those tiny glasses of gin she kept coming. "I'm asking you how you were able to hold out against the brujos? Look at your husband, what they did to him."

Yes, what had they done to Bonny? He lay away from the fire, asleep it seemed, watched over by the McHair girl. They must have really knocked the stuffing out of him. "Do you think he'll be all right? He got quite a dose of the drug—much more than I did. Will he recover soon, do you think?"

"Of course he will!" The old lady smacked her lips. "So will the priest, who must be in worse shape than he is. It's all in the mind, you know. They never touch them. All they do is drug them and let their own guilt do the rest. The Indians in Colombia do the same thing; among primitive people there are no executions as we know them in this barbaric country. Every death of a criminal is, in a sense, suicide. So, if either Father Alvarez or your husband had committed a mortal sin, they would have jumped off that rock." She sucked at the cigar, gave her another of those gimlet looks and asked, "What about you? Are you without sin?"

"I should think not." She was not about to discuss her personal history with the old woman. She had had only two glasses of Geneva so far, but already the fire was beginning to swing under the stars.

"And Anagonga?"

"Anna who?"

"The chief brujo. He must have tried every one of his tricks to stop you."

"You mean Sanchez?"

"Is that what he called himself? He's an old man, very skinny and very wily. He was all-powerful, until you emasculated him; for after what the women did, his power is gone. You realize that, surely?"

She said she didn't. It didn't matter to her. All that mattered was the baby, and sleep.

"Well, Anagonga knew, even if you didn't. How come he didn't bring you down before it got to that?"

"I had the baby," she said curtly. "I had something to hang on to." Then she looked at the deformed little creature in her wicker chair, the high-button shoes, the cigar, and suddenly she felt a sense of kinship. "He showed me my father, brought down by a dog and beaten to death by the Kapos. I must have seen it when Dr. Schmidt carried me away, but had no memory of it. Till now." Suddenly she felt a chill on her chest and saw that the baby had fallen asleep in her arm. "She'll need a wet nurse soon," she said. "She hasn't had any food since she was born."

"Don't worry," the dwarf said. "They're as tough as squirrels. It's going to get some water and honey soon, that should tide it over. At the hacienda, Manuela will take care of the thing. There must be a nursing mother somewhere in the quarters. Now, tell me: how did you manage to get past Anagonga?"

Indeed, what exactly *had* she done to defeat the old man who had wanted to take the baby? Nothing. She herself had done nothing. All she had done was call for help, to all of Schwalbenbach. Including Dad. It had all come back to her. No wonder she had never dared remember before, for she had murdered her father as surely as if it had been she who set the dog on him. "It had to do with my father," she said. "Something he did."

"What did he do?"

"He gave his life during the war for other people's babies."

"In that case," the child's voice said, slurring slightly, "that little critter owes its squirrel's life to *him*." She raised her glass. *"Salud!* To a true *hombre.* Every true *hombre* has a streak of Don Quixote in him. Wherever he is: *Salud!"* She knocked back another little glass. "Wherever he is, *chica,* he must be proud of you. Proud. In heaven, with God, he must be proud of his daughter and grateful."

"Grateful? What do you mean?" The fire slowly rose and fell.

"Because he didn't die for nothing! That's the one thing men cannot stand: the thought that they die for nothing. We women don't care. We don't ask why, why, all the time. We say *poof!,* and look at our children."

Was it true? Was it true that this child owed its life to Dad? No, to all the people of Schwalbenbach. A mystery, but there it was. 'He did not die for nothing.' Suddenly the thought struck her like a stone in the face. The Seed! Old Ethan Woodhouse! *'In your father's apparently senseless death there is contained,*

somewhere, a seed waiting to grow a harvest of light and love;
what happens to that seed is up to you now.'

"No," she said angrily. "One baby is not enough! A hundred,
a thousand babies would not be enough!"

"For what, *chica?"*

"To make sense of my father's death! Not even a million babies would!"

"So it takes two million," the dwarf said, and made a grandi-
loquent gesture at the stars with her cigar. "It's not the number
that counts, it's the fact. If he had not given up his life for other
people's babies, you would have said *Poof!* and Anagonga, the
old skunk, would have danced that baby off the rock, as they did
its chicken-hearted father. At least one man stood up to Anagonga and his bag of tricks: your father. *Salud!"*

No! She'd be damned if she would ever accept that Ethan
Woodhouse had been right. However, for the sake of the poor
old woman in her basket, and out of respect for the miracle of
identification, she said, "It's a thought."

The fire rose slowly, the sky with its stars shifted, then sank
slowly back again. She woke up with a jolt because somebody
took her cigar away. It was the dwarf. "Before you burn a hole
in your baby. The time has come for sleep."

"Doña Ana?" she said drowsily; then she forgot. What had
she been about to ask? She tried to recapture the fleeting
thought she had had just now, but all she managed to recall was
'possible?'

The dwarf looked at her with total, drunken understanding
and said, *"Chica,* for the Dove, anything is possible." She threw
the cigar into the fire, and waddled back to her basket on the
other side.

Laura lay down, the baby in her arms. The foreman came and
said, *"Señora,* here's some honey for the little one," and covered
them both with a blanket. She thanked him, dipped a finger into
the warm sticky liquid and tried to make the baby suck it. But it
wouldn't; it would only take it if she smeared it on her nipple.
She did so, a few times; then they both fell asleep, exhausted.

The night was still, the valley tranquil. A coyote howled on
the mountain, close by. Far away, the faint yapping of ranch
dogs answered its call.

The dwarf sat gazing at her in the firelight, looking very old.

BOOK FOUR

UNITED STATES,
BIAFRA, COLOMBIA
1961-1969

CHAPTER ONE
U.S. Atlantic Seaboard, Summer, 1961

THE General Conference of the Religious Society of Friends was held in June 1961 in a genteel little town on the Eastern Seaboard of the United States. The small resort was virtually taken over by Quakers during the four days of the Conference; the natives, a hardy lot with a keen eye for the dollar, had adapted their charming, whitewashed little town to the invasion of well over two thousand Friends, just as they had adapted it a week before to an invasion by the Southern Baptist Conference, and the week before that to the Benevolent Order of Moose. The shopwindows were full of signs saying WELCOME FRIENDS! The indoor skating rink offered reduced rates to Quaker children, and Pinky's Bar had put out a special sign showing a black hat and the inscription *"In Ye Olde Quaker Hat, Wines and Spirits."*

The participants of the Conference, Friends of seven different Yearly Meetings, milled about the narrow streets and the boardwalk skirting the ocean in discreet high spirits. The biennial Conference was like a huge yearly meeting where everyone met old friends, relatives and weighty members of the Quaker establishment. There were over a dozen workshops in which one could participate, ranging from "The Relevance of the Friendly Persuasion in Present-Day Social Conflicts" to "Approaching the Militant Minorities with Love." There were featured speakers twice a day in the large auditorium, but, as it had always been, the main attraction was Quaker gossip, carried on in small groups scattered on the beach and on the benches lining the boardwalk, which faced stern signs put up by the city fathers: "MALE BATHERS OVER THE AGE OF TWELVE WEARING BIKINIS WILL NOT BE TOLERATED ON THIS BEACH."

The keynote speaker, who was to address the Conference that first night, was Dr. Laura Martens, famous Quaker pediatrician, who would speak on the subject of "Quakers and the Children of the Third World." There was great interest in her lecture, for she was one of the few living Quaker saints. Her exploits over the past ten years had been eulogized in Friendly periodicals all over the world. She had, singlehanded, saved thousands of children from starvation, disease and death; her vast bulk, draped in budget fashions for dignified maturity, was familiar to all Friends. Photographs of her, which adorned many an adolescent Quaker girl's bedroom, showed a huge, disheveled female who, to the delight of the young, smoked cigars.

Everybody knew that she would wind up her performance that night with a plea for donations; even so, the house was packed well in advance, and the huge hall buzzing with voices quickly hushed when, finally, the familiar bulk, swathed this time in unsuitable pink organdy, climbed the stage and took her place on the facing bench among the Conference luminaries, who instantly folded their hands and bent their heads to indicate the beginning of the ten minutes of silent worship that opened every gathering.

To Laura, the feeling of being exposed as exhibit number one evaporated the moment the hush fell over the house and the silence dived to a deeper level. She was still a little groggy after the transatlantic flight; to her, it was two o'clock in the morning. It really was nonsense to expect a person to stand up and address a crowd at such an ungodly hour, and she hoped that some of the weighty Friends with whom she shared the facing bench would rise to give vocal ministry, thereby fending off the specter of sleep. It would not do for the keynote speaker to keel over during the opening silence of the Conference.

Luckily, as she had anticipated, one of them did rise and start to speak in hushed but clearly audible tones about "the age-old Quaker concern of the nameless helping the nameless." He had barely sat down when the ball was caught by the next luminary, who proceeded to hold forth about "our duty to minister to the suffering of mankind." Neither of the two, obviously, had read or heard of William Blake's devastating observation: *"He who would do good to another must do it in minute particulars; general good is the plea of the scoundrel, hypocrite and flatterer."* It seemed a suitable quotation with which to begin her lecture.

When the hands were shaken, breaking the meeting, and she rose in her full roseate splendor to walk toward the lectern, she was received with thunderous applause. Here and there starry-eyed youngsters leaped to their feet and shouted, "Bravo!" and she found herself smiling deprecatingly at the elders behind her. She managed to quiet the cheering crowd with a gesture of blessing, and decided that, after all, it might be better not to open with William Blake, but plump for Isaac Pennington. There was no reason to antagonize the Establishment more than was strictly necessary.

" *'Our life is love, and peace, and tenderness,' "* she began, " *'and holding one another up with a tender hand.'* This, Friends, was written by Isaac Pennington three centuries ago, and I think it still describes the essence of our Friendly calling." There she went: the rolling phrases, the wry jokes, the harrowing descriptions of children dying of hunger and disease a continent away. She soon sensed that she had their attention and proceeded to soften them up to have their pockets picked; for what all this boiled down to, of course, was money. Money for various hospitals in the Third World, for children to be saved and children who needed saving and for the children who were beyond saving, which, alas, were the majority. She built up to what she hoped would be a stirring appeal, but tonight she felt very weary. Oh, well, all she could do was try.

*   *   *

To Boniface Baker, seeing Laura up there from the anonymity of the audience in the darkened hall was a profoundly upsetting experience. He had pictured in his mind the moment when the girl he had married would appear on the podium and he would hear that voice again, so strong and resonant and yet, on a few occasions that were unforgettable, so full of tenderness and concern. But the experience, when it finally came, was an anti-climax. The huge woman on the stage had nothing to do with the Laura of his youth. It seemed incredible that in the eleven years since he had last seen her she could have changed so dramatically. Domineering, aggressive—she had already been that toward the end, but she had also been an eighteen-year-old blonde who turned men's heads in passing. Now it seemed as if she were deliberately mocking her own femininity, for he could not believe that the caricature she presented was not deliberate. She must have known what she was doing when she let herself go to this extent, divested herself so ruthlessly of all physical attractions to end up, at an age when other women looked their best, as a shapeless bulk, an immensely powerful, laconic female who seemed to be saying, 'All right, Friends, I am taking care of your consciences for you by the work I am doing, so you'd better cough up some dough if you want to go on sounding off in meeting for worship about that of God in every child, and the Family of Man.'

As he listened to her oddly unmoving evocation of the horrors she had seen—dying children, orphans lost in burning cities, abandoned babies crying in the jungle—he was surprised by his own lack of emotion at this first encounter in eleven years. To go to Friends General Conference this year had been a last-minute decision. He was visiting his mother with Gulie, Himsha and the three youngest children when he heard that Laura was to be the keynote speaker. The temptation to go, to sit in the audience unnoticed and speak to her after her lecture had proved irresistible. Gulie had not been too happy with the idea, but she had understood and come along, to keep Himsha and him company. Now he wished he had let it pass. He would have kept his illusion of Laura as the fiery young Florence Nightingale, phoenix risen from the ashes of Camp Schwalbenbach. Now he no longer felt like going to speak to her; but she was sure to hear that he had been present. The Quaker grapevine never failed.

But what was the true reason for his negative reaction? Uncouth and blowsy as she might be, she was a formidable woman who did admirable work. Was it because she held up a mirror to him, showing him the way of all flesh? He had never been exactly slender, now he was a fat man. His tousled boyish hair was gone, his jowls had thickened, his chin doubled. But he was not old yet, not as old as the woman on the stage wanted him to believe. 'Oh Laura, Laura,' he thought, 'what have you done to yourself? What have you done to *me*?'

It was too dramatic a sigh for him not to feel that he was indulging in self-pity. Wasn't he a happy man, rich in worldly goods, blessed with a happy family, a loving, beautiful wife? He looked at Himsha, the strikingly beautiful sixteen-year-old girl who had been the baby that Laura and he saved from the pueblo. She was listening to Laura with obvious rapture, bewitched, like the rest of them, by her power and the monumental good works that had made her a legend in her own time. Then he looked at Gulie, on his other side. She too was listening with rapt attention, but he saw on her sensitive face an expression that surprised him. She was looking at the monster that had been young Laura with an expression of concern.

*   *   *

Gulie did not quite know why, but the woman on the stage moved her deeply. She had been apprehensive of meeting Laura again; despite the gulf of years and the promptings of reason, she had been haunted by a feeling of guilt. After all, whatever way you looked at it, she had taken Bonny away from Laura; now that she saw her again, the overwhelming emotion she felt was pity, an intense concern for the lonely creature up there, so manfully trying to hide her desperation behind a blustering provocative manner. Gulie did not for a second succumb to the spell Laura had thrown over the audience. She did not see in her the tower of goodness, the irresistible power of love. All she saw was an intensely lonely woman, haunted by the unspeakable horrors of her past, who had, in an effort to escape from them, plunged into the horrors of the present, the dying children of Asia, Africa, South America, the mere contemplation of whom would break any mother's heart. Poor, poor Laura—Gulie wished there were something she could do to bring some solace to the suffering of that huge female up there, who anyone could see was desperately vulnerable, crying out for help, for love.

*   *   *

Seeing the magnificent woman up there in that ludicrous dress, her graying hair piled untidily on top of her head, decided Himsha Baker: this was the only person in the world who could help her. Dr. Martens looked exactly as she had expected her to look after all the stories she had heard about her: huge, coarse and very, very tough. She did not look like a Quaker saint at all; saints were supposed to be gentle, self-effacing, abstinent. She had doubted that she would have the courage to approach her. But now, seeing her in the flesh, she not only took heart, she was certain that her instinct had been right: of all people, this was the one person to go and see.

As she sat listening to that powerful voice, feeling that marvelous courage, that overwhelming compassion, Himsha's eyes filled with tears, something which had only happened once before, the day she had heard Bach's Passion of St. Matthew for the first time in a concert hall. When the final chorus exploded in its hymn of mourning and joy, she had been stirred to the very depths of her soul, and the tears had flowed freely despite Hannah Clutterbuck, who she knew sat watching her, beady-eyed, ready to slurp up any show of emotion. It had always been Hannah's complaint that Himsha was a cigar-store Indian who never showed what she felt and never indulged in normal feminine exuberance or delicious gloom. Now, listening to that magnificent voice, overwhelmed and inspired by that majestic and yet tender personality, Himsha indulged in daydreams: herself as a doctor, like Laura Martens, a saint, an angel of Mercy, moving among the suffering children of the world, the very embodiment of the elemental Quaker tenet: *'All He has is thee.'* For the time being, all God had was Laura Martens; but that night Himsha felt certain, for one brief hour, that God would soon have two of them.

*   *   *

There was one person in the audience who watched the speaker with professional detachment: Dr. Alfred Wassermann, now a well-heeled New York psychiatrist, specializing in the post-concentration camp syndrome. In his large practice he had never come across a survivor of the camps who had been able to shake the curse; after reading about Laura Martens' lecture to the Quaker convention he had come all the way from Manhattan solely to hear and watch her. For she appeared to be the exception, the one victim of the holocaust who had managed to rid herself of the psychological scars and the permanent emotional trauma all ex-inmates shared, at least those who had come to him for help.

But as he sat there, listening, watching, his professional objectivity waned. My God, was that the wisplike girl he had known? What had she done to herself to end up, at age thirty-four, looking like a walrus? It indicated that, despite the positive power which was unmistakable from the moment she opened her mouth, there still must be a problem. Well, of course there was. It had proven impossible to eradicate those years, but possible, in theory at least, to sublimate the experience. That, it appeared, was what she had done; of all the people he knew from those nightmare years she was the only one who had found the strength and the will to turn the destructive experience into a creative power. There could be no doubt she had done a lot of good for a lot of children. She must, in terms of numbers, have saved a battalion of them, single-handed. Admirable, and yet . . .

Maybe these were spiteful thoughts. Maybe what he took to be professional doubt was envy; for what she had done was what he had tried to do: turn the curse into a blessing for as large a number of people as possible. In his case, all he had managed to do was opiate some of his fellow victims and turn them from emotional cripples into people who functioned in society and were in other respects at least apparently normal. None of them really were, none of them ever would be. Was she the exception? Anyhow, what he was witnessing was a miracle of persuasion. Look at these people, they were completely spellbound, even though they knew full well that all she wanted was their money. Well, he was ready to part with a few bucks, when it came to that. She was pretty impressive.

As she wound up her peroration, lining up her willing victims for what she called "a gift of love," he decided not to go back to New York that night as he had planned. He must have a word with her in private, however briefly. He had to assure himself by observation from close quarters that what he now saw from afar was true: that Laura Martens, the chameleon who had survived the camp only because of her incredible powers of adaptation, had truly turned into a creative force and was not acting out the greatest role of her life, that of Quaker Saint.

*   *   *

Ethan Woodhouse had refused to sit on the facing bench because he wanted a frontal view of the speaker, not sit staring at her behind. He had worried about not being able to hear her from the hall, but, thank God, the woman had a voice like a foghorn, he even had to turn down his hearing aid.

It was fascinating to see her there, exactly as she had been sitting in the courtyard of MFS all those years ago. She was virtually still wearing that T-shirt warning you to keep a safe distance, and the cigar was now her standard attribute. She hadn't changed one bit: heavier, maybe, more mature, but otherwise she could have got up from that bench in the courtyard sixteen years ago and marched straight onto this platform.

Well, for better or for worse, there stood the Religious Society of Friends, year of our Lord 1961. It could be better, it could be worse; but that was how it had always been, from the very beginning. How many Quaker women had stood, over the past three hundred years, haranguing Meetings about suffering children, feeling totally unsuitable, impostors, mistakes of God? He saw, profiled behind her, an impressive row, all of them different, all of them driven by the same mysterious, soul-consuming impulse. She was a specimen of an old breed, Margaret Fell in latest disguise. He savored a feeling of pride at having been right when he first saw her, at a time when everybody, even blessed Stella, thought she was mentally disturbed. He had seen the tree in the stunted sapling, the magnificent battle-axe of the Lord in the mutely rebellious child who had sat in front of his desk, giving him the evil eye because he dared to suggest that there might be in her father's gruesome death the same seed of absolute good Ann Traylor had failed to discern in the death of Bonny Baker in the dungeon of Lancaster Castle. Now look at her! Would her father, in heaven or hell or wherever he was, be granted the awareness that it was he who had propelled this juggernaut of mercy on her way? That his crucifixion had brought about a spark of light and love for innumerable children who otherwise would have been swallowed mercilessly by the ocean of death and darkness? She herself might not accept that yet; she certainly hadn't at the time. She had stood up, eyes blazing, and all but spat in his face before slamming out of his office without a word. He had rummaged among his old diaries that afternoon, looking for the one in which he had made a note on their first encounter. "Laura Martens Baker: will make a good nurse eventually, when the chips are down. Once her motherly instincts are aroused, she may even turn into one of those lionesses who are so admirable from afar. Have no problem recommending her to the Steering Committee as the right person to extend to the infants in the Huni pueblo the sheltering arms of the Society of Friends." It had come true; only, for "infants in the Huni pueblo" read "infants of the Third World."

The more he looked at her—for he had stopped listening—the more he felt himself thinking about her sad father. How the man must have been destroyed, seeing his child raped and abducted! He must have died in unimaginable, total despair. 'Ah, God,' he thought, 'give the poor man this night! Give him the knowledge that, owing to his gruesome crucifixion, there will never be an end to the concern for which he died!' For, look at the faces of the rebellious young: the sneering adolescents, the grim unbelievers! One of them, at least one, would be burdened tonight with Jacob Martens' concern, maybe without realizing it as yet. It was the secret, the seed of life in the womb of the always seemingly moribund Society of Friends: *'let your lives speak.'* And, my God, what a life was speaking tonight! It was a privilege to be allowed to sit here, at the age of eighty-three, and see that row of glorious women rise behind the tartar on the podium. She might not be quite what elders, past and present, had in mind as the image of the Weighty Friend, but they were stuck with her, thank God. For as long as she would last, she was the leader of the peculiar people who never acknowledged any leaders, the present beacon to the children of the light. The perennial holy experiment was now in her hands, until some now mutely rebellious adolescent among the next generation would have the torch forced upon him or her on the day she would fall.

It was so immensely satisfying, so full of hope and glory, that he turned off his hearing aid and went into meeting for worship all by himself while the foghorn voice harangued the crowd.

* * *

When, finally, the pizzazz was finished, the collection had been made, the weighty Friends flattered, the starry-eyed young fans successfully evaded, Laura fled to her hotel, feeling very, very tired. And no wonder: apart from the usual exhaustion after one of those evangelistic speeches, it was three o'clock in the morning now, her time.

The vision of her hotel room was like an oasis; but as she collected the key at the desk, she was accosted by a fat man who said, "Laura? How are you?" She turned around with a snarl, and had to do a double-take before she saw who it was. "My God," she said.

He smiled. "Not quite. Do you remember Gulielma?"

A tall, Indian-looking female advanced on her, rather diffidently, and held out her hand. "Hello . . ."

As she shook the woman's hand, she wondered why she did not remember her at all. The Gulie McHair she recalled was a gangling, myopic creature with glasses, acne and oily black hair, smelling of horse; this was a stunning beauty. "Well, well," she said, "we haven't all made pigs of ourselves, I see. What happened to your spectacles?"

The woman blushed and answered, "Contact lenses."

"Good for you! You're a knockout, baby."

"Can we sit down for a moment?" He pointed at the wicker chairs in the dimly lit lobby.

"Well . . ."

"Oh, just a few minutes. Just to touch base. I—we would love to chat with you, just for a little while, before you make off again to—where is it this time?"

"Latin America," she replied, with a sinking feeling. She couldn't very well turn him down. She might be hanging on by her gums, but she had to see this through. He had always been one for moving massively, he would be mortally hurt if she made light of this. And, after all, she owed him half an hour. "Tell you what," she said. "I'll just go upstairs and get a glass of water, and—"

"Oh, but I'll get you one," he said. "Let me—"

"Bonny!" his wife warned. Her meaning was clear: Let her go, the woman wants to visit the bathroom.

"I'll only be a moment. Make yourselves comfortable."

"Well—I guess I'd better get back," the wife said. "Our eldest daughter is waiting in the car, and my mother-in-law is baby-sitting our three youngest children."

"I understand, dear. Off you go. Nice seeing you again."

Her abruptness, as usual, flustered the other party. "I mean—maybe the two of you would like to have some time together first. I—why don't we all have dinner, tomorrow or the day after?"

God forbid. "I'm sorry, I'm going to have to leave again." She had two days, but this threat was enough to make a pregnant sow run.

"Oh—I see. Well, goodbye, then. Nice seeing you again, Laura. You are doing wonderful work."

"Thank you. Goodbye." She shook the slender hand gingerly. It was very soft; whatever Gulielma McHair Baker did to fill her days, it wasn't laundering or washing dishes. And why should she? She must be a multi-millionaire since her grandmother died. The woman fled. She turned to Bonny. "Boy," she said. "You look splendid. Together we must weigh about four times as much as when we started."

"Yes," he said, and laughed uncertainly.

"Be right back." She bounded up the stairs—well, 'bounded' was an illusion: 'charged' was the word. In her miserable, bleak little room she opened her suitcase, took out an earthenware crock and filled three quarters of the tumbler on the washstand with Dutch Geneva. She could not possibly face the meat-grinder of reminiscence without some fortification, certainly not in the state she was in. She wondered if he would mind if she smoked a cigar, but decided against it. To bury his illusions was one thing, to bury them under a landslide was unnecessary. Well: into the fray once more.

"Here I am!" She hoped she sounded appropriately enthusiastic as she advanced on him. He was embedded in a wicker armchair that was so tight it stuck to his hips when he got up. "Don't mind that," she said. "It happens to the best of us fatties. It's the basketwork that makes them hang on."

He laughed, and she sensed that he had hoped to make her forget his size and see only the dashing young Knight in Shining Armor, or the Wicked Young Dog—whatever it was men at conventions hoped to achieve, whooping it up with funny hats. "You're a rancher now, I gather?"

"Yes. Can I get you anything? There may be some Coke or some soda at the desk . . ."

"Bonny," she said, suddenly moved to pat his knee, "take it easy. I am not your ex-girlfriend. Not even your ex-wife."

"No—er—yes . . ."

"How many children do you have now?"

"Six, altogether."

"All adopted?"

"Yes."

"Why? Which one of you is to blame for that?"

"Neither of us. We decided, or, rather, Gulie did, that she didn't want to risk adding another dwarf to the family line. Also," he added, somewhat portentously, "we felt that there were enough children born into this world as it is, and that we should take care of some who had no parents, and help them to fulfill their potential."

"H'm." She eyed him quizzically. "You inherited the McHair empire, didn't you?"

"Gulie did, not I."

"Okay. She did. How many millions?"

"Are you asking that because you want to determine your ransom? Or to make me feel guilty?"

"Guilty of what? Marrying a rich woman?"

"Well, on the face of it, opting for a life of material comfort."

She took a swig from the tumbler, after stopping herself at the last moment from raising it and saying 'Cheers.' "Oh, I don't know about that," she said. "We all live the way we like to live, if we can afford it. Anyone who tries to sell you the idea that he's doing selfless service and feels deprived is a huckster. I wouldn't change places with you for a million bucks. I'd go out of my mind in ten days flat, sitting on my moneybags out in that desert. And you would go out of your mind if you took on my job, believe me."

"Never mind all that, Laura," he said, recovering some of his old authority. "What have you been up to since we last met?"

"You'll have to help me there. When was that? So much has happened since."

"Last time was at Granny McHair's funeral."

"Ah, yes. I fled before the banquet, as I remember."

"That's a nasty dig."

"No moral judgment implied. I was still in the age of illusion, when I went in for diets. One look at that cold buffet waiting in the hacienda . . ."

"Laura, you're as transparent as ever."

"Ah? I never was aware of being transparent. What do you think I was up to, that time?"

"I think you had a fair dose of holier-than-thou in those years."

"Maybe." She took another swig. This was turning into an eldering session. She had to restrain herself from saying what she thought of him and his gentle rebuke, backed up by six million bucks. At least.

"And, mind you," he added, "rightly so. It was fantastic, the way you slogged your way through college and medical school. At your age, and with your background . . ."

"Nothing wrong with my background," she said. "It's not a rags-to-riches story. My father was a bank manager. I went to high school in Holland. I received a most generous restitution from the Dutch government for the house in Westerdam, and the money the Germans stole. And I sold the houseboat."

"Your amnesia is a thing of the past?"

"I should hope so."

"Did you ever remember who Winnetou was?"

Fancy that! "Yes," she said. "He was not a horse at all, but a character from a children's book about Indians my father read aloud to me. His friend was a trapper called Old Shatterhand."

"You were planning to visit Holland, when we last met."

"I did. I saw all the sights, including a woman called Clara van Loon Babbersma, who used to be a neighbor, and who asked if I was likely to see you sometime, in which case she asked to be remembered. Seems you rolled her over in the clover during the war, while talking about me and dear old Dad."

"Laura, what's the matter with you? You're as prickly as a cactus."

"I see. We're into desert slang now, are we? You wear high heels and chaps at home? Roping in the calves, bringing in the greenbacks?"

"Laura, stop it."

"Well, hell, old buddy! You're a classic example of the old adage: the Quakers came to America to do good, and they did very well."

"Sure. Shall I get you another glass of water?"

"No, thanks. I don't like the tapwater here. I have a bottle of spring water in my room upstairs."

"Bottle, or crock? You are still a lush, by the smell of your spring water."

"Were you serious?"

"About the glass of water? Give me your key and I'll get it for you. How much spring water do you want?"

"Oh, about half of this. It's the third room to the right, second floor. Thanks."

"It's a pleasure."

He took the tumbler with him as he jellied up the stairs. Boy, look at those buttocks! She stretched, and put her feet on the wicker coffee table. It squealed in refined protest. Ah, she was beginning to relax. He was all right, really, old Bonbon. Bit of an ass, of course, but as solid a citizen as *lieb' Vaterland* could want. Suddenly she heard them again, across the *Paradeplatz,* bellowing it in their cups on summer nights, when the windows of the mess hall were left open because of the heat. *'Lieb' Vaterland mag ruhig sein, fest steht und treu die Wacht am Rhein.'* If seeing him was going to bring that kind of stuff back, she had better beat it right now.

There he was, carrying a full glass, the dear calf. "Oh, Bonny, that's too much!"

"Since when?" He was out of breath after his little jaunt of mercy.

"Listen," she said, mollified, "you should shake a fewscore pounds. Overweight kills more people—"

"Look who's talking."

"Well, hell! If I'm digging my grave with my teeth, that doesn't mean it's okay for you! I know just the place: a fat farm in the south of England. Boring as all hell, but they do get them off. The address—"

"Laura! We haven't seen each other for years! What are we doing, sitting here, talking about fat farms?"

"Sorry, old chum," she said, sipping. "I was just trying to save your life. And I'm past the point of no return. You may have to carry me up, in a minute. That'll put an end to your suffering. Overweight bird in gilded cage. Canary dies of exertion."

"No, Laura. You're not going to weasel your way out of this by pretending to be drunk. Remember? I'm Bonny Baker, who—"

"Yes," she said wryly. "I remember. That was quite a night, wasn't it? The night you lost your virginity?"

He flushed crimson.

"I don't mean your unsuccessful effort to emulate the *Obersturmführer.* I meant the first violence you committed. Was it your last?"

He looked unhappy. "Why bring that up?"

"Look, old chum. Either we talk about fat farms, or—"

"Surely there is a happy medium?"

"You name it."

He smiled. "All those years, and we're at it again."

"At what, schnozzola?"

"Bickering. Needling each other."

"Hell, boy—I tricked you into damnation and you tried to wring my neck. Call that 'needling each other?' We damn near hurled each other into the pit. If that baby hadn't been foisted on us at that particular moment . . . Talk about *deus ex machina.* Anyhow: cheers." She drank.

"How many more babies have been foisted on you since then, would you say?"

"Don't be an ass. That's what idiots ask: 'How many?' " She mimicked the idiots, tipsily. "I haven't counted them, God forbid. And they aren't foisted on me; I'm foisted on *them."*

"It must be ironic, to see this wealthy, affluent crowd after—"

"Bonny, stop probing your aching tooth. Believe me, I don't consider you a shirker who has betrayed the cause, just because you are a millionaire. I think you did a swell thing, adopting six kids and giving them a home. I couldn't have done that in a thousand years. Remember George Fox? He converted them, and never wanted to set eyes on them again. All evangelists are the same. And you'd better face it, that's what I am: an evangelist, a female Billy Sunday, with a bedpan instead of the Good Book."

"That's what that general went on calling me: Billy Sunday."

"Which general?"

"The one with Hitler's name. The one who ordered us married."

"Ah, the one with the bee in his bonnet about Heinzl. He said he wanted to 'understand' him. I wonder where he is now. I could have had a different life, had I but known."

"You think so?"

"Hell, I know so! I could have zeroed in on him with my mad, empty mind, instead of on you. If I had, I would have married him, of that you can be sure. I would be living in Japan now, or in the Canal Zone, and worrying about my kids getting hung up in the electric fence playing baseball."

"Would you have liked that?"

"Why not? You seem to like it, why shouldn't I?"

"But you said yourself, a moment ago—"

"A tumbler ago. I'm on an honesty kick now. The next stage is tears, then a few haymakers, and kerplunk! You're in no fit condition to hoist me up to my room unaided. So, either line up a few service-oriented Friends, or get the hell home to Mom. With the contact lenses. The fact that you only adopt doesn't mean that you don't screw her, I hope?"

"Laura, honey . . ." He put his hand on hers. It nearly undid her.

"Knock that off, Boniface! I told you, tears are next!"

"What's the matter, Laura? I'm your oldest friend. We went through an awful lot together. You're as unhappy as sin. Why?"

Oh, boy, here it came. The dirty laundry. Well, one chute was as good as another, and he'd asked for it. "Want to know? Okay. I'm lonely. Lonely as hell. All I have is admirers, and smelly babies who insist on dying. Nobody dares get any closer than sticking their heads around the door. I wish I had married that goddam general. I wish I had married a gorilla. I wish I had stayed married to *you*. I wouldn't have accepted any adoption nonsense. The hell with the population explosion. I would have wanted my own kids, torn out of my guts, a whole litter of them. We would have been as poor as dirt farmers, you and I, and we wouldn't have done a single good deed, but we would have been *alive.*"

"Well, aren't we?"

"You're a bird in a golden cage, and I'm impersonating St. Francis in drag. Call that living? Hell, man! You don't know what it means, to be a monolith of virtue. A Blarney Stone for enraptured Friends. 'Selfless love.' That's their incantation, when they come to genuflect and drop their pennies in the well. 'Friend Laura Martens, thee has restored my faith in selfless love.' And instead of saying: 'Listen, buster, as it happens, I don't believe in selfless love,' I say: 'Thank thee, Friend; but, remember, I am not alone in this; without thy help . . .' And that makes a difference of at least two hundred bucks. A neat trick. Yet, without that money—what the hell. Get me another glass, will you?"

"No, Laura. You've had enough."

"Hey, listen! Who do you think you are? My husband? Get me another glass!"

"No, Laura. In that case, I'm going home." He rose in his full, corn-fed splendor.

"Okay, Bonny, okay." She waved a hand at him. "Sit down. I

can stand you without being doped, I guess. Now I can. Sit down!"

"I think you should be in bed. How late is it, your time?"

"Never mind that; I'm fine. Sit down. Dammit, man! I've just *told* you! That's what everybody does: stick their heads around the door, and as soon as I make a move in their direction they beat it. You're just like the rest!"

"Laura, I know you. Yes, yes, I realize it's been years, but I know you. I'm sorry I fell for it and went to get that glass in the first place. You must go to bed now. We'll see each other tomorrow. Come, let me help you upstairs." He stretched out his hands.

She looked at him from below, slumped in her chair. Imagine, she had been married to him. Enough to scare the shit out of anyone. Like being married to the Goodyear Blimp. "You must have problems with the missionary position," she said. "And don't pull that face on me, I'm a missionary myself."

"Laura, I know you're drunk, but not that drunk. Stop acting like a spoiled child. Come, I'll take you to your room."

"Spoiled?! Spoiled with what? Love? Companionship? Little playmates? Let me tell you, Nanny: I—"

"Hush! There are people asleep in this hotel. Tomorrow—"

She got up, refusing his outstretched hands. "Shall I tell you something, you coward? You came here to poke a stick at me, like the rest of the little boys, to see if I was real. And the moment I snarled, you—"

"Come, dear. Quiet. People—"

"Oh, shit!" She needed his help getting to her room like she needed a hole in the head. He was a bastard. A yellow-bellied, miserable . . . "Good night, Bonny. Sleep well. And when you get home, don't wake up wifey. Or the kiddies. Or your mother-in-law. Or the dog."

"Bless you, Laura." He kissed her.

"Now, what the hell did you do *that* for?"

"Because I love thee."

"Don't use Quaker baby-talk with me!"

"Sorry. We use plain language in the family because we thought it would help bring us together. Also, it's difficult to get mad with someone you call 'thee.' "

"Want to try?"

"Hush. Good night. I'll give you a call tomorrow." He fled. There was no other word. He bloody well fled. She must be as cozy to be with as a buzzard.

"Good night, all," she said to the empty lobby, the empty desk, the empty revolving door. "Please put your contributions in my shoe, outside my door. Bye-bye." She made herself sick. But what do you want? There was no one else to make sick. Not one damned miserable soul.

Off to bed with you, you maudlin, fat broad! To bed, St. Laura. *Masturba, madre.*

* * *

Instead of going to the car, where Gulie and Himsha were waiting, Boniface crossed the boardwalk outside the hotel and sat down on a bench. The surf hissed in the translucent darkness; a harvest moon made a path on the ocean. There was a smell of seaweed and warm sand, and a taste of brine in the air. He shouldn't keep them waiting; Gulie had been very patient and understanding. But he needed a few moments to himself.

My God, the loneliness of the poor woman! How stupid not to have understood that at once, as Gulie had. Laura was as unhappy as sin, with all her good works and her dazzling fame. A monolith, she had called herself. That's what she was: as lonely as that giant rock in the Huni valley, before it became a Mecca for tourists.

But she had wanted it that way, whatever she might think now. She had hurled herself into her studies like a woman obsessed. She had deliberately cut off all ties with him, once they were divorced. Should he have been less hasty? Waited a few months longer, as he had been prepared to do, instead of having himself strong-armed by Gulie's grandmother into marrying so soon, without any courtship worth speaking of? But then, Gulie and he had known they belonged together almost the very first night, when she took him to see the stables. Laura had guessed that, even if they hadn't, at the time. How sad, to see Laura like this, to hear her still swearing like a trooper. But would she have been much different if he had stayed married to her? Had children? Lived heaven knows where; wherever Meeting for Sufferings would have sent them? She would have driven him around the bend. She was not only much too strong a personality, she was, obviously, emotionally damaged forever. And no wonder . . .

He sat for a while longer, staring at the sea in the moonlight; when finally he returned to the car, Gulie reached over and opened the door for him.

"Sorry it took so long," he said. "Let's go."

"We can't," said Gulie. "Himsha isn't back yet."

"Where the devil is she?"

"She wanted to see Laura too. She must have waited until you left."

"Why did she want to see her?"

"Because Laura carried her out of the pueblo and saved her life."

"Oh, boy," he said. "That's unfortunate."

"Why, darling?"

"Laura is drunk."

"Oh—how sad . . . What shall we do? Shall I go after her?"

"No, let her find out for herself. She's sixteen. She must learn how to handle a situation like that."

"Drunken saints, thee means?"

He put his hand on hers. "Laura is a terribly lonely woman. Thee was right."

"Even so—I'd like to go and get her."

"Don't. She won't come to any harm. On the contrary, she might learn something."

"Like what?"

"That to be God's instrument doesn't necessarily mean you have to be a flawless human being."

"Bonny, darling—she will be barging into the room of a drunk, not going to Sunday school! Laura needs a nurse, not a teenager with a crush on her."

"If Himsha has a crush on her," he said, "all is well. Mind if I put my head on thy shoulder while we wait?"

*   *   *

In the seclusion of her dismal little room Laura undressed and took off her girdle, which was always a blessed relief, although it gave her the feeling of suddenly being three feet tall and four feet wide. Giddy with booze and fatigue, she washed her face, but that was all she felt up to right now. She would undress and all the rest later—first a blessed moment of just lying down, maybe read awhile. A thoughtful soul had put some reading material on the bedside table: George Fox's Journal in the Ellwood edition, still expurgated by Margaret Fell after three centuries, and a pamphlet, entitled *The Sound of Silence,* by a woman Friend with the incongruous name of Bangs-Fripan. She sighed, took out her glasses and chose the pamphlet; if that wouldn't put her to sleep, nothing would.

She was just nodding off over the preface, which, after three centuries, still asked gloomily, "What *is* a Quaker?" when there was a soft knock on the door. She refused to be roused, drowsily hoping that whoever it was would have the grace to go away. But there came another knock, louder this time, and she bellowed, "Who the hell is that?!" The blast of her voice and the blessed power of blasphemy seemed to chase away the intimidated caller. She tried to recapture her drowsiness, but there, damn it, the creature was knocking again.

"All right," she said, with grim resignation. "Who is it?"

"Aunt Laura . . . "

A girl's voice. Aunt? She had no nieces. Muttering unquakerly language, she got up and opened the door. A small, slight Indian girl was standing timorously in the dark hallway.

"What do you want?"

The little creature whispered, "I am Himsha Baker, Aunt Laura . . . I—I'm the baby thee carried out of the Huni pueblo. May I—may I talk to thee?"

For a moment Laura gazed at the girl without speaking, overwhelmed by the momentousness of the occasion. Well, well, the Huni baby. The first of a long, long line. Now, there she stood, a ravishing young woman, obviously totally unaware of her striking beauty.

"Come in, dear, and close the door. Forgive me—I didn't expect any visitors."

"Oh, but I—I'll come back tomorrow if thee prefers, Aunt Laura . . ."

"Don't be silly. You've waked me up now, so you might as well come in. Close the door, honey. Sit yourself down—no, wait, before you do, get me that box of cigars, will you? Over there on the dresser. And hand me my lighter from my purse. Just open it, honey, just open it, take it out."

The girl obeyed, nervously, yet clearly excited that she had managed to penetrate the lioness' den. It must have taken a good deal of courage after tonight's blustering performance. She proffered the cigars with sturdy equanimity and, after Laura had selected one, helped her light it.

Laura blew a cloud of smoke at the ceiling, relaxed on the skimpy pillow and said, "So you're the baby! Tell me—what can I do for you?"

The girl sat down on the edge of the solitary chair, gazed at her with those stunning black eyes and said, with the solemnity of youth, "Aunt Laura, would thee advise me to study medicine?"

Dear God, it was going to be one of *those* conversations. "Do your parents know you're here?" Then she added, as an afterthought, "They aren't waiting for you, by any chance?"

"Yes, Aunt Laura . . ."

"Well, then we'd better make this short, hadn't we? So you want to study medicine. Why?"

"Because—because I want my life to be of service to humanity—follow thy example . . ."

She gazed at the exotic little creature who now sat staring at her like a desert owl from the Llano Estacado. What a beauty! Study medicine? Before that one knew what happened to her, she'd have her picture, with turban and scowl, on the cover of *Vogue.* "Well, Himsha," she said, mollified, "that's a tall order. You'll have to put on a few pounds, to start with. But okay, tell me about yourself."

*   *   *

Himsha looked at the fat woman on the bed with trepidation. Had she gone too far? Should she just have said, "I want to study medicine," and left it at that, rather than gush over her? Obviously, Aunt Laura was not happy with the fact that she wanted to follow her example. She looked very forbidding as she lay there, puffing at her cigar. Her eyes, which seen from the audience had looked so pure and radiant, turned out to be shrewd and secretive and cold. Her jolly, good-humored self-deprecation that had been so admirable during her lecture now appeared to have been a sham. The woman on the bed, scrutinizing her uncompromisingly while sucking at the obscene cigar, did not seem self-deprecating at all. She exuded an enormous authority, a tough, aggressive power; there was no tenderness there, no feminine softness, not a shred of the motherly warmth she had seemed to have on the podiùm. And yet she had done all those magnificent, compassionate things in Africa, South America . . .

"Look, child," Aunt Laura said suddenly, as if she had come to a decision. "Before you start idolizing me for what I've done, I think I owe it to you to tell you how I came to do it. It's all very flattering, but I think you should know the truth."

"Oh, Aunt Laura," she protested courageously, "I know all about thee. My father—" She stopped, embarrassed, wondering whether Aunt Laura would want to be reminded of her brief, unhappy marriage.

The woman on the bed smiled wryly. "Well, what did your daddy tell you, honey?"

"Mother did, really—and many other people who saw thy witness."

"Saw my what? Oh, yes—sure." She tipped the ashes of her cigar messily on the floor, a contemptuous gesture to the maid who would have to clean it up in the morning. She continued, "Child, let's face it. To your mother and your father, and to eager young Friends like yourself, I'm a prime example of the Quaker *persona* or whatever you want to call it. But you must forgive me, baby. The world in which I live and operate has little use for abstract definitions. Your father is a dear man, if there's anyone who knows that, it's me. But he hasn't any idea of where I am, or even who I am; I don't think he ever did." She hiccuped. "Scuse me." She waved the cigar. "All those weighty Friends, led by your father of all people, decided long ago why I'm doing what I'm doing: it's in order to provide, quote, a posthumous sense to the apparently senseless death of my father, unquote. One old, weighty Friend even had the gall to say to a young girl who thought that she had murdered her own father and who had, as a result, been an amnesiac for three years, 'The Seed, child, the Seed! You must nurture the Seed of light and love in the evil death of your father!' Well, you've heard the story. You know my father went berserk after seeing me raped, that he attacked his tormentors when I was carried off in the arms of an SS officer, and that he was clubbed to death in screaming insanity. Sweetie—" the fat woman looked at her with terrifying eyes—"the Seed may have lived on during the three centuries of the Society of Friends, but, believe me, that Seed, that God, that God of Love, that saintly bore is *dead!* Himsha, baby, my first baby—" the woman shakily pointed at her with the cigar—"I can, as I did to that hall full of people tonight, spoon-feed you the cough syrup of a God of Love. But, believe me, I saved you from death *not* because I called upon a God of Love to protect you, but—now, you listen carefully—because—" she belched "scuse me—because I begged for the protection of the devil as well as God. Henchman as well as victim. My father's murderers as well as my father himself. I don't know who Margaret Fell called on for help when she needed it, but one thing I know for certain: it was a God who, through her, went on acquiring identity. Himsha, baby—" she puffed at her cigar—"if you want to become someone like me, someone whom silk-tongued bores minister about in meeting, you must understand one thing: God needs you as much as you need Him. Forget about Yearly Meetings, Friends' pamphlets, professional—*shit!"* She had dropped the ash of her cigar into her cleavage, and tried unsteadily to dust it off her brassiere. "Blast, hell! Did you see where those ashes went? Realize what that means? I'll have to get up now, take a bath . . . Well, what the hell? As I was saying . . . What *was* I saying?"

Himsha suppressed the urge to flee. "Thee—thee was describing thy—concept of God . . ."

"Ha!" the drunken woman sneered. "I would! Honey-bun, little love, don't mind my slobbering nonsense. I'm tired. I'm sozzled. I'm no preacher. I—I—" Suddenly she glared, a frightening, glazed look of anger or impatience; in any case, not the look of a motherly saint. "Himsha, sweetie," she cried, with tears in her voice, "go home and pray! Pray: 'Lord, have mercy on the sinner without whom I would be dead now! I and all those others!' All of them, all of you, owe your lives to two men, one a saint, the other a soul in hell. The saint can take care of himself, he's with God now, wherever that may be, but the other needs your prayer! The other, beyond forgiveness . . . soul in hell . . . my poor, poor Hei . . . Heizz . . . Huzz . . ." Without transition, the fat woman fell asleep.

Himsha looked at her for a long time, motionless, full of awe and pity. Then she got up, tiptoed to the bed, gently took the cigar out of the sleeping woman's hand, put it on the edge of the bedside table, turned off the light, tiptoed to the door and closed it softly behind her.

* * *

The next morning Dr. Wassermann set out, looking for Laura. He had discovered what hotel she was staying at and found she was not in; nobody knew where she had gone, but the town was not all that big. He was sure if he just walked down the board-walk he would come across her. He had been here less than twenty-four hours and already he had begun to recognize people.

After last night's performance, his opinion of the Quakers had improved considerably. They might look pedestrian and some-what woolly, they might despite their admirable works be one of the most closed and esoteric sects in the world; in the case of Laura Martens they had worked a miracle. He remembered her as she had been that last time he had seen her, on the eve of her wedding to that young Don Quixote Baker. There had been no doubt in his mind then that she was emotionally damaged for life and might well end up insane. The American boy marrying her had been the height of folly; he would end up either berserk or a saint, but castrated in both cases. There had been a vicious, de-structive streak in her which, he had been certain at the time, would increase in virulence once she escaped from the scene of her nightmare. The woman he had observed from the audience the night before had been a beacon of positive, creative power. And it had been the Quakers' doing.

Without doubt, Laura Martens was the only one among the ex-inmates of the concentration camps he knew who had man-aged to shed their curse and rise, not as a maddened pain-crazed Lucifer, but as a rough, tough angel of mercy. Despite his scien-tific detachment and the low opinion in which he held men in general, listening to her last night, observing her throwing her considerable weight around and yet radiating that creative pow-er, had made him feel good. In a sense, it made him feel better than he had felt in a long time. It even seemed as if, in her, there was hope for himself.

So he smiled broadly at all the Quakers, the way they smiled at him, although he didn't know a soul among them other than by sight. He felt buoyed up by their infectious kindness and their obvious enjoyment of the occasion. The boardwalk was crowded; on the beach groups of bathers sat clustered together in the shade of huge colored parasols, a gay and summery scene. Surely, Laura must be somewhere near, there simply was no other place she could be. Then he saw her.

She was lying on her back in a tiger-striped bathing suit, her voluminous limbs and bulging belly aggressively displayed. She was lying on a towel without the benefit of a parasol; he spotted her in the first place because she was alone. Groups of people surrounded her, chatting and laughing; it was as if she had drawn a circle of emptiness around her. Obviously, she was being avoided out of awe for her forbidding fame, intimidating authority and her desire to be left alone, unmistakably expressed by the way she lay there. Even he, surely the last person on earth to be intimidated by her, had to overcome a reluctance to disturb her privacy. He waded toward her motionless bulk through the soft sand, his unsuitable shoes filling at once, making him feel awkward and alien with his city suit, raincoat and Homburg hat. "Hello, Laura," he said manfully, braving the vacant stare of a pair of rhinestone-studded sunglasses. He realized that she did not recognize him; maybe because the sun was behind him. He took off his hat and said, "It's been a while since we last met. Just to refresh your memory: I am Alfred Wassermann, the doctor, fellow inmate of Schwalbenbach, the one with whom your father worked—for a while."

She removed her sunglasses. She did not move, she did not say a word, but his trained eye spotted the uncertainty that defused the tough, ice-blue stare which must have chilled many a bureaucrat trying to bar her way. Those eyes were unchanged; it was as if the real Laura Martens, the sleepwalking girl of Schwalbenbach, were still there, still asleep, hiding in that mountain of lard.

"Well, well," she said at last, unenthusiastically. "What are you doing nowadays?"

"I have a practice in New York as a psychiatrist. A rather specialized psychiatrist, it is true, but a psychiatrist all the same. Do you mind if I sit down?"

She obviously did, but he was beyond being intimidated now. He took off his raincoat, folded it and sat down on it by her side.

She smelled, rather unappetizingly, of sun-oil and perspiration. She was really an unappetizing female. He wondered how many people realized that it was a deliberate disguise.

"Well, what is your specialty?" she asked in a tone of resigned boredom.

"The post-concentration-camp syndrome."

She gazed at him for a moment, then she rose on an elbow, rummaged in her purse, which looked like an overweight mongrel dog, produced a cigar, and after she had bitten off the tip in a masculine manner and spat it out, obviously expected him to light it for her.

"Sorry, I don't have any matches," he said, observing her. "I don't smoke."

She rummaged some more in the shapeless bag, produced a Zippo lighter and lit the cigar with its aggressively large flame. She snapped the lighter shut, tossed it back into the bag, lay down again, bulbous and brazen, one arm under her head, puffed at the cigar and said, "That must be a prosperous practice; you look like you hit the jackpot."

"Indeed there are rather more ex-inmates around than one would have thought," he said pleasantly. "And most of them need help."

"And are you able to give it?" Her tone was scathing, but those eyes gave her away. Poor, troubled woman. There was no doubt now, the Laura Martens he had known was still there. As he looked down at her, smiling, he had the chilling notion that in a sense she was one of the most tragic cases he had come across. He wondered what it was, still lurking within her, what unspoken terror, what repressed horror from the lightless deep gave her that haunted, tortured look.

"Well?" she asked. "What is our common denominator, if we have one?"

"Guilt," he replied.

*   *   *

She gazed up at him unblinkingly, trying to look bored. "Guilt of what?" she asked, smoking. "Of having been raped in front of my father at the age of fifteen?"

"Of having escaped alive while others died," he replied. "Of the dark deed that assured our survival."

Her cheeks stiffened. "Deed? What deed? Or are you speaking for yourself?"

"I am speaking for all of us, without exception. We all have done something in order to survive, which cost the life of someone else. Or so we believe." He was completely relaxed, urbane, sure of himself.

She felt a sudden return of the reluctant awe in which she had held him in that other world, the world of Schwalbenbach. It seemed hauntingly real still, more real than the sunlit beach, the faint hiss of the surf, the famous doctor Laura Martens, savior of children. Suddenly it all seemed a fragile fancy: the power, the fame, the toughness, the disdainful negation of her femininity. With shocking vividness she recalled the girl she had been; she relived her, from within, as if that girl were still there and had now been flushed from the dark nook where she had been hiding. She wanted to fight back, shake this ridiculous feeling of exposure. "Speak for yourself, friend," she said in her gruffest voice. "I have no sense of guilt. Sorry. But you can't win 'em all."

"In that case," he replied, smiling, "you are the exception that confirms the rule." He looked away, at the sea. "I've heard about your admirable work, of course. I was there last night, in the audience. You are an inspiration to us all. I often mention you to my patients as an example."

"Example of what?"

"Of the possibility we have to shake the curse and turn it into a source of creative power. Rather than suffer it as a destructive paralysis which is the case, alas, with most of us."

To her alarm she felt her eyes fill with tears. The chill of them ran down her temples into her ears. It became her undoing. "Jesus Christ," she said hoarsely, not caring about the cry of pain that he would recognize instantly for what it was. "Why don't you fuck off and keep your bedside manner for your patients?" It was a pathetic effort to escape. If he was half as good as she thought he was, he must be on to her like a ferret.

He looked at her, his eyes full of the peace and the serenity of the sea. "I know," he said. "It's the very devil of a load to carry. All I can say is: you are doing it better than most. At least, you have something to show for your life."

"Oh screw it!" she cried, sticking her cigar in the sand. She put back her sunglasses, but that only brought him closer, a maddeningly understanding, objective observer. "Sometimes it still makes me sick, the memory of my father," she said, melodramatically, telling herself she was testing him.

"I can understand that. It was obvious at the time that this was something you would have to carry all your life."

"The trouble is of course that among all your patients, to which I gather I now belong, I am the one who carries a real guilt. If I had not followed him, driven by that insane desire to be with him, he might be alive today. And even if he weren't, he would not have died that way."

"You followed him out of love. Are you sure it isn't the love that gives you a feeling of guilt, rather than the fact that he died as a result of your intervention?"

He was even better at his job than she had thought him to be. "Of course, I know all that," she said, wearily. "You don't think I would have got this far in our profession without realizing I was in love with my father? But the trouble with you Freudians is that, like evangelical Christians, you believe that the truth will set you free. It doesn't, alas. Not in my case at least. I still carry that burden of having been the cause of his murder. For the way he died, his despair, the hatred that engulfed him, after he had tried to combat it all his life."

Even as she said it, she felt a reluctance. She was not normally a gushing woman; she could not remember ever having spilled the beans about her inner life to such an extent. But there he was, he knew what she was talking about; he was a professional psychiatrist, and she'd never see him again, so what the hell.

"This is what I meant when I said our common denominator is guilt. I can prove to you, rationally, that you cannot be held responsible for your father's death; but I'll never be able to convince you because by now your guilt is one of the basic components of your life. All I can possibly say is that, maybe, you are going at it too hard."

"Now what does that mean?"

"Look at myself. The guilt I carry is that I bought my life by extracting information from dying patients about their hidden assets, and passing on that information to Kroll. Fairly innocent, to the rational mind. But we are not dealing with the rational mind, we are dealing with the dark waters of the soul. And in that hidden world, from which all my power and my weakness spring, I still carry a sense of guilt. Nobody, no rabbi, no doctor, no sage, will ever be able to convince me that I am not guilty, least of all my own rational mind. So, all I can say to you is: carry your cross as comfortably as you can, without riling at it too much, and thank the Lord or your lucky stars or your sturdy nature or whatever you have to thank for it, that in your case the cross induced you to save the lives of thousands of children who otherwise would have died. Surely, that is a concept you can live with in some degree of comfort?"

"I did, until you turned up," she said unfairly.

"I'm sorry about that. I'll leave you now, if you wish."

He said it a little too glibly for her taste. But then, it had been a childish retort. You cannot unburden the secrets of your heart like a sixteen-year-old without being treated like one. "Tell me about yourself," she said. "What have you been up to all these years?"

He proceeded to tell her, in greater detail than she had bargained for. Then she told him about the work she was doing and tried to crush him with the nobility of her achievements.

But she knew that she did not impress him in the least, that all he saw in her pathetic effort to resurrect the image of the great doctor Martens was a little girl on a bicycle, still trying to flee from the nightmare of Camp Schwalbenbach. Even so it gave her a small satisfaction that, despite his uncanny insight, he obviously had not been able to identify the man she had really loved, and what her true guilt had been.

*   *   *

While the three of them were having dinner in a restaurant on the waterfront, Himsha suddenly said, "I've made up my mind. I want to study medicine."

"Medicine?" Gulie's eyes were heartbreaking to watch. Boniface himself was shocked by the child's decision, but it was Gulie who worried him at the moment.

"But—but I thought thee was going to continue in art?" Gulie said emotionally. "Thee has such a wonderful, creative talent! Thee has a gift from God to give to people!"

Poor Gulie; she would never realize that to protest against it was the surest way of confirming a child in a decision. She simply could not remember in moments like these that she was dealing with an adolescent, whose basic urge was to achieve independence from her parents.

"I know," Himsha said coldly, "but I changed my mind. I want to specialize in pediatrics and work among the underprivileged children of the Third World."

It sounded rehearsed.

Gulie's face hardened. "And what, pray, inspired this sudden turn around?" She sounded on edge and added, alas, "As if I didn't know!"

That settled it, of course. Boniface sighed. Maybe Gulie could help herself as little as the ravishing, rebellious girl confronting her.

Himsha glowered at her. "If thee knows, why does thee ask?"

"Because I do not believe thy decision to be valid if it's to emulate Laura Martens! Thee is not Laura Martens. Thee is a gifted, sensitive child, much too sensitive because of thy artistic talent to go in for the kind of gruesome work Laura Martens does. Look at her! Look at the size of her, the—the shape of her! Then look at thyself. Thee should shield and nurture thy God-given talent, and not be side-tracked by the glamour of a woman who is above all an indomitable battle-axe!"

It was lovely to see her so passionate, it always was. But she was not doing her case any good.

"If it weren't for that battle-axe," Himsha retorted, "I would not be alive."

"But thee *is* alive!" Gulie cried angrily. "Thee has received a gift from God to cherish, to develop! I might as well say that I should have studied medicine myself because I was saved by an appendectomy! Without the surgeon who performed that operation, I too would have been dead!"

"There is a difference, Mother, between having an appendectomy and being carried out of a pueblo full of rabid males bent on killing you. By a woman who in doing so risked her own life! At least that was a risk the surgeon who operated on thee did not run, I presume."

"Now, now, Himsha!" Boniface said, appeasingly. "Thee knows very well that thy mother is only thinking of thy own good."

"Why must she? Why may I not think of my own good? How does she know what is good for me?"

"Because I am thy mother!" Gulie cried.

"I am sorry to remind thee: thee is not. Thee is my mother as much or as little as Laura Martens is, who saved my life at the risk of her own."

"Himsha! Gulie—"

But Gulie had risen, her eyes suddenly full of tears. "I—I—"

"Gulie, please. . . !"

But she threw down her napkin and stalked out of the restaurant.

Boniface should have followed her. But there were all those people looking at them curiously, and there was Himsha, now looking pale and drawn, obviously sorry for both Gulie and herself. She needed him as much as Gulie did—more so right now.

"Thee shouldn't have said that, Himsha." He tried to soften the reprimand by putting his hand on hers. It felt fragile and slender, an artist's hand. Gulie was right, of course. The child had talent, but even if she hadn't, she certainly was not made to brave the horrors Laura Martens battled with the power and the perseverance of a tank.

"I am sorry," Himsha muttered. "But it's true! She isn't my mother! If she is, Laura is!"

"Now hush, hush. Thee knows that is not so, thee just knows it. Mom has nursed thee, looked after thee all thy life. Thee could never have wished for a more gentle, tender, loving mother. All Laura Martens did was carry thee out of the pueblo."

"Risking her own life in doing so!"

"Absolutely. But it was not thee she carried out, Himsha. It was a baby. A symbol."

"Of what?"

"Of her—well—I was going to say 'recovery,' but I think that's too clinical. Let's say: her discovery of what to do with her life."

"Her name was Laura Baker then, wasn't it?"

"Yes, it was."

"Why did thee divorce her?"

"I did not divorce her, she did not divorce me. We both decided that she should lead her own life and I should lead mine. Also, it had never been a real marriage in the accepted sense of the word. . ." The moment he had said it he was sorry. Why bring that up?

"Thee means it was never consummated?" She looked at him coolly, daring him.

"That's right."

"Then why did thee marry her in the first place?"

"I married her because, at the time, it was the only way in which she could acquire a visa for the United States."

"Why thee?"

"Because I happened to be the only U.S. citizen around."

"Well, I'm glad thee's not saying 'because all God had was me!' "

Despite his understanding of the plight of adolescence, he felt he was getting angry. "That's a little gratuitous, sweetie, even for thee in thy present mood."

"Sorry," she said, "but I'm getting sick of everybody dragging God into everything around here. They can't go to the bathroom without God willing it. Aunt Laura never talks about God willing anything, she just goes ahead and does it. I must say, I prefer that."

"That's okay," he said. "For that's Aunt Laura's way. But I don't think we should be too ready with our judgment of how people try to cope with the mystery that surrounds us. Each of us comes into this world alone, a unique, irreplaceable individual, never seen on earth before, never to be seen again. Thee too is an individual the like of which has never been before, and that brings with it an essential loneliness which ultimately we cannot break. Thee is in the difficult process of leaving the family and the parents that have nurtured thee ever since thee arrived in this world. I cannot guide thee as to what to do with thy life, not any longer. All I can do is hope that thee will mind the Light."

And then she said, "Oh Dad . . ." and suddenly bent her head and kissed his hand. He was flooded with an eerie awareness of the momentousness of this moment, as she sat there, her long black hair spread out on the table, kissing his hand with all those beady-eyed people covertly watching. It was as if something were being decided that would fundamentally change their lives. But there was no knowing what it could be.

* * *

Gulie did not know where to find Laura. She only realized that she was looking for her when she found herself on the boardwalk, gazing up and down the now-deserted beach, shading her eyes with her hand. This was where she had spotted the woman that morning, in a bulging bathing suit, talking to a man in a business suit sitting on his haunches. Of course she was no longer there, nobody was, everybody was having dinner.

Gulie set out for the hotel where the speakers stayed with grim determination. Never mind how famous and weighty Laura Martens was, she would face her down and call her to task. The gentle, sensitive, gifted child! She had all the artistic inventiveness and delicacy of her late father, Atu, even the art teacher at Kissing Tree High School, who was as academic as they came, had in the end admitted that Himsha had an exceptional talent. Her drawings of animals and desert flowers, her water colors of the Huni Valley and the Llano Estacado were true works of art, the kind of thing she herself would have loved to be able to do. Maybe that was why she was so furious with Laura Martens for turning the child's head.

She spotted Laura, alone at a table in a corner of the dining room, smoking a cigar over a cup of coffee, and her heart sank. The woman was such a blustering bully—what could she say to her? Well, whatever the words in which she would express her indignation, she should not dither now and lose steam. She should confront the intimidating woman while she still had the gumption to do so, not let herself slide back into the usual, pussy-footing Quaker identification with the adversary. She strode, with a show of purpose, to the corner where Laura Martens sat enthroned in splendid isolation with her preposterous cigar. The ham! Of course she smoked cigars only for effect, not because she liked the taste—only stogie-chewing rancheros did that.

"Good evening, Laura Martens."

The fat woman looked up stonily. At the sight of those cold, sky-blue eyes from close quarters, Gulie's courage faltered. But she persevered determinedly. "Mind if I sit down? I'd like a word with you." Without waiting for her majesty's permission, she pulled out the other chair from under the table and sat down.

Laura Martens said nothing. All she did was observe her with those ice-blue eyes, expressionlessly, through the smoke of her cigar. To her dismay, Gulie felt herself becoming intimidated by this contemptuous scrutiny; then it occurred to her that maybe Laura had not recognized her. The lobby last night had been dark. "I'm Gulielma Baker. Bonny's wife."

"Of course." Laura tipped the ashes of her cigar onto the saucer of her coffee cup. There was no ashtray on the table— Friends did not approve of the addiction to tobacco. "Care for coffee?"

"No, thank you."

Laura drew in a mouthful of smoke; Gulie could not help watching the process with reluctant fascination: the huge bosom expanding even more, the fleshy shoulders rising, then the bulging cheeks blowing out the smoke, theatrically, like a Wagnerian dragon. "You are wise. Americans drink too much coffee. Bad for the cardiovascular system."

Despite the patently stagy cigar business, Gulie took heart. Laura was trying to bully her already, before a serious word had been spoken, but it was all hollow bluster. It might work with government officials of backward nations, or intimidated Friends, it did not work in her case.

"Laura Martens," she said, "I hear from my daughter Himsha that she has decided to give up her career as an artist, for which she has been coached since the age of five, after a conversation with you last night. I think you have done her a disservice." It was lame, as accusations went, but at the last moment the Quaker understatement got the better of her.

Laura looked at her without expression. For a moment Gulie thought that she was not going to answer; then she said, "As far as I can recall, I tried to dissuade her."

"But it's since she talked with you that . . ." Gulie stopped, bewildered. "You mean, you didn't encourage her?"

"I sure didn't. The girl seems far too delicate for my kind of work."

"But—but I certainly agree!" Gulie exclaimed. "She's a very artistic child. I don't know whether you remember, her father was an artist too. I—I'm sorry, I honestly thought you had encouraged her!" She could not help it; she was incoherent with relief.

Musingly, Laura Martens drew on her cigar. Then she blew out the smoke again, this time not at the ceiling but at Gulie, and the heavy scent of the tobacco suddenly triggered a memory in her: old Juancho, lying wan and pale under his blanket after Hidalgo had kicked him. She had knelt by his side, terrified, and asked, 'Juancho, what can I do? What can I do for you?' His already bloodless lips opened and he whispered, 'Light it for me,' and his shaking hand went to his breast pocket, from which it took a half-smoked cigar. Revolted, yet driven by a desperate courage, she put the cigar in her mouth, lit a match on the seat of her Levis and sucked in the thick, heavy smoke. When it finally had taken fire, she held out the smoking stump to him, but as she did so, she saw that his eyes were glassy and his mouth had frozen, half open, in a vacant smile.

She looked at Laura. It was as if the memory opened another dimension behind her, the teeming world of the past of which this moment was the apex. Behind those cold blue eyes, the theatrical prop of the cigar, she suddenly discerned a multitude of children, all the suffering children in the world, to whom this odd, warped woman had ministered with the passion and the relentlessness of an obsessed soul. She saw her again as she had come down that trail, carrying the baby; she remembered the look those cold blue eyes had given her when she had asked where Bonny was. Now, here were those eyes again, looking at her with that same impersonal gaze. "I don't think anyone can tell your daughter what to do," Laura said, putting the cigar on the saucer. "Not if she is burdened by a concern, as the Friends put it. You may think her the most unlikely person to take on this particular concern, but there it is."

"Well, maybe we shouldn't take it too seriously," Gulie said, clutching at straws. "It may be just a fancy the child took, after listening to you last night."

"I took a similar fancy after listening to your grandmother. Somebody has to light the fire. And, once it's lit, it never says: it is enough."

"But—but she's so unsuited!" Gulie cried, in the face of all those children whose presence she sensed in the shadows behind Laura Martens. "She's so sensitive! She—she . . ." Miserably, she felt her eyes fill with tears. "I wish you would go on trying to dissuade her!" She realized too late that she was pleading, no longer battling.

"You don't mean that," Laura said calmly. "You know as well as I do that she should be allowed to decide what to do with her life without our interference. It's a pity that she won't live your life for you, vicariously, but not many daughters oblige their mothers that way." She blew out the smoke, at the ceiling this time. "What's more, I don't know that you actually need a vicarious life lived for you. Boniface and you must have a good marriage."

"What—what makes you think so?"

"You have the radiance of a well-laid woman."

Gulie felt the blood rush to her cheeks. She had never felt so embarrassed in her life, so outraged. She was about to say something unquakerly, when, for some reason, she was struck by the same sensation she had felt the night before as she watched Laura Martens on the platform: a sense of loneliness and desolation. Suddenly she was filled with compassion for the lonely woman, still dragging the burden of unspeakable horrors. She remembered how she had wondered long ago, before meeting her, how a girl her own age could have survived the gruesome cruelties Laura had endured. She had wondered what would become of someone like that. Now she saw the answer gaze at her through the smoke.

"Well—I think I'd better go," she said, pushing back her chair. "It was—it was nice talking to you, Laura. I'm sorry I rushed to conclusions about you and Himsha."

"Forget it," Laura said dryly.

"I—I—" She didn't know what she wanted to say, some reassurance, some words that would convey to the lonely woman the fact that she understood, an explanation, a wish. But all she could do was smile and make off, weaving her way past the tables where the Friends sat watching.

* * *

Laura watched the tall, slender figure as it hurried to the door and vanished in the lobby beyond. Hard to believe that this swan had emerged from the awkward duckling with the thick glasses—if ever there was a testimony to love, and contact lenses, it was Gulielma Baker. Of course, she should not have shied the poor soul away with her earthy remark, but the woman did radiate the kind of physical completeness that lovers share with nursing mothers and well-fed babies.

Puffing at her cigar, she reminisced, cautiously, about those mornings, those afternoons, those nights when she herself must have looked like that: sleek, somnolent, sensuous, every fiber of her body alive, in full bloom of womanhood. She remembered walking to the window, slowly, half asleep, her limbs heavy with the delicious languor of love, and then peeking through the frame of the glass curtains at the *Paradeplatz,* the motionless rows of inmates who had been standing at attention for hours, the Kapos prowling among them, waiting for someone to topple over with fatigue so they could beat and kick . . .

She rubbed her eyes. At the time, the young Laura in love had shown little emotion at the scene outside the window; only after the present Laura had come to life and learned to deal with it had the memory filled her with a cold horror, as if the monstrousness had been preserved in ice, to emerge as fresh as the day it happened. She had loved a man who had turned into a sadistic, cowardly swine, but, whatever he had done to others, he had turned her into a woman.

The emptiness of life without him suddenly seemed to be summed up by the dirty saucer with cigar ashes, the half-empty, unappetizing cup, the crumpled paper napkin, the lonely table in yet another impersonal hotel dining-room, surrounded by anxious people who did not dare approach her because of the legend, or because they did not want the image they had of her to be disturbed.

Now, come, come, she thought, lighting her cigar again, you are becoming maudlin. All it is is pure envy of Gulie Baker, who sat there crushing you with her triumphant womanhood, brandishing her bedded bliss, her *pluralis sexualis*. Well, Bonny finally had his hands full. She remembered, with unsentimental detachment, the boy she had deliberately tantalized into a frenzy and finally driven to the point that he had shrieked 'Whore!' and almost throttled her. All that because of the insane notion that thereby she would prove Heinzl to be a mere victim of circumstance, helpless hero, slowly battered to his knees, fighting to the bitter end. Poor Heinzl had—Oh, for God's sake! All she was doing was to argue the case for the defense, and not Heinzl's, but her own. The guilt she carried was not that she had been the innocent cause of her father's death. She had long since accepted that for what it was: the reckless act of a young, loving tomboy who idolized her father. No, her true guilt, the one that could not be forgotten nor argued away, was that—amnesia or no amnesia—she had writhed in sexual ecstasy while outside her very window prisoners were being tortured and beaten. She had cried out in rapture in the embrace of the man who every Wednesday had selected the week's batch for the extermination camp. She had loved those people's executioner with an abandon totally detached from morality, conscience, decency, faith. She was a child of violence, and the violence had left an indelible mark on her that no good works, no self-sacrifice, no dedication to the suffering children of the world could ever erase.

And now she lived out her days in the unutterable melancholy of widowhood. Heinzl was still there, sometimes almost physically, when she woke up weeping, her hand groping in emptiness, to have the dream-like reality of his flesh elude her, tauntingly. These last years, she had begun to feel a sense of kinship with her grandmother Stella, who had mourned her murdered husband for over forty years of lonely torment before she finally, mercifully, died. My God! If people only knew. . .

Sick of her own musings, she got up and ambled off, defiantly plump and graceless, daring the purse-mouthed Friends or their snotty children to accost her with some mealy-mouthed platitude. Well, what do you know: one of them barred her way, a bald-headed beanstalk with glasses. "Where next, Laura Martens?"

She was about to answer 'Wherever next man indulges in his favorite vice of infanticide,' but the fatuousness of it all overwhelmed her. "Wherever way opens," she said dutifully. "Excuse me," and, waving him aside with her cigar, she made off into the night, where the surf hissed in the silence and the stars stood, bleak and lonely, over the empty sea.

CHAPTER TWO

New York, Kennedy Airport/Biafra, Summer 1969

<hr>

"ATTENTION, all passengers," the loudspeaker bellowed, drowning the tired tinkling of the piano. "The departure of Pan American Flight Number 607 to Bogotá will be delayed one hour. I repeat . . ."

"Oh, dear," Boniface said worriedly. "I wonder what the trouble is. Well, maybe my plane will be delayed too. Shall we order another glass of wine?"

Himsha smiled mischievously in the candlelight. "Thee is going to be pickled, Dad," she said. "But all right. Let's live it up. Neither of us has to drive tonight."

He tried to catch the waitress' eye, not knowing what to call her. She was taking down the order of the table next to theirs and refused to look in their direction; when she moved away, he finally called, "Miss—er—Friend!"

The woman stopped in her tracks, as if he had whistled. "Sir?" Her face was wary.

"We'd each like another glass of this delicious wine," he said ingratiatingly. "It really is delicious. So was the meal."

"Glad you enjoyed it," the waitress said, obviously deciding that he was harmless. She picked up the empty glasses.

"Let's make it a carafe," Himsha said.

"Large or small, dearie?"

"Large, please."

"But, Himsha . . ." The woman had already made off. "Thee knows no moderation," he said. "If thy mother could see us . . ."

"Yes, why isn't she here? Thee was going to tell me."

"Joshua has the flu, and Carrie may have to be taken to the doctor because of her knee. The usual scrimmage. What's more, she thought it too expensive to come all the way from Kissing Tree. But thee knows she would have liked nothing better."

"Nonsense," Himsha said. "I know how she hates farewells. She never took me to the station either when I left for camp. Thee did."

"Well," he said appeasingly, "here we are again. Another summer camp, you might say. Does it frighten thee? I mean, is thee nervous?"

"No."

He should have known better than to ask. It was obvious that it did frighten her, to leave for her first assignment in the wilderness.

"Is she still angry, in her heart of hearts, that I gave up art to become a doctor?"

"No, no, for heaven's sake! She resigned herself to that years ago."

The waitress came with the carafe and put it between them. "Anything else?"

"No, thank you, Friend." He saw the woman give Himsha a quizzical look, then a shrill, commanding voice at the next table yelled, "Waitress!" It was a blue-haired, elderly woman, obviously in her cups, spinning an empty glass with an olive in it.

"Well, love," he said, pouring the wine, "here's to thy safe return." He raised his glass and she followed suit. The wine was cold and tart, he began to enjoy it. On the small dance floor a few middle-aged couples shuffled timidly to the tune of "Wagon Wheels" hammered out by the pianist. Himsha gazed at them, obviously miles away, already with the epidemic in those mountains. He gazed at her as she sat there dreaming in the candlelight. She was no longer a girl, but a lovely young woman. Memories crowded in on him: the pueblo, dancing with the squalling infant in his arms, while outside the drug-crazed Indians hooted and banged their drums, working up to the gruesome rite of human sacrifice. Then all those years that followed, the baby, the child, the adolescent, the college girl; and now here she sat, a young woman, poised, courageous, about to leave on her first assignment as a medical student with a Quaker mission among the Indians in the mountains of Colombia.

Slowly, he became aware of the piano playing in the background. It had been playing all the time, but only now did it catch his attention: the music was "The Tennessee Waltz."

Overcome by the momentousness of the occasion, the memories, the wine, he rose and, holding out his hand, said, "Come. Let's dance."

She looked up, puzzled.

"Doesn't thee recognize the tune?"

She frowned, listened, and said, "Ah, yes—of course." Then, obviously only to please old Dad, she put down her napkin, rose and walked ahead of him between the tables to the small dance floor, where they joined the other shuffling couples.

He took her in his arms, so slender, so fragile, and together they waltzed to the tune that meant so much to them; at one moment he could not help himself, he kissed her hair.

As he did so, a harsh, drunken female voice yelled, close by, "Ugh! Sick old lecher! Should be ashamed of yourself, dirty old man!"

Bewildered, he stood still, and saw that they were beside the table with three men and the blue-haired woman, the one who had waved the glass at the waitress. The embarrassed males at her table tried to hush her, but she was not to be hushed. She went on, "Yeah, I know! I know I'm not supposed to say that kind of thing! But it's time somebody said it! Just because we're at war in Vietnam doesn't mean that any old lecher can help himself to Asian girls!"

It was all so ridiculous that he could not help smiling. But the wine and Himsha in his arms and the wonderful fullness of the moment made him decide to approach the drunken woman after the manner of Friends.

"I can understand your concern," he said. "But I assure you that you are mistaken. Do you mind if we sit down with you for a moment? There is a story I would like to tell you . . ."

The woman muttered, "I bet there is!" But she was obviously taken aback.

"Come, Himsha," he said, "let's sit down and tell our friend what this particular tune means to us."

* * *

Oh, my God!

It was one of those moments when Himsha loathed her father

and all he stood for: the sentimental Quaker mollification that had anodized her all through her childhood. It was an aspect of Quakerism that had almost made her an agnostic.

Embarrassed beyond words, she felt like grabbing her purse and flight bag and fleeing to the gate of Pan Am flight 607 to Bogotá. He was totally without shame or even self-consciousness when it came to 'speaking to people's condition.' He wasn't even aware, as everyone else was, of the foul-mouthed old woman's condition; she was too drunk to sit upright, let alone absorb a Quaker sermon about that of God in "The Tennessee Waltz." But, oh, well, she might as well suffer through it, it was Dad's evening, after all, and he *was* on his way to South Vietnam; in his case, it wasn't all faith and no practice. The farewell was much more poignant to him than it was to her; in her mind, she was already in Colombia, sick with apprehension, suddenly convinced that the whole thing was a ghastly mistake.

While her father began to hold forth, with irritating unctuousness, about the meaning of "The Tennessee Waltz" in their lives, Himsha asked herself, despairingly, why she had not listened to her mother instead of to Laura Martens. Now it came to translating all that beautiful talk and all those romantic dreams into action, stark reality stared her in the face: she simply did not have what it took to see it through. She was too frail, too sensitive; already the children in the University Hospital had moved her to tears sometimes, what would happen once she was confronted with real suffering? Laura Martens had warned her long ago, it took an exceptionally tough kind of person to do her kind of work; what had given her the idea that she could even begin to emulate the formidable woman who, single-handed, was putting the true essence of Quakerism into practice? And there Dad went, yakking away, oozing over that awful drunken female as if he were a gypsy violinist. Himsha sighed; there was nothing she could do about it once he had the evangelical bit between his teeth. This time, it might also be that he had drunk more wine than he could handle, and that was her fault. So with a feeling of contrition she listened again to the whole story of the pueblo and "The Tennessee Waltz," and how she was now off as part of a medical mission among Indian children in Colombia, where there was an epidemic, and how he was on his way to visit Dr. Laura Martens, the woman who had carried her out of the pueblo, now working in Biafra among the child victims of the Nigerian civil war, after which he would continue on to South Vietnam.

It was embarrassing, but after a while she could not help being touched. Despite his incurable sentimentality, she loved him dearly. He looked like nothing on earth; he was fat, bumbling, an uncomplicated calf of a man, and yet, as he sat there telling their story, she realized that she was listening to the sum total of three hundred years of the Society of Friends. For better or for worse, he embodied the Quaker faith, the way Laura Martens embodied the practice.

The woman, of course, was captivated by the story, but she was also drunk and tears ran down her face as she listened, shaking her head, rolling her eyes, sucking her glass several times although it was empty. When the story ended, she blubbered, incoherent with apologetic fervor, "Oh, dear, dear baby, I'm so sorry! I didn't know, by God I didn't know! I just thought he . . . Oh, God . . ." She put a dry, claw-like hand on Himsha's, who had to keep a tight hold on herself not to yank it away. "Where exactly are you going, dearie? What's the address?"

"Oh, I don't know . . ."

"I know," Father said, of course. "I'll give it to you. Here, I'll write it down."

"Listen, honey, I've got orchards in California, let me send you some canned fruit for those poor Indian babies! It's the least I can do, honey. It's the least. God bless you, honey. God bless you, sir. God bless you all, goddammit, God bless everybody . . ." She broke into sobs, and dropped her head on her arms on the table. Within seconds, she was snoring.

Himsha rose, but Father carefully wrote down the address and put it beside the woman's hand before he followed suit. His arm around her shoulders, he took her back to their table, radiating the peculiar *bonhomie* that elderly Friends defined as 'being in the power of the spirit of love' but which she suspected, tonight at least, to be the result of the wine. "Well, sweetie," he said, "wasn't that a strange moment of guidance?"

"Yes," she said. "Very strange."

That was the moment the waitress saw fit to present him with the bill. He put on his glasses, his eyebrows rose, and his ministry was silenced.

*   *   *

"No, no—it's right here, just around ze corner . . ." Despite the thick Scandinavian accent, the disembodied voice sounded shrill with nerves; Laura thought she heard his teeth chatter in the darkness.

The Biafran night was pitch black; over the strained whine of the truck's engine she could hear the massive chirping of the crickets disturbing the African night with their restless racket. Suddenly the driver turned on his headlights; the very moment he did so, dark figures jumped out of the thicket brandishing rifles. "Turn off your lights, mother-fucker!" they yelled. "Turn off your goddam lights or I'll shoot your balls off!"

Well, well, the voice of 'progress, peace and patriotism,' as, this time, the slogan went. The driver yelled back something patriotic, she could not make out what; the lights were switched off and the truck pitched and wallowed on in the darkness, down the bumpy track.

"Zey are right, of course," Dr. Einarsson muttered apologetically. "Ze moment ze plane sees a light, zey bomb it . . ."

"Sure," she said. The man's nervousness was so obvious that a soothing sound seemed to be indicated. She herself felt no fear, no tension, nothing at all, just a bone weariness which was old hat and a tearful melancholy which was new. She must be more tired than she had realized, for ever since she had set foot in this tragic, blood-soaked corner of the forest she had been overcome by melancholy. Yet it was no worse than the other places of sacrificial slaughter she had visited over the years—the same sense of futility and mindless cruelty, the same sickness, famine and drumhead executions, the same slogans, the same raucous voices yelling obscenities in the night. It was only from a distance of a hundred miles behind the front that words like 'freedom' and 'independence' began to achieve a semblance of meaning. Here, where the ancient lunacy of war raged in full virulence, there were just the blood, the violence, and the dying children, wide-eyed, pot-bellied, and in some cases blond with kwashiorkor, the terminal stage of malnutrition. The blond African children were doomed, as were, probably, the soldiers of freedom roaming the forest with U.S. guns or Soviet guns, or English, or French, or Belgian guns, crying, "Mother-fuckers!" before firing at headlights, or low-flying planes, or just shadows haunting the night. She had seen and experienced it all a hundred times—why should it, this time, affect her as if it were the first? This was no worse than Indonesia during the Dutch police action, Indochina during the Vietminh war, the massacre of the Congo, the torture chambers of Algeria. Why should she, now, feel overcome by this paralyzing melancholia? Must be something she had eaten. That infernal stockfish, probably. It always made her feel nauseated, despite its splendid protein content. Or maybe it had been the sickening dip with which they had landed on that airstrip. Or maybe she was just getting too old for this.

"Here it is, ze hospital," Dr. Einarsson said, with a sigh of relief.

The darkness had become translucent, indicating that they had entered a clearing. The truck slowed down, the driver yelled something, she could hear the sound of an iron gate screeching open. The truck started up again and finally drew to a halt in front of the ghost of a low white building, seemingly roofless in the night. There was not a light to be seen, legless ghosts roamed the darkness, one of them said with a pleasant female voice, "Oh, hello, I thought you'd never come. Have you got the stockfish with you?"

"Yes, and the fat lady," the driver said, as if she were part of the menu.

"Zat will do!" Dr. Einarsson cried, with a hollow show of authority. He could not have been here long, or he would have realized that the African always called things by their proper names. She *was* a fat lady, that way at least the legless ghosts in the darkness could visualize what was now crawling out of the truck. "Hello there," Laura said, addressing the ghosts. "I'm Dr. Laura Martens. I've come to collect the children."

"Ha, die Dokter!" It was the same jolly voice, now greeting her in ebullient Dutch. "Do you remember me? I am Nurse Hardveld, we met in Ramallah, Palestine. Remember?"

"Of course," Laura said, groping in the darkness for the hand she knew was held out toward her. "How are you, Nurse Hardveld?"

"Oh, jolly good, Doctor, jolly good. It's a nice hospital here, you know, really not bad. But wait a minute, let me introduce you to the other nurses. We're all Dutch, we all work for *Terre des Hommes.* Girls, this is the famous Dr. Martens."

There was a polite mutter in the darkness, and Laura was presented to four legless, headless shapes, each with a moist hand.

The heat was oppressive; now the truck engine had fallen silent, the crickets in the forest were deafening.

"This way, Doctor," the jolly voice said. Wearily, overcome by another wave of melancholia, Laura trudged behind the voluminous ghost, who, now that her eyes were getting used to the darkness, was developing a pair of sturdy legs and a head with a nurse's cap at a rakish Italian policeman's angle. When they entered the hall of the hospital and Laura could discern the woman's features in the light of a candle lantern on the wall, she did indeed remember her: one of those immensely capable, remorselessly cheerful nurses who seemed to thrive on emergencies that would drive anyone with normal sensibilities to desperation. As she was shown around the hospital, Laura noticed in Nurse Hardveld's enthusiastic, jolly comments the familiar symptoms of the disaster syndrome: all modern nursing standards abandoned, all improvisation demonstrated with pride, as if coconut shells were preferable to sterilized bottles for giving formula to starving infants. It had been the same in Palestine, India, Algeria, the Congo, Indonesia—emergency situations in which the practice of medicine was thrown back a hundred years, and out of the woodwork came these incredible nurses, radiant with confidence, indefatigable, cheerfully hailing their desperate improvisations as triumphs of common sense and ingenuity, which indeed they were. The only trouble was that, once the proper instruments arrived and the proper procedures were re-established, these same nurses would wilt and pout and ultimately pack up, muttering about 'bureaucrats' and 'computerized nursing.' They reminded her of those peculiar pine cones in the American Northwest, that die barren under normal circumstances and sprout only after a forest fire.

"Of course," Nurse Hardveld said cheerfully, as she marched ahead of her down a shadowy corridor toward the wards, "we've had to improvise. These buildings really were a school, you know, which was evacuated because it wasn't camouflaged, so the Nigerians went on bombing it. We've turned the classrooms into wards, and we have camouflaged the whole of the compound. Covered the roof with palm fronds, that kind of thing. We also had to fence in the whole shebang, for we are a nutrition hospital in the first place. We are well stocked with food and we had raids on our stores almost every night until we turned the place into a fortress. We still are bothered by theft, of course; we have Biafran personnel, who always try to smuggle out food for their families, or pieces of soap, or diapers. Diapers they wrap around their waists, you know, so I've had to appoint one woman guard who frisks them at the end of every shift. And if something is found, they're fired. I know it is harsh, but it's the only way. There are hundreds of people who want to work for us, so . . . Here you go, this is Ward A. The moderate cases." She threw open a door, and Laura entered the dimly lit room. At once, she was struck by the familiar smell of disease, neglect and death. She had smelled it a hundred times before, but this time it hit her as if it were the first. Inexplicably, she felt her eyes fill with tears. What in the name of God was the matter with her?

"Mind if I smoke?" she asked roughly.

"By all means, Doctor," Nurse Hardveld said, beaming. When Laura lit a cigar and blew out the first smoke, the woman gushed, "Oh, now I *know* it's you! I was waiting for this!"

"Fancy that," Laura said dourly. Then, her cigar clamped between her teeth, she walked with sturdy speed past row upon row of pathetic little faces, emaciated bodies, bloated bellies, lying two and three to a cot, with underneath, on mattresses, another layer of misery and suffering and haunting black eyes gazing at her in mute incomprehension.

"Normally we have something like two hundred and fifty beds in this place," the head nurse continued cheerfully, "but, as you can see, we are so overcrowded that we had to double and triple the occupancy and even start putting them underneath the beds. We can't turn them away, can we now? What's more, these children are used to this, you know. African families . . ." And there she went, displaying the dismal symptoms of the disaster syndrome with breezy gusto. As front-line hospitals went, this was not one of the worst, but the fact that it contained nothing but children made it a haunting disgrace. By the time they had visited Ward C, the terminal cases, hundreds of blond little Negroes with matchstick limbs and bulbous bellies and old, old faces with the saddest eyes of all mankind, Laura felt she could stand no more. She was about to turn on her heel and march out, brandishing her cigar, impersonating the legendary, belligerent Dr. Martens, when there were shouts and shrieks in the courtyard, and the sound of shots. A young nurse came running, eyes wide with fear, shouting, "Deserters! Deserters! They're raiding the stores!"

"Well, *godsalmebeware!*" Nurse Hardveld cried, hitching up her girdle under her nurse's smock. "I'll teach them!"

"No, no, I don't want you to go! I absolutely *forbid* you to go!" It was Dr. Einarsson, whom Laura had forgotten, and who now stood, arms outstretched like a scarecrow, barring the woman's way.

"While you two fight this out between yourselves," Laura said, brushing the delicate man aside, "I'll have a word with those critters." Neither of them realized that it was a flight; they followed her, protesting halfheartedly, as she strode down the corridor, puffing at her cigar, and took down a lantern from the wall in the lobby.

"No lights, no lights are allowed outside . . ." Dr. Einarsson's voice was feminine with nerves.

"Like hell," Laura muttered, playing her classic role for all it was worth. Then she strode to the door, ripped it open and emerged in the warm miasma of the tropical night, as blind as a bat. She heard shufflings and whispers all around her, and beyond that the deafening swirl of the crickets. "Stop that!" she bellowed into the night. "Stop that, and get the hell out of here!"

The shuffling stopped; from somewhere came a stifled cry; then, with heart-stopping suddenness, the muzzle of a gun was poked at her stomach and a sweaty, pop-eyed black face emerged in the lantern light; the eyes were bloodshot and crazed with the lunacy of war. "Shut up, fat whore!" he screamed. There it was again, Harlem's gift to the world, the *patois* that had become the language of revolution in the Third World.

"Calm down, baby," she said, puffing at her cigar, noticing the bewilderment on the poor boy's face. "Don't yell at me, man. Get your arse out of here before it's too late. Those motherfuckers stopped us on the road just a few minutes ago. If they catch you here, they'll shoot your balls off, as you damn well know." Well, there it was: the approach to conflict after the manner of Friends, St. Laura's version.

The crazed, bloodshot eyes blinked; she became conscious of the utter exhaustion of the poor boy, facing her with his little gift from the Western world. It was an M6 rifle, this time bestowed by the United States.

"Where was that?" he asked hoarsely.

"Hell, I don't know, just a few minutes away from here. So call your little friends and scram, there's a nice boy."

"Listen, you fat—" She recognized the tears in his voice. From her breast pocket she took a cigar and stuck it in his mouth.

"There," she said gruffly. "Now get the hell out of here. Goodbye." Without waiting for his reaction, she turned on her heel and marched back to the door of the hospital and the small cluster of intimidated spectators in white smocks. She did not look around, for she knew what would happen. And it did. There was a sharp whistle, a call, a secretive shuffle, the sound of running feet; before she reached the door, she heard the gate screech shut behind her. Thank God for that.

"Well," she said, as she pushed Dr. Einarsson aside with the fist holding the cigar, "that's that. Now, where are those children I'm supposed to collect?"

To her alarm, two huge arms were thrown around her neck, a wet kiss was placed on her cheek. *"Godverju,* Dr. Martens!" the ebullient Nurse Hardveld exclaimed enthusiastically. "You are terrific!"

The other nurses laughed nervously, the tittering laugh of relief. "Well, Dr. Einarsson?" Laura said malevolently.

"I didn't realize . . . I would have gone—I mean, I was about to go out there," the poor man said, making things worse.

"I know, I know," she replied appeasingly. "I meant, 'How about a kiss for the conquering heroine?' " The nurses tittered, and she swung around. "Now, where the hell are those children?"

"In the orphanage," Nurse Hardveld replied.

"And where is that?"

"Down the road. Maybe ten minutes away. Would you like to go there now?"

"If you don't mind."

"All right, Sisters," Nurse Hardveld said, using the bizarre English term for registered nurses. "Back to your wards. I'll take Dr. Martens down the road, I'll be right back."

"You cannot go alone," Dr. Einarsson protested, in a vain effort to recoup some of his male prestige.

"Don't you worry, Doc," Nurse Hardveld said, with degrading condescension. "I won't be long. All right, Dr. Martens, this way please."

Laura wondered whether she should do something about the Swede, who stood gazing at them as if in shock. But let each man handle his moment of truth with his own resources. In Stockholm, or wherever he came from, he probably was an excellent pediatrician, with a lot of empathy for his patients. In order to cope with man's inhumanity to man on this vast scale, you had, alas, to be a bit of a bastard.

When they crossed the courtyard, the sky above the forest had turned blue and the first faint glow of daybreak brooded beyond the wall of trees. The chirping of the crickets seemed to be subsiding, and somewhere nearby the first birds of dawning began to take over the wilderness from the cicadas of the night. There was no sign of the thieves, they had been swallowed up by the forest.

"Doctor," Nurse Hardveld said, as they walked briskly toward the red streak of the dawn over the forest, "there's something we need your professional advice on."

"Oh? What's that?"

"It's a problem we've been having for some time, and neither Dr. Einarsson nor we know the answer. But you've probably come across it before. We've an awful lot of tetanus here, and they do bring their children for the first injection, but when they see what we do to them, they refuse to come back for their boosters. We've tried everything: little mirrors, beads . . ."

"That went out with Stanley and Livingstone."

"Then what do we do to make them come back for their follow-up?"

"What would be a lot of money to them?"

"Well—I don't know. A pound is an awful lot. You think we should pay them?"

"No. Make them pay you a pound for the first shot."

"Doctor!"

"They will come for their first shot, won't they, even if they have to pay?"

"I—I suppose so. But one pound!"

"Give them half the money back for the second shot, and the other half for the third."

Nurse Hardveld walked in silence for a few moments, then she said, *"Godverju,* Doctor, you are really something else! Terrific! Doc Einarsson will be behind himself with joy!"

"I wouldn't bet on it," she said dourly. "But it'll work. It worked in New Guinea, in the case of frambesia. You know: three shots of Salvarsan, intravenously. Hurt like hell. But they came. Boy, did they ever come!"

As she tramped along, cigar between her teeth, she remembered that other forest, those other Stone Age people forced into the twentieth century at gunpoint.

"Must have been fascinating work, Doctor—New Guinea," Nurse Hardveld said politely.

"Sure. What I remember best is my first Papuan chieftain. On a mobilette, with bifocals and a penis sheath." So much for homesickness and loneliness in those forests of hell. Then, as now, somebody had insisted on liberating somebody else; the result had been one thousand nine hundred children, by the last count, killed, maimed or orphaned.

Day broke brusquely; by the time they reached the orphanage, they could see where they were going without the aid of the lantern. And by that time Laura had lost the brief elation of action; she was again overcome by that odd melancholy, that feminine sensation, almost forgotten, of feeling tears warm in her eyes, the growing compulsion to break down and bawl about nothing, everything: the endlessness of suffering, the ultimate loneliness of each child that had, over her long and weary lifetime, gazed at her with the mute incomprehension of those children underneath those beds.

"Well," Nurse Hardveld cried, with a cheerleader's early-morning briskness, "here we are!" She pushed open the door of another of those low white buildings with a camouflaged corrugated iron roof and SCHOOL written all over it. As she did so, she uncovered a cacophony inside, the crying of a multitude of little voices, each one of them a wail of hopelessness.

"For God's sake," Laura muttered, overcome once more by the impulse to turn and run.

"Oh, don't mind *them,*" Nurse Hardveld cried, "it's breakfast time, you know."

"Fancy that," Laura said, her gruffness more directed at herself than at the pathetic, war-numbed woman.

A black nurse came to meet them, what she said was inaudible because she left the inside door open and the yelling and screaming drowned all other sounds.

Nurse Hardveld brought her mouth close to Laura's ear and shouted, "She has them sorted out! They're all in there! All yours!"

Laura lifted a hand in acknowledgment, stuck her cigar between her teeth, chomped down on it and strode toward the din.

The moment she entered the long, low room, the screaming

subsided somewhat. As in the case of the pilferer, her mere ap-
pearance penetrated the anesthesia of shellshock. She was aware
that she must present a menacing and intimidating spectacle as
she stood there in the doorway, broad-shouldered, big-breasted,
huge-hipped, an elephantine apparition in her unsuitable pants
suit, blowing smoke from her nostrils. And then, out of the dim
confusion, a tiny figure came scurrying toward her, a naked
black toddler, bawling his little head off, stretching out his thin,
emaciated arms toward her in a bewildering gesture of recogni-
tion.

"Well, well, who have we here?" she grunted, then she shifted
her cigar to the other side of her mouth, bent over and picked up
the tiny creature, which turned out to be much too light even for
its size, and delicate as a bird. "Well now, well now," she grum-
bled in her deep voice, "what is all this about? What is this nonsense?" She pressed the crying child against her breast and her
pocket with the cigars. The child threw its arms around her neck
and clamped down with such force that she knew she'd have a
devil of a time dislodging it.

But she didn't want to, not straightaway. For the trembling
little body, the wobbly head resting on her shoulder gave her
that old feeling of purpose, power, joy. 'Well, here we go again,'
she thought, trying to fool God with her gruffness as, like sunrise
dispelling the dark night of the soul, He manifested His presence
once more.

* * *

"The airport is a strip of road in the wilderness," the pilot
shouted. "You'll be able to see it in a minute, over on your side!"

Boniface peered out of the little window, but all he could discern below was virgin forest, stretching from horizon to horizon,
each giant tree no more than a whorl in an ocean of whorls. The
stench of the cargo of stockfish was stifling in the heat; the shirts
of pilot and navigator were blotched with perspiration. The tension in the air had increased notably; obviously, they were in
danger of enemy attack now.

He peered nervously at the darkening sky, looking for the
black, deadly spot of an attacking plane. But all he could see was
one solitary hesitant star in the blue emptiness. The pilot and the
navigator, the only crew of the cargo plane in which he was the

only passenger, were scanning the sky too, and their evident apprehension was such that Boniface felt it in the pit of his stomach. What kind of men were those, to have volunteered for this highly dangerous duty of ferrying medical supplies, milk powder and stockfish to the beleaguered, enemy-encircled sliver of forest, all that remained of Biafra? They were both Scandinavians; they struck him as adventurers rather than humanitarians, but that was a self-righteous assumption.

"We'll have to circle awhile out of range of their ack-ack!" the pilot yelled. "Still too much daylight!"

Boniface nodded and leaned back in his seat, feeling slightly sick. He had not slept since he had left New York, thirty-six hours before. The airport terminal in Libreville, Gabon, had been much too noisy and the benches too sticky with heat to sleep on. Now, as the plane began the first of what would probably be many slow, wide circles, he was, in spite of his apprehension, overcome with drowsiness.

He must have dozed off, for when he came to with a start, it was dark. The plane's engines, which had been droning monotonously, suddenly sharpened in pitch, the plane dived down at an alarmingly steep angle; its searchlights flashed on, lit up for a few seconds a narrow landing-strip surrounded by trees, then the lights were switched off again and they soared down in total darkness in what seemed a reckless, desperate plunge. Boniface gripped the arms of his seat with apprehension; then the wheels hit with a bone-jarring jolt and the machine, yawing and wobbling, came to a messy stop.

"Whew!" the pilot said in the darkness. "Lucky again. Okay, Mister—end of the line."

The door flew open and a black shadow appeared in the gap of lighter darkness, the upper half of a man, "Out!" a voice urged hoarsely. "They're overhead! Out, out!"

"Okay, okay," the laconic pilot said. "Give me a chance to unstrap this kite from my ass."

Boniface unhooked his own belt and discovered his hands were shaking. Somewhere overhead sounded the steady drone of a plane.

"What's the EB load going to be this time?" the navigator asked.

"Sixty children East-Bound," the half-body replied. "And one fat escort."

That must be Laura, Boniface decided; then, suddenly, the night outside changed into white, glaring day in which the trees of the forest and a row of trucks stood out sharply.

"Jesus Christ!" the African in the doorway cried. "Get the hell out! They're throwing flares!"

Someone pushed Boniface roughly out of the door, he missed a step, fell, and sprawled on the ground, which smelled like the reptile pavilion in the Philadelphia Zoo.

He was yanked to his feet and carried more than pushed toward a low, earth-covered air-raid shelter at the edge of the forest. As he stooped inside, breathless with fear and exertion, all hell broke loose behind him. The crashing thuds of explosions, the rattle of machine-gun fire, the staccato barking of cannon nearby. Then, in the semi-darkness of the flare's eerie light which seemed peopled with motionless bodies, a child began to cry and a familiar voice drawled, "Well, well, look who's here!"

So she was here too. And ready to slit her own throat rather than show she was as scared as he was. He had asked Operations in Gabon to announce his arrival by radio; the disembodied voice, mocking him in the darkness, evoked the Laura he had known, not the famous humanitarian of whom he secretly stood in awe. "Don't tell me you didn't get my telegram," he said, shivering with a sudden chill as bombs exploded in the forest all around them, their dull thuds setting the earth aquiver. The crying child seemed to infect others with its fear; on all sides, high, tremulous voices began to whimper and wail.

"As a matter of fact, I did," Laura's laconic voice replied in the darkness. "What's all this about an urgent message?"

Heart pounding, he explained that Meeting for Sufferings had delegated him to approach her about a new and exciting project. They were planning a program of medical missions all over Latin America, and they wanted her to be the head of it. They had already started with a pilot project in Colombia, where a small expedition was working among the Indians right now. "As I was the only menber of the Steering Committee who knew you personally, they felt that I should—should—" But the bombs were crashing closer, spraying the shelter with a hail of debris, and the vicious rattling of a machine gun nearby drowned out his voice.

"Hush, babies, hush!" Laura shouted to the crying children. Suddenly a flame sprang to life and her face floated, round and old, in the darkness as she lit her cigar.

"Turn out the light, turn out the light!" a hysterical voice yelled from a corner.

"Take it easy, baby," Laura said, between puffs. "Don't yell, just let yourself go. We all do. I've got plenty of diapers." The cigarette lighter snapped shut; the darkness that fell seemed deeper than before. Boniface was overcome by a sense of hopelessness, a feeling of apocalypse, as if here in the virgin forest, thousands of miles from home, some fire had been started that would ultimately consume their world. He was obviously exhausted and jittery.

"Now let me see if I've got this right," Laura's voice said calmly. "You've risked your life getting into Biafra, just to bring me a proposal that could have been taken care of by letter? There must be a double bottom to this."

"There isn't, Laura. It's just that Meeting for Sufferings wanted to make sure you didn't take on another assignment before you'd heard of this one."

"Bullshit," she said.

Outside, the thudding bursts of the bombs had ceased, the machine gun had fallen silent; from somewhere in the forest came the sound of voices. The wailing of the children quieted to a whimper.

He sighed. "All right," he said. "I offered to come and see you myself because—well, because Himsha has just left for Colombia. She's only in her second year in medical school; this is her first assignment. She's young and inexperienced and very delicate; we—I am terribly worried about her, in that epidemic in the jungle. She—well, if you were to agree to head the program, you might go and have a look at the pilot project and maybe— well, that's what I hoped you might want to do, go and see . . ."

"You and your wife aren't bankrolling that new program, by any chance?" she asked. She was the most uncomfortable person to deal with. He began to feel sorry that he had gone to all these lengths. "We are on the board of—of a trust," he said.

"Don't tell me it's the Gulielma Woodhouse Trust, the one *Doña* Ana nearly pulled from under the Quakers?"

"It is," he replied wearily.

"And I know Meeting for Sufferings, stingiest lot I ever came across. They aren't likely to send anyone on a junket into the African boondocks if they could settle for a postage stamp. So you paid for this trip yourself, didn't you?"

"No, not entirely."

"What does that mean: not entirely?"

He smiled. It was her old game. This was how she must browbeat pompous officials and stuffy bureaucrats; she was a tremendous powerhouse; lucky that the power was used to a good end.

"This is just a short detour on my way to South Vietnam," he replied.

"What on earth are you up to there?"

"If you must know, a number of Friends back home have decided to adopt Vietnamese-American abandoned children who have no future, some are living in the streets like beggars. I am on my way to collect sixteen of them and escort them back to the U.S."

"You haven't adopted a Vietnamese kid yet?"

"We may."

"Well, well," she said mischievously, "you're going at it with a collector's zest." In the darkness, the red glow of her cigar brightened and dimmed. Then she asked, "By the way, does the girl know about all this?"

"What?"

"Your financing her first assignment and haring off into a jungle war because you are worried about her?"

"No, of course not!"

"Well, that's something," she said. "She'd never look at the two of you again. I'd cool it, if I were you. She's a big girl now. Toss her into the hot water and stand back. That's how it works. Let it work, and get your parental nose out of the pot."

"You—you will accept?"

She chuckled. "Wouldn't it be something if I said no? And do you know what? That's exactly what I do say." She looked around. "Well, the worst seems to be over."

The entrance to the shelter was blacked out as someone peered inside. "Okay!" a jolly voice shouted. "All clear! You can come out now! Come out!"

In the corner someone stirred; a dark shape stumbled past, retching, stooped and vanished in the night. Boniface himself felt sick, sicker than in the plane when the fear had first struck him. He had better get used to this; Vietnam must be much the same.

"Thanks," Laura's voice said calmly, "but I don't think I'll go out yet. The kids have settled down, they might as well stay here until it's time to board the plane." Then she said to Boniface, "Let me light the lantern, so I can have a look at you."

Again the lighter sprang to life, she held it out to him.

"Here, hold this. I'll hand you the lantern. I've only got one hand at the moment."

He obeyed, lit the candle inside the lantern she gave him; as the flame grew and steadied, he saw her sitting against the wall, surrounded by sleeping children. They seemed to fill the entire shelter; she held one of them to her breast, its head on her shoulder. The child had thrown its arms around her neck, and seemed to hang on to her with all its might, even in sleep.

There was something harrowing about the spectacle of the big, flaccid body, the double chin, the sagging flesh, the messy, untidy hair stacked on top of her head. He felt compelled to say, "You look fine, Laura."

The cold blue eyes surveyed him mockingly. "You were always gallant, Bonny," she said, smiling. "You don't look too bad yourself."

She couldn't have been serious when she said no, just like that. She was teasing him again, one of her morbid jokes. He wanted to reason with her, but the nausea wouldn't subside; he might have to rush outside soon, like that other guy. The children were quiet now, they must be exhausted too. "Who's that you're carrying?" he asked.

"Oh, just some little brat who jumped me when I came to collect this bunch," she said. "He's been hanging on to me ever since, like a monkey to its mother. I'll get rid of him in Libreville. What was the ride like?"

"Hair-raising."

She chuckled. "And all that because you worried about your daughter? You're an oddball, man." She sucked on her cigar, blew the smoke at him and grinned. Except for that child in her arms, she looked dissipated, bloated with self-indulgence. But he was too old, they both were, to go on playing that game. "You are a fine one to talk," he said. "Who did the same thing, long ago, taking out after her father on a bicycle because she was worried about him?" Then he saw her eyes. "That—that's what love is all about," he added gently. So it was still a sensitive area, even after all these years. What a cross she carried underneath all the coarseness, the tough façade! He put his hand on her arm. "It hasn't been for nothing, Laura. You had to go through an awfully dark valley, but now, you know—now you exude the Light."

She peered at him through the smoke, scowling. Then, shaking off his hand, she ground out the cigar in the dirt by the lantern, and said, "You're an incurable romantic, Bonny. You're just dazzled by this poor little critter I'm holding. Take him away, and what's left?"

"Yes, Laura," he said, "that's exactly what I mean."

* * *

Well, he certainly still knew how to turn on the schmaltz! But she was unable to shake the spell he had thrown over her. There he sat, a fat man in a seersucker suit, as preposterous in this air-raid shelter as she must have looked with her faked pregnancy on that bicycle. She remembered the customs officers who had stopped her at the border, her fall into the brambles, the woman who had questioned her, how they had washed their hands of her and let her bicycle on to her fate, which they must have guessed, if not foreseen. Things would have been very different if they had had the guts to stop her, lock her up, anything to keep her from pedaling right into the arms of *Obersturmführer* Kroll. If Bonny, then a mere boy, had stopped her at the border, he wouldn't have washed his hands of her. Here he sat, the medic, once more on an errand like the one to which she owed her life. That girl needed Aunt Laura breathing down her neck like she needed a lion with halitosis. But it wasn't the girl that counted, it was he. The sentimental, reckless ass! Those Quakers, if they were the genuine article, were truly fools of God.

Out of the blue, she was overcome by a surge of idiotic envy. He didn't know how fortunate he was to be able to sit there, radiating goodness, without the suspicion that all his goodness amounted to was a futile effort at atonement. What would she give for one moment of his guiltless, honest love! No wonder the Huni baby had worked out well. It was not she who had saved it, but those doting parents. Owing to that caprice of fortune, the squalling child she had carried out of the pueblo was now on her way to becoming a second Mother Theresa, instead of a second Lizzie Borden.

When a voice called, "Plane's ready, all aboard!" she rose; so did he. "Okay," she said, "Latin America it is. Tell Ethan Woodhouse I'll be over, the moment I've taken this lot to Libreville and, if there's no escort there, on to Geneva."

"That's wonderful," he said. "We'll talk about it on the plane."

But this was too good a chance to miss. "No," she said, "we will not. I'll take the assignment on one condition: that you go and visit the children's hospital here and give it a hefty donation. There'll be a truck going back there as soon as my plane leaves. The doctor is called Einarsson, and there are some nice nurses, Dutch. So get with it."

"All right, Laura," he said wearily. "I—I will. Then I'll see you in Philadelphia."

"Good for you. But if your donation is less than five figures, you can stuff Latin America."

He gave her a lopsided grin. "You were always good at blackmail."

"Holy blackmail," she said. "It makes a difference."

With shouts and shoves and raucous admonitions, she roused the exhausted children and began to herd them through the low doorway of the shelter into the night, where the plane stood waiting, a ghostly white bird glinting in the starlight.

*   *   *

Well, he had brought it off—even though it was going to cost Gulie and himself this outrageous ransom. The rogue! So *this* was what she called 'fund-raising!' The Mafia at least never used that expression.

He watched, feeling gypped and moved at the same time, as the children, a herd of stumbling pygmies, were shepherded into the plane. She was the last to get in, still carrying the sleeping child. Before vanishing inside, she waved at him, at least he thought she did. He waved back.

The engines roared to life; the plane rushed past in a wobbly takeoff, and he heaved a sigh of relief when it skimmed the tops of the trees. He heard the plane climb, and was watching the small blue fires of its exhausts vanish in the sky when fireworks exploded among the stars. It was a festive sight, but he realized with horror that they were anti-aircraft shells. The plumes and fountains of light went on bursting in the sky; then there was a huge explosion, a vast blinding star that seemed to hover for a moment before it plummeted down and disappeared. There was a dull thud, a second explosion deep in the forest; then an awful silence.

Stunned, horrified, he stood staring at the distant fire in the jungle while in the silence a thin cheering of voices sounded, far away: apemen, cheering the fact that they had re-established the night.

But he recoiled instantly from the violence he felt surge within him. 'That of God,' he thought, 'I must answer that of God in the men who killed her, or all will be lost.'

That night in the children's hospital, to purge himself of the feeling of senselessness and waste, he wrote a letter to Himsha, telling her about Laura and the way she had died.

CHAPTER THREE

T HE sky was vast and deep cobalt blue, deeper than the sky had been at home over the Huni valley. In the far distance, unimaginably far, were snow-capped mountaintops, so tiny and yet so brilliantly clear that they looked like small animal teeth, glistening in the sun. The whitewashed church, long since deserted, which they had planned to use as their emergency hospital must be centuries old, older than the church of the hanging Christ in the pueblo; its walls were five feet thick, its stubby towers blunt and slitted with gunports like the turrets of a fortress. The mountaintop itself, strewn with huge boulders tossed about in some prehistoric cataclysm, seemed more remote than the pueblo where she had been born. The whole scene suggested remoteness, solitude on a continental scale, and the view was of a stark, forbidding beauty. But, for the moment, it was lost on Himsha.

She watched, with mounting horror, the slow procession of Indian women carrying their dying babies, climbing the trail toward her. There she was: young Quaker physician about to start a lifetime of service to the suffering children of the world, and already she felt like sneaking away from the battlefield, to vanish among those boulders and rush blindly back to the valley. She watched the slow procession of mothers with horror because she did not have the medicine that had been promised to her. She had nothing except the small first-aid kit she carried; she was alone except for two Indian nurses whose language she barely spoke and who had not caught up with her yet. She had been assured in the valley that the medicine would be here when she arrived; she had even been told it was here, yet when she reached the little church there had been nothing.

What could she do? How could she help those women in bowler hats, with their stolid closed faces, carrying their dying babies? She should feel kinship with them; she had been selected for this assignment because she was an American Indian, a full-blood Huni. Yet, as she watched the flat, closed features and felt upon her the inanimate gaze of those pebble-like black eyes, she realized that she had never faced so alien a crowd before. It seemed to her at that moment as if these people were inhabitants of some distant planet onto which she had been thrown without any preparation, without the power to cope with the disaster she was now facing: the wholesale slaughter of innocent children in an epidemic of, of all things, German measles. The disease had long since been conquered in the civilized world, but still caused ravages among the young in these remote regions, where humanity itself did not seem to have been established yet, where the representatives of the Roman Catholic Church, like the scruffy priest in the valley, seemed more akin to the shamans in the pueblo than to the priests she had worked with in the ghettoes of American cities and who, to her, had not only seemed more Christian than she herself, but more Quakerly. Here she was, facing her first real test, and by merely looking at the closed faces around her she knew that she had already failed. Not only did she not have the medicine and there was simply nothing she could do for these people at this point, but in some eerie fashion the very core of her being, the essence of her personality were laid bare by those unglinting eyes—and the eyes perceived nothing, no person, no identity, only a fake, an illusion who, under their monolithic stare, evaporated into nothing.

As she sat there, motionless, returning their motionless gaze, it appeared to her in a welter of self-destructive emotion that she had been living a lie. She was no Indian. She had nothing in common with those people, nothing at all, except the color of her skin, the set of her jawbones, the sheen of her black hair. What the Quakers had done to her was to rob her of her identity; they had turned her from an Indian into a homeless, raceless child, a vaporous monster of virtue and kindness and docility and godliness; they had stuffed her with phrases which, at this moment, exploded in her face: 'Go for that of God in the other,' 'Ap-

proach every conflict after the manner of Friends,' 'Death is a
horizon, and a horizon is nothing but the limitation of our sight.'
Here she was, confronted with reality at last, not with the stagy
quasi-reality of Quaker work camps, barn-raisings after hurri-
canes and baby-sitting after floods. Here it was, reality as it had
existed on this planet ever since man began: here were the mothers, their faces closed and secretive, their eyes dull and inanimate, confronting her with their dying children, not hoping, not
believing, just seeing her as she now saw herself: a dark-skinned
gringa who had no idea what it meant to bear a child and bring
it into the world, clad in some flimsy white fabric, carrying a little satchel with her voodoo. It needed only one look at the creature to know that the voodoo was worthless, that the creature
herself was terrified out of her wits. There she sat, swallowing
nervously, her hands tightly clasped, trying, tense with panic, to
control the crazy impulse to flee. She knew she was getting hysterical, that the questions she was asking herself at this moment
could only evoke the wildest of emotional answers, but she could
not help herself. Those brilliantly white teeth in the haze of the
far horizon must be the highest peaks of the Andes, an incredible
three hundred miles away; to talk about 'death being a horizon'
in the face of that unimaginable distance summed up the sentimental unwordliness of her "mission." She was no "jungle doctor," she was a vacillating, artistic creature who belonged behind
a drawing-table, as everyone who really knew her had tried to
make her realize all along. Safe from reality inside the 'garden
enclosed' of the Society of Friends, she had been able to indulge
in daydreams of 'angel of mercy,' 'all He has is thee,' but here—
    She suddenly became conscious of the tinkling of bells in the
distance. Her first thought was that they must be church bells in
the valley; then she realized that she was too high up for that.
The valley and its church and its now almost nostalgic remnant
of civilization was more than a day's climb away—impossible to
hear church bells from that distance. Then, with a whoop of joy,
she sprang to her feet and ran to the edge of the precipice. Yes,
it was true, it was true! There it came, the caravan of mules,
each carrying a double pack of cardboard boxes! She turned
away to wipe the tears from her eyes without the mothers seeing
it, and uttered a prayer of thanks.
    A half-hour later the mules arrived at the old church. After
she had welcomed the two Indian nurses volubly as if they were

long-lost sisters, they began to unload. One of the nurses had a letter for her, which she glanced at: from Daddy, mailed somewhere in Africa.

Hands shaking, she opened the first of the cardboard packs, because she desperately needed some reassurance, some contact with the world of medicine in which she had a function. Then, as she extracted the first can from the cardboard pack, her heart sank. She gaped at the label with unbelief. *"Grade A Morocco plums, pitted, deliciously stewed in their own juices, another delectable delicacy from Plattfuss Orchards, Rutford Village, California."*

In growing panic, she ripped open the next box of the load, and the next, and the next, until, hands shaking, sputtering with rage and confusion, she had to conclude they were all the same. Every single one of those cardboard boxes contained one dozen cans of prime Morocco plums, deliciously stewed in their own juices. In the last of the boxes she found a letter, which she ripped open. *"Plattfuss Orchards, at the well of nature's goodness, Rutford Village, May 2, 1967. Dearie! Here are the plums I promised you that night when your father told that beautiful, beautiful story of how you were saved from that pueblo by himself and that wonderful woman, and why you were dancing the Tennessee Waltz. I have never heard such a wonderful story in my entire life, it is so inspirational that I told our pastor, Dr. Heinemann, who used it in a sermon that brought tears to the eyes of the entire congregation and believe me, dearie, we are not the weeping kind, this valley is full of hard-nosed fruit-growers, all of German extraction and as dry-eyed as they come. So, bless you in your beautiful work, and I am sure you will be able to find a good use for these delicious plums among your patients. How fortunate they are to have you! If you can find the time, drop me a line and tell me what you did with them. But even if you don't, dearie, blessings on you from myself, and from all the people of our congregation, especially Dr. Heinemann. What an ashamed old bag am I! Forgive me, will you? I was a little in my cups, I'm afraid. But you sure are a beautiful human being, as is that lovely Daddy of yours. Come back soon and let's all dance to the Tennessee Waltz! Yours faithfully: Selma Plattfuss."* There was a postscript. *"Ha-ha! I knew you would ask that! Where is the can-opener? Of course you haven't got one there in the wilderness of those mountains!*

*Well, sweetie, you'll find it in this very case. And just to make
sure, I included two."*

Stunned, she dug among the stuffing paper of the box and
found indeed two can-openers. Her knees gave way; she sat down
where she stood, a can-opener in her hand. Conscious of the nervous scrutiny of the two Indian nurses, she picked up a can and
pretended to read the label. *"Morocco Plums are an exceptionally sweet and saftig kind that was popular in England in the
second half of the seventeenth century. After having lain dor-
mant for centuries, Plattfuss Orchards . . ."* She suddenly felt so
nauseated that she was sure she was going to be sick. But she
must not communicate her panic to those two nurses, who stood
close together, watching her, not sure what to think of her odd
behavior. She took Daddy's letter from her pocket and tore open
the envelope with trembling hands. She had to smooth out the
paper on her knee and hold it down so as not to betray to the
watching nurses how her hands were shaking.

*"My darling Himsha, I am writing this in a makeshift chil-
dren's hospital in Biafra. I have just seen the plane with Laura
Martens and sixty little children shot out of the sky and crash
in flames in the forest. It is quite obvious that not a soul will be
found alive.*

*"I don't know how to go on or what to say to thee, all I know
is that at this moment I feel the need to write to thee and to tell
thee about this, maybe because she was to some degree indeed
thy mother as thee once said in that unguarded moment, much
to the sorrow of my dear Gulie. Maybe she is—was—thy mother because, as far as I can see, thee is the only one who is continuing her work.*

*"There have always been in the Quaker movement extraordi-
nary women, not by nature or by birth, but extraordinary by virtue of the concern with which they were burdened for the suffering children of their generation. Margaret Fell was the first of
these, after her came many others, each with her own distinct
personality, and of that long row of Quaker women, who all had
in common that they refused sainthood, Laura Martens was the
last. Now that she has fallen, it is thy turn to take on this ancient load that has always been the lonely burden of some
Quaker woman in each generation. I know that the news will
shock thee, I also know that thee must, at this moment, be full
of inner doubts and uncertainty and lack self-confidence. But I*

want to assure thee, beloved Himsha, that whatever it was that
sustained women like Margaret Fell, Gulielma Woodhouse,
Lydia Best and Laura Martens will surely, surely be sustaining
thee . . ."

Himsha closed her eyes and sat quite still. In that stillness,
during which she seemed to be suspended in space, some small
strength, some beginning of a new, serene power began to communicate itself to her. It grew within her, it seemed to fill her
slowly with an unemotional tranquility, a stillness that was not
silence but fullness, a fullness of light, a growing awareness of
the reality of the infinite ocean of light and love that was God,
which now communicated itself to her and needed her to communicate itself to those stolid women in their bowler hats, squatting on the edge of infinity, their dying babies in their laps.

There was nothing she could do for them, nothing at all; but
surely the medicine would soon arrive, soon they would be given
all the benefit of modern science. For the moment, all she had to
give them was—yes, what? How to go about communicating to
others the reality of the infinite ocean of light and love if you
were experiencing it yourself for the first time in your life? She
picked up the can-openers, rose to her feet and went to the two
Indian nurses who were watching her nervously, not knowing
what to think of this strange, emotional creature who looked so
much like themselves, yet with whom they had nothing in common. "Here," she said, in Spanish, "if you will start opening
those cans, I'll hand them out. We might as well make use of
them now we have them."

Eagerly, the two nurses started to open the cans, kneeling on
the ground. Himsha picked up the first two and carried them to
the women gazing at her with those expressionless, inanimate
eyes. She gave a can to the first two in the row and said in Spanish, "Here, take this. It's not the medicine for your babies yet,
but it is very nice and it will do *you* good. Here, try it, it is
sweet."

The two women, with a suddenly human timorousness,
glanced at each other. Then the first one, the bravest, dipped two
graceful fingers into the syrup and brought out a round, wet
plum.

"Go ahead, eat it!" Himsha smiled at her, sure now that this
was the answer, that this had broken the ice between them, that
this was what she should have done.

The woman cautiously nibbled at the plum.

"Well?"

The woman smacked her lips and tasted it, watched nervously by the whole row. Himsha realized that though she might tell them a hundred times that this was not medicine, to them this was the beginning of the voodoo. Then, with a bold, greedy bite, the woman popped the rest of the plum into her mouth and started to chew voluptuously. Her neighbor followed suit.

Trying not to run in her elation, Himsha went back to the two nurses, who were now opening cans with dedication, and picked up the next two. As she carried them to the row of Indian mothers squatting on the edge of infinity, she had the overpowering feeling of a human presence. She did not know whose presence she felt—only that it must be a woman, and that whoever it was filled the sky with laughter.

ENVOI

NEW MEXICO

November, 1973

WHEN the train slowed down, Ethan Woodhouse woke jerkily as the black attendant touched his shoulder. "Kissing Tree Station, sir," the man said apologetically, as if it were a fault of his. Well, it was; he should have called him earlier! The train came to a clanking, clattering halt and his bags were still in the rack!

"Take it easy, sir," the attendant said soothingly. "Plenty of time, sir, we have fifteen minutes."

"Oh, all right, all right!" Ethan could not help himself, he hurried fussily as he tied his shoelaces and fidgeted with his tie in front of the little mirror that reflected an ancient, carved face full of cracks, like a prehistoric pot. Whatever old age might have to offer in the way of rewards, it certainly was not the most handsome period in a man's life.

The attendant took his bags and vanished with them down the corridor. Outside, on the platform, a veritable host of people seemed to be waiting in the bright winter sunlight to welcome the new arrivals. He donned his overcoat, jammed on his hat without checking whether it was back to front and shuffled down the corridor in a senile hurry which, for some obscure reason, seemed to give satisfaction to his baser nature. He climbed down the steps arthritically, tipped the porter, who saluted with such a flourish that he thought, alarmed, he must have given the man too much. Then he scanned the faces, hoping that one of them would be waiting for him. But he might have known it: here he was, main speaker at the opening of a new Quaker hospital in the desert, and they hadn't even taken the trouble to . . .

"Ethan Woodhouse?"

In front of him stood a young man with a shaggy mane of black hair, flat nose and inordinately wide cheekbones, beaming from ear to ear. Must be an Indian of some sort. Well, after all, the hospital was intended for Indian children. "Yes?"

"I'm Joshua Baker," the young man said cheerily. "Are these your bags?"

He was tempted to retort, "Who else's?" But he realized this was the cantankerousness of the Golden Years; probably something to do with hormones. Or gas. That food on the train . . . !

"Yes, they are," he said. "Thank thee, Joshua Baker."

The young man picked up the suitcases as if they were empty. "We have a car outside, sir—er—Ethan Woodhouse," he said, in the jovial tone that was an attribute of Quaker youth. When he himself had been that age, he must have been as nauseatingly cheerful and oppressively loving. It was drummed into one with the steadiness of rain: love that of God in everyone, Ethan, love that of God . . . Who was it, in the dim past, who had said on one memorable occasion that he loved that of God in someone but very little else? Probably George Fox. No man had ever recorded his own thoughts and maxims with more zest. "What tribe does thee belong to, Friend?" he asked in a grudging show of interest. "Huni?"

"No, sir, er, Ethan Woodhouse," the youth replied. "I'm an Eskimo."

"You don't say." It came out before he could help it. Oh, those Bakers! He knew it was unfair, but the demonstrative multi-racial make-up of their adopted family rubbed him the wrong way. If there were something to the flying saucers and Boniface Baker were to stumble on one of the little green men, his first question to the extra-terrestrial visitor would be, 'May I adopt thee, Friend?'

"Are we going directly to the hospital?"

"No, no, Ethan Woodhouse," the youth said, tripping up the steps of the underpass with the agility of a mountain goat despite his load, "we are having meeting first, and then a covered dish luncheon, and then, I believe, the official opening."

"I see. And when am I supposed to sound off?"

"Excuse me?"

"When is my speech scheduled?"

"Oh, I don't know—er—Ethan Woodhouse. You—thee will have to ask Amanda Clutterbuck."

"And who might Amanda Clutterbuck be?"

"The clerk of our Meeting, sir—Ethan. But it is sure to be after lunch."

God, those luncheons! What was it in the Quaker personality that equated holiness with indigestion? He remembered receiving a complaint that some Meeting on the growing edge of Quakerism had flippantly called its hospitality committee "Committee for Sufferings." His reply had been, "If the hospitality expresses itself in the usual Quaker fare, it would seem to me the committee has been aptly named." There had been a few chuckles about that reply among the mandarins in Philadelphia, senile chuckles admittedly, but chuckles all the same. My God, the solemnity of some of these newly convinced Friends!

They emerged into the bright sunlight of the station square, and the young Eskimo headed toward a low-slung, bright red, shark-smiling machine. "Is that yours?" Ethan asked alarmed. It seemed too cramped to house a cat, let alone the *enfant terrible* of Philadelphia Yearly Meeting.

The young man beamed. "Yes, Ethan Woodhouse!"

"Is there a taxi?"

The young Eskimo's face fell. He looked like a three-year-old whose favorite toy truck had been taken away from him.

"Surely, young Friend, thee does not expect me to sit in *that?*"

"Oh, but, yes, sir—yes, Ethan, look, it is very roomy . . ."

He stifled a cry as the young brute turned a knob which made the whole top of the machine flip up, like the lid of a box, exposing two leopard-skin bucket seats and an instrument panel reminiscent of the Zeppelin, which he had visited the day before it burned to a crisp.

"See?" the boy asked, pleadingly. "There's plenty of room!"

Grimly, he collected his old bones and eased himself into one of the exotic buckets. After doing something with his baggage behind his back that gave rise to apprehension, the boy got in next to him. "Would you—thee mind fastening thy seat belt, Ethan Woodhouse?"

"My what?"

The boy bent across his lap and pulled up a strap with a buckle the shape of a slavering lion, whose lower jaw snapped into place when the strap was closed. "There," said the boy.

He grunted, "Whatever this infernal machine may be, it certainly is no witness to the Peace Testimony."

"Excuse me?"

"Let's go." He sighed. The trouble about senile wit was that it tired the comedian more than it bewildered his audience.

The car leaped forward with a malevolent growl; he grabbed the strap with the lion and closed his eyes. It was not the fear of death that beset him; this would be as good a way as another. It was anger with the timorous fragility of old age, the infuriating feeling that instead of the vigorous, male body of his youth which he had always taken for granted, he was now carrying around a glass cupboard full of china, on legs that had once played soccer and now seemed as wildly unsuited to the act of walking as the stems of clay pipes.

It was a blessing when finally, after a drive that seemed to be executed mainly on two wheels, they stopped with a jerk in front of one of those adobe bungalows that had sprung up by the thousands around every New Mexican city. "The Meeting House," the boy said proudly.

The usual delegation came out to welcome him, young women with beads, youngish men in sport shirts and sandals and a few older Friends wearing bolo ties. There were also a lot of children, running around in an undisciplined manner. He allowed himself to be hoisted out of the machine, adjusted his pince-nez and was suddenly overcome with the usual neurotic terror, common before every speaking engagement, that his dentures would slip. They never did, but it was always better to retire into the restroom for a moment, before the beginning of meeting for worship, and sprinkle his uppers with Snap-a-Grip.

This time, when he finally reached the blessed privacy of the men's room after a welter of greetings, pleasant inanities and his own mendacious cries of "Of course, I remember thee!" he felt suddenly inexplicably sad. He had no idea why; normally old-age melancholia did not trouble him until after supper. But now it hit him in plain daylight, with the blank, cobalt blue New Mexican sky framed in the little window. The very idea of having to stand up in front of this crowd of people with their unruly children and their scowling adolescents made him feel inexpressibly weary. Dear God, what was the point of it all? Why did he have to live to this idiotic age, washed up in this graceless new world like a dodo, last remnant of a lost species? These people, now waiting for him to give them an uplifting address like a spiritual orthopedic sole, had nothing in common with the Friends who had been his contemporaries and who were by now all gone, and if not gone, senile. People like Stella: how she would have enjoyed the way they had named the hospital, which he was about to open officially! For years, Stella had been haunted, as he himself was at times, by the ephemeral ghost of the long forgotten Jacob Martens to whom Laura had owed the inspiration for her godly works. After the Judge Martinez Hospital for Indian Children had been bought from the State of New Mexico for a song because of its dilapidated condition, refurbished and spruced up, a special meeting of the Steering Committee had been called to discuss the new name. Of course, someone proposed 'Laura Martens Hospital,' of which there were already a fair number. Then he had a divine inspiration, and suggested it be called after Laura's father, Jacob. When unity could not be reached, simply because no one had ever heard of the man other than in the vaguest sense, he played his trump card. Together with the building itself, they had bought its contents: linen, cutlery, crockery, realizing too late that all of it was marked indelibly with the initials 'JMH.' "Friends," he said, "imagine what it would cost us to have all that replaced just because of the initials? 'Jacob Martens Hospital' would mean they can stay the same!" After a reverent silence in which the Quaker spirit of frugality manifested itself, the Recording Clerk was ordered to write a minute of approval, containing the proviso that 'The name would be prominently displayed above the entrance of the building in sturdy, semi-permanent lettering.' How Stella would have savored the 'semi-permanent'! How they would have laughed together, two gaggling old dodos, in the Snack Shoppe across the road from the office, as had been their wont after each meeting of the committee! Ah—Stella . . .

He stood for a moment eyes closed, hands folded, in a sudden, eerie awareness of the Presence; then there was a knock on the door and a nervous voice asked, "Ethan Woodhouse? Is thee all right?"

For God's sake! They must have thought he had slipped into eternity by way of the toilet! "Of course, of course!" he replied, hastily. "I was just—er—er—putting on my glue."

"Oh?" The voice sounded bewildered but reassured. No wonder; what must they have thought he meant? Well, better get on with it.

When he entered, they had already started meeting. Everyone was seated on rows of uncomfortable-looking folding chairs, the hallmark of the growing edge of Quakerism, and there was a facing bench of sorts, also made up of chairs, where one seat was left between a woman with glasses and a middle-aged Friend in an open-necked sports shirt. The woman looked at him and pointed meaningfully at the chair. She must be the Clerk, Amanda Clutterbuck. Of course, the infernal chairs were made of metal, which meant that he would in all likelihood be bothered by his bladder again. He wondered whether he could ask for a cushion or a newspaper to sit on, but decided that he had caused enough of a stir as it was. So he sat down resignedly, bent his head, folded his hands and entered the silence.

He had expected to sit there with the usual idiotic babble burbling in his mind, but to his surprise he felt the sudden deepening of the stillness that was the sign of a covered meeting. There, within him, came the irrepressible call to rise and minister, a rare occurrence indeed. He wanted to talk about Jacob Martens and his daughter. He was about to do so, when from the hushed meeting came a child's voice, sighing in unbearable boredom, "Oh, boy . . . !"

He opened one eye and spotted right in front of him a ravishing, dark-haired young woman with a most becoming blush of embarrassment and, beside her, an Asian toddler, feet dangling. The child's black eyes gazed at him with the innocence and the perspicacity of a bird. The call to minister shriveled. Maybe not so much because of the interruption, but because the dark-haired young woman, who sat there mortified and abashed, was a joy to behold. Jacob Martens would have to do without his fatuous comments.

No one said a word; meeting was over with blessed speediness. He rose stiffly and staggered across the open space in front of the facing bench toward the young woman and the child. "Well, well," he said, his voice croaking already with disuse, "and who have we here?" He stood, his huge frame swaying, gazing down on the child.

"I'm Gulielma Baker, Ethan Woodhouse," the ravishing young woman said, "and this is our son Boniface. He is only three years old, from Vietnam, he doesn't really speak English yet. The rest of our family would have been here too, but my husband—"

Ethan held out his hand, which to the child must have seemed the size of a frying pan, and growled, "Pleased to meet thee, Friend Boniface. And thank thee for thy ministry. Thee spoke to my condition."

Even as he said it, he realized that it is of such things that a man's memories are made, and his pride of belonging. God knows, he might have contributed to yet another Boniface Baker growing up to be a Friend.

"Some non-alcoholic punch, Ethan Woodhouse?" the woman from the facing bench asked.

"No, thank thee, Amanda Clutterbuck," he replied, "I'm afraid I'd come unglued." With that, treading gingerly, he headed for the sunlight and the covered dish luncheon, offered by Kissing Tree Monthly Meeting's hospitality committee.

That afternoon, under the bright New Mexican sun, while traffic roared by on the overpass and freight trains rumbled clanging through the desert, he unveiled the plaque on the façade of the hospital. It read:

> *To the memory of Jacob Martens, Dutch Quaker, born 1889, died 1942 in Schwalbenbach Concentration Camp, Germany. His martyrdom inspired his daughter Laura and all those who follow her example to do their work of mercy among the suffering children of the world.*
>
> *May there never be an end to the good he has done.*

About the Author

Jan de Hartog, born in Haarlem, Holland, the second son of a Calvinist minister and a Quaker mother, ran off to sea at the age of ten. At sixteen he entered Amsterdam Naval College, but during the Depression he returned to the sea, ending up as a junior mate in the Dutch ocean-going tugboat service. When war broke out in 1940 and Holland was occupied by the Nazis, de Hartog was trapped in his native country. During this time he wrote and published his first major novel *Holland's Glory*, which became an instant and historic bestseller and made him a symbol of the Dutch Resistance. (The German occupying forces banned the book in 1942, but it went on selling in large quantities in the underground market.) When he escaped to London in 1945, he was appointed war correspondent for the Dutch merchant marine. There he gathered the material for his postwar novels *The Distant Shore* and *The Captain*, of which over a million copies were sold in the United States alone.

In 1956 he and his wife, Marjorie, crossed the Atlantic on assignment for a number of European magazines, and after a year decided to become permanent residents of the United States. In 1962 de Hartog accepted a post as professor of English at the University of Houston, teaching creative playwriting there and at all-black Texas Southern University. His wife became a volunteer nurses' aide in the local charity hospital; de Hartog followed her and served three years as an orderly in the emergency room. Later, after publication of his book *The Hospital*, conditions in the charity hospital vastly improved and, for the first time, blacks were admitted as members to the board.

In the late sixties de Hartog, himself a Quaker, undertook the ambitious project of a multi-volume novel on the history of the Religious Society of Friends. *The Peaceable Kingdom* was the first book, now followed by *The Lamb's War.*

De Hartog has written many plays, among which the most famous is *The Fourposter* (later turned into the musical *I Do! I Do!*), and several volumes of essays, the best known being *A Sailor's Life* (memories of life at sea before World War II) and *The Children* (a personal record for the benefit of the adoptive parents of Asian children).

Mr. and Mrs. de Hartog live on a farm in Bucks County, Pennsylvania, with their two daughters from Korea.